I0722957

Also by Joanne E. Zienty

The Things We Save
Children of the Revolution

sequel to
CHILDREN OF THE REVOLUTION

THE
NIGHT
PROPHET

joanne e. zienty

WHEATON, ILLINOIS

This is a work of fiction. Names, characters, places, and incidents either are the
product of the author's imagination or are used fictitiously. Any resemblance
to actual persons, living or dead, events or locales is entirely coincidental.

FIRST EDITION

Designed by Cecily Pincsak

Library of Congress Cataloging-in-Publication Data has been applied for.

ISBN 978-1-7336881-4-7

For all the kindred spirits, fair and foul,
who shape our souls and make us who we are.

HURON
region
lower
SUPERIOR
region
ONTARIO
region
MICHIGAN
region
the
OUTLIER
the
OUTLIER
ILLIANA
region
ERIE
region
map of the
PROTECTORATE

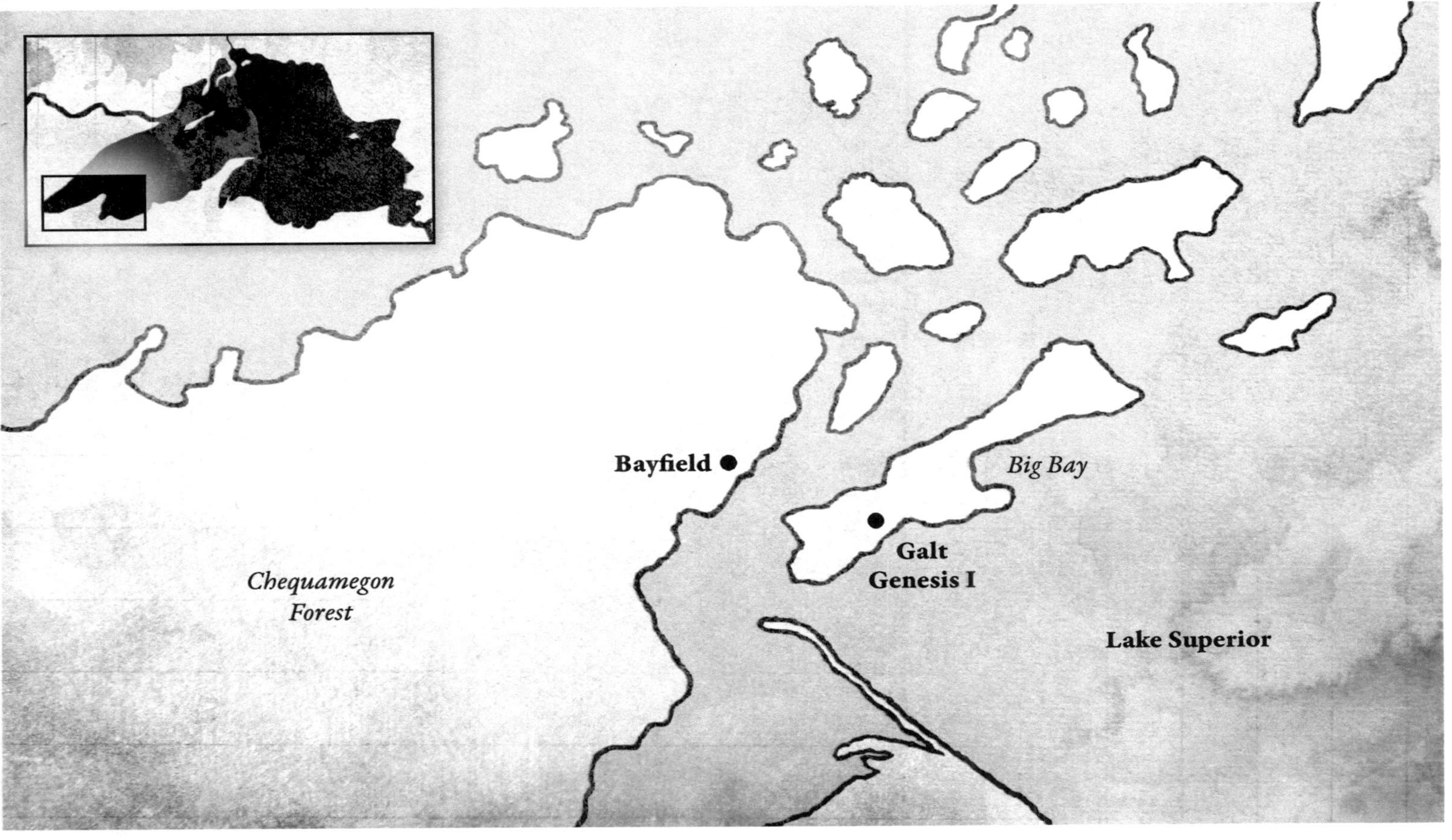

Bayfield
Big Bay
Galt
Genesis I
Chequamegon
Forest
Lake Superior

PART ONE

Vox

Year 82 – December

"Surely, whoever speaks to me in the right voice,
him or her I shall follow,
As the water follows the moon, silently, with fluid steps,
anywhere around the globe."
—Walt Whitman, *Voices* (1871)

1

A Vox in Twilight

IT'S THE VOX HE COVETS. Or so he tells himself.

Not the body. Not the face. Not the long-legged strut with a certain swagger, a tantalizing assuredness that suggests she's been broken, maybe to the core, and come out stronger. Has had her world rocked and is now out to rock the world.

That does intrigue him. But he's warned himself to put it aside for now. For now, the primary driver is the vox. Soothing to the ear, like a blend of honey and home-brew is soothing to the throat. Oozily smooth but with a bite, an afterburn on the way down.

He's dreamt of a vox in the night, a siren song, a banshee wail, a cry from the heart. A vox with the will to break through, to bash walls, smash bricks, shatter glass, to tear down the curtains that separate the flesh from the spirit. Dreamt of whispers to wind through the narrow passages that lead from the brain to the heart. Has dreamt of pain, of tears, of nightmares. Nightmares induced by, brought forth by, this vox. Beautiful and terrifying as the lightning that arcs across the sky.

He knows of a story, a legend, a myth. Handed down through millennia. Words passed from vox to vox, from ear to ear. A story long lost except to the memes and those lucky few who hear it from their lips. A story of a face that launched a thousand ships and left a fabled city in ruins. A face that inspired men to madness. But what of a vox? A vox disembodied, a vox that leaves it to the listener's imagination to conjure the face? What havoc might that wreak?

Since the leaves began to turn he's played the spy, watching her go through the motions of her days. In Dealers' Alley, haggling with the bartering rats. Bent over a bike, wielding her wrench like an artist wields a paintbrush. Wrestling with a recalcitrant generator, fingers black with grease. Wandering the aisles of the Galt-Mart, those same fingers spotless, snaking out and surreptitiously tucking a sweet down the waistband of her jeans. She always pays for the staples—rice, beans, flour—flashing the vouchers she's earned in exchange for her services. But the little sweet treats—those she steals.

He's idled for hours here in the park that borders a strip of beach. She comes here two or three times a week with the toddler and the young man in tow, even on the knife cold days when the polar vortex dips south, bringing a bone-chilling freeze along with it. While the man and the child frolic, she sits on the bench nearest the beach, just the black ribbon of bike path separating it from the sand and the forbidding, steel gray expanse of Lake Superior. Positions herself in the middle of it, her lithe body wrapped in a sleek down jacket—obviously a swag hand-me-down—one leg bent, tucked in close, her chin resting on her knee, staring out at the water from behind a pair of blackout shades.

Or he imagines she's staring. For all he knows, watching her from afar, her eyes might be closed as she dozes in an afternoon siesta. Occasionally, very occasionally, she'll be the one pushing the toddler on the swing, and then it's not a frolic but a lesson aimed at eventually relieving herself of the task.

"Pump. With your legs. Get going! Stretch 'em out, pull 'em in. Stretch out, pull in. That's it," she orders, the honey and the bite in that vox enticing, goading—willing—the little girl's limbs into obedience.

The trio usually leave as they arrive, hand in hand, the little one in the middle, her turbulence of black curls bouncing and short legs churning to match the others' strides, until she whines and the young man scoops her up and settles her on his shoulders. She always squeals, pumping her blue-mittened fist, a queen clutching an imaginary scepter, straddling the world.

But not today. Today the fem perches on the bench, back to her companions, resistant to their entreaties to join them, and when they are tired and presumably hungry for supper, she waves them away. After a pause, they wander down the smooth asphalt path that winds out of the park back towards the manse and the town beyond.

A part of him, the part that his mother often called bold as brass, wants to sidle over to the bench and settle his lanky frame down on one edge or the other, just to see her reaction. Would she hop up and leave? Unfold her leg and give him the once over from behind those shades? Tell him to frack off, the bitter in her vox overwhelming the sweet?

Fortune favors the bold.

Or so he tells himself—another of his mother's sayings— but he waits. And waits. Until the sun eases down past the towering firs and oaks that border the western edge of the park. Until his legs start to stiffen and his back to ache in its casual slump against the unforgiving slats of the bench he occupies. Until he's cleaned every piece of bike gear in his backpack three times— his ostensible excuse for sitting there—wiping, oiling, rewiping, stowing them in the pack, taking them out again. All the while watching. Observing. Waiting to take his cue from her.

When she does finally move, it is the slow unfolding of a butterfly out of its chrysalis. The stretch of a leg, the flexing of an arm. The luxurious arch of the back before the body is set into full motion in that sauntering, long-legged stride that he admires, like a swag might admire the gait of a fine piece of horseflesh.

He waits to make his move until there's a bit of distance, until she's on the path. Then he swings his own long legs into motion, knee joints cracking. Out of the park, on the streets of town, the bees are sparse, most of the workers already ensconced in their personal hives, swags tucked away in their manses. Bayfield is a smallish enclave to begin with, and it's late, nearly curfew, which drops so quickly in winter.

Fly away home.

She's not in a hurry. Pauses to peer in the darkened shop windows, the places where imminent parentals awaiting their spawn bestowals drop v-cards on quaint trinkets crafted by the locals. Beach glass bracelets. Beeswax candles—how apropos—studded with the needle-like leaves of lavender or balsam. Adorable embroidered bibs and tiny onesies fashioned in androgynous grays and greens. He knows the route by heart, so when she turns down the alley between the bakery and the oilers, where the sweet aromas of sugar, yeast, and butter compete with the bracing scents of bergamot and wintergreen, he doesn't worry when he momentarily loses sight of the back of her head with its dark braid coiled high like a sleeping serpent. Instead, he breathes deep.

He rounds the corner, anticipating having her in his sights again, when the raw clench of a strong hand jerks his right arm and forces it up behind his back with a swift savagery that leaves him gasping. With equal speed, a fine line, a knife blade steel-sharp, ice-cool, rears up, poised, menacing, at his throat.

"What d'you want?" Her mouth up against his ear spews flames.

Fortune favors the bold.

"Right now? For you to let me go." Bravado. He kens she'll appreciate that. Or so he hopes.

But no. The steel slides, just a whisper, and he feels a warmish trickle down the skin of his neck.

"Whoa."

Her stance rivals that of a ball-breaking trap. He takes a moment to admire the secure hold she's got him in, pressed tight to her body, her foot keeping his splayed, pinning him off-balanced.

Fem's got some skills.

When the trickle of blood reaches his collarbone, she lifts his chin with the flat edge of the blade. "Something to know about me. I never ask for anything more'n twice. What—do—you—want?"

He weighs employing the joke again and decides against it, like any canny man with a knife to his throat.

"Your vox," he states, as flat as a fact, expecting her to fling him away at the outlandishness.

But the steel of her grip only grows stronger as she digs a thumb into the space where the veins meet at his wrist, and the steel of her blade balances on the thin veil of skin that curtains his carotid artery. Yet he senses a certain tremor in her body pressed so intimately against his.

"You heard that before, ain'tcha? Someone's toldya you got a lovely vox."

"And that man's dead," she spits.

But he hears the catch.

Fortune favors the bold.

"Not by your hand."

A violent shove puts him on the ground, cheek to cheek with the serrated edge of broken concrete, a patch the sweeps neglected to repair, the pebbly bits grinding his skin raw. He scrambles to his knees before her and pauses, unable to read the look on her face, her skin basked in the rose and violet glow of the early winter's twilight, eyes still hidden behind those blackout shades.

Which she lifts. Perhaps to get a better look at him.

But it also affords him a better look at her. At her wide-set eyes, flecked with green and gold and a tinge of unease. Unease that she masks with a blink.

She's good.

"Who are you?" she whispers. "What d'you want?"

He feels a smirk stretching his lips and tries to restrain it, but succumbs to its power. *That's three,* he longs to say. Instead, he shrugs. "I'm just a pathfinder."

"A pathfinder," she repeats, peppering the word with scorn.

"A pathfinder," he echoes. "Just lookin' to find a way to remake the world."

2

Pathfinder

"Heard that before, too, huh? I see that, even through this murk."

Rude and brazen as a splash of ice water to the face. There's a temptation in Angel's hand, where her hunting blade still rests.

It would be so easy. So easy. Just one lightning slash.

Except it wouldn't. Be easy. She can feel the heaves bubbling, the sweat beading, the panic crawling around her bowels. Slithery. Snakish.

Angel stares at this man who's been trailing her for weeks. A man with a seemingly infinite amount of time on his hands. Time not owed to or kept track of by the Galt Corporation. Time that belongs to him and him alone. In this dangerous proximity, she can see the strength of his jawline, the crinkles around his eyes, the hawk beak sharpness of his nose. It's a face that triggers nothing in particular. But the words that slip from those plumpish lips, purple in the twilight, are a different story.

"Why've you been following me?"

"So you noticed?" A chuckle.

The bravado, the sheer insolence. Who dares to palaver like this when a knife is one quick jerk of a hand from his throat?

"I could kill you—Pathfinder—so—"

He doesn't let her finish. "Oh, I think if you were gonna,

you'd already done it."

It burns like a lick of flame to a finger, knowing he's right. And bold enough to say it. She grabs him by the scruff of his flannel jacket and hauls him up, slamming him face first into the wall, surprised not by her own strength but by his lack of heft, tall and wiry as he is, but light, as if hollow-boned like a bird. She pats him down, fishing a small multi-tool out of the front pocket of his jeans along with a pair of blue Galt water vouchers. Swipes a hand along his legs, feeling for a knife or a burner tucked away in an ankle holster.

Nothing.

"Thorough, with just a hint of the ol' ruff'n tuff," he says. "Whoever taught you to do a pat down taught you well."

She jerks him around to face her. "Look—"

"Look—"

They say it together, the sounds and their breath mingling in the inches of space between their faces.

"In winter's darkest days, have you asked yourself how you can be a light in another's life? How you can be a light in the Protectorate galaxy? How you can bring your shine, use your light for the good of the Protectorate?"

The fem alto that blares from the feedcoms mounted strategically across the town is modulated, temperate, only a shade synthetic. Close enough for Corporate work. Perhaps the CQO was not personally available to record the curfew message, so her robo-proxy was pressed into service.

The man smiles, a true smile now, not a smirk, teeth gleaming. The straight, artificially aligned teeth of an elite.

Swag? But trying to hide it?

He waits until the voxcast concludes, then continues. "Your vox. I want your vox." He gives a shuddery shake of his head. "No. I need your vox. Your amazing, compelling, fully human, ultimately listenable vox. For a job. No, no," he rambles on, shaking his head again. "it's more than that, really. I hope you'll find it—" his dark eyes roll up and around as he searches for a word and then center on her face "—a calling."

She stares, dumb-silent as the trunk of a tree, mouth set in a frown, like a cleft in the bark.

"I know you," he continues. "Not better'n you know yourself, no, I won't go so far, but I see you. The way you flick a hand to send your man and the little one away. The way you sometimes gnaw on the end of that braid when you let it hang down. The way you need to wait 'til the mart door slides open. The way you go in through the out door. The way you can hang at the park 'til the sun eases into its crib, cuz you're not worried about an embed scan seein' that you ain't up in your own. Cuz you ain't got one, do ya? An embed, that is."

His words are a splash of fuel on the spark of fear in her belly.

"Who are you?" she whispers again, taking a step back.

"Already toldya. I'm a pathfinder."

"That supposed to mean something to me?"

He shrugs. Lifts a hand to his throat, wipes the dribble of blood with his thumb. "Sorry my reputation don't precede me. Proceed me? Whatever." He grins quizzically. "That's why I'm neither the wordsmith nor the orator. Ain't got the chops. I'm just the troublemaker, the instigator. The pathfinder." He chuckles low—a short *heh-heh*—before he inclines his head toward her, gives a little half-bow, constrained by the still-narrow gap between them. "You can call me Path for short."

"That's not a Corporate name."

"Neither is Angel."

"Look, I don't know what your game is—my vox is my vox and for all I know, you've just had one too many sips of oblivion. They say the home-brew eats away your brain, eventually."

"Never touch the stuff. And this ain't a game. There's someone you need to meet."

"I don't need to meet anyone. Stop dogging me or the next cut'll be deep."

"Don't doubt it. But all I'm askin's for you—"

"No." Angel closes her blade and slips it into her cargo pocket. "And now I'm gonna vanish and so are you and this never happened."

She turns, but is astonished to feel the claw grip of his fingers snag her elbow and jerk her back around.

"This the world where you want to raise that precious lil' one?" He doesn't hiss in anger, or throw the question in her face like ice water. Just asks, like he's asking if she'd like a second slice of bread or prefers the color green to blue.

"You know you'll have to be movin' on soon. Cuz the numerators'll be combin' their way through here. And the missus won't let you stay, she's not gonna risk it, no matter how good your man bakes that bread and whips up that stew or how many garden beds you can plant and weed. That wanderin' life, never knowin' which bee or swag you can trust, always lookin' over your shoulder. Is that all you can hope for that little fem? Is that the future you want to see when you look into that sweet face?"

Under the burn of her glare, he releases his grip, but slowly, one bony finger at a time. Yet she still feels held in check, a captive of the challenge in his suddenly solemn eyes and the gauntlet thrown down by his words.

"Tomorrow. Noon. I'll be on the bench," she hisses as she turns and strides away, but as she goes she thinks she hears the words, a hushed incantation.

"To remake the world."

A glance over her shoulder reveals the confirmation. The man standing, fist pressed to his chest, before twilight drops its shroud over him, over her. Over the world as she knows it.

3

Words to Form Memories

IF ANGEL SLEEPS THAT NIGHT, it's only a sleep in pieces. Of minutes knitted together here and there in the midst of gaping holes of black terror and memories. Lying in bed, her fingers creep up the arm where the wounds have long since healed, the skin smooth again, but where pale scars linger, the ghosts of deeds she's tried to forget.

But triggers will be pulled. And the past two years have seen many restless nights. And dreams that begin and end in trees. Always in trees. Running, walking, stalking, being stalked, the trees so close, bullying around her, bark razor sharp against her cheek. Sometimes she sits bolt upright, startling awake with a rattling gasp, as if a giant exhalation in the darkest depths of night can expel the beast writhing through her innards. Sweat beading, hot, then cold. Finding her arm outstretched, hand gripping nothing, fingers clutched around...nothing.

Other times, she finds herself staring down at the child as she sleeps, uncertain of how she got from her own bed to this one, far across the room. The child has been a restless sleeper since birth, pawing and twisting, little whimpers punctuating her frets. What does she dream of?

Once Kuba had spouted off some drivel about how he could remember taking his first steps, leaving his mother's grip and tottering toward the outstretched hands of his great-great grand-mother. He said he could distinctly recall the way the skin folded in wrinkles around her knuckles and joints. The lady of the manse, the widow, Mrs. Wright, had scoffed, asserting it was an impossible memory, that one can't have memories from a time before one has language, before one can talk.

"We need words to form memories."

Kuba, his back to the old fem, had rolled his eyes and later, alone with Angel, insisted the memory was true, so very real was it in his mind, the warmth of the ancient matriarch's fingertips, the glitter of pride in her eyes. But Angel had been secretly relieved, thinking back on that first winter after her daughter's birth, sheltering at the decrepit manse, a stone's throw from the lake called Michigan, living in the midst of a pack of squatting Bartertown rats and scoundrels. She and Kuba had slept in shifts, not trusting a single rotten soul, even as they shared their roasted raccoon and stewed squirrel and pilfered tates and onions willingly enough. But too many of them, fems and men alike, wanted to hold the infant, to coo in her face, their lips and noses dangerously close to her little bow of a mouth, her snub of a nose. Come spring, the three of them had shoved on. Would she want Lark to have memories of that?

That's been life for two springs now. Finding shelter, leaving shelter. Sliding in on the willingness of swags to overlook certain things. Sliding in on the inclination of old swags to not want to lift one finger of their own if they can find someone else's to do the job for them. The tedious work. The dirty work. The sweet and savory of Kuba's kitchen magic veils and softens Angel's surliness. The honey that balms the bee's sting. And, like the B-town rats, the fems fall for the child. Every time. Fawn and fritter. Foolish, hungry. Yearning for what they can't have.

It was frightening at first, but Angel has come to recognize the subversive beauty in arousing those painful longings. The jagged trail from start to conclusion. *I am without. You have something I want. Yes, I am angry at you for having it. But I could have this thing, just like you, if it wasn't for them. They, not you, are the real obstacles keeping me from my desire.* The amorphous "they." Because does anyone know who truly determines these outcomes? Who makes the determinations of who is bestowed with the keeping and raising of a child and who is not? Just another decision handed down from behind the glass and steel veil of the Hive. Stoke that anger long enough and hot enough and some sort of spark might ignite.

She has learned to spot vulnerability and turn it to her advantage. Angel had zeroed in on the widow immediately. Something more than gravity weighed heavily on the old fem's shoulders. Grief, maybe. Regret, surely. And oh, there was a longing in those deep-set eyes, a longing that settled in the ash-colored hollows under them.

What are you missing? What do you want?

The swag had made no effort to disguise the fact that she was watching them at play. The town, like so many in the Protectorate, had so few children that the park was deserted most days that whole damp week back in May, except for the old fem's brooding presence. She'd sat with her silver-streaked hair twisted and braided in an elaborate wreathe around her aging face and stared, not even bothering to hide her hunger behind a pair of blackout shades.

A fem with time on her hands.

And so Angel knew she'd found their next safe house. She just needed to create an entry point. She detected that the fem had no man to gum up the works. She deciphered the pattern of activity with which the fem filled her empty days. A trip to the GaltMart on Mondays, a pampering day in town on Wednesdays, catching a sedate live act at the small bandshell near the marina on Fridays. But her movements were mechanical, joyless, as if she regarded it all as a slog, something to get through and over with.

And then, as it turned out, Nature played its lovely, trickster hand. Rain. Days of it. It was a simple matter of standing in it. And playing coy. Refusing aid. Letting the old swag insist on giving them a lift. *To where? Nowhere.* Letting her have her way, as swags are wont to do. Letting her take them in.

It didn't hurt that Lark's tears had ceased the moment the three of them had eased into the stylish hot yellow transport that marked the fem as a former tech sector employee. That Lark had smiled at the music playing from the feedcom. That the fem had sighed over the child's blue eyes ringed in amber. These blandishments reduced the problematic fact that they were sitting, dripping wet, in the plush interior, bottoms soaking the fabric, to just a piddling matter. In any case, Angel had known she'd be the one to clean it all up.

And here they were, eight months later, their longest stay in any particular place. Oh, there'd been a feeling-out period. A length of time required to construct a narrow bridge of trust. But the widow has grievances aplenty, above and beyond the Corporate refusal to allow her and her late husband the opportunity to spawn. She writhes in the Corporate grip and it didn't take long before she began to fume within Angel's earshot.

"You bees think we have it so easy—the bushwa life, the swag life, you call it—well, I could tell you stories of all the strictures that come tucked into the posh box, wrapped in glitter foil and topped with a satin bow."

Relocations at Galt's whim. Why, she and her adored spouse, a supply chain engineer, had suffered through ten of them in the span of forty years. In fact, she was sure the stress and strain of it had contributed to his early and unexpected demise. Why, the man was just sixty-five!

Five years more than any worker bee ever gets, Angel had thought, even as she nodded sympathetically.

And then to put them here, in Bayfield, staring out at Galt Genesis I day-in and day-out, well, it just smacked of cruelty on Corporate's part. Further evidence of the vileness of the minds in the Hive. The widow is certain the decision came directly from the desk of CQO Zinni. Or at least from the desk of one of her mincing toadies. She had met the CQO in the flesh once. At a conference for the logistics team leaders. Well, she was not actually introduced, but the widow saw her standing across the ballroom. Quite the striking figure. *"Her suit—long jacket, short skirt—was as silvery as her hair. Beautiful—in a fake kind of way, you know?"* But even from afar the widow could feel the nastiness radiating from the fem, like the chill rising from a block of ice. After that, she'd made a point to avoid all the 'tronic signs with that evil face staring out—even if it meant walking or driving blocks out of her way to do it—*"just to avoid that shivery feeling, you know?"* And she is certain the last housekeep she'd employed had been some kind of Galt spy, as if the embeds weren't enough to keep the Corporate eyeball apprised of one's comings and goings. When that fem had been severanced, the widow didn't put in a request for another, swore she'd make do on her own.

"I couldn't wait to retire and stop hearing that damn feed all day long. And the relief of not having the two-way stream listening in on me. Say whatever I damn well please without them overhearing it. It's been two years now. Two years that I should have been enjoying with my dear Cam."

A roll call of swag problems. But Angel did what she's done her whole life, stayed quiet and listened as she cleaned and planted and weeded and repaired and let the widow yammer on and play the benevolent queen with her braided crown and insist they call her 'Mam'—in the maternal sense, rather than the formal—and sink her pink-polished talons into Lark's daily upbringing. The widow sometimes seems to forget that the three are not her actual children. She slips into stories and remembrances of the past as easily as stepping into a pair of well-worn slippers.

"My grandparents were in the Galt tech division. That's the only thing that saved them when the old Republic fell apart. One, they had the knowledge and skills to serve Galt's purposes and two, they had the money to insulate themselves from the nastiness that befell so many others. And they were loyal."

She's let it slip that she was a child born in the second decade of the Protectorate's existence. So, like Angel's old mentor, Debs, she holds its history in her living memory. Angel regrets not asking more questions of Debs before he passed, regrets not pressing him for more of his memories. She vows not to make the same mistake twice. And yet there is a risk involved here. Of presenting a mind too bent on inquiry.

Playing with fire. A dangerous business, Kuba fumes at least once a month, both wanting and fearing this illusion of domesticity.

Angel frowns more than smiles at him, though she knows he has the child's best interests beating in his heart, throbbing through his temples, guiding his hands. It's a regret, for sure, but a shallow one that she can't waste a lot of precious time worrying about. He has mastered the craft of the father, while she beats back night terrors and dreams of mothering the rough beast of rebellion.

4

Silence Speaks Volumes

WITHOUT THE SUN to help her plot the hour, Angel digs the gold timekeep out of the front pocket of her cargos and flips the thin disc open. Quarter til. Just enough time for her to slip out of the garden shed where she's passed the winter morning sharpening the widow's myriad utensils—pruners, loppers, shovels, hoes, and trowels—and trek down the bike path to the lakeside park.

She flicks the clamshell lid closed and rubs her calloused thumb over the image etched into its surface, that of the bullet train's great ancestor, a cloud of smoke caught in a forever billowing belch from its curious pipe. The face of the boy who owned it—stole it—drifts into her mind's eye. His bushy black eyebrows cocked above his mismatched eyes. One brown, one amber. Suraj's vox drifts in as well.

Shorty points to the hour, the long one to the minute. Here endeth the lesson. Time out of mind.

She shivers in the icy drizzle that's been leaking from the overcast sky all morning. Casts an eye towards the house, sprawling and hideous. Dips her hands in the water bucket. Wipes them on the rag hanging from her belt loop. Sets out down the muddy trail through the thickets bordering the property, choked with ninebark shrubs and overgrown lilacs, leafless and dispirited, the promise of lush spring blossoms only a forlorn anticipation.

The bench is empty. As she settles there, she checks the time again. Both black hands point straight up. Five ticks—that's all she'll give them.

"Nice timekeep. Where'dya snatch that?"

Angel keeps her eyes fixed ahead, forcing him to come around. The man is even scrawnier in the harsh daylight. But he's hulking compared to the wraith who hovers beside him, a figure of skin-wrapped bones, swallowed up by an oversized gray parka.

I want to fatten you up with Kuba's black bread and three bean stew.

The thought almost makes the leap to her lips but she lassos it, wrestles it down with a cough she hopes doesn't sound as fake as it feels.

"Punctuality is the politeness of princes," the man who calls himself Path says, with a bow and a flourish of his arm.

"Time and tide wait for no man," Angel spits back, waggling the timekeep at him before tucking it back in her pocket.

"Patience is a virtue," Path replies, grin plastered.

Rolling her eyes, Angel turns her attention to the skeleton man, whose eyes are fixed on her with that sort of intensity that sparks flame in cheeks and heat in the secret parts of the body.

"Cat got your tongue?" she snaps at him.

A flinch, a wince, a side eye, all in the tick of time they've been bantering about. Gravity grabs hold of the muscles of Path's face, everything suddenly sagging. Another awkward silence. The bag of bones with the fierce eyes adjusts his red paisley bandanna, which has slipped a bit. He tucks the faded fabric carefully up around his chin.

It's not that cold. But when you have no fat to insulate...

Path puts a hand on the skeleton's shoulder where Angel imagines a knife-edged collarbone juts, but the man shrugs it off immediately, with a glare that could pierce armor.

Hmmm, a mean squint and a short fuse. I predict this will go nowhere fast.

"Angel, I'd like you to meet Word—Wordsmith—my brother. From another mother," Path says, again with a flourish, dripping smarm like a backwater master of ceremonies dreaming of snagging a spot on the live stream.

Does it hurt to make that expression—it's not a smile, more a grimace—with such a hollowed-out face, skin stretched too tight across sharp bones? The skeleton man mouths a word—hello?—and give a salute, a motion of his hand that seems as if he's flicking away a gnat rather than extending a greeting.

Oh.

Angel swallows, trying to clear the ignorance from her mouth.

"Word isn't much of a talker—right now—but he's still got a lot to say, savvy?" Path lowers himself onto the bench beside Angel. "And that's where you come in."

"What happened to him?" Angel avoids looking at the man, shifting her body and gaze toward Path.

"He can hear you just fine. You don't need to talk to him through me. In fact," he continues, bounding back up, "I'm gonna let my kicks wander on down to the shore. Maybe dap a few stones. Let you two get to know each other." With a parting wink, he crosses the strip of winter-brown grass in two long strides, heading toward the water, kicking up clumps of wet sand in his wake.

Word eases himself onto the far end of the bench, keeping his gaze fixed out toward the roiling gray lake.

"So, you been mute since birth or..." Angel lets the thought trail off, regretting its harshness immediately.

She's not looking at the man beside her. Instead, like him, she stares ahead, watching Path at the water's edge as he squats to snatch a rock and then rises to sling it with an agile sidearm. The stone dances across the water.

Bony fingers waggle in front of her eyes. Angel shifts, turning to face the man, the icy fire in his eyes. He leans over, fishes in his black backpack and removes a marks-all and a compact board, its white surface mottled with gray smears. Uncaps the pen and scribbles on the board in a firm, crisp hand. Shifts it so she can see.

I hope you can read

She sizes him up. His eyes, a melding of green and gray, hold a wealth of secret amusement and malice, behind lush black lashes. The drizzle has subsided to a fine mist, which beads on his tumult of tawny hair like tiny, glistening pearls. He drags the marker across the board again.

Path sometimes forgets the little details

He gives a shrug, an oops gesture, a lift of his eyebrows.

Angel nods, just a slight dip of the chin, her body tight, muscles poised for flight.

He signals, hand to head, but instantly recognizes her lack of comprehension. Fishes a rag out of his pocket and swipes it over the board, wiping away the writing.

Why do you come here—you and the man and the little one

Angel hesitates, then shrugs. "It's a beautiful spot, yeah? Why wouldn't I?"

Lots of beauty here But you sit and stare and sit and stare Out there

Angel turns her gaze back to the water. Lifts her chin as if pointing. Knows she should say nothing, knows she should be as silent as him, should swallow down the urge to speak. She's always been so good at that. Too good.

Miss Stillwater. Mr. Cain's nickname for her. Cain, the fusty bikeman from the Illiana Bartertown, always teasing. *She never speaks. Just walks in beauty like the night. Agua quieta. Where the river runs smooth and quiet, that's where it's deep.*

But she's been so good at keeping quiet that she feels swallowed up with all her swallowing. Buried alive under the weight of all the unspoken thoughts. Only daring to steal moments, the briefest of moments in the sheltering dark, when she'd whisper, lips pressed to the crown of the infant's head or the nape of her neck, letting the words seep out like blood from a wound. Venom from a rattler's fang. But now the child is older and knows many words, learns new ones daily, spews them forth. And it's no longer safe—and not fitting—to let the ugly ones fall upon her innocent head.

She breathes in. Holds.

Stop. Breathe. Focus. Think.

Leap.

"I was born there." Angel stares at the islands offshore, slabs of green and gray in the mist, calm as leaves floating in a puddle.

Word sweeps the board clean. Writes.

Not likely Youd be blinking hot on the embed scanner in my pack

"Long story short. It happened. My mother made it happen."

Mother. That fem, barely more than a girl, who exists only in the inch long fragment of memory that Angel keeps tucked away in a pocket of her own black backpack, the pack she's carried since the day the world fell apart. The day that Eben, her father, the man who raised her, who saved her, revealed her origin story. She pulls the imagekeep out sometimes, when rain pelts the windowpanes or the child frets in her sleep, prodding Angel into consciousness, eyes wide open, ears focused on the child's restless breath. It's then she'll ease herself out of bed, careful to avoid the squeak of the mattress and the creaks of the floorboards, to pluck the treasure from its secret place in the corner of the closet and flick on her maglite so its tiny circle of brilliant white light frames a face. Her birth mother's face.

Angel has looked for that face in crowds, in the stalls of dealers at B-towns, in the aisles of GaltMarts, and slouched at tables in gobble-n-gos all along the trek north through the lower Superior region, the odyssey of the past two years. She's tried to age-up the cheekbones and contours, to etch crow's feet into the corners of those hazel eyes, but the image resists change. Sometimes, seeing a set of swaying hips from the back, Angel imagines they belong to the fem she seeks. Wouldn't a fem possessed with such singular bravery strut just like that? But when she hurries down the next aisle over and turns the corner to catch the front view, the face above those hips is always wrong.

A tap on her knee. The board in Word's hand.

Tell me the long version

Angel shakes her head. "Distant past."

Whats past is prologue

A grimace slashes his face. ***Not my line btw—read it in a biblio***

As he shifts, swiping the writing away, the bandanna around his neck shifts too, the gap revealing a streak of vivid angry red, bright and raw in contrast to the dullness of the fabric. Angel's stomach clutches, but she can't drag her gaze away, until he notices and draws the fabric tighter.

"Prologue, huh?" she prompts, finally raising her eyes to his.

He holds her stare for a moment before he writes.

Long story short—I survived

Angel digs the timekeep out again and checks it.

"Look, I gotta get back to work. Not even sure why I agreed to come—"

"Cuz you want...to remake...the world."

The sound is the wind, if the wind had bones. Labored and airy, tight-made and rattling. Driving her to flee yet holding her fast, in bonds made of iron and breath.

5

We Are All Damn Otis

THE PLAN IS SIMPLE. The plan is outrageous. His words. Her vox. Because the voxcasts in the Superior Region have been silent while he struggles to heal. This silence must not be allowed to stretch on and on. Not now, not when they've come so far. Not now, when their message has spread like an oil slick across the Protectorate. When they know they have a multitude within their grasp. In fact, now is the time to up the ante, to extend their reach. To send the message out into the night, over and over and over again.

Angel, slack-jawed, dumb-struck, cannot believe this revenant is the man who's spoken to her out of the crackling night all these many months since she first heard the voxcast on that Halloween night at Kuba's family compound in Illiana. Throughout their journey north, they've been listening with the rabid dedication of the true believer and the convert ever since Kuba traded a couple loaves of bread and a water vee for a battered 'tronic receiver with a solar cell and a hand crank that she'd had squawking again in blink time. Kuba knew just what frequency to dial up and then they huddled by it, volume turned low, night after night, outsmarting the 'tronic curfew, waiting for the sleek prow of a vox to slice through the rough sea of static.

"You're listenin' to Radio TCT, three chords and the truth."

Warm, deep, resonant, but with ripples of tartness here and there, a savory tang encompassing the listener like a bath of warm lavender oil.

"You're Damn Otis?" Maybe—probably—a hint of disappointment colors her words.

He frowns. A tired frown. Scribbles.

One of many We are all Damn Otis I can see you were expecting someone

He hesitates, the swipeable marks-all hovering over the board. Finishes.

different

"Sorry to disappoint. Another time, another place," he rasps. "Well, maybe I was looking for someone...different, too." The effort needed to vocalize is draining him, the energy seeping away before her eyes, and when their eyes meet, it is Angel who looks away first.

"But," Word continues after a swallow, "here we are."

Path is striding across the beach towards them. When he reaches the bench, he pauses, boots crusted with sand, a question on his face. "Well, do we have a match made for utopia?" he asks, eyebrows arching over his sly smile.

Word wipes his board with the tail of his shirt, scribbles again.

Yeah a match made for no place

Path cocks his head, frowns. "No, no, eu-topos, bro, the good place."

Word erases the words and thrusts the board into his backpack. His shoulders rise and fall, lips tight, eyes set in a grim squint.

"I don't know anything about making a voxcast," Angel stammers.

"You can talk. And you have a vox that's made for the airwaves. That's all you need," Path reassures in a coaxing lilt. "We'll do the rest. Well, mainly Word here. He's the media whiz."

"I have responsibilities," she murmurs.

"No more than anyone else in the movement." Path jerks a thumb in the direction of the manse. "You really feel allegiance to that swag you been swabbin' for? Seriously? Guess maybe I misread—"

"Not her. My daughter. And my—"

"You can't bring them into this," Path cuts in. "You can't tell—"

"I have to. Kuba, anyway. I'm not going to sneak out at night—"

"I see," Path interrupts again. "Worried he'll sus you're playin' him?"

"No!" Angel jabs back. "It's not like that. We're not—he's not..." She glares. "It's none of your deal what he is or isn't. But I won't keep this from him." She pauses, looks Path straight in the eye. "*If* I decide to do it."

"If?" Path glares from Angel to Word. "You didn't close the deal?" He shifts his weight from one foot to the other, like a child impatient for a sweet. "You didn't close?"

Word grabs his backpack and stalks across the grass, shoulders hunched. Path heaves the gusty sigh of a party host who's been left to clean up the empty bottles and spattered candle wax the morning after. Settles himself on the bench, close to Angel. Too close. She's up against the armrest, with no room to scoot over to avoid the press of his thigh.

"He's not a charmer," Path says, as if in explanation. "Never has been. Even before."

"And you are?"

Path grins. "I have my moments."

When he reaches down to dust the sand from his boots, Angel catches a glimpse of the small scab where her knife nicked his neck.

"Look," he says, straightening. "I won't lie. There's some danger involved. Maybe more'n some. Damn Otis is a wanted man. Always on the move."

Angel stares at the scab, pondering.

I know what it feels like to be hunted. To have a hound at your heels.

Path notices where her gaze is lingering. Fingers the scab. Smirks. "But you seem to know your way 'round a knock-about. You'n that blade. As for the vox, it's not like you'd be out raidin' or rowdyin'. We generally leave the—" he pauses, lets that annoying smirk seep across his face again before he continues. "The more physical side of the movement to others. Those more suited to that line of work."

Angel watches him wipe his hands on his jacket. "Then how'd he get his throat slashed?"

Path stares at his fingers. Inspects his fingertips. Picks at a hangnail. Rubs at a curious pale scar that runs down the back of his left hand from his knuckle to nearly his wrist. Glances over at her, then out at the lake, where a herring gull skims along just above the waves. Turns his ferret eyes back to her. "That's a question you'll have to ask him. My question to you—are you in?"

The Safe House

"ARE YOU NEUROFRACKED?! Or just totally hellafried?"

Kuba is giving her the stink eye, like he's already decided the answer. Angel just takes another sip of home-brew, savoring its heat on her tongue. They are tucked into opposite sides of a hammock that droops year round between a pair of oaks at the far corner of the manse's acreage. It's cold and damp, but it provides a refuge where they can talk in private, without the potential of the widow overhearing. They've been arguing in whispers for close to an hour. He keeps circling back to insanity. And Lark.

Living for two. Responsible for someone other than herself. Responsible...

Responsible.

"She's the very reason I'm gonna do this," Angel says, swishing another sip of the boozy concoction around her mouth.

Although that isn't the whole truth.

Don't deny the thrill. Because once it's under your skin, it's burrowed in there but good. Like a tick. And it's just as near impossible to root out.

Kuba's anger runs hot, flaring and then flaming out just as quickly, while Angel's builds in a chill, layer upon layer, like ice freezing over a pond. Opaque. Persistent. Solid. Cold as the north side of a gravestone in winter. He tries all the ways he knows to melt that frozen surface. Logic. Reasoning. The likelihood of failure versus the small chance of success. The danger. To her, to him. To Lark. In the darkness, he can't quite make out the expression on her face, but he can picture it nonetheless. Jaw set, lips firm. Eyes fixed on something only she can see.

That thousand-yard stare.

After he's spewed aggravation in fits and starts, he settles into silence, exhausted.

"You knew back at the Chicago garrison my work wasn't done. You knew. And you traveled the road with me," Angel states, her vox flat, matter-of-fact. She shifts her body, causing the hammock to sway. "You want out now, fine, but you know bailing won't change my mind. And—you bail—you know I won't let you take Lark."

The sigh is the sound of air escaping a punctured tire. A sound of frustration. Defeat. And just as the young man knows her expression, Angel knows his. The resignation that hangs in his eyes and drags down the corners of his mouth. Surrender.

"I've sacrificed things for you," he says.

"I didn't ask you to."

That truth hangs like a curtain between them.

"You're a stone cold killer," he whispers.

"You knew that, too."

The missus is not a stickler for obeying curfew. Why should she? She is old—as old as some of the fems of Kuba's family back in Illiana, nearly as old as Debs had been, and her swag status will allow her to pass on from this world in the natural way of things, when the time comes, rather than through Corporate-directed severance. However, two years since his passing, Mrs. Wright still mourns her husband. So while some nights she lingers in the living room, knitting by the light of a lavender-scented candle, more often than not grief chases her to an early bed, not long after Galt CEO

Blanche intones the nightly Vesper message and the electric circuits are cut, leaving power only for the dormant feed in case of emergencies. Tonight's message about perseverance in the face of adversity had brought a smile, secret, inward, fleeting, to Angel's lips.

Lark is more recalcitrant at bedtime, fighting off the nods, wheedling just one more story or song, pink lips set in a semi-sweet pout. But Angel has long ago handed that task over to Kuba. Her stories aren't fit for the telling. And so it's not difficult for Angel to slip out of the manse and take the trail to the park under the violet glow of the solar lamps.

Path is waiting for her on the bench. "And so, it's on," he says in greeting.

Angel makes no reply and they head off in silence. The neighborhood here is silent, too, without even the hum of renegade generators. Its streets are lined with the corporate-built boxes, encased in plastiwood siding in monotones of gray and tan, edged in ubiquitous white trim, that the bees call home. There is nary a glimmer of candlelight in the windows. An outward show of obedience to Protectorate rules.

Their path heads uphill, away from the lake, into a neighborhood of older homes of a pre-Protectorate vintage, each unique in architecture and color palette, marking it as bushwa territory. Bayfield, with its roots in the old Republic as a swag vacation spot and, before that, a fishing town on the shores of Lake Superior, is now essentially a way station between childlessness and parenthood. The couples who successfully navigate the minefield that is the Galt approval process—the physicals, the mentals, the proof of moral character and devotion to the Corporate Way—arrive for one last inspection by the assignment bureaucrats. One final round of questions posed by fems in sleek gray suits and matching ear buds, whose deadpan expressions and vocal tones are at odds with their proximity to joy. Potential parentals who manage to squirm through the course of ever-narrowing hoops are never actually eliminated by this final examination. It's just another form of torture designed to keep the populace in line. Parentals-to-be arrive two days after their child is birthed, which allows for a physical inspection of the infant and the insertion of the embed which will monitor the whereabouts of the child throughout his or her life. And track and regulate his or her emotions.

The success of this brain smoothing is disputed within the Corporate hierarchy, with the scientists claiming the process works, while the bureaucrats point out all the instances when it apparently doesn't. The riots at GaltMarts in the Illiana and Erie Regions last fall. The rash of break-ins at medicenters in the Huron Region. The strange disappearances and slayings of goliaths—an entire platoon—in lower Illiana in the summer of Year 80. The as-yet unsolved murders of the Chief Water Engineer and the Director of Special Services at the water plant in the Chicago garrison two Decembers ago. Unrest ripples through the Protectorate, originating from stones cast by unknown actors. But in Bayfield, a sense of joy abides. At least on the surface. At least among the bees who buzz in empty-handed and buzz out, arms filled with their heart's desire.

Path and Angel turn down a lonelyish winding strip of crumbling asphalt lit by a set of evenly spaced solars. At the end of the long driveway sits a two-story house with a high-peaked gabled roof and a broad veranda, not unlike the wide porch of Angel's childhood home. The porch back in AgSector 21 where Eben taught her to play chess, where Serafina strummed her guitar, and they all sang songs handed down through time out of mind.

Angel blinks away the memory.

"How do you come to be here? Whose house?" she asks warily, hesitant to set foot on the wooden stairs. They sag to the left, and the splintered treads look as if they've felt the weight and scrape of too many shoes. As if they are long overdue for a visit from the sweeps with their hammers and paint.

"Sympathizers. A retired couple," Path says, leading the way.

Angel nods and follows Path up the steps and through the heavy steel door, a seemingly much newer addition to the house.

"But they're...out of the loop," Path continues, his vox taking on the silky tones of a Bartertown rat trying to distract a customer from the dings and dents on a chain guard. "You know how it is. Some are only willing to go so far in support of the cause. You don't need to meet them or interact."

As with the widow, retired status makes the feedcom less problematic. Retirees can listen to a limited stream of infotainment and not worry about being overheard by an omnipresent Galt ear. Or so it is said. The Hive mind appears to lack the imagination to conceive of threats from its privileged geriatrics. After all, living out their days in cushy digs with the bounty that Galt provides, what bitterness could they possibly harbor? What intrigue could they possibly plot? They are the Grateful Generation, blessed with Galt's beneficence. Or so it would seem. The widow, in a pique of anger after her husband's death, had stuffed her feedcom into a closet and had bragged about its unorthodox, unapproved location to Angel. It makes Angel wonder whether Galt's omniscience is truly all-seeing and all-knowing. But she also kens that surveillance could easily persist on the down-low.

"Where's the feedcom?" she asks, feeling the need to whisper.

Path picks up a maglite from a bench in the dark foyer, flicks it on, spotlights a door. He opens it, revealing an ordinary closet with an assortment of coats and jackets. He swings the lite upwards to illuminate a shelf on which rests a rectangular black pouch.

"Faraday bag," notes Path in a matter-of-fact tone, before closing the door again. "Which—shocked, not shocked—the couple conveniently had in their possession. Rebels at heart, underneath the swag skin. Saved us the trouble of stealing one."

He swings the maglite to highlight a narrow staircase, its treads covered in threadbare carpet.

"Up we go," he says, and they climb the flight of stairs, turn a sharp right and head down a long hall. Near its end, Path opens a door and ushers her into a disheveled bedroom. The splashes of light from the maglite highlight an unmade bed tucked in a corner, sheets wrinkled and bunched, a puddle of t-shirts at its foot. The laggard leg of a pair of jeans hangs down the front of a small dresser.

"He's a slob," Path murmurs apologetically. "But we all have our faults, yeah?"

The light continues its arc, spilling over a set of coppery metal bowls resting atop of battered chest of drawers, then landing on a small door knob. Path opens the narrow closet door. Pushes aside some sweaters and shirts hanging haphazardly from a rod, reaches up and pulls a cord attached to a light fixture, its empty socket a black hole ringed in white. The narrow rectangle of ceiling swings down, revealing a space above, a space suffused with a mellow glow. Using a hanger, Path snags the end of what turns out to be a rope ladder.

"Treehouse we were denied as kids." He focuses the maglite on his face, where a smirk lurks in the harsh glare. "Just boys at heart." He gestures. "Ladies first."

Angel notes the speculation—almost a dare—lurking beneath that smirk and wonders if her own face is revealing something she'd rather conceal. Fear. Hesitancy.

"Fortune," Path says, sweeping a salute, lip curled in a taunt.

When she sets her foot on the first dowel rod, a frisson of excitement and trepidation sets the skin on the nape of her neck to tingling. Two rungs up and her head breaches the opening into a confined, damp chill. Into a smell of new wood and a sense of dust recently unsettled. A triangular space with sharp slopes and angles. At the far end, in a splatter of light cast by a battery-powered lantern, Word sits at a makeshift table fashioned from a wood plank laid across a couple of sawhorses. The plank is stacked with 'tronic gear and biblios. His grimace suggests he's not particularly glad to see her.

Same here and frack you very much.

Angel boosts herself into the attic. Stands too quickly and clonks the top of her head on a rafter. Blinks away the sudden shimmer of stars. Scowls at the amusement that tugs at Word's lips. Amusement that he quickly covers with his own scowl.

"Bump your head?" Path says as he pokes his through the opening. "Do it all the time. Ain't been here long enough to get the auto duck motion ingrained in my brain. Yeah, so—"

Word draws a hand across his neck. It's not swaddled in the red bandanna, but the angry scar is hidden in the shadows. Pushes his hand out as if pushing something away.

"Sure, bro, I'll go. Thought you might want an interpreter— or a chaperone, but—"

The shadows can't hide Word's seething glare.

A mad man. A madman.

The hand that dismissed Path beckons her. The plywood boards shift and flex under her feet, causing her to walk slowly, carefully, as if feeling her way across a newly frozen pond.

Not nailed to the crossbeams. Slipshod. Temporary.

But the equipment at the improvised table looks totally slick. A black 'tronic box with slim buttons and fat knobs, smooth screens and all manner of ports. A vox setup with a bulbous-headed mic. Another black box that resembles the one she fixed for Ms. Salinas, the meme, back in Illiana. Way back in the day. The one that played heavenly music from shiny discs. There's also another piece she doesn't recognize. Some type of ancient tech with a low square base fitted with a round black platter and an arm-like attachment.

"All this"—she gestures to the gear—"lets you be Damn Otis?"

Word considers her. The lantern light does nothing to mellow his taut face. Indeed, it sharpens the contours, the hollows.

Do you ever eat?

Angel curses herself for not bringing a hunk of bread and a slice of cheese with her, as one might do to placate a feral dog. To prove that he's not some spirit creature, but an actual flesh-and-blood man who requires and takes in sustenance.

He applies marks-all to whiteboard. Shoves it around so she can read.

It'll let anybody be anybody

Jewels

Words.

Tumbling around her mouth like stones for polishing. Agate and obsidian. Strings of them. Like necklaces. Glittering. Calling the eye. Printed on a scrap of cardboard, in a scrawling hand, tight in some places, loose in others. In the creation of certain letters—the dotting of i's, the crossing of t's—the pen must have been pressed down with such force that its tip punctured the surface.

She stumbles as she reads them. Over and over again. A slashing hand. Stop. A rolling hand. Begin again. The man sighs. Shifts on his stool. Runs a hand through his unkempt hair. Tugs at it as if he hankers to pull it out by the roots. Perched on a stool not three feet away, Angel feels the waves of his exasperation rippling through the narrow space, washing up against the shore of her own frustration.

"Look, dial it back," she growls, slapping the rectangle of cardboard off its easel. It flops face down in front of him on the makeshift table. "You can't expect me to get it perfect the first time."

He glowers. Scribbles. Shoves his whiteboard in her face.

Ive lost count

"First," she repeats.

He shakes his head, wipes, scribbles.

At least 10 times

"This is the *first* time I'm here doing this in this frackin' attic with you staring at me and—right now—I'm thinking it'll be my last." She glares back at him, mouth set.

Silence crackles until Path's vox breaks it. "You been workin' hard. Time for some 'blivion and snacksies." His head pokes through the entry hole, followed by his hands and arms, which set a jug and a plate of bread and cheese on the plywood. " 'A book of verses underneath the bough, a jug of wine, a loaf of bread—and thou beside me singing in the wilderness. Oh, wilderness were Paradise enow.' " He winks and boosts himself into the attic. Cocks his head. "Hmm, I sense discontent. Smell it in the air."

He stoops to pick up the jug and plate. "He can be quite the taskmaster when it comes to his words. Almost as relentless as a Corporate overseer." Path sets his offerings down, right on top of the piece of cardboard. A fresh, yeasty aroma wafts from the thick slices of bread.

"A genuine frackhole."

Word grabs the jug, downs a long swig, and slams it back down. The plate rattles. Path sighs, scans the table and pulls a mug out from behind the 'tronic box. Gives the inside of it a cursory once-over, wipes the rim with his shirttail. Pours a generous portion into it and offers it to Angel.

"Good shit," he coos, as she hesitates, eyeing the mug with barely disguised disgust. "Don't worry. It'll kill any germs lurking within."

Don't mock me.

Angel snatches the mug and, before any second thoughts can intervene, takes a deep swallow. The liquid is smooth on the tongue, but flares like a match against a striker on the way down. The burn provokes a shudder. Path grins. More mockery. So she takes another sip and wills her face and body into a freeze.

"Make sure you eat somethin'. Need to head back soon and I don't wanna have to sling you over my shoulder. In case we run smack into a night patrol."

"I'm ready to go now," Angel says, draining the mug and rising to her feet, wincing a little as the liquid courses its fiery way down her throat. She half expects Word to make an effort to stop her. To insist they continue. But he doesn't.

Downstairs at the front door, Angel turns to Path. "I can make my own way."

He shakes his head. "Manners maketh the man," he says, ushering her out.

"Maybe you should remind your—brother—about that."

Path takes her elbow, guiding her around a deep crack in the pavement. "Aww, give'm a chance. He's really got the eti-skills. Genuine, b-town rat, con man level. He could probably charm the burner out of a goliath's hand. Scratch that cynic and he'll bleed the red blood of a romantic. Well, maybe that's—whaddaya call it? Hyperbole? But, seriously, he's been through a lot. And the thing he loves was taken from him."

Angel wants to retort that she knows a thing or two about that, but she holds the words in her mouth, where they feel like pebbles that will remain rough-edged and ugly no matter how long they tumble in a polisher's drum.

He gives a little bow as he leaves her at the park bench. "I have just three things to teach: sensitivity, patience, and compassion. These three are your greatest treasures."

Something in her expression makes him grin. "No, didn't come up with that on my own, either. Biblios, all from biblios. If I didn't read, I'd probably have nothin' to say. Now Word, he's the one who writes his own great lines. And now they'll be yours." Another bow accompanied by a flourish of his hand. "Will you be here tomorrow?"

Angel considers. Stares hard at his face, skin cast with a purplish tinge from the solars. Thinks about the ravaged neck of the man back in the attic.

Nods.

One week. Seven days. One hundred sixty-eight hours. The time allotted for Angel's transformation from a street-smart fixer of things into...

What?

The voxcast. It's all about the voxcast. And the date. January fifteenth. It has to happen then. When Angel asks why, why the rush, the pressure to be ready—what's the deal?—Word squints at her as if he's examining something growing out of her chin. Something a tad disgusting. She's so certain something must be there that she swipes a hand over it. Feels nothing but smooth skin.

He gestures to Path, who's leaning against the rafters at the far side of the attic.

"January fifteenth," Path says with a certain emphasis, then shrugs. "Well, why would you know anything about it?" He shoots Word a look as if to remind him to lower his expectations. To remind him of the nature of the raw material he's molding.

Angel has told them little about herself, other than a few glancing allusions to her childhood in Illiana and the Corporate removal that set her feet on her journey north, keeping her answers to their infrequent questions clipped, dispassionate. And in return, Path hasn't spilled much on his side. He's joked about dragging himself out of the elite gene pool. Bragged about his technique for perfecting his backwater drawl and his cojones for removing his own embed with nothing but a fish gutter and a couple of lethe pills to kill the pain. Hence the scar on his left hand. But he's let nothing drop that would identify his parentals. Nothing about his life before. She assumes this is the way of the guevara. The less you know about someone, the less you can spill under the glare of the goliaths' interrog lights and the spell induced with a jab of Veracivaxx.

"The fifteenth marks the birthdate of an ancient prophet of the Old Republic. A man who knew the beauty and power of words. Blessed with the gift of the gab. Speechifying. Although a bit too pacifist for my taste." Path shrugs. "Even heroes have feet of clay. Alas, just one more dangerous name wiped from the memory banks." He casts another glance at Word, who slumps at the 'tronic box, chin in one hand, fingers of the other drumming the top of the plank table, eyes skittering. "So the fifteenth it is."

"If no one knows, what difference does it make, this date—"

"All the more reason to do it. Because it should be known." Path's tone is suddenly drained of all snark. "It's part of the history that's been erased. And some may know—the memes and those who hear them—they may recognize the significance. It's the principle of the thing." He catches the arc of Angel's rolling eyes. "Yeah, some things we do for principle." He smirks, the snark creeping back. "Even us rogues and outlaws."

Word snatches a worn biblio from his pile. The cover is missing, the binding frayed, the paper fragile and brown-tinged. He shoves it in Angel's face as it falls open to a page with a small black and white imagekeep of a dark-skinned man in profile, his fist resting against his chin. He has a meaty face and close-cropped hair and a pensive look in his eyes. But he's wearing swag clothes and if Angel passed him on the street, she wouldn't identify him as a fellow traveler on the rebel path.

Word snaps his fingers. Shuts the book. Beckons.

"So, no time to waste, yeah?" Path's eyes give her a push.

Word is indeed a taskmaster, bordering on tyrant. The speech he's prepared is not long, just three paragraphs. The sentences are forthright, not flowery. Short and pointed, not meandering and riddled with clauses. But Angel stumbles. Misses the inflection he desires on a particular word. On a particular syllable. Doesn't articulate a phrase with the emotion—the passion—that he expects. That he demands. These instructions he conveys not with shouted commands, but sharp hand gestures and disparaging rolls of his eyes. With shakes of his head. Snaps of his fingers. An abrupt rap of his open palm on the plank.

Begin again.

And she does.

When their hour together is over, she's always near to tears and more than halfway to hating him, though she's loathe to let any of that seep out in front of him. Or Path. But she suspects that Path notices, since he's always quick with an encouraging word.

"You're doing fine, yeah. He just expects—perfection. Lives in a different world than you and me," he says as he leads the way down the staircase, swinging his maglite.

The moon is near full and its silvery light slants through the windows in the room opposite the staircase. Angel can make out the frame of a fireplace and the bulk of two chairs set before it. She stops in mid-step when she perceives a rounded form above the back of each chair. What appear to be the tops of heads. Path hears her sharp intake of breath and turns around. His gaze follows hers. A soft chuckle purrs in his throat.

"That's right. You ain't met the mister and missus."

The maglite cuts a path across a scuffed wood floor and a floral-patterned rug. Path keeps it pointed down until they reach the fireplace and step in front of the chairs. Then he sweeps it in a dramatic arc and focuses on the occupant of the chair to the left. Angel sucks in another gasp.

She's staring at the blank visage of a mannequin.

Path pats the top of the smooth, egg-shaped head. "This is Mrs. McCarthy. And here,"—he swings the maglite to spotlight the chair on the right—"here is her darling husband, Mr. M."

The male mannequin sports a threadbare plaid shirt and khaki trousers; the fem, a shabby scoop-necked nightgown that stretches to the floor.

"Mrs. McCarthy don't get out much," Path says by way of explanation. "Well, neither does the mister anymore." He shines the light in Angel's face, gauging her reaction. She swats at it like she would an annoying mosquito. Path swings it out of reach and laughs. "However, their embeds do get out upon occasion."

The maglite spotlights a gold oval locket resting against the fem mannequin's flesh-toned chest.

"Swags and their glitz, yeah?" Path lifts the locket and releases its clasp. Inside, held in place by a bead of grayish stickum, lies a tiny seed-like embed chip. "Luckily, she had two. One in gold, the other"—he sweeps the circle of light to the male mannequin's chest with the aura of a carnival barker—"silver."

This locket is heart-shaped, the silver tarnished. Angel reaches out and flicks it open. Another chip is glued inside.

"How'd you come by these?"

Path rests a hand on the male mannequin's head. "Snagged 'em from a GaltMart teardown before the sweeps came through. Awesome find. Fully poseable."

"Not the dummies. The embeds."

Path holds the maglite under his chin, throwing shadows in all the wrong places, highlighting all the wrong features. His skull-like visage sends a ripple through the hairs on the back of Angel's arm.

"I'll never tell," he murmurs, grinning, teeth too prominent in the shadows and light.

Angel taps the minute chip with the tip of her finger. "I had one of these." She snaps the locket shut and lets it fall. The clink as it collides with the mannequin's molded chest is a sad, hollow sound. "I know what you'd have to do to get 'em."

Path holds the light under Angel's chin. Winks.

"Then why'd ya ask?"

8

Everything is Personal

LARK BOUNCES ON THE WIDOW'S KNEE, munching gleefully on a piece of toast. The slab of bread and the toddler's plump cheeks both sport magenta smears of raspberry jam. The old fem takes a napkin and daubs at the stains, cooing.

"Oh, who's the messy eater?"

Lark resists, bobbing her head, curls tumbling. With Angel, it would have turned into an angry standoff, full of no's on both sides. But under the widow's touch, it becomes a giggling game. The fem has a way with the child.

"She's just starting to know her own mind," Mrs. Wright asserts, as she always does when dealing with the fractious child. "I may not have had the Corporate blessing to be a mother, but I've had the chance to observe the children of others and I've kept it all up here." She taps her temple with a fine-boned finger that ends in a glossy pink varnished nail. "Maybe the whole time I was preparing for this little sweetie to come into my life."

Illegally. Against the Corporate mandate. But Angel swallows down the little frog of resentment burrowing in her throat. *Gratitude. Gratitude for this haven. Gratitude for this fem's desire to mother your child. To do the kind of work—the mothering kind of work—that you feel so unprepared to do.*

"And every day we are thankful for that, Mam," Angel says,

as she pushes back from the breakfast table and bends to brush a kiss on the top of Lark's head.

"Mama go," Lark warbles.

"Yes," says Mrs. Wright. "Mama will go work in the greenhouse and Mam and Lark will build something with those new blocks we found at the whimsy shop." The widow inclines her head toward the sunroom off the kitchen. "Those windows need cleaning, too. Rain spatters all over. I can barely see out them. And it's such a beautiful view. My husband was so proud of his gardens, even in winter. I only wish we'd get some snow."

"Snow?" Lark repeats.

"Snow," the widow nods. "Oh, when I was your age, in the winter, the snow still piled up and ice still ringed the lake shores. Why, there's even a crazy legend about an ice bridge that used to form between here and the big island. But nobody's around who actually remembers that. I don't think I believe it. But snow, yes."

Angel puts her bowl in the sink and stares out the window at the gray landscape, remembering Serafina's tales of winters long ago, the passing of knowledge from meme to meme. Things long past, things intended to be forgotten but held tight by rebel minds.

Could this old fem be a secret meme?

"Go bye," Lark says, waving with the soggy toast still clutched in her fist.

Angel pauses, regards the child. Bends and gives her a second, more lingering kiss, her eyes meeting the old fem's, holding the look for a moment. Then she turns away to begin her work day.

Mid-morning, Angel takes a break from cleaning the exteriors of the windows. She drops her squeegee into the bucket of sudsy water, lifts her blackout shades to check for streaks. Closes her eyes and arches her back, enjoying the slanted rays of weak sunlight penetrating the grim slab of clouds that's been pelting the region with sleet for days on end. Rolls her neck and shoulders.

"Late nights startin' to show on your face."

Angel opens her eyes to find Kuba standing there, offering her a tumbler of water.

"Just sayin'," he remarks with a studied air of indifference. Which hides nothing.

Angel positions the shades on the bridge of her nose again, hiding the plum-gray circles that muddy the skin under her eyes. Takes a long swallow of water.

"Now ya see 'em, now ya don't. Can't wear those inside." Kuba nods toward the house.

Angel shrugs. "Her attention is focused on one thing and one thing only. Caught in the web of the little spider's charm."

"Yeah, well, that's worrisome, too."

"It's the price I—" she catches herself, seeing his glare—"we pay. Her need protects us all."

Kuba shakes his head. "This is a dangerous game we're playing."

She drains the glass. Hands it back to him. Wants to roll her eyes at what has become his favorite expression of late. But bites her lip and bends to fish the squeegee back out of the bucket. "Not a game," she murmurs and gets back to her task.

She's sick to death of the whiteboard and its black commands.
Feel it If you dont feel it you cant make others feel it
Louder
Softer
Too fast
Too slow
Feel it Live it Live the words
Nothing satisfies the man. She can recite the words, phrases, sentences now without a stumble or a hitch, but Word sighs and frets, tapping the marks-all, clenching his fists. Raises his hands in the air and gestures like a conductor directing an orchestra. *Trying* to direct an orchestra, but, in reality, dealing with the

limitations and vagaries of one imperfect instrument.

For the past two nights, Angel has tried to be docile, to be the passive lump of clay for him to mold. In an attempt to ingratiate, she's brought him all manner of leftover delicacies from the widow's table. Kuba's brown bread, his vegetable ragout, a thigh of herb-roasted chicken. He's eyed them with the same sullen glare with which he regards everything. Pushes them aside, gestures for her to begin. And to stop. And then to begin again. And to stop. Jabbing and slashing the air, swiping and filling the whiteboard until the sharp odor of the ink wafts to the rafters, filling the space with rancor.

Tonight she's pushing back. In a passive-aggressive sort of way. Deliberately repeating the words with the same inflection and tone that he's just criticized, to test whether he's really noticing, whether he'll jot down the same litany of complaints and correctives for each run-through. He is. He does. Seething. So she abruptly changes tactics. And tries, genuinely tries, to get it right. To deliver the speech the way he wants it delivered. To say the words that he's put in her mouth in the exact way he wants them said. To take the pebbles and bring forth pearls.

It's a fail. Again. And when, again, he grabs the board to scrawl the latest criticism, Angel leaps off her stool, rips it from his grip, and slings it across the attic. It smacks against the far wall and lands with a clatter in the dark tight corner where the slanted roof meets the floor.

"Talk to me!" She jabs a finger in his face. "Trash me all you want, but if you're gonna flame me, be a man and say it out loud. To my face—not that frackin' board. If I'm not the vox you want, then just spit it out and be done with it, and this is over. But I need to hear it. To hear you say it! I need to hear a vox other than my own!"

His is the stung look of a man whose most intimate companions are bitterness and misery. He blinks. Lets the marks-all drop from his hand onto the table. Angel looms over him, tight in his space, so that he has to cock his head back to look her in the face. Baring his neck to the lantern light. Her hand, with a will of its own, is drawn to it—that neck and the angry scar that runs its length. Trembles toward it, hovers just above the disfigured skin. Feels its heat radiating into her fingertips. She expects him to slap her hand away. Braces for the smack. But he lets it linger there, his eyes, glittering in the mellow light, locked on hers. Daring her? Begging her?

Until the spell is broken by the sound of Path ascending the rope ladder. In the split-second before she hears the creak of the plywood as he boosts himself above the opening, Angel's hand flutters to her chest where it rests above her galloping heart and slowly curls into a fist.

"Time's up," Path says.

"Be right down," Angel replies, not looking over, keeping her gaze steady on Word, holding his. Only after Path descends again, and Angel hears the soft thud of his feet on the closet floor, does she let her eyes slide away. Turns to make her own descent. And then she hears that rattling, rasping skeleton wind.

"I always eat the food you bring."

"Don't look for praise outta him. Most you can hope for is a lack of criticism—or nothin' at all. It's in his nature. Hell, it's in his bones. In the frackin' marrow. His eyes are always drawn first to the flaw," Path says as they descend the porch steps.

The weather's turned in the past couple of days, a wind from the northwest bringing a biting freeze that encases the tree limbs in rime. They look as if they've been dipped in a thick coating of sugar, the crystals glowing an unearthly violet under the solars. A sudden gust nips their cheeks.

"I don't need praise," Angel snaps, tugging on her gloves. "But I do need to see a reason for doing something. A goal."

Path's usually brisk pace slows, as he tests the icy surface of the pavement. "The goal? To. Remake. The. World." He enunciates each word with precision, but there's something mocking in his air.

"That's a slogan, not a goal," Angel scoffs. "What's the goal? The result?"

His hand closes around her elbow and he tugs her into the shadow of a towering pine. "You want me to spell it out?" His mouth is so close to her ear that his breath seems to curl inside it, hot and damp against the crisp night air. "Do I know enough about you to ken you're no Corporate spy? Maybe. Maybe not." His cheek presses up against hers. "I'm not spilling our ops to you yet. But you want me to say we're out to overthrow Galt? To take the Protectorate out of its grip? Consider it said."

"You and whose army of goliaths?" she taunts, shrinking away from the intimacy of his skin on hers.

"There's plenty of us," Path boasts, his grip holding her tight to him.

Angel considers. Sometimes the McCarthy house is rank with the smell of unwashed bodies, when other members of the cell crawl in to replenish supplies, shower, and get and give the latest info dump. Path has intimated they are squatting out in the Chequamegon Forest. Has vaguely suggested they are running sabotage ops. Angel never sees them, only senses their presence by their odors and the faint murmurs and vibrations she hears and feels emanating from the basement. It would seem there's never more than two or three at a time. Perhaps they spread out their comings and goings to avoid telltale spikes on the utility meter.

In the garage there's a gray personal transport that Angel presumes belonged to the McCarthy couple—or whatever their names really are. Were. Biofuel vouchers are hard to come by, and with security stations on the north and south stretch of Highway 13, the dealers don't swing by Bayfield to barter very often. The security traps make overland travel through the forest on foot the safer bet for interlopers of all kinds. Does the transient nature of the town, bees coming and going, picking up their infants, make it easier for the guevaras to blend in when they do come in out of the woods? When she's inquired about meeting them, Path always gives a crooked grin and a subtle brush-off.

"In time. They're never in one place for very long. To be a gue-vara is to be ever on the move. But you already know that, doncha? Right now, it's best you remain hidden behind a veil of mystery, too. The vox. Only the vox. More power in that, you ken?"

Now he throws a taunt. "Showed you mine. So show me yours. What's your goal?"

Angel breathes. Lets her shoulder sink out of their hunch. Rests her gloved hand over his and slowly slips her fingers under his, gently prying them open one by one until her arm is free, though the heat of his touch lingers through the fabric of her jacket. With her cheek near to his, it's her turn to whisper steam. "I'd say my goal is more concrete. More achievable. I aim to put a hurt on the bastards who put a hurt on me and mine. A permanent hurt."

A dismissive grunt gusts from Path's lips. "Vengeance is just a personal vendetta. Small beans in the grand scheme of things."

"Everything is personal, with me."

In her waking dreams, it's clear, easy, straightforward. Free the ovas, the fems of the Breeder Islands. To honor her mother. To remove that cog from the reproductive wheel of Galt. And then, move on to the Hive. But there, it gets a little foggy, even though the faces that slip in and out of the haze are a constant. The pallor of the skin, the brilliant blue of the eyes, the slick of black hair, the swoop of silver. The vastness of their imag-es designed to make them something more than human. But even without a plan, Angel knows in her gut that CEO Blanche and CQO Zinni will bleed out just like the goliaths down in the Shawnee. Carrion for crows.

At the bench, she pauses, her gaze drawn to the searchlights that rise from the cliffs of the islands, the beams skimming the surface of the lake in lazy arcs.

"She's most likely dead, your birth mother. Long dead," Path says.

Oh, yours is a face that's asking to be slapped. But Angel resists her fingers' reflex to curl and clench. "So when I smash those lights and ferry every last one of her sisters across the water, the taste of it will be that much sweeter," she mutters.

Path rests his arm on her shoulder, pondering. "Well, from one guevara to another, it'd be easier to just cut the power. And necessary, too, from a communications standpoint." Angel shrugs to dislodge his arm, but he shifts with her, keeping it firmly in place. "Too bad the lake between this shore and the islands doesn't freeze over anymore. Some claim it did, long ago. Might be tough to rustle up an armada round here."

"There's boats out there. Crews still fish the lakes. There's people to be turned. That's what these voxcasts are for, yeah? Winning over hearts and minds? Planting the seed. Watering it, feeding it. That's what you said. So it's possible," Angel insists.

"Theoretically, yeah, anything's possible. Provided they— the ovas—want to. Leave, that is. You do understand they live a pretty swag life over there? Pampered, to say the least. How d'ya know they want out? Seems like you're bettin' it all on one fem that you never even knew the rhyme and reason of."

"I just know," Angel snaps. "I know that no fem wants to be a baby-making machine."

Path smirks. "Galt would phrase it more elegantly. A vessel of reproduction, perhaps," he ventures, in the pompous tones of a Corporate proclamation. "But you have a point. And I like a fem with the courage of her convictions."

Angel hardly notices that the arm on her shoulder slips around her back into an embrace. She's too busy pondering.

"I have the conviction. It's the doing...the how of it," she murmurs, half to herself.

"Well, that's where I come in. Fortune—"

"Yeah, yeah, the bold. Blah, blah, blah."

"And the gods help those who help themselves," Path replies, nudging her hip with his. "Whoever the gods are. But for logistics, baby," he whispers, his lips grazing her cheek. "I'm your man."

9

The Singing Bowls

Now that she has put it into words, and put the words out into the world and into someone else's ears, the plan—or the idea of the plan, the germ of it—becomes an obsession. The scene plays in the theatre of her mind throughout the day, interrupted only by brief intermissions when she's forced to consider other things. The grocery list. The widow's hankering for the scent of her husband's pipe tobacco. Lark's sudden resistance to shoes. But the image soon rushes back to center stage, in panorama.

A line of fems clothed in filmy white, flowing shifts, feet bare, hair streaming, crossing the water under the blue sheen of a full moon in a trail as sinuous as a wisp of smoke and just as quick to disappear.

Her logical brain scoffs, tells her all the ways it won't happen like that. Can't happen like that. That in order to make it happen for real, she needs to think in concrete terms and banish the romantic, gauzy vision crap from her waking thoughts. And yet, that vision remains, of a trail of barefoot fems in white.

It's the vision she holds when she swoops Lark up in her arms, away from Mrs. Wright's grim insistence on forcing the toddler's foot into the tiny blue sneaker. "Maybe the shoe doesn't fit," she laughs, twirling around as Lark arches her back, giggling.

"It fit just fine a few days ago," the widow scowls.

"Growth spurt, Mam, as you so often say," Angel replies, still spinning with Lark, whose little fists are jabbing at the air.

Mrs. Wright tsks, but the corners of her downturned lips are softening.

Angel gives Lark another twirl, then pulls her close for a fierce kiss. "No kicks today!"

"If she stubs her toe, it's on you," the widow says, a half-hearted scold.

"So be it. I'll bear that burden."

It's the vision she holds when she pours herself a second mug of home-brew, ignoring Kuba's frown. She'd picked at her dinner, pretending to eat, moving the food around on her plate, tossing and re-tossing the greenhouse-grown kale, arranging the orange coins of carrot into a lopsided stack, peeling the crust off her slice of bread and fashioning it into a corral for her peas.

"You're worse'n her," Kuba gripes, nodding at Lark, who has made a happy mess on her plate. "Good thing the missus's out tonight or she'd be putting the questions to you."

"Yeah, so don't you take her place," Angel warns. She's cursed herself for spilling the voxcast date. Knows he'll be listening tonight. It's churning up her nerves, sending waves of nausea rolling through her belly. She longs for an impossible cloak of total anonymity. Finds it maddening that she has to share this secret with a trio of others.

It's called trust. But do I?

"To liquid courage," she says out loud, raising her glass and downing another long swig, finishing with a grimace.

"Since when do you need that?" Kuba mutters, clearing their plates from the table.

Fems, wraiths clothed in white, skimming the silver lake, veils trailing, ghosting pale, silent, sheer. Likes brides. Brides of freedom.

It's the vision she holds when she climbs the rope ladder,

ducks into the attic and strides across the plywood. The vision she holds when she perches on her stool, takes a sip of water, and clears her throat. The vision she holds up until the moment when Word pushes the mic in front of her face, using his index finger to measure the distance between its bulbous mesh head and her lips. And then it's gone, like mist in sudden, scorching sunlight.

Something is in her throat, obstructing it, throttling it from within. Jagged and frozen, like a monstrous hailstone. She struggles to swallow, to force down whatever is stuck there. But it's fierce. Resistant. Frozen.

Word is pressing buttons, twisting knobs, powering up the 'tronic boxes. He's planned to start with her speech, stark in the night, to startle listeners with her vox, fresh and new to their ears. To smash them in the face with his words, wake them up from their midnight languor. Rile them up and then keep their blood at a boil with a selection of tunes. He's been as exacting as ever. But since the night she whipped the whiteboard from his hands, he has made an effort to vocalize his demands, to disguise them as requests in his breathless ache of a vox. To hear it stirs a sense of pity, and of shame, which Angel struggles to tamp down with justifications for her own behavior.

He's a brute. And so he only understands brute force.

Now she steels herself for his fury, as the grip throttling her throat settles into paralysis, a numb closure of every passageway and opening in her body.

He will see. He will see and stop this before it goes live.

But he doesn't see. Doesn't notice the stark terror that clamps and holds her mouth shut as cruelly as a muzzling hand. His fingers curl in front of her face in a countdown.

Five. Four. Three. Two. One. His index finger flicks as if flipping a switch.

Go.

Her lips open and close behind that invisible hand. Open and close. Open and close. A gaping silence. It's only then that Word looks at her, truly looks her in the face. Into her unblinking eyes.

She braces for something that never comes. Forces her eyes closed against the wave of his anger that must surely crash over her. She hears the click of a button being pushed. The sudden hush that replaces the steady low hum from the 'tronics. Silence that goes on for time. And then the faraway shudder of a door slamming and the thud of feet on a staircase. It's Path, who's been banished to the shed to monitor the generator and the quality of the voxcast. She hears the rasp of rope against wood as he climbs the ladder. The nasal quality of his vox as he pokes his head through the opening and whines, "What the frack? You're late!" And then the sibilant hiss as Word slashes the air to dismiss him. And then they are alone again.

What she least expects is there in Word's hand as it closes over hers. A gentle tug drawing her to her feet. The aching whisper. "Come."

When they are down the ladder and standing in his room, she realizes that, besides their first meeting on the bench in the park, this is the first time she's seen him outside of the attic. It's odd and a bit cringe-inducing, but at the same time strangely comforting to see him in the midst of his mess, in the funk of his man smell, t-shirts drooping from door knobs. But she's still swallowing and swallowing, still unable to dislodge the frozen blockage. And still bracing for the lash of his scorn.

Path, leaning against the doorframe, folds his arms across his chest. "What gives? Are we on? We're burnin' precious fuel waitin' on—"

Word shoves Path into the hall and holds up a hand, fingers spread, before closing the door in his astonished face.

"Lie down," Word rasps. He turns to the chest of drawers and fiddles with the knob of the lantern, dimming the light. When he turns back to Angel, he's holding a metal bowl in each hand.

His eyes flash, cranked that she hasn't followed his command.

"Lie down," he repeats. "Or sit. Whatever. Works better if you lie down."

She wants to ask what's happening, what he's doing, but the hailstone is still stuck and she can't breathe a sound.

"Yeah, you will make me talk, won't you? Spell everything out," he hisses, setting the bowls on the rug, pushing a tangle of denim out of the way. Gestures to the cleared space. Eyes her steadily. Shakes his head, steps forward into her space, and places a hand on her throat.

Angel shrinks back, but in the narrow room there's no place to retreat, and she finds her back to the wall with his palm, warm and dry, up against her skin.

"Happened to me. My first time. Beginner's curse. Stage fright. Whatever. Ball of ice right there." He draws his fingers down until they rest in the hollow at the base of her throat. "We can melt it. Lie down."

Angel sits, her back against the wall and knees drawn to her chest, arms clasped tight around them, warily watching as Word sits cross-legged on the rug and arranges the six bowls in a tight arc. He beckons her with a flick of his hand.

"No, be open to it." He fists a hand tight and then slowly unclenches it to present an open palm. "Be open."

In the end, the singing of the bowls is what convinces, what gently presses her shoulders out of their hunch. When he taps the first bowl with a small wooden mallet, the low tone shimmers and spreads like a ripple from a pebble tossed into still water, widening, ever widening, until it washes up on the immovable shore. He taps it again, and then a third time, creating tone on tone on tone, spreading, spreading, spreading, until they wash up on the shore of her body. With open-mouthed beauty, the simple sounds morph into something complex and glimmering, drifting over and around her, encompassing her, pulsating through her. The hum is a great yawning maw to swallow her, but not as a ravishment. As a gentle enveloping.

How the bowls sing, how he coaxes their music with the lightest tap of the mallet, prolonging the vibrato by lifting a bowl and swirling it through the air, drawing the mallet around the outer rim, encouraging, cajoling with the deftness of a lover. And the bowls sing. Of fear and doubt, and the casting away of those feelings. Of the need to let fear and doubt seep out and drain away. Of the need to draw out fear and doubt like poison from a snakebite. Of the need to push fear and doubt aside, like the warm winds of spring drive out the chill of winter.

When the singing fades and the last vibration calms to a hush, when Word sets the mallets down and looks at her, the question settling in the shadows under his eyes, he doesn't have to utter a word. Angel swallows, free, easy, the hailstone melted, the fear and doubt vanquished. At least for now. She nods her answer.

"Yes."

When she's seated on her stool, the vox mic just inches from her lips, he startles her by taking a multi-tool from his pocket and slashing the cardboard script, hacking it in two and flinging the pieces into the same far corner into which she'd slung his whiteboard. He adjusts and readjusts the mic, avoiding her eyes until he finally has formulated a reply to her astonishment. To her unspoken question.

"Speak your truth. As you see it. As you live it. You are the Night Prophet."

His fingers flash the countdown. He flips a switch on the 'tronic box. Nods.

10

The Night Prophet

I AM FROM BIKE GEARS, from respys and copper mesh and a talis round my neck, from Faraday cages and Bartertowns. From dust on the porch, dry, drifting, gritty as sandpaper. From barren fields that stretched gray when they should have been green.

I'm from the upturned chessboard and the twang of a guitar, from Eben and Serafina, from the medic who cared and the meme who remembered. From stop breathe focus think and hasta siempre, from forever is not come, will you leave your work undone? From thirteen's your lucky number.

I'm from the deepest part of the river, Miss Stillwater to some. From the wisdom of the Son of the Mississippi, from Joachim, the man of science, from Debs of the iron hand, from Em's sass and Mars' smile and Suraj's blood. From Illiana by way of Superior, mulberries and MREs, from the night a fem gave birth alone, in pain, in terror, and in one moment of bravery, set me on a path to freedom. I am not there yet because we are not there yet.

I am from nowhere and everywhere. I am no one that you know. I am everyone you know. The bee in the field and the factory. The swag with a longing in the heart and a craving in the belly that all the things in the Mart cannot satisfy. I am the wolf who walks alone, the she-wolf with the fang of carbon steel. I have looked evil in the face. And sometimes the face was staring at me in the mirror.

I am the girl with the gun who slew the goliaths, and I have the scars to prove it.

I have walked the roads from south to north, and I have seen the despair in your slumped shoulders, and the way you scramble for the crusts thrown from the master's table, fighting like dogs among yourselves, when you should be turning that snarling anger elsewhere. I have seen you and I have walked and I know that I have many more miles to walk before I rest.

In the past, I have walked with a single companion. But I see now, that to bring a change into this world, I will need many to fall in stride beside me. Will you walk the road with me? Be my companion? My brother? My sister?

Hasta siempre...forever has not come. There is still time. To remake the world.

So sayeth the Night Prophet.

The attic is a study in contrasts. Path's jubilation bounces to the rafters and ricochets off the slanted walls. Abandoning his post in the shed, he bursts in before the first song builds to a crescendo, shouting his approval.

"Amazing, yeah!" Grabbing Angel's hand and pulling her to her feet, he twirls her into an awkward dance. "Knew it!" he exults, jabbing a finger at Word. "Toldja she's the one! Fortune favors the frackin' poet!"

Word is stoic, hunched on his stool, swapping out small silver discs in one 'tronic box and flipping a large matte black disc scored with concentric grooves onto the revolving platter, concentration etched on his face. The songs tonight are wordless, but the instruments that play are singing a message just the same.

Angel's mood lies somewhere in between. Gobsmacked that Word pulled the rug of his words out from under her feet. Burned that he left her hanging like that. Revved that he trusted her to come up with something coherent on the fly. Relieved that it's done, that she didn't stumble, that she somehow managed to mine rough stones from deep in the cavern of her heart and polish them into jewels. A giddiness drives the staccato rhythm of the blood coursing through her veins, the noise of it ringing in her ears. Breathless and dizzy as Path spins her again and again.

The music peaks and dies and Path pulls her into a swaying, shaking hug, all laughter and bumping heads, until it begins to calm into something sinuous and entwined. Until a cough and a gust of the serrated wind cuts them apart.

"Don't want to waste that precious fuel, do we?"

She's ravenous. They all are. So rather than walk her back to the park, Path sets to scrambling eggs and toasting thick slices of bread.

"Home-baked, not off a GaltMart shelf," he brags, pouring them each a mug of home-brew.

"Thought you didn't touch the stuff," Angel teases, watching his Adam's apple bob as he downs a generous swallow.

Path winks, raising an eyebrow. "I lied. Get used to it."

Mid-sip, Angel bursts into a guffaw that sends brew spewing out her nostrils like liquid fire, sending Path into his own gale of snorts. He flings her a dish towel to mop up. Word shakes his head, shovels a forkful of egg into his mouth, then pushes Angel's mug aside. When she reaches for it, he pushes it again and makes the slash signal.

"Oh ho, no more for you, says the adult in the room," Path taunts. "Can't hold your 'blivion—least 'til you get some grub into your belly."

As they eat, talking through mouthfuls, Path and Angel engage in a celebratory post-mortem, dissecting every moment of the voxcast, every pause, every little vocal nuance. Angel bathes in his praise, his smiles, his gestures. Word is silent, raking his fork through his mound of eggs, nibbling around the edges of his bread, eyes down.

"Hearts, minds, and a cause, baby. Raise their consciousness and they'll raise their arms," Path exults, mopping up the last bits of egg with another hunk of bread. "They'll join in. Hell, they're already joining. More recruits. More cells every month. Hell, every week. 'Surely whoever speaks to me in the right vox, him or her I shall follow, as the water follows the moon, silently, with fluid steps, anywhere around the globe.'"

Angel shakes her head. He's speaking in tongues, in riddles she can't decipher. "But it was just one story, not even a story. They'll need more."

"Yeah, yeah, yeah," Path says dismissively. "And you'll tell 'em. But you need to ken more of what we're doing here, the nature of the train you're riding." He pushes back from the table, jabbing his finger in Angel's face. "I've got just the ticket."

The floor creaks in protest as he dashes out of the kitchen. Then come the staccato thumps of his feet running up the stairs. More creaks overhead. The sudden silence that settles over the table feels itchy and constricting, like too-tight sleeves on an ill-fitting sweater. Angel scrapes up the last of her eggs and chews slowly, pondering how she can drag a compliment, even just a single word of praise, from Word without being obvious. She refuses to fish, much less beg. Word's gaze is fixed on his plate.

The sounds of Path's movement fill the void. He bursts back into the kitchen, brandishing a biblio like it's a knife. He shoves Angel's plate aside and slaps the biblio down in its place. A man's face stares out from the cover, handsome, beautiful even, with full lips and brooding eyes fixed on something in the distance, perhaps something he's yearning for, something for which he's been waiting a long time, something that maybe he's not sure will ever arrive. His wild hair flares out from under a beret, only half-tamed. Below the face, in white, the words **Guerrilla Warfare** and a name. It's a slim volume, well-thumbed, its rust-colored cover creased and dog-eared, soft in the corners and along the spine; its inner pages, like all the other biblios that Angel's ever seen, delicate and brown-tinged with age.

"Guevara?" Angel mumbles, confused.

"The original," Path gloats, tapping the cover. "Lived the life. Wrote a damn biblio about it. Why do you think the bushwas and corporates call us 'chés'?"

Angel traces the outline of the man's face, as if reading its contours. "This him?"

"Read it," Path taps the biblio again. "Read it. Every guevara should."

"But Debs was the original guevara," Angel mutters, blurting out the thought sloshing around her oblivion-soaked brain.

Path stares at her as if she's a stubborn nut he's trying to crack. "Debs? Debs was an amateur compared to Ché." He hoists the biblio. "Debs could've learned from studying Ché. Might have better understood the need for a more active form of persuasion." He slaps the book back on the table. "But 'nuff 'bout guevaras of the past. Dead and gone. Tonight, we're celebrating the guevaras of the present. And future."

Eyes gleaming, he picks up a little vocoder from the kitchen counter and thumbs it to life. Music surges from a squat black vox cube tucked next to a basket of onions and garlic bulbs. Path swipes and taps until he comes to the song he desires. Lilting, yet slightly frenetic in its undulating rhythm.

"'Tonight," he says, pulling Angel to her feet. "Tonight, we dance to some tunes Ché would have appreciated."

When the candles have burned down and the jug of home-brew is empty and Path is a stumbling wreck, it's Word who insists on walking her to the park. He does so without a word, pushing Path down onto the living room sofa, where he lies, arms splayed, struggling to right himself like an overturned beetle until Word tosses a shawl over him.

"Sleep it off," he growls, snuffing the candles between his thumb and forefinger. He moves to take hold of Angel's arm, but she shakes him off as he slings his own backpack and Angel's over his shoulder.

"Fine, I'm fine," she mumbles, swatting his hand away again. But she puts a foot wrong on the porch stairs and he grabs hold of her elbow and doesn't let go on the silent march through the empty streets all the way back to the park. Night is ebbing, leaving a blue residue, the morning light just beginning to slip in front of the stars.

Angel plops down on the bench, frowning at the horizon across the lake where a pink glow is beginning to unfold like a fan. She doesn't want this night to end. Word stares down at her. Flicks his hand, as if telling her to go. She shakes her head. Every movement still feels sloshy and slo-mo.

"Can't go home yet," she mumbles.

Word settles himself on the far end of the bench.

"Don't hafta mind me like I'm a child. Go." Gives the air a swat, dismissing him.

But he sits there, hunkered down as if anticipating a battle, eyes fixed on the spread of dawn.

"Why'dya cut the script?" Angel asks, talking slow, trying mightily not to slur.

Word sits for a moment, then tugs open his backpack. Retrieves the whiteboard and marks-all. As he begins to write, the board propped on his bent knee, Angel wraps her fingers around the top of the marks-all, staying his hand.

"No, talk to me."

He tries to twist out of her grasp, but her grip, remarkably strong, holds firm. He throws a glare. She parries it with her own.

"Hurts," he finally rasps.

"Yeah, that's how you know you're alive," Angel growls. But she relents, releasing him with a jerk, as if scalded. "Whatever."

She turns back to the horizon, then puts into words the thought that has been hounding her. "Didja want me to fail?"

Silence thickens, then his serrated vox slices it open. "How can you ask me that?"

"Then why'd you put me there, with nothin' to say? Couldn't bear to hear your precious words comin' out my mouth?"

"The words... it wasn't good."

"The script? Yeah, it was."

"Wasn't true. For you. It's why you couldn't read it—the way I wanted it read."

Angel feels the last glow of triumph tarnish and fade. In its place, a dull ache begins to throb behind her eyes and a suffocating heat to pulsate through her body. She struggles to shed her close-fitting jacket, panting with the effort, heaving a deep sigh as the biting air envelopes her in its cold embrace.

"I have to learn to trust people," Word finally continues. "It's on me. To trust that you get it, that the people listening get it, without me spelling it out down to the letter. Trust they'll see it hiding in plain sight. I need to be as honest as you."

Angel massages her forehead, desperate to hold the pain at bay. "I'm not—honest. I lie all the time. Like Path."

Word reaches over and runs a finger down her left arm. The place where the scars are etched in a pale row. "To others, maybe. Not to yourself."

His touch, here and then gone, feels as if it has carved another scar along her skin, invisible, bloodless.

They sit in silence in the growing light of dawn until Word flicks a hand toward Angel's backpack. "Path is neurofracked to give you that biblio. Got a place to stash it, out of sight of that fem?"

Angel nods. "Know my way around a hidey-hole. Though I don't think she'd get all up in my face 'bout it. Got a touch of the guevara about her." She stares at the pale orange smear slowly spreading where the water meets the sky, then turns her gaze back to Word. "Your biblios. Where'd you get 'em?"

"My father."

"How'd he get 'em?"

"His to begin with. From his family. He was one of the Handed."

His words are a splash of ice water to her flaming cheeks. "He knew Debs?"

"Yeah, Debs was like a father figure to him. They were tight 'til Debs took off. Said it was safer that way." Word drags a hand through his tangled hair. "That's the story I heard from my mother after my father took off, too. Don't have a reason to doubt her."

"How old were you when he left?"

"Fourteen."

"You never saw him again?"

"Saw him? No. Caught him on a voxcast every now and then. He was still in the movement, planning ops, running a sabotage crew. Recruiting. But it's been years since I've had any word of him. Maybe his luck ran out."

"I'm sorry."

"Or maybe he's just gone deep incommunicado."

"At least you have his biblios. So much lost. Will we ever get it back?" Angel muses, half to herself. "I was s'posed to be a meme, but I don't know a teaspoon of what I should. My mother, the one who raised me, gave me a history, but it was just a story, just a tale she told. A legend. Full of holes."

"History is identity," Word rasps. He uncaps his marker and scribbles on the board. Thrusts it toward Angel.

Without it you are whatever those in power say you are

"Is it out there... somewhere?" Angel asks.

Bits and pieces

Angel sighs. "Like a puzzle waiting to be put together."

Word erases and scribbles. ***Maybe at the Hive Those swags may be arrogant enough to think they can keep it locked away like some private treasure***

Just waitin' for a pirate to come along.

"You should get home," Word says, shoving the board back into pack. He stands, silent for a moment, regarding the burgeoning dawn. "It was beautiful. What you said."

And then he's gone, slipping into the blue-cloaked morning.

11

Parables

EMOTIONS CHURN INSIDE KUBA in the wake of the voxcast. Pride in Angel's accomplishment manifests in the smile that splits his face when she slips in through the sunroom door, where he's been waiting—drowsing, dreaming, jerking awake—for her return. Relief heightens the ardor of the embrace in which he wraps her as she crosses the threshold. Awe drives his impulsive kiss of the lips from which her fierce truth spilled. Jealousy bubbles up when she gently turns away and he smells the tang of home-brew on her breath and the musty residue of sweat and adrenaline on her skin. Unease clenches his stomach when she whispers that she needs to grab some sleep, so will he tend to Lark when she wakes? Disappointment weighs on his shoulders when she slips from his grip and pads quietly to the stairs. Fear seeps into the recesses of his heart at the thought that she has taken the first steps down a path where he can't follow.

When he peeks into her room, she's passed out, sprawled across her narrow bed, still in her sweatshirt and jeans, backpack slumped on the floor. His own body is drawn to the small oval rug next to the bed, where he sits, cross-legged, the rough texture of its woven braids reassuring to his fingers. He presses his temple to the bony knob of Angel's knee, savoring its hard reality.

Kuba is a man who enjoys domesticity. A tiller of the soil.

A planter of seeds. A reaper of the harvest. He has never learned the skills of the hunter—has shied away from learning. He has no appreciation for the hunt and she has always been an elusive quarry. He often wonders what she was like before. Before the nightmares that the shave-head devil Tanner and his goliaths wrought. He's tried to draw out stories, like drawing out toxin from a snakebite or pus from a wound, but what trickles out are just sentence fragments.

Her childhood fear of bugs, particularly those of the many-legged, creepy-crawly persuasion. *Flee and scream don't even begin to describe...* Smiley faces she drew on her bedroom wall as a reminder to make better choices, to get with the program. Reminders she failed to heed. *Could never be a grinbee as much as I tried...* Serafina teaching her the ways of the screwdriver and the wrench. The first bike she repaired on her own. *An oh-so-sweet black and silver fat-tire all-weather with a saddlebag in back and a basket up front...*

He pictures her child-self plucking a cherry tomato from a vine drooping under its scarlet burden. Tearing a mint leaf from its stem on a hot summer day and crushing it under her nose to get a whiff of its invigorating scent. Ambling through a field of ripening wheat, her hand skimming the spikes, feeling the tingle of hardening seeds on her palm. But he realizes these are all his memories. That he is imagining her in his own childhood, rather than visualizing hers. And he blinks back a tear because wishing and picturing can't make it so.

His head jerks and bobs as he struggles against sleep. In a waking moment, he spies the corner of a biblio jutting out of a pocket of Angel's backpack. Fishes it out. Flinches at the juxtaposition of the words 'warfare' and 'guevara.' Studies the man's partial face in the half light. Could be one of his güeys back home in Illiana. Could be him, if the widow didn't insist on a clean-shaven face.

He digs his multi-tool out of his cargo pocket and thumbs its mini-lite to life. Opens the biblio and begins to read.

When Lark stirs in her small bed across the room, he rouses himself and goes to her quickly, shushing.

"Mama still sleepy?" she asks, rubbing a fist across her eyes.

"Yes, Mama's still asleep. So we'll be very quiet."

"Kuba make brefist?"

"Not yet, but I will, as always. And you can help me."

Lark smiles. Kuba smiles back. But his heart always catches a little when she calls him by his name, as Angel has taught her, instead of Papa or Daddy.

Blinks away another tear, because wishing and picturing won't make it so.

The revelry of the night's triumph is short-lived and what's left in its wake feels more like a hangover than afterglow. Path and Word squabble over future plans. The content of the next voxcast—and the one after that. Path argues for more of the same. Another riff, free-form, stream-of-consciousness. Word insists that a little shot of that goes a long way, and requires a heavy dose of substance as a booster to truly make a difference.

Path drums his hands on the table. "True that. Never underestimate the ability of a hoary cliché or a well-worn trope to move the masses to a frenzy."

Word scowls as he tears a hunk of bread from a half-eaten loaf.

Angel sits mute, mesmerized by the strange way the disagreement unfolds, hearing only Path's side, seeing Word's gestures, frowns, and fraught scribbles as he silently advocates for his plan. She's still unsure of the origin of the words she spoke, knowing only that they rose from the depths and spewed forth like molten magma from the earth's core. And, like magma, she senses they are unpredictable, not given to being summoned on command.

On someone else's schedule.

What the men do agree on is frequency. If they've jolted their disciples' psyches like they think they have—like they hope they have—then they need to get back to a rhythm. A regularity. To keep hold of those ears, those psyches. They have insiders in the Tech bureau who help them bleed the voxcasts into the feed stream. Insiders whom they have trusted for a long time. Insiders who can estimate how many listeners were gathered around feedcoms and 'tronic boxes. A fifth column they hope can continue this dangerous sabotage. A fifth column they hope will remain true to the cause.

So much is founded on hope. On wishes and expectations. Desires. They know that this voxcast definitely bled into the local area feed. Path heard Angel's vox ooze through the mesh of the McCarthys' feedcom. But how many bees dare to defy the curfew? How many dare to defy the Morametrics monitors? Dare to stay awake on the off chance they'll catch a Damn Otis vox? All they really have is hope in the dark.

But Path and Word are willing to walk by faith on this journey and so they argue and talk smack, slinging ideas and insults, until they eventually compromise on a plan for the Night Prophet to invade people's spaces. To crawl up inside their heads. The sixth midnight of each week shall belong to the voxcast, as yet another day of servitude to the Protectorate morphs into the one day of rest, a night when the bees are primed for some release, for some revelry. What better time to remind them something better could await. Could arise. If they are willing to fight for it. The very act of listening is a defiance.

A gardener went out to sow her field. As she walked, scattering seed, some fell along a path where the soil was hard-packed, not prepared for planting, and the birds swooped down and snatched it. Some seed landed on the rocky places at the edge of the garden, places that lacked rich soil. That seed sprang up quickly, but under the summer sun the plants were scorched, and they withered because they lacked the deep roots to sustain them. Some seed fell among weeds. It sprouted, but the weeds grew faster, choking the young plants. But much of the seed fell on good soil, where it flourished and produced a crop—a hundred times what was sown.

Many who have sight do not see. Many who can hear do not listen. For some this will always be their fate. To hear, but never understand; to see, but never perceive. Their hearts have become as calloused as their hands; they wander through their days as if blind and deaf. But I am calling out to you who are blessed because your eyes do see and your ears do hear.

When anyone hears the message to remake the world and does not understand it, they are captive to the evil that binds them and their spirit is snatched away, like the seed sown along the trodden path. Many who hear the words will be roused in the moment but will fail to follow through and keep the spirit of revolution in their hearts, like the seed that falls on the rocky ground and grows ragged without sinking deep roots. They do not persist. When trouble comes, they desert their comrades. Some will hear the word, but will be tamped down by fear and worry and empty promises from Corporate lips, like the seeds that fell among the weeds and thorns. Which are you? Do you see and hear and understand? Are you the seed falling on good soil? Will you yield a crop, a hundred times what was sown?

Ask yourself why they call it 'severance.' Ask yourself why those who board the trains are never heard from again. Why they are the vanished. Are you ready to hear the answers, the truths, however painful they may be? And then will you be prepared to remake the world? For on this night, your brothers and sisters are readying the path, gathering the supplies. Do not be surprised to find the shelves of your GaltMart empty. But seek out your brothers and sisters and they will provide.

So sayeth the Night Prophet.

Word says the greatest revolutionaries have always talked in parables. That they have trusted their followers to glean meaning from the harvest of words. That stories have the power to persuade. Path prefers a blunt approach, a direct call to action. Word employs metaphors and similes to diss his brother's style of propaganda. Says it's like taking a bludgeon to a walnut, like using a machete when a scalpel is needed. Says *this* is what it is to be a prophet. To be a vox crying in the wilderness to prepare the way. Path always has a sly retort. To be a messiah, one must move among the people, be willing to get your feet dirty in the muck.

"That's not where we are," Word rasps. "Not yet."

"And we'll never get there at the rate we're going," Path fires back.

Word draws his inspiration from biblios, sometimes lifting words directly from the pages, sometimes filtering them through his own lens, mingling, mixing, mutating. In time, he offers the texts to Angel, invites her to edit and embellish, to add her views to the melange. He insists that what they send out into the night must be the breath of hope. He says despair, the belief that a situation is fixed and unchangeable, is a paralyzer, a toxin that freezes the body, a noxious fog that clouds the mind. Says hope is the true antidote because it breeds action. Says optimists think all will end well without them having to make it so, while pessimists believe things will end badly no matter what. So neither take action. But hope lives in a space of uncertainty, in the idea that one cannot know what will happen. To hope is to wrap your arms around the unknown. To embrace possibilities that lie beyond the brink. To believe that what you do matters.

One summer's day, a bear, fur thick and glossy, teeth yellow and sharp, lumbered through the forest in search of berries. It happened upon a fallen tree. Tucked away in its rotted core, a hum of bees had built a hive. The bear, looking to steal the fruits of their labor, nosed around to ken if the bees were standing guard of their golden treasure. One of the swarm, the lowliest of workers, came home from the clover field, burdened with nectar. Knowing what the bear sought, the bee flew at his head and stung with a ferocity she never knew she possessed. The bear roared in pain, and sprang upon the log, claws and teeth bared and gnashing. But the brave worker, tiny as she was, stared death in the face and sang out the alarm to rouse her sisters.

The bear swung his mighty paws at the buzzing mass of fury, then took to his heels, fleeing to a nearby lake. Pursued by the winged storm, he plunged into the water. Still the bees swarmed, the bravest of them, in the ultimate sacrifice, diving to sting the bear's nose and ears and eyes, until at last, the bear, exhausted and fevered by the venom of so many stingers, drowned. The bees flew back to their hive and mourned the loss of so many of their comrades. But none said the loss was not worthy of the cause.

There may be losses tonight, as your brothers and sisters rise up to free that which is the source of all life, the liquid gift that is your birthright. Whisper it if you must, shout it if you may. ¡Liberen el agua! Remember, there is a fate worse than death.

So sayeth the Night Prophet.

Path insists on adding what he calls the 'Cassandra shit' at the end of the voxcasts. The predictions of mayhem wrought by the brothers and sisters of the movement. At first Word tries to dissuade him, pulling a thick biblio from his shelf, paging through it.

"The thing about Cassandra, güey, is that no one ever believed her. She was spewing prophecies left and right and she was laughed out the door by her countrymen."

"Yeah, yeah," Path scoffs. "And how many bees out there within vox range have ever heard of her and her story? Nada, güey, muy pocos, a coupla memes, a few locos scattered here and there with a stash of biblios under the floorboards. We're writing our own history here, the real thing, not some crazy myth. And these 'prophecies' are all real ops in motion."

Angel takes the open biblio from Word's hands, skims the lines on the page, struggling a little through the formal, flowery language. "So what I'm *saying* will happen, will *actually* happen?"

"*Is* happening," Path purrs. "As the words leave your lips."

12

The CQO

Chief Quality Officer Mora Zinni begins each day with a meditation. On the wall of her office, a narrow, cell-like space painted in a vague shade of greige and relieved only by a floor-to-ceiling window at its far end, hangs a vast painting depicting a scene with its origins in the mythology of an ancient culture. The bees who come to clean in the after-hours snigger with a prurience to be expected of their ilk when they refer to the piece of art as the bare-assed fem on the half-shell. They cannot read the small plaque inscribed with the artist's name and other matters of provenance posted just to the left of the painting. A sensor which monitors any movement across its invisible 'tronic tripwire prevents them from doing the vulgar things they would like to do, high-fiving or fist-bumping certain parts of the fem's body. The bees aren't fond of their jobs but the alternative is even less appealing. They've heard the rumors. But they also know a friend of a friend of a friend who's heard the voxes in the small hours. And while the swags may think them lacking in intelligence, the bees are whip smart at sensing under-currents and the way the wind is blowing. The CQO may suspect their muddy thoughts, but, given the fact that Galt, while making great strides in the use of hormones to influence behavior, has yet to perfect the art of reading minds, she can't be sure.

Her meditation on the painting does indeed center around the conundrum of perfecting the human form—mind and body—in all its marvelous, maddening complexity. The exaggerated anatomy of the fem in the painting dominates the viewer's attention. Every part of her being is elongated, from the serene yet slightly melancholy face and curving neck, to the sweep of her arms and the stretch of her perfect torso, to the length of her fine legs. She is willowy and yet not, for there is a substance to her body, a sense of solidity that assures the observer that she is more earth than air. The mythology purports that she was the goddess of love, the embodiment of beauty, and the artist, as a man of his time, must have taken a muse, some fem from within his own circle, as a model for this Venus. Perhaps a fem with milky, unblemished skin and golden ropes of hair that hung almost the full length of her body. Perhaps a fem with whom he was enamored, for the CQO has no doubt that he enhanced his model's appearance through the wiles of his paint and brush, just as the imagers tweak the pixels in her own digital portraits to achieve that smooth, flawless perfection that she insists on for the 'tronic boards.

This was the very question that CQO Zinni had brought to the scientists at the breeder program when she schemed to add it to her portfolio. *Why are we doing this, if not to refine and enhance the product aesthetically, as well as materially? Yes, brawn and brains and docility and ruggedness are all very important, but why can't we have workers that are pleasing to the eye as well?* The quality control metrics for diet and exercise are in place to keep bodies healthy and fit to a reasonable standard, but they can't change physical traits. And yes, form may follow function, but things can be functional and beautiful at once. People as well. Why not at least try?

The CQO is not a scientist, per se, but she is a thinker and has enough knowledge and understanding of the technology involved to undercut the argument of the gene pool researchers that they can only go so far, that there is only so much manipulation that can be done. She is certainly willing to admit the mistakes that have been made in this pursuit. After all, it was she who terminated the unfortunate androg experiment when it became apparent that the project expectations were unrealistic and the cost overruns of trying to fix all the issues were prohibitive. Drama and melancholy belonged onstage and in the entertainment stream, not in the average workplace.

Oh, where are the Einsteins and Darwins willing to take up the gauntlet she has thrown? The men and fems of genius with the drive and stamina to solve any problem placed before them? This lamentation tends to lead to another question. *Can genius be bred?* These are the problems that wheel in her mind as she contemplates the fem born of the water and borne to the shore in the cradle of a scallop shell, encouraged along by the gentle exhalations of the personified winds. Oh, for the answers to arise as fully-formed and full-grown as Venus from the foam-flecked sea.

Thus the CQO doesn't appreciate the interruption when the cultured but slightly nasal vox of her aide seeps through the feedcom perched on a corner of her sleek desk, announcing the unexpected arrival of the Communications Control officer with the Protective Services director in tow. However, duty waits for no one.

"Gentlemen," she says crisply, greeting them with an expression that suggests they have a high bar to meet in order to justify this unscheduled intrusion.

Without waiting for an invitation, the CommCon, a slender, fierce-eyed weasel of a man, right down to the sharpish canine teeth in his frowning mouth, eases his body into one of the low bucket-shaped chairs facing the CQO's desk. He gestures to the director, a barrel-chested man who walks with the swagger and sway of a bulldog, to take a seat in the other.

It is not lost on the CQO that these two specimens are classic examples of life-forms that are definitely in need of aesthetic refinement. But, of course, she doesn't let a hint of that notion show on her face. She merely gestures for them to proceed with a flick of her elegant, long-fingered hand with its immaculately manicured nails, as opulently white and shimmering as pearls or the shell that Venus rides.

The CommCon understands the CQO's aversion to small talk with underlings so he gets right to the point. "We're seeing an uptick in instances of feed hijacking again, the chés trying to stir up the swarm. We've pinpointed the most recent to the Superior Region."

CQO Zinni stares in that penetrating way that she has perfected, a stare that can find the flaw in anything and zero in with the intent to crack that flaw wide open. "Superior is a very large region, Mr. Emmons, as I am sure you've noticed in the daily course of your duties."

"Yes, ma'am, it is, and we are in the process of trying to narrow the area where the voxcasts are originating. Indications are the northern sectors, but we can't be sure yet."

"Yet," the CQO echoes. "And what is the nature of these new intrusions?"

The CommCon shoots a look at the ProServ director, who clears his throat with an ostentatious growl. "Similar to those coming out of Erie and Illiana. And some of the Ontario Region bleeds as well. An intent to foment discontent, provoke disorder, insubordination. A classic tactic of insur..." His vox trails off as if he catches himself remembering something. He adjusts his shoulders before continuing. "The usual ché propaganda."

"The usual propaganda," repeats the CQO, trying not to let the boredom she's feeling creep into her vox. From a meditation on the struggle to perfect the human form to this. Truly from the sublime to the ridiculous. Every month brings the same report. These ludicrous transmissions breaking into the feed, sending static-tinged messages of hope and the call to uprising. A scramble by the comms team to pinpoint the origination venue. A mad dash by security forces to secure the location and round up the perpetrators. A stunning lack of success.

"When you flick the light on, the frackin' chés scatter like cockroaches."

That was an excuse offered by one team after coming up empty-handed. A team she'd summarily busted and reassigned to Border Patrol down on the far southern reaches of Illiana, in the cleared-out Shawnee, where maybe—just maybe—they could be trusted to spot a living, moving body in that vast, drought-dead no man's land. It was an inexcusably lame defense. Perhaps she should have severanced them. Does she suffer fools gladly? Perhaps this is her blind spot, this penchant for giving security forces second and third chances. This appreciation she has for the physical form of the goliaths, as the bees, in surprisingly apt but typically florid language, call them.

To make matters worse, the ché cockroaches that they do catch refuse to talk. Perhaps because they know they are destined for severance no matter what they do, no matter what bits of information they spill or how many other cockroaches they implicate.

The CQO carefully tucks back a swath of silvery hair that has fallen over her eye as she considers this problem. Could it be time to change strategies? Offer the promise of clemency? Pardon? Second chances? Would the cockroaches be susceptible to those allurements, no matter how fake they might be?

"However, there is one new wrinkle," says the CommCon, intruding on the CQO's silent ponderings.

"A wrinkle," she echoes with a sigh. "Are we discussing fabric, Mr. Emmons?"

"It's a fem's vox. Calls herself the Night Prophet."

As she drums her fingers on her desk, CQO Zinni's nails click like the barrel of an old-school burner as it spins. "A fem. I'd call that a twist, Mr. Emmons, rather than a wrinkle. And is it possible that it's just the product of an audio manipulator? A man masquerading as a fem through a little techno-wizardry?"

"The idiolect and modulations sound authentic. Doesn't have the flatter pattern of a robovox. This one, she's a bit more of a storyteller than the usual Damn Otis vox. Maybe a bit more subtle."

"Calling oneself a prophet is hardly subtle, Mr. Emmons."

The CQO is tempted to ignore these skulking provocateurs like one ignores a wasp, letting it hover and flit and sense and sip, standing ground without swatting it in fear. Showing fear just breeds more disrespect, feeds the foolishness. Stirs the beast to strike back. For truly, how many bees are actually listening to these bleed-throughs anyway? They're breathed out into the night air, when presumably very few are awake to listen.

But presumption is a risky business. And there have been incidents. The CQO refuses to think of them in any other way. She's sharply corrected the ProServ director when he's used the term 'insurgency.' A pack of the rabble running amok through a GaltMart is not an insurgency. A mob overrunning a water facility is not an insurgency. A crazed individual assassinating a Regional Director is not an insurgency. The problem is that she cannot find a suitable word to describe these events, which she insists on viewing as singularities, unrelated occurrences, each driven by a unique factor. Anger at a temporary scarcity of goods. Frustration at the failure of the water filtration system and the lack of a placating response. A personal vendetta.

And yet.

Some of these incidents have reached the ears of CEO Blanche and she's had to bend and twist in uncomfortable ways to reassure him that every episode has been properly dealt with, facilities secured, perpetrators severanced. Except, of course, for those who manage to elude the security teams. Still, he had remarked in passing about quality slippage. It had only been in passing, she's sure of that, and on something, some little matter, completely unrelated.

And yet.

The CommCon is rambling on about locus factors and connectivity patterns and neural divisions when she blinks and holds up her hand.

"Gentlemen, it's your job to put out these little fires before they spread and unite into one huge conflagration. Erie, Illiana, Ontario. Now Superior. It would appear to be moving closer to Corporate. This is troubling. CEO Blanche would be troubled to learn of this. So my expectation is that you quash this and quash it now before we have to trouble him with it. He's a busy man, much preoccupied with keeping Galt Corp running smoothly for the good of the Protectorate. He doesn't need one more thing added to his plate. So I expect you to step up your game and take care of this. If you need additional resources—tech, equipment, boots on the ground, as the Director might say—let me know and all will be provided. But these feed intrusions must end and the perpetrators must be severanced immediately. Are we clear on the mission?"

The CQO finishes with a smile and the men nod, like children reminded for the hundredth time that they must eat their dinner before they can have any expectation of dessert. She's ready to dismiss them, to return to her meditation, or pick up the business of the day, when she's suddenly seized by a notion. A notion that intrigues her.

"I assume we have audio of this new vox." When the men stare blankly, her fingers start to tapping again. Click, click, click. "Captures of the feed intrusions?" Her tone becomes more forceful. "These voxcasts?"

The CommCon's head jerks up and down, like a child's bobblehead and just as ludicrous. "Yes, ma'am, we do."

"I'd like to hear them. Well, perhaps not all of them. How many have there been?"

The CommCon and the ProServ exchange a look. "Not sure—"

"Well, send me what you have and I'll pick and choose. You have them by date?"

The CommCon nods. "Yes, certainly."

"Good. We're done here," the CQO says in a clipped tone that signals they should leave.

What was that silly slogan she'd discovered while trolling the semaphore visual archives?

Get it? Got it. Good.

13

A Hymn to Water

No hay lágrimas en la revolución.

There are no tears in the revolution. Something my mother, one of my mothers, told me. But she was wrong. There are tears. There will be tears. Many tears. Streams and rivers of tears. Tears to fill the lakes by which we shelter. For I have not come with a message of peace on my lips. I have come with a knife in one hand and a burner in the other. He who loves the false security offered by Galt more than freedom is not worthy of freedom. I am here to set a man against his father and a daughter against her mother, if necessary, if they prove pledged to Galt instead of freedom. For I say you may find your foes living in your own house, breaking bread with you. Know your enemies. For they may be sleeping under your roof.

Look around. Ask who will march with you to the Hive. Who is willing to fight with you to cast out the oppressors and puppet masters? To hunt down the enablers and all those who traffic in human life? To destroy the queen and her drones? That is the mission. Accept it and join us or step out of the way. Change is coming. You may not see it. It will take faith to believe it's happening. You may be asked to walk by faith and not by sight alone. But you must believe it can happen before you can make it happen.

Tonight, some of those in power who direct the action, who pull the strings and manipulate the misery, will be brought low.

The news of this will not be broadcast on the feed, for Galt does not speak of such things. Does not reveal its weaknesses. But the word will spread from lips to ears that these men and fems lie where they were slain, in ever-expanding pools of red.

I have come to burn bridges, not build them.

So sayeth the Night Prophet.

Creeping through the dark manse is second nature to her, with her intimate knowledge of the placement of furniture and creaking floorboards to avoid, gathered from days of dusting and vacuuming and sweeping. But she nearly stumbles on the threshold to her room when she hears the widow's crooning vox floating around the edge of the door as it stands ajar.

And I saw a new land
The first had passed away.
And there came a great vox
Comforting words to say.
Wipe tears from your eyes
No sorrow and no cries,
For these pains are vanquished
The old world has passed this day.

The song flows in a minor key, soft and melancholy.

To those who thirst I shall give
Water without price,
From the mighty fountain
Of the water of life.
And a shining nation
Shall rejoice in exultation.
Rise this day in victory
On the lake of the water of life.

With a trembling hand, Angel pushes the door aside to find the widow standing in the dim molten glow of the bureau candle, swaying to and fro with Lark in her arms, the child's head nestled on her shoulder.

"Ah, there you are, now that the storm is over," the old fem murmurs.

Angel blinks.

Why didn't Kuba…

It's as if the widow can read her thoughts. "I was up, pacing. Sleep is sometimes elusive for me. And for this little one, too, or so it seems. And for you as well," she whispers. "But I believe I have lulled at least one of us back to dreamland." She bends and tucks the child back into her bed, drawing the coverlet up to Lark's chubby cheek.

"I could ask the whys and wherefores," the widow says, her mouth near to Angel's ear, her hand on her shoulder, so close that Angel can smell the balsam-scented hand cream she applies day and night. "But I won't. I've found that sometimes the less one knows, the better off one is, in the grand scheme of things. I believe it's called 'plausible deniability.' Of course, the simplest explanation would be that you have an admirer whom you wish to remain on the down-low. But I sense the real explanation is far more complex. Nefarious, even."

The candlelight glints in the old fem's eye like the twinkling of a distant star. Angel catches the wink and the light but firm pressure of the hand squeezing its subtle message.

"Mind you, there's no need to abscond in the middle of the night. And not just for her sake." The widow inclines her head toward the little lump in the bed, then casts Angel in a long stare. "I think we understand each other. So I will see you in the morning." And without a smile and without waiting for a reply, she slinks around the door like a cat on the prowl and closes it with such stealth, the latch makes the barest of clicks.

At breakfast, while Lark half eats and half plays with her oat kibble and the widow sips tea and smiles her most indulgent smile, Angel idly tortures herself by picking at a hangnail as she tries to contain the thoughts swirling through her mind like the winter winds whipping around the corners of the manse.

"That song you were singing," she finally blurts when the pain crosses over from distraction to goad.

"What song?" the old fem replies, a study in obfuscation.

"From last night. What was that?"

"Oh, did you hear my croaking?" The widow chuckles. "Twas hardly singing. That was just a little ditty my nanny used to sing to me. You've never heard it before?" When Angel shakes her head, the widow shrugs. "I'm surprised. It's a hymn to water. And in praise of the beneficence of Galt."

"My mother, the woman who raised me, never sang it to me, as far as I know. And I've never heard it on the feed."

"Well, it's not a sanctioned Galt song. Far as I know, it's a folk song from the early days. When the Protectorate was new. A song of the bees. Who weren't called bees back then."

"Where did it come from?"

"Who knows? Some anonymous fellow or fem hummed it up and it stuck and then spread." The widow takes a sip of tea. "It's a simple melody. Easy to sing. I'd guess it probably rose out of the people's joy at finding some order made out of the chaos."

"It sounds more mournful than happy. And it's a lie."

"What's a lie?" The widow's eyes flash as she sets her mug down with a thump.

"Water without price."

"Ah." It's an off-hand utterance, one that could be aimed at Lark, who's built a tiny cairn of granola clusters on her plate and is quite pleased with herself, or at Angel and her presumption. "Perhaps. If you're inclined to think that relinquishing a bit of freedom is a high price to pay for security. Perhaps that's why your mother never sang it to you." The widow lifts her mug as if in a toast. "Was she a rebel like you?"

When Angel opens her mouth to launch into what would almost certainly be a lie, the widow holds up her hand and arches her eyebrows. "Oh, don't even try to deny it. You are young. With a fiery heart. I've seen it, though you try to keep it under wraps. Well, let me tell you, as one who has seen much—even through the bushwa lens that you so scorn—when people fear death, most will gladly go along with measures they think will save them. Even if that means, yes, a loss of freedom." The widow takes another sip of tea. Her eyes are unreadable as she stares at Angel over the rim of her mug. "Or so I've been told."

"You're a meme." The words spill out and scatter before Angel can catch them.

The widow blinks and for another moment her expression is inscrutable, her eyes mirrors instead of windows. Then a tiny curve bends the corners of her lips and a sigh escapes, as if she's been waiting for this tick of the clock. Waiting for this realization to finally dawn.

"Such could be said of anyone who lives long enough and pays attention while they do. All the more reason to respect and honor your elders," the old fem says, taking another sip of tea. "So, tit for tat. You are an aspiring guevara," she purrs in a tone that just might be tinged with admiration. "If you are not one already." She raises a hand. "Don't confirm or deny it. Remember, plausible deniability."

Angel can only imagine the changing mosaic of her face as the feelings race through her mind and body. Shock that she has been so transparent. Disbelief that this whole time she has been convinced the widow, besotted with the child, was completely unaware of what was going on, while the old fem has actually been reading her like one of the forbidden biblios that Angel suspects are hidden somewhere in the manse.

"Will you answer my questions?" she asks when she finally finds her tongue. "Tell me what I want—what I need—to know?"

The widow's lips bend into that tiny curve again. "I will. As long as you don't tell me anything in return."

14

The Mark

"THAT'S HER."

Path cuts a side-eye to the left, dipping his head ever so slightly in the direction of the tall willow of a fem poised at the bike rack in front of the bakery. She's twisting her sleek tail of ice gold hair while she waits for her dark-haired companion to open the security lock that prevents her sweet, swag, top-of-the-line fat-tire ride from being pedaled away by an enterprising Bartertown rat.

Angel has glimpsed the fem before. Once, back in late autumn, she'd crossed her path while strolling with Kuba and Lark along the main drag on a mission to fulfill the widow's craving for chocolate rarities. Lark was clutching her favorite stuffie, a fuzzy pink rabbit gifted by the widow. In her excitement at pointing to some delicacy displayed in the sweetshop window, the child dropped the toy just as the fem and her companion drew alongside. It was the man who stooped to retrieve the rabbit, but the fem plucked it from his hands and held it out to Lark, a coaxing, honey-dripping smile curving her plum-colored lips.

"Here, you darling thing." Her eyes were hidden behind blackout shades, but Angel could imagine the covetous look lurking in them.

Lark, shy with strangers, had ducked her head, so Angel

accepted the stuffie, mumbled her thanks and hurried into the shop. It was Kuba who had given the fem a second glance.

"Looked kinda familiar, yeah?" he'd asked as they bent over the display case of fancy handcrafted confections.

Angel, luxuriating in the delicious, enveloping smell of cocoa, had just shrugged and pointed out the desired goodies to the clerk.

But she'd seen the swags again, on an overcast afternoon at the beachfront park while pushing Lark in a swing. The couple, in matching black thermal skins and scarlet thermal jackets, were pedaling lazily down the path. The fem had glanced in their direction and pedaled on. Angel had idly wondered if biking was a passion of one or the other or if they were just fulfilling their Morametrics quota. When the pair made a loop around the park to pass by a second time, the fem again turned her head to observe them. There was something about the face, its piquant heart-shape, the curve of the jaw. And the eyes, this time not concealed behind the shades.

Those eyes. The look in them. That's what's familiar. Just another baby craver.

Observing her now, Angel decides from the fem's posture that she's accustomed to being waited on. That she thinks her fingers are meant for the display of rings, not the completion of menial tasks. After the man tucks the bike lock into his saddlebag, the two secure their helmets, straddle their bikes, and pedal off.

"He doesn't have the look of a securitycrat," Angel muses, watching the retreating figures.

Path shakes his head. "Not security per se. Intel says facility manager. Show runner. Button pusher. And a side hustle as her bike man. Never see her without him." Path sniggers. "Slick if you can luck into it, huh? With a moniker like Flint Frazier, what other line of work would suit that dude?"

Angel lowers her blackout shades, lips set in a scowl, eyes pursuing the couple until they round the corner.

Looks like the type of man who would call any fem who catches his fancy 'baby girl'.

Out loud she asks, "Spawn?"

"Never seen with any."

*So she **is** a baby craver.*

Path makes a sliding motion with his hand. "We need an infiltrator, someone on the island, inside the facility. Been tryin' awhile to get an inroad through security or medic placements, but it's impossible. Place is locked down. Very little coming and going. With the staffers, security is all brainwash and mind control. Frackin' embeds. No way 'round 'em. No way to turn anyone already there."

As a cluster of high-dressed swags in their winter fabrics saunters toward them, Path slips his arm around Angel's waist and guides her across the street. "But Promise Frazier, the swagstress, she gets what she wants, yeah?" He throws a sneer at the backs of the couples as they enter the café. "Like them. Intel says she lost her house bee to severance and hasn't taken a new one. Yet. But you know just by lookin' she ain't one to lift a hand, other than to have some bee manicure it. So, you just have to get her to want you. Or that sweet lil' thing who calls you mama. And then you're in."

"No," Angel says flatly, instantly.

Path winks. "Of course that should be the first thing out your mouth. You'd be neurofracked to answer yes on the first ask."

"You recruited me to speak the words. Words. You said it wouldn't involve actions."

"And you told me the reason you came here. Your goal. Takin' that facility down. You gonna really be all talk and no action? Just the prophet and not the messiah?" He grins. "Just let yourself steep in it for a bit. Is it so far a leap from what you're giggin' on now? Your hustle with the widow?"

Angel's turning on her heel, about to flee, but he anticipates it and clamps a hand on her wrist. "You need to ask yourself how badly you want it. Takin' it down, lettin' the ovas walk free. And how far you're willing to go to make it happen. Yeah, we need the buzz to stir the swarm, but we also need that brave little bee to make the first sting."

She struggles to pull away, but his grip is too strong. Keeps her off balance. Sets her flesh to tingling, like the time she forgot to unplug a 'tronic box before setting to work on its broken innards and the pulse and buzz of current surged through her fingers. He brings his face closer to hers, his lips brushing her ear.

"You've done worse things. Or have you lost your nerve?"

The widow's geodesic dome, a greenhouse her husband had built and lovingly tended to satisfy her craving for fresh veggies in the off-season, is an oasis of warmth, color, and life in the midst of bleak late winter. The raised beds sheltered under the polycarbonate panels harbor a variety of cold tolerant crops. Emerald heads of lettuce that grow in pretty rosettes of tender-crisp leaves. Sprawling ruffles of kale. Bluish-green fans of sturdy leeks. The carrots are Lark's favorites. She loves to tug at the bright green feathery fringe to reveal the vibrant orange surprise hidden beneath the soil.

"Pop!" she burbles.

"Pop!" Kuba repeats. "Then it goes—plunk—in the basket."

Angel sits on the cozy wooden bench in the center of the greenhouse, where the fig and lemon trees stretch nearly to the top of the dome. She smiles, watching the two harvest, but the smile is small and feels tight on her face. Like the hammock in the yard, the greenhouse is a space where they can have privacy, but she can never really settle into these moments. When she's inside the dome, where the view of the world is smeared and indistinct, a tension keeps her back ramrod straight and the bones grinding in her neck as she cranes her head to peer out the open door and scan the perimeter of the garden for—what?—Lurkers? Intruders? Goliaths? It's always there now, in her gut—this need to be aware, to be alert. It keeps her eyes flitting, like a pickpocket rambling through a live act crowd searching for an easy mark.

Kuba peeks out the open door, as if he, too, is checking for eavesdroppers. They catch each other's eyes and grin. It's a little ridiculous, all this thrillweep subterfuge. Despite the fact that she's surrounded herself with gardens and outfitted her vast stone patio with an elegant wrought iron table and a set of matching chairs, the widow is not a fan of the outdoors in any season. In the spring, she shelters from the days of pelting rain. In summer, she abhors the heat. The flittering insects. The crawling ones. In autumn, she will take her personal transport for drives through the changing trees, but slips into melancholy remembering this was the time of year when she lost her husband. In winter, she burns the lights throughout the day, flouting Corporate guidance, burning through E-vouchers to chase away the gloom while she completes the prescribed brain puzzles on her tablet and the fitness regimen on her full body platform, ear buds plugged and face set in grim determination as she strives to follow the commands flowing through the feed. Quite likely this is what she is doing as the three bees who she has come to think of as her children putter around her greenhouse. The greenhouse she can hardly bear to look at now.

Angel hasn't broken the news to Kuba yet. That the widow is a meme. That the old fem has sussed out that they are not just homeless waifs that she gathered under her wing. And Angel also hasn't told him that she's weighing whether or not to buy into Path's infiltration scheme, whether or not to make a move on Promise Frazier, to lure her with the bait that Path believes the fem craves. That she's pondering whether she's truly ready to embark on the bigger plan to destroy the breeder facility. To set the ovas free. Kuba would disapprove. Try to talk her out of it. For Lark's sake, of course. And he would be right. So rather than plunge into that conversation, Angel sidesteps it like a muddy puddle.

"Found out who that fem is," she says, fingering the smooth gray bark of the fig tree.

"What fem?" Kuba replies, preoccupied with snipping spinach.

"The blonde swag who bikes around with the dark-haired dude. The one you were givin' the twice-over outside the sweet shop."

Kuba reddens. "Wasn't givin' her the twice-over. Just said she looked familiar."

"It was definitely a twice-over." Angel shrugs. "And why not? She's very beautiful. Name's Promise."

Kuba's hand stops in the midst of hoisting his harvesting basket. "Well, that's frackin' corporate."

"Her man—the one who's hip-tied to her—he's high up in the breeder facility."

Lark pads over, climbs up on the bench and thrusts a torn leaf under Angel's nose. "Smell," she demands, waving the offering back and forth, so close it tickles.

Angel takes a big sniff of its sweet, spicy scent. "Mmm, basil."

Lark brings the leaf to her nose, mimicking Angel. An intake of breath, a sigh.

Angel turns back to Kuba, now snipping herbs. "But that still doesn't explain why she has the look of someone I've seen before."

Kuba tucks sprigs of thyme into the basket. "Well, I guess it's a mystery we'll never solve, cuz now that we know who and what she's attached to, we'll make sure whenever we spy her comin' to turn tail and haul aa—" Kuba catches himself with a grimace toward Lark. "Whatever we're haulin'—in the opposite direction." His eyes shift to meet Angel's. She holds his gaze for an instant before letting hers slide away and resume a scan of the peripheries.

"That biblio you brought home has some interesting things to say," Kuba ventures, overly casual. "About rebellion. Taking the fight to the goliaths."

Angel can tell he's inviting her to join an internal dialogue that he's been having. She reluctantly takes the bait. "Interesting?

That's kinda vague."

Kuba sets down the basket laden with vegetables, scoops up Lark and sits in her place on the bench, settling her on his knee. But, feeling explorish, she immediately wriggles down and sets off to pluck and sniff more herbs.

"Look, til you showed up at Grey-Grey's farm, I never gave too much thought to what was happening outside our fences. Yeah, I knew we took care of our own and if Corporate poked a nose around, we'd lop it off right quick and bury the evidence. We were definitely operating in the blur. The farm was my world and it was like there was this veil separating us—me—from whatever else was out there. Me and my bros, my güeys, yeah, we caught a Damn Otis vox every now and then. And that was slick, like a taste of danger."

Kuba picks a finger-length jalapeño from the basket. "But it was like this hot pepper. Stings your tongue for a bit, then the burn fades." He tosses the pepper back. "Grey-Grey had some biblios—she called 'em history books—but I could never see the point of reading about what used to be. I mean, it's gone, whatever the past was like, and all we have to deal with is the now. The biblios I liked were about quests—with random, ordinary people—bees—rising up to do extraordinary things. But even though I liked reading them, I knew they were just stories."

Lark toddles back with a fistful of lemony-tart oregano, clambers onto Kuba's lap, and nestles in the crook of his arm.

"Then old man Debs hauls up with you and you're lookin' like someone tried to slit you open and you've got a baby, this baby"—he drops a kiss on the top of Lark's head—"up inside you, and that was a little tear in the veil. And then you told your story, the massacre in the AgSector, Tanner, the goliaths. That was another tear in the veil. But what really ripped it to shreds was when you left for the Chicago garrison. I don't know why I went after you that morning. Something just..." He pauses, shrugs. "Just drove me. Maybe it was the thought of you trying to go it alone. Or maybe it was the notion that here was my chance to step into the story. To be one of the ordinary bees who do extraordinary things."

They're almost too much to bear, his earnest eyes in his man-child face.

Why am I always prone to break your heart?

Angel sighs. "In those stories—and the ones you tell her," she says, nodding at Lark. "Good always triumphs, yeah? The bad guys are the only ones who die. The good live on to tell the tales, pass them along from one generation to the next. That makes for a pretty story, but it's just a story, not the truth. The world, this world, it's not like that."

Kuba won't be dissuaded. "No, it's not, but we need the stories all the same. Because we need something to feed our dreams, to make us think the world *could* be like that. To make us feel that it's worth fightin' to make the world like that. Fightin' to turn the ideal into the real."

Angel takes the sprig of oregano that Lark offers, holds it to her nose, inhales deeply.

Is that what I'm doing, fighting for ideals? Doesn't feel that way. It all still feels very personal. Maybe one day that will change. Maybe not. Does it really matter?

What is more personal than your own survival, the widow had said, when Angel asked for a memory of the early days. And then the old fem had murmured a story that her parents told her. A story of pure chaos.

"That's how they remembered it. They were just children, but there was nothing their parents could do to keep the truth from them. It was all over the screens of the time, something they called streaming, a type of feed called the internet. The collapse of their country. Which had been on edge for years. Wildfires burning uncontrolled in the west. Hurricanes ravaging the coasts of the east. Millions of

refugees from cities under water. Millions more from areas with no water at all. All crowding inland and northward. Mixing with people—depending on the largesse and goodwill of people they'd been hating for years. The bombs exploded and the rumors along with them. It was anarchists on the far-left. It was extremists on the far-right. No one knew who was truly responsible, least of all the government, which was paralyzed by extremists on the inside. Things fall apart very quickly when the infrastructure—the power grids, the food supply chain, the local governments, the systems of a civilized life—are sabotaged and all you've depended on to keep your life regulated and in balance is broken and stripped away.

"But some corporations, the mega-megas, had planned for just such a catastrophe. Had the prescience to stockpile. To man their own paramilitary forces. To protect their own. A conspiracy theory posits that they even had a hand in setting the world on fire. Precipitating the downfall. Well, however it all went down, Galt seized territory early, protected it, expanded it by seizing control of military bases and equipment. Providing shelter from the storm. It took years to build the Protectorate, but they had the resources—and one of the most essential resources—the lakes.

"No doubt they were seen as heroes at the time. And I'm sure those at the center of the Hive still think of themselves as heroes. After all, everyone is the hero of his or her own story, yes? I'm sure that holds especially true of villains. How else do they justify their acts of treachery? And even heroes do things in extremis that can never—and should never—be forgiven.

"Good and evil reside in every human heart and what separates them is not an abyss, a chasm, but a line as thin as a vein, and just as fragile."

A look had passed between them. A chill had twined itself up and around Angel's spine, like a viper on the hunt. Even now she can feel its icy, serpentine trail. She shivers, and knows it's not on account of the wind that gusts through the open door.

"Well, enough talk of stories and ideals," she says, hefting one of the baskets full of their harvest. "There's dinner to be made and dishes to be washed. Everyday heroics, yeah?"

15

In the Air

Beware false prophets, who come to you clothed as sheep to hide the ravening wolf inside. Who claim to be as one with you, but whose loyalty lies in the palm of Galt. Stop your ears to their words. Words that drip with a honey that masks their evil core. Keep your eyes on their actions. Actions will reveal the truth. They are like trees that bear rotten fruit. They will be cut down.

So sayeth the Night Prophet.

Path is pressing for a decision. The window of opportunity is narrow. They can only occupy the McCarthy house for so long before the numerators arrive for a sweep. And then he and Word and most of the cell will be moving on. There are other targets to aim for, easier targets with a higher probability of success. Angel knows the reason for her hesitation has a cascade of black curls and enormous eyes that see the world as something new every single day. A reason that occupies a space where love, fear, fierce protectiveness and wary ambivalence mingle and clash. When, on their long trek north, in a moment of candor, she had finally revealed to Kuba the manner of the child's conception, the violent act of a malevolent man that brought her into being, his response had been uncharacteristically cold-blooded.

"She's here. He's dead, by your hand or mine, we'll never

know. She's not him. That's all that matters."

For Angel, it's not so black and white—and never will be. She knows when she thinks of Lark as a murderer's child, it's not always Tanner's face that looms in her mind's eye.

After the night's voxcast, lingering in the attic for a post-mortem and a snack, Path tosses the question as casually as he tosses a slice of bread onto his plate.

"Are we a go?"

Word's look asks a different question.

"I believe the facility has found its infiltrator," Path responds, with a nod toward Angel.

Word's reaction stuns Angel. He slings his own piece of bread down and stares in mute disbelief for a moment. Then he rages silently, retreating to his white board.

He didn't know.

And he's furious at the idea of losing the vox they've just found, accusing Path of rushing the action before the groundwork's been laid. Path insists hotly that they'll find a way to keep the Night Prophet on the vox. They've run into roadblocks before and have always managed to overcome them. Now is no different.

"She'll find a way to get to the mainland. Once a week might be doable. You'll just have to trust her to prep on her own. She's a savvy critter, yeah."

Word blows out an exasperated sigh, rolls his eyes. Starts scribbling.

Angel, frustrated at being the object of the conversation, raps her hand on the table. "I didn't say I'm doing this." She trails off.

Word fixes her with the eyes of a snarlsome dog straining on a short leash.

"Yet," she finishes in a mumble, lowering her gaze, avoiding those eyes.

However, the decision had indeed come to her, just that morning. It was there—the smell of it—in the air that rushed in when Angel had lifted the window sash to wipe the winter's filth from the sill. The turn of the seasons.

"Please clean the windows again," the widow had practically pleaded. *"Today. Life looks so much better through clean windows."*

Oh, that bushwa mentality.

But she'd set to the task on a gray morning just this side of spring, a morning that had threatened rain but turned sunny. The scent in the breeze had set Angel's heart to racing. The odor of the earth awakening, of the thaw that sets the freshets flowing, of the melt that swells the streams and rivers. A scent of arrival. And of leaving. A scent that roused a hankering for going. For leaving the widow's cavernous house, like a bear coming out of hibernation, shaking off the winter's slumber and the funk of its den. A scent that impels motion, growth, change. A scent that had made her decision clear.

"But I am," she continues, raising her vox and her eyes. "Doing this. I am. It's what I came here to do. It just took awhile to see a way forward. And now I see it. I can't destroy it working from the outside. I have to go inside and kill it that way. Like a virus invading the body. It's the only way."

Her sudden vehemence hits Word as hard as a slap, his face flinching away, eyes squinched tight. Path pumps his fist in the air, bashing his knuckles on the rafter over his head. He laughs, even as he hops around, shaking the pain off his hand.

"This calls for a frackin' sipperbration," he snorts, clambering across the floorboards. With a wink, he drops through the opening.

Word wipes his board with long, slow sweeps of his shirt tail. He's shaking his head as he presses the marks-all to it. When he's done, he shoves the board into her hands, eyes flashing in a fierce squint.

You dont have to do this Give the vox more time Pipeline has it that its starting to stir the bees this tapping on their hives

But Angel only sees doubt in the turned down corners of his

lips. And that brings a swell of anger thrumming through her core.

Do not doubt me. Do. Not. Doubt. Me.

"Some dream, some talk, some do," she says, placing the board on the table.

As a clank and clatter heralds Path's return, Word leans forward, closer and closer, as if he will lay his doubting lips upon her cheek. But he leaves just a whisper, fiery as a brand.

"Tonight you spoke the words of a revolutionary who died for his cause. But this movement—our movement—needs a prophet, not a martyr."

16

The Play

A RECONNAISSANCE OF the Fraziers' comings and goings reveals that every other Thursday morning at 10 sharp, the man gets his square jaw close-shaved and his slick of brown hair trimmed at the quaint barbershop along Route 13 on the outskirts of town. The shop, tucked next to a fish market and with its spinning pole striped red, white and blue, is charmingly retro and adored by the swags, residents and visitors alike, eager to throw their spare V-cards around. While Flint idles in the chair, his face swathed in a steaming hot towel, Promise bikes alone along the lakeside trail, past the empty slips of an abandoned marina, into a secluded area thick with scrub trees and pines.

And so the plot is hatched.

Kuba's a tight ball of walking fury as he and Angel tread the red brick path to the shed where their bikes are stored. "Stone loco," he's hissing, over and over, half under his breath but just loud enough to ensure she can hear him.

"You don't have to ride this with me," Angel replies, the calm of her vox belying the wild thumping in her chest.

"You know I do," he snaps back, jerking the shed door open.

She lets that settle without a response while she eases her silver and blue cruiser down the ramp. Part of her wants him along.

The other part wants him to stay at the widow's, to be there for Lark. In case.

Her mind won't go farther than the words.

But he will go. Because of the vow he'd made, even if she's not of a mind or heart to hold him to it.

Wherever you're going, there I am. Your enemy is mine. That's the way it is. The way it's gonna be. Even if it brings me nothing but pain.

The brother born for adversity.

In town, with the strengthening March sun turning the lake into a glinting mirror, Angel and Kuba loiter outside the cafe at the corner of Manypenny and 2nd Streets, along the route the Fraziers take to the barbershop. Bent over their bikes, they pretend to examine spokes and chains, but keep their eyes, hidden behind their shades, on the periphery. Minutes ooze by, but Angel resists checking her timekeep.

And then their targets round the corner. Even with hints of spring in the air, both still sport their winter biking gear, red jackets, black skins. However, the fem's not wearing her usual sleek red helmet and blackout shades. Her hair is swept up in a messy topknot and her face is flushed, eyes pink-rimmed as if she's been crying. As they sweep past, Angel and Kuba straddle their bikes and push off in a slow pursuit. They round two bends in the road and Flint glides to a stop at the bike rack just steps from the barbershop. Promise, instead of stopping with him to bestow her usual parting peck on his cheek, just pedals on without a word or glance.

Angel frowns.

Frack. This isn't business as usual.

But even as she watches in dismay, the fem turns off the main road and heads down 7th Street in the direction of the trail. The usual route. Sighing in relief, but without uttering a word, Angel and Kuba follow at a discreet distance. The street dead ends, but the fem keeps going, veering to the right, off the asphalt and onto a narrow boardwalk, riding it down a slope to the trail. Pulling up to the path, Angel can just spy a moving flutter of scarlet, the fem's jacket cardinal bright amidst the still-bare branches. Even where the brush thickens, the brilliant dot of color pierces its tangled veil.

They pause at the trailhead for a moment before starting down the path, swerving left and right to avoid pockmarks of mud and puddled water from the night's rain. They pedal slowly, almost idly. Timing is everything.

Angel feels a thrum coursing through her body, a swelling, not unlike the swelling of the tiny buds at the tips of each branch of the shrubs and trees lining the trail. A swelling that echoes the stretch and spread of the rhizomes and roots of wildflowers just below the surface of the soil. Anticipation. And then a slight murmur of fear buzzing just beyond her ear. Too far. They've pedaled too far. Just a ways farther down the trail, where a swag manse sprawls atop a hillock, the scrubby forest has been tamed, the trees felled to open up a stunning vista of the lake to the east.

C'mon. C'mon. We're too far. This can't happen in the open—in view of—

Then it comes. A fem's startled cry.

Don't hurt her. Don't you frackin' hurt her.

Accelerating around a bend, they find the fem on the ground, bike overturned and back wheel still spinning, a ragged man looming over both, his black-gloved hands reaching.

Kuba skids to a stop as Angel leaps off her bike, shouting. A flash of chaos. Kuba's switchblade glinting in a thin ray of sunlight. An arc of silver. The crackle and swish of the underbrush as the ragged man retreats, like a crow flapping tattered wings, his filthy shirttail snagging on a dead branch, snapping it, the crash and caw echoing as the underbrush swallows him whole.

Angel kneels beside Promise, shielding her view. "Are you hurt?" she asks, surprised at how real her concern sounds. The fem shakes her head, but her eyes are enormous and ruddy blotches of fear stain her cheeks.

Kuba stands the bike upright. "What happened?" he asks, flicking the kickstand down.

The fem accepts Angel's outstretched hand as she clambers awkwardly to her feet, like one not used to spending time flat on her ass on hard, damp ground. Especially in the company of strangers. Especially in front of a pair of obvious bees. She recovers herself, combing her fingers through loose strands of hair, tucking them behind her ears, brushing splotches of mud and wood chips from her jacket and riding skins.

"He—that man—came out of nowhere. He was just there in front of me. I swerved and—I think—I don't know—I think he grabbed my handle bars." Her vox is shaky at first, but steadies as she regains her composure. "I was thinking, well, I may have to apologize for almost running him over and thank goodness I was pedaling slowly, when he just lurched toward me, as if..." Her words trail off. She does a curious little twist of her neck. A small adjustment of her spine. Angel swears she hears the crick and grind of bone and cartilage.

"Well," the fem continues. "It's enough to say that I wasn't at fault here."

Angel does a quick inspection of the cruiser. "Your bike looks okay—more than okay." She doesn't have to reach too deep into her bag of tricks to pull out some flattery. "This is one sweet ride."

The fem smiles, pride gleaming as bright as her teeth. "One of a kind. Made just for me." Her eyes narrow. "You know bikes?"

Angel nods. "Bikes and me go way back. First things I learned how to fix." She can almost feel the fem's eyes slide over her, as if taking her in for the first time.

"Aren't you the one with that little sugar cube of a girl? The cutie with the tumble of black curls," the fem says, as if she won't take no for an answer.

Angel nods, forcing a shy smile.

"You the minder? A housekeep? You're newish to our little enclave, yes? I don't recall hearing about a move-in or any family additions to our dirty neck of the woods. I tend to be in the know."

Angel lets her eyes slide, ducks her head a touch, looks up from beneath her lashes.

Deference. Be the bee.

"Work for Mrs. Wright, a widow up on Front Street. Cleaning, cooking, gardening. Repairing bikes. Started last spring." Angel pauses, casts her eyes down. "Child's mine."

A mix of speculation and admiration glint in the fem's eyes. "However did you manage that? You look awfully young to have gone through the approval process. And a service worker, at that."

Angel sits at the fraught crossroad of two paths: to tell the lie now and be discovered later or to present the truth upfront and risk all. So instead, she forges a third.

"I don't know."

A crooked little smile purses the fem's plump lips. "Hmmm, interesting," she murmurs, drawing out the syllables. "I'm Promise, by the way, otherwise known as Mrs. Frazier." She arches an eyebrow expectantly.

"Angel."

"Angel?" Promise repeats, a question in her tone, as if expecting more.

"Just Angel."

"Just Angel." Promise cocks her head. "No, not 'just Angel.' Angel, mother of?"

Angel hesitates before uttering her daughter's name.

"Lark, that's pretty," Promise says. "Lark." It's as if she's rolling the word around on her tongue, savoring it.

Kuba clears his throat, as if to speak, though Angel has instructed him to keep it zipped unless spoken to. The fem drags her eyes from Angel, gives him the once over. "And you are?"

"Jakub," Kuba mutters, using his given name, ducking his head before throwing in a "ma'am."

Promise nods dismissively and glances at the silver retro time-keep that encircles her wrist, a possible physical manifestation of her thoughts. "Well, that just spoiled my few minutes of peace. And so, away I go." She nudges her kickstand up and wheels the cruiser back around in the direction of the town center.

"We'll ride back with you," Angel blurts. "Just in case."

Does a wrinkle of distaste crease the corners of the fem's lips and eyes?

"We'll stay back a pace or three."

Promise blinks, nods, straddles her bike and pedals off.

They follow her back to the boardwalk trailhead, keeping a respectful distance, then pull to a stop and let her go on alone down the street towards the barbershop. She never once looks back as her scarlet form turns the corner and disappears.

Kuba kicks a pebble. "Well, that was in-ter-est-ing." He mimics Promise, drawing out the word with the same inflection and tone. "And just what did we achieve by that?"

Angel shrugs. "Time will tell."

Kuba toes another pebble. "Yeah, sure. And that goon on the trail? Ever met him before?"

Angel shakes her head.

"That s'posed to protect everyone involved? One of those 'need to know basis' things? Plug the leaks before they happen? But how do you ken who to trust?"

"Path said a guevara would be there on the path. And he was."

"So you trust Path?"

Angel has no answer. *Does* she trust Path? Word? She doesn't want to consider those questions now. Her mind is pondering the changing expressions that had animated the fem's face, the inflections that had rippled through her vox. Pondering whether she will take the bait.

"Quite the attitude on that one. As if she thinks she can tell birds where to fly. And y'know what else?" Kuba continues, on a mission now. "Didja notice? The frackin' fem never even said thank you."

17

The Rope

IT IS A COURTSHIP OF THE EYES. Silent. Significant. A courtship of the gesture. A dip of a chin. The flutter of fingers. An arch of an eyebrow. And it is never quite clear who is courting who. Who is the seducer and who is the seduced. Or if the seduction is mutual.

The sites of these trysts are achingly public. At the park. In front of the shops along Rittenhouse Avenue. On the pebbled shore. The one constant is the child, who is sweetly oblivious to the dance of deception. Oblivious to the truth that she is the pawn, the prize, the precious. All the child knows is the love that spills over her like cool water in the heat of a summer's day. That envelops her like a warm blanket in the depths of winter. And yet, perhaps she does somehow sense the import of the situation, because, throughout, she is docile, showing only the angelic side of her persona, hiding the obstinate devil's spawn that lurks within.

As March slides into April, impatience twitches in Angel's limbs. She tries to tamp it down by working harder, throwing herself into the tilling of the widow's modest vegetable garden and the sowing of seeds for basil, bell peppers, and eggplants in the tiny biowrap peat pots she's acquired at the Bartertown that popped up south of town. In another week or two, it will be time to start the tomatoes and the broccoli in the protected environment of the dome. If she is still at the widow's in late May, she'll transplant the seedlings to the outdoor plot. She's determined to play the long game. To finish the job.

Path is more impatient, rambling on about prods and tipping points and the need for an instigating event and an agent provocateur, which he never defines or explains, talking in loops and circles, tracing an invisible pattern that Angel knows will come to some malevolent fruition. Word broods, retreating into a voxless condemnation, scribbling his few words across the white board, his silence gruff, harsher than any roar. Kuba, under the spell of the guevara biblio, has adopted the pose of a stoic dedicated to keeping all the volatile fems in his life happy. Coddling the widow's whims. Channeling Lark's boundless energy and enduring the whiplash of her changing moods. Following Angel's lead to an uncertain destination.

And so Angel courts. And is courted. Smiles and nods. And flutters her fingers in a barely perceptible wave.

The wooer and the wooed.

One summer's day, a cruel child trapped a bee and a fly in a glass bottle. He stood inside a dim shed, his thumb over the opening, and watched as both insects frantically banged against the walls of their prison, seeking a way out. Called to dinner, he stood the bottle on the floor and ran off. By chance, he left it in a shaft of sunlight. The bee, driven by instinct to follow the light, floated up and shot out of the opening, leaving the fly to fling herself against the sides of the bottle. Eventually, after much fumbling, the fly found her way up to the opening and freedom.

The next morning, the malicious child repeated his cruelties, again trapping a fly and a bee to watch their struggles. Soon he was called to lunch. Planning to return to his sport, he turned the bottle upside down in the grass so its opening was blocked. The bee, again following her instinct, sought the light and flew up, only to crash into the closed end of the bottle. She banged and banged, over and over, in the direction of the sunlight, an exercise in futility. Meanwhile, the fly flitted here and there, up and down, in her haphazard manner. Sensing the smell of grass and soil, she stumbled down to the opening. There, the blades of grass parted for her and she slipped under the rim and crawled to freedom. The unfortunate bee, unable to follow a different path or let go of the call of the light, kept banging her head, trapped forever.

The path is rarely broad and straight and filled with light. It is often narrow and winding and long, cloaked in darkness and hardship and struggle. But it ends in freedom. Some of your brothers and sisters are walking that path now, as I speak, as you listen. The path leads to a battle with giants. But even the smallest among us can take up her makeshift weapon and strike a fatal blow. And the goliath will be felled like a mighty oak and lie at the feet of his conqueror.

This is the path to freedom. Are you prepared to walk it?
So sayeth the Night Prophet.

It's all hiding in plain sight. No, not even hiding. It's there to see and hear, as bold and bright as polished brass, as loud and clear as a taunt from a heckler.

The CQO has listened to the audios, has heard the vox of the Night Prophet and the messages sent into the night air. She knows the power of a good turn of phrase, knows the value of an idiom, knows why a cliché becomes a cliché. Understands the effectiveness of leaving the ears and the mind wanting more. Has fretted that the Corporate dailies, once so potent, are now just aural wallpaper. Has struggled to recall long-dead words erased from the general memory, and entered endless keyword searches into the knowledge management system until the phrase finally pops up, lines from a long ago biblio written by a long ago man.

Now I make a leaf of Voices—for I have found nothing mightier
than they are,

And I have found that no word spoken, but is beautiful, in its place.
O what is it in me that makes me tremble so at voices?
Surely, whoever speaks to me in the right voice, him or her I
*   shall follow,*
As the water follows the moon, silently, with fluid steps,
anywhere around the globe.

She has read the words and trembled. Because these voxcasts are more than exhortations. More than the usual ché propaganda, as the ProServ director had so casually referred to them. Yes, some are stories that one would tell a child. Some sound like the ramblings of late-night therapy sessions. Rabble-rousing, cheerleading, full of less-than-half-truths. And yet. To the susceptible, to those looking for any excuse to morph into a swarm, to form a mob, it may just be the right type of tinder and kindling.

In addition to meditation, the CQO's preferred method of problem-solving is visualization, which often takes the form of creating data tables. The orderly patterns of columns and rows, alphabet characters and numbers, focus the brain and steady the rhythm of the heart and the pulse of blood. She has entered the dates of the voxcasts in the first column, and in the second the gist of each message and the text immediately preceding the sign-off. For the third column she's had to do a little digging in the incident logs, not normally part of her purview. In the past, she's been content to leave that task in the hands of the ProServ director. However, it's fast becoming evident that the man is not up for the job. If he truly was competent, if he truly had the initiative required to meet—not exceed, just meet—expectations, he would have created the spreadsheet himself, brought it to her, and pointed out that these voxcast prophecies were not wishful prognostications designed to breed false hopes in the listener, but were, in actuality, the equivalent of feed newscasts, relaying events as they happened. Yes, they were couched in the vague yet florid language of the soothsayer, but the references would be clear to anyone with a half-discerning mind.

"Shelves of GaltMart empty..." That evening there had been a rash of break-ins at Marts in all six regions of the Protectorate. *"Liberen el agua..."* Attacks on water facilities in two regions. *"Those who pull the strings and manipulate the misery will be brought low..."* Simultaneous assassination attempts on several Regional Directors. *"Battle with giants..."* Multiple attacks on goliath patrols and garrisons in three regions.

The table reveals all. Some of these forays have been successful, the looters and brawlers carrying off merch and gumming up operations, while others have been easily repelled, with the rioters—one can hardly call them combatants—subdued and severanced on the spot. The loss of the two directors is concerning, a measure of the savagery of some of these chés. The CQO doesn't want to believe an affiliation exists between all these events, between these saboteurs, yet how else to explain the messages—yes, the propaganda—all coming from this one vox.

> *All wait for the right voices;*
> *Where is the practis'd and perfect organ? Where is the develop'd*
> > *Soul?*
> *For I see every word utter'd thence, has deeper, sweeter, new sounds,*
> *impossible on less terms.*
> *I see brains and lips closed—tympans and temples unstruck,*
> *Until that comes which has the quality to strike and to unclose,*
> *Until that comes which has the quality to bring forth what lies*
> > *slumbering,*
> *forever ready, in all words.*

> *What lies slumbering.*

The CQO prides herself on her reasoning skills, her logic, her dispassionate approach to dealing with life's complications and, yes, its inevitable disasters, keeping her head when everyone else is losing theirs. These characteristics, these personal qualities, got her to where she is today, the Chief Quality Officer of the Galt Corporation, the second in command, sitting at one end of the long gleaming table in the tall-ceilinged room with walls of glass where all the decisions are made.

They call us bees. We call ourselves bees. And so let us embrace the nature of the hive and its hierarchy of power. For it rests not with the queen, but with the workers. And when necessity arises, to save themselves and their small world, they will overthrow and execute a failing regime.

So sayeth the Night Prophet.

There is a tremor in the CQO's hands as she reaches for her water glass, a tingling in her fingers as they curl round the tumbler and lift it to her lips.

18

The Cell

KUBA HAS RACED THROUGH the slim biblio on guerrilla warfare and gone back to reread sections, his imagination susceptible to its variety of seductions. He's a man aflame, reciting phrases, intoning passages, burning to be a member of the vanguard. He talks of breaking old molds, establishing new. Of social justice. Of remaking the world. Of achieving the ideal. It's at his insistence that Angel demands Path provide the down-low on the other members of the cell, as well as an introduction to the guevaras hiding in plain sight. Except it's not in plain sight at all, but a longish trek to the west. Obstinately, Path insists the meeting take place on the one day of the week that the widow religiously devotes to personal care, which involves an extended visit to town, so she's not available to gather Lark to her bosom and mind the toddler. Angel is not happy about this wrinkle, but Kuba shrugs. Reminds her they've been toting Lark around on their backs and bikes since her birth. What's a few more miles?

Kuba's introduction to the faux bros takes place on the edge of town. It's as awkward and twitch-provoking as the sight of poison ivy rambling along a path where one has just stepped foot. Path leans against a tall cedar fence, so new its yellow planks give off a fresh, tart scent that almost masks the odors wafting from the biodumpster behind it. Word is bent over his bike, testing his tire pressure. They both give Kuba the twice over, taking his measure like dogs sniffing out a rival.

"Just let 'em try to stick their noses up my ass crack. I'll give 'em what for," Kuba mumbles under his breath.

"Don't," Angel hisses as Path saunters over, cutting Kuba the kind of glare a mother throws to head off potentially embarrassing behavior by her spawn.

"Didn't know you were bringin' a guest," Path drawls. "Uh, guests," he corrects, casting a skeptical eye on Lark, strapped into her carrier on the back of Angel's bike.

Lark's expression seems just as skeptical.

"Body man," Kuba retorts.

Path and Word exchange a look. "Yeah, look like you'd be handy in a rumble."

"Handle my own and then some," Kuba replies, still bristling.

"Sure, we can always use another hothead," Path chuckles, throwing Word another smirk. He nods. "Vamos."

They take off down the main asphalt road but soon veer onto an unmarked trail tucked behind a thicket of scrubby brush and the brown tangle of last year's vines. The path is narrow, hemmed in by the spindly branches and contorted trunks of understory trees struggling to claim their share of sunlight. It's rough going, bumping over roots, ducking under random limbs until they reach a stretch of pine barrens where the land unfolds and a vibrant green patchwork of sprouting stems and newborn leaves spreads amidst stands of scrawny, twisted jack pines. Path, at the head of the entourage, quickens his pace in this open area and there's a rise to the land that Angel can feel in her thighs and calves.

Soon they are enclosed by woods again, awash in the misty green of swelling leaf buds, a hue that seems to waft on the fresh breeze and spread cool across the skin of their cheeks. The trail squeezes around the massive gray trunks of maples and oaks and the slender bodies of aspen and birch until it narrows precipitously, too tight for safe passage on wheels. Path pulls up and dismounts. The others follow his lead. A pile of limp brush slumps to the side, a stack of twigs and limbs that looks suspiciously manmade. Angel squints at a metallic glint amidst the browns and grays.

The spoke of a bike wheel?

Path follows her focus and grins. Leans in. "Don't miss nothin', do ya, sweetheart?"

He leads them down what is scarcely a path, just a thread of rust-colored soil woven through the sentinel trees and the brown and green fabric of leaf litter, skirting the still-curled heads of sprouting ferns and the heart-shaped leaves of wood violets. He is a silent hiker, placing his feet precisely to rouse nary a whisper of footfall. Kuba, just behind him, is far less precise, his boots finding every stem, twig, and cluster of dry leaves, sending up a chorus of clicks and crackles. Lark, tired from her rubberneck-ing on the bike ride, is close to nodding out in the carrier on his back. She doesn't seem to notice the noise, but each sound sends a shiver radiating up Angel's back.

The woods. Always the damn woods. So many frackin' trees.

Suddenly sweat is beading across her forehead, pooling in the hollow of her neck, trickling down her spine and belly. Fear trickles with it. The breath catches in her throat when out the corner of her eye she sees the dark mass looming. She pulls up short, drops to a squat, reaching for the burner she doesn't have, panic clutching her stomach until her frantic fingers find the other weapon that's always with her. She whips it out of her cargo pocket, thumbs the release, brandishes its carbon steel blade in the direction of—

Nothing. Just the empty air filled with the tang of pine and the mellow odor of decay in the midst of rich new life.

Panting, sucking in, but unable to truly breathe. To get enough of that empty air. To throw off the weight of all the baleful trees bearing down on her, hemming her in, a prison of trees.

Trees through which the masses, the black-clad and helmeted goliaths, crawl and stalk and slither.

Angel... Angel...

"Angel?"

Her name echoes in voxes as drenched in fear as her own body, throats and mouths clogged with it. And yet a hand dares to descend upon hers, to cover her trembles with a steady, enveloping calm. A hand to ease the knife out of her white-knuckled clutch, and carefully fold the blade back into the grip. A hand to slip around her shoulder and gently uncoil her body from its defensive crouch.

When he turns her body, when they are face to face, there is no question in Word's expression, just a hint of recognition and a patient acceptance, as if he already knows the answer. Though she tries to swallow the words as she's always been able to do in the past, to keep a tight hold on them and a vice grip on her vox, they slip out.

"Trees. I've been in trees. In woods like this. With evil. Always evil in the trees. On narrow paths." She flinches even as she utters the words, the trees in her memory looming, crowding, until there's no space to even breathe. "Too close," she gasps. "The narrow path always leads to evil."

He cocks his head, puts a steadying hand on her shoulder. "Not here. Here, we walk a path that leads to a better day, to a new life. It's narrow, yeah. And difficult, the road we walk." He brushes a strand of hair away from her cheek, lets his thumb rest there for a calming moment. "And only a few will walk it. The broad road and the wide gate—the path that many take—that's the road which leads to destruction."

Did the words even come from him? Or were they merely the rasp of the still bare branches in the wind?

He takes her hand, unfurls her fisted fingers, and places the knife in her palm.

The masses here are not dressed in black, but gray and brown and dappled green, as they step out of the thickness of the forest and into a tight clearing at the base of a low sandstone outcropping. They are mesmerizing in their slow movements and in the patterns of light that play over them, patterns that shift as the breeze shifts the treetops, patterns that make even the drab leaf litter ripple like water.

Five. Seven. Nine. They encircle the intruders, their hands resting easily on hips, just above where their holstered burners sit at the ready. Jut-jawed, blank-faced, inscrutable as empty walls, resembling nothing so much as a platoon of ex-goliaths, unleashed from their corporate chains. Then a guffaw splinters the tense silence as a tenth man, immense and swarthy, with a tangle of black hair escaping his worn red bandanna, vaults from the top of the ledge into their midst. He pulls what could be an embed scanner from his chest pocket, casually eyes the slim black device, then stuffs it back inside.

"Llegan tarde," he grunts, folding thick arms across an even thicker chest.

Scrawny Path, who could easily fit two of himself inside the man's frame, shrugs, glancing back at Kuba and Angel. "Some of us are used to the more leisurely bushwa pace of life."

The tenth man's eyes sweep over Kuba, widen when they take in Lark's face peering over his shoulder, but slow to a crawl when they land on Angel. Cheeks burning, she holds his gaze when it finally reaches her face, a steel rod of defiance stiffening her spine. When he steps up to her, she's forced to tilt her head to maintain her stare. The stare stretches until a grin splits the man's face and another guffaw explodes from his lips. He takes a knee, wrapping Angel's hand in his huge paw, bringing the back of it to his lips, gazing up at her from behind lush black lashes.

"La profeta nocturna. The lovely vox in the night."

Angel is frozen, limbs fearful of making an awkward move,

of provoking laughter in the circle of guevaras, until the man lets out yet another hearty laugh, stands, and steps over to Word, crushing him in an embrace.

"Güey, lo siento, but your words, that whole palabra, sound much better coming out a fem mouth. In liquid gold."

Then it's laughter and man hugs all around, a tossing of names, few of which Angel catches in the rapid-fire volley, and then a rush of bro chat, although it becomes clear to Angel's discerning eye that some of the grizzled men are actually fems. Or androgs who've somehow slipped free of their chemical bondage, hair cropped, armpits and legs furred, renouncing Corporate strictures not only in word and deed, but with their bodies.

Path and the tenth man, who goes by the nom de guerre of Armor, lounge against a fallen tree trunk, heads together in deep chat. Kuba has fallen in with a trio, a couple of younger-looking dudes and a fem, a shocked but gleeful expression animating his face. Lark, who earns a casual inspection from everyone but none of the usual fuss, squats in the dirt between his feet, contentedly digging with a stick. Word is huddled with the rest of the band. Angel drifts along the periphery of each small cluster, gathering bits and pieces of the conversations.

Sabotage. A torching of a feed line tower. A break-in at a Galt Mart. An ambush of a pair of goliaths just off the main road. The dirty work, the necessary work of insurgency, told as tales of glory to make a young man's heart pound and his hands burn to take up arms and march into the fray, more urgently than any biblio could do. Did she calculate this would happen, when she pressed Path for the trek out here? Did she anticipate the gleam that would spark in Kuba's eyes? Is she already so certain that this time, where she's going, he won't be able to follow? That their paths must diverge? And so to help him find his own?

Under the rumble of all the palaver and chewing of the fat lies a hissing thrum, a gush, a burble. Following the sound, Angel edges out of the circle of camaraderie and around the contour of the outcropping, the stone damp, cool, and rough under her hand. Beyond its curve, the slender path, studded with rocks and roots, switchbacks down a steep slope. At the bottom, a gorge cradles a boulder-strewn creek bed and a churning cascade of water. As it spills over a mossy ledge and fans onto the slabs of red sandstone below, the gush of it soothes and riles at once. Holds her in its thrall until a hand pressing on her shoulder startles her.

"You can walk behind it," Word says, his rasp an echo of the water's strident song. Without waiting for a response, he takes her hand.

They hop from boulder to boulder across the shallow creek, creep over the rust-colored mud to the curving rock face, and then inch across the wet ledge until they stand behind the waterfall. From there, looking out, the red rocks of the creek and the green of the woods beyond are veiled by a liquid wall of white.

"Peaceful, yeah?" Word muses. He reaches out a cupped hand to catch a bit of the spray. "You know, it wasn't fake. Or meant to be a joke. What Armor did back there. Droppin' the knee. He wasn't ragging on you."

The water pours. Angel's cheeks grow damp, caressed by the fine mist until it feels like a second skin.

"You're striking sparks with each vox—and so it will grow, from a spark to a fire. Small at first, but then it spreads and grows into a conflagration—a wildfire— "

"Burning out of control," Angel interrupts. "I've seen a wildfire. Ran from one. Can still taste the smoke and ash in my mouth."

"It's just a metaphor," Word replies.

"I'm not afraid of what's coming—or what you hope will come. I've walked through fire." She extends her fingers into the icy cascade. "But I've more to think about now."

"We could find a safe house for your girl. There's—"

"No, she stays with me," Angel says, bringing her teeth down hard on the words, cutting him off.

They lapse into silence, while the churning water roars on. After a time, Angel feels his hand on her shoulder again.

"You know, if you ever want to talk about it. The woods. What happened. Before."

Angel can't imagine that time will ever come. To talk about it would only be to relive it. To take a knife and cut deep into old wounds, places now scarred over. Places best left untouched. She brushes past him, leaving the liquid veil behind, and startles to see they have a witness.

Perched on a boulder at the creek's edge is a tall, big-boned fem clad in weathered fatigues, with a faded red bandanna taming her spray of salt and pepper hair. Although much of her face is hidden behind a respy, from the way the crinkles stretch out from her speculative eyes, there's a likelihood she's smiling.

"You know what they say about those who slip behind the waterfall. Together," the fem says, amusement lending a lilt to her muffled, low-pitched vox. She glances beyond Angel's shoulder as Word appears. "Mated for life."

"And you know what they say about fems who believe in superstitions," Word rasps, his face reddening. "Esa mujer está como una puta cabra."

As he strides past, the fem kicks her booted foot out, hooking his leg and sending him sprawling. In another swift move, she's got a knee firmly wedged to his back, pinning him to the red dirt.

"No digas loca a una mujer a menos que quieras verla ponerse loca, ¿si?" The fem punctuates her speech with a shift of her weight for emphasis and Word groans. She nods at Angel. "Don't call a fem crazy, unless you wanna see her go crazy. ¿Lo entiendes?"

19

La Tigresa

"No, POBRECITO, THE FIRST WORDS out your mouth should have been an introduction, not an insult," the fem scolds, as she eases her knee off Word's back.

Word grunts as he pushes himself to his feet, shifting his posture, tossing his head like a petulant steed with a bit clenched in its teeth. "Oh, so we have manners out here now?" he huffs.

"Manners always and everywhere. What keeps a civilization civil," the fem responds cooly, and then, in a tone that exudes genuine warmth, introduces herself to Angel. "I'm Teeg. Welcome to our little corner of—" Teeg pauses, casting a shady side-eye at Word. "Civilization." She extends her fisted knuckles for a bump.

Angel answers with a tap and a nod. "Angel."

She can feel the fem taking her measure, much in the way Armor had. Much in the way that she herself is doing with the fem. Like a cat eyeing the distance between the floor and the counter before making a leap, head bobbing, paws shuffling, calculating carefully to avoid disaster. The fem, this Teeg, wears her skin like it's the mantle of a goddess. Fully inhabits her solid-bodied space. Owns it.

"Forgive this," she says, gesturing to the respy. "Was up near the Duluth garrison. Some nasty business going round there. Doing my part to keep our güeys safe."

"Teeg—La Tigresa—is the mother of us all," Word says with an affectionate flourish of his hand. "Spiritual. And practical."

"Oh, please—and you dare to imply that I am old enough to be your mother?" Teeg says with mock indignation. "I should be offended—but, of course, I am—old enough, that is." Her lilt suggests she is as comfortable making fun of herself as she is baiting Word. "I'm glad you are recovering your vox, my son," she continues in that impish tone. "Practical mother, yes, I stitched you up real good, but spiritual, not so much—anymore." She glances at Angel. "I think another has relieved me of that burden."

Angel blinks at the implication, stammering, "I'm just a vox."

Teeg shakes her head. "Not just. No, yours is a vox that turns each word into compelling music to the ears. That is a gift. But I must admit, I pictured you—different. Funny how the quality— the texture—of a vox can paint a misleading portrait."

"How did you picture me?"

Teeg shrugs and shakes her head. "That matters not. Because now when I hear the vox, this"—she makes an encompassing sweep of her callus-hardened hand—"is what I will see." The lines around her hazel eyes crinkle again, suggesting another smile behind her respy. "Maybe we should rejoin the güeys before they have time to craft their own crude jokes about your mutual disappearance." She raises her eyebrows and cocks her head at Word. "Because you know they will."

Teeg leads the way up the steep path back to the top of the gorge. Her dark eyes flash surprise and a certain wary delight when she catches sight of Lark, who is whacking her stick against the trunk of a birch and letting out intermittent hunger whines.

"The littlest guevara?" Teeg fishes in her backpack and pulls out a protein bar. She turns to Word. "Have you and your compañero been hiding something this whole time?"

Word inclines his head towards Angel.

Teeg squints, tilting her head. "Ah, yes, the resemblance is there. The chin, the nose. Especially the eyes."

Angel shakes her head. "She doesn't have my eyes."

Teeg shrugs. "Maybe not the color, but I see you in them." She squats down at eye-level with Lark and hold out the bar. "¿Tienes hambre, mi dulce niña?"

Lark scampers back to Kuba, wriggling into his arms, hiding most of her face. Only her eyes, wide and full of doubt, peer over the sleeve of his jacket.

Teeg tears open the wrapper and waggles the snack. "I know a cry of hunger when I hear one."

With Kuba's encouragement, Lark stretches out her small hand. "Yes, please," he prompts. What Lark burbles shyly sounds more like 'yepplee' but Teeg grins and hands over the treat. "Thank you," Kuba prompts again, but Lark is too busy nibbling.

Angel moves to sit beside them, but feels Teeg's hand on her elbow, guiding her apart from the others.

"You bring the loca—got to be more than a little crazy toting your pequeña along—and you bring the bravura, or so we hear. And a big idea," Teeg says. "But you are light on plans."

"I need help in that area."

"A lot of help," Teeg says with emphasis. "This would be a big op—no, a huge op."

"But doable?"

Teeg stares off through the trees to the east, where, miles away, the lake and the Breeder Islands lie. "Anything is doable. But achieving success is another story. Make no mistake, we've talked about doing something along these lines before. Sketched out scenarios. But nothing's come of it. So far." She turns her gaze back to Angel. "Path tells me you're willing to go inside."

"Working on it," Angel replies, casting a glance at the scattered guevaras, whose eyes seem to follow the two of them as they walk. "You've got thirteen in the cell? That's all?"

"Fourteen. One is out—on business." Teeg flicks at a

hovering fly. "Cells are small by design. It's how we stay mobile. Fleet. How we can strike and disappear and reappear and strike again. Like this annoying buzzer here," she chuckles, swatting again. "But there are other cells—many others—spread across Superior and the other regions and plenty of allies on the inside and, if it please the Maker, the Night Prophet is helping to recruit more," she adds with a wink.

"No embeds?"

"Not in this cell. Many of our allies have them, of course—and we use those connections carefully."

"Where do these people—these 'allies'—come from?"

Teeg stops and fixes her in a stare as binding as a trap's steel bracelets. "Where do you come from? Do you assume you're the only freeborn? That's a big assumption—and wrong." She falls back into her rolling swagger. "Some guevaras were born here, free. Some came from the Outlier. Borders are porous. And water is life. The Protectorate may not have freedom—yet—but it has water."

"But the insiders—why would they want to help?"

"They are not just helping—they are part of this movement."

"But what's their motivation?"

Teeg smiles the tired yet patient smile of a teacher faced with a student whose questions are never-ending. "You're a young thing with many questions, yeah, but here's one for you. Tell me this. Is it your experience that people here are generally—oh, let's not even say *happy*, let's just say—content with their lives? That they feel an allegiance to Galt?"

Angel doesn't have to pause to consider this. "Well, no, but still, they're part of Corporate, they're in the system. They may question it and grumble and complain, but in the end, for the most part they comply." Yet even as the words leave Angel's lips, she knows the exceptions to that statement, all the little defiances she's witnessed and heard over the years. And so she persists.

"Do you trust them?"

Teeg shrugs. "The simple answer is yes, I do—I have to. Until they break my heart. I've read the biblios. Listened to the memes. It's a rare movement that can emerge victorious by only working the outside game. You need people on the inside helping you break the walls. Is your experience so different? Did you make it to this day all alone?"

In the face of Angel's silence, Teeg continues. "We have certain things in our favor. We have a nexus, a funder, multiple funders to work the inside game." She holds up a palm. "Do not ask me to name people, places, or things. I will not. Cannot. But just accept that the eye of Galt is surprisingly weak and easily distracted by bright, shiny objects. And the mind of Galt lacks a certain—shall we say—imagination? Refuses to believe that the people to whom it distributes such *largesse*—sarcasm, mine— could possibly be discontent. It's a complacent mind. And this is all to our advantage." She readjusts her respy. "So don't be as unimaginative as Galt. The obstacles in our path are many and they are high. We won't overcome them without a plan."

Angel blinks at the implication in Teeg's words. "So my— idea—it's a go?"

"Your idea? I'll have you know I've been hankering to take down one of these facilities for years," Teeg replies in a clipped tone, her eyebrows arching. "We've disrupted a few water and power facilities, but never had a complete take down. And that's what we need to do—a complete take down—to level up our game. But I'll give you props. This op starts with you and I want to see what you bring to the table for us to work with. Go back to Bayfield. There's things we need to know." Teeg ticks them off on her long fingers. "How many fems are in the facility? How many are ripe for leaving? What's the security presence? How many goliaths are we going to have to take out? On my end, I need to ask a few more questions. What happens when we get the fems out? Do we have the safe houses to shelter them? What kind of additional firepower can we secure?" Teeg swings a fist through the air, smacking it down into her palm. "Security will come down swift and hard. Once we go in motion, we've set the storm loose, the winds'll be like nothing you've seen or felt, I guarantee, and we're not gonna have a lot of time to run this before the funnel cloud touches ground and comes bearing down on us."

Teeg's words spark a memory. A twilight trek through an October landscape, trees turning, the smell of decay rising with every footfall, Angel's maglite sweeping in a narrow arc across an even narrower path. A track forged by beasts on the hunt. Coming upon a raccoon, its masked eyes glowing orbs on its fear-frozen face. She senses that wild, wide-eyed look is bleeding onto her own face now as more memories surface. Of the trees and goliaths in black. Goliaths advancing. Advancing like the tornado that Teeg has evoked. A relentless, evil, irresistible whirlwind from which she's spent the last two years dodging and dashing and cowering.

She tries to keep her game face in place, hold the fear-wild look in, blink it away, but Teeg must spy a glimpse of it because she puts a reassuring hand on Angel's shoulder.

"It's a lot. We're talking a lot of lives. All precious. None to spare. We never want to engage in a prolonged firefight if we don't have to. We hit 'em hard and then we run away to fight another day. But when we must, then we lay it all down. Leave it all on the battlefield. And that's why we put our trust in others, because we can't do this on our own. But we don't trust blindly. We have a system to verify. People who are placed to pass along information, some of it true, some false."

"Informants?"

Teeg nods. "It's like the test watertechs use to find leaks in the pipe and valve system. They toss some dye into the water network and watch to see where the red spills out. Look, talk with Word. He's a little rough around the edges, but he's a veteran and he's got a good head on his shoulders. And he's durable. Like steel. He's been forged in the fire of failure."

"I thought Path was the logistics man."

"Path?" Teeg scoffs, a chuckle bubbling low in her throat. "Path has a very dangerous mind, but he has no interest in the intricacies and tribulations of building the bomb." She winks. "Metaphorically speaking. He's impatient. Wants everything to happen now—or better yet—yesterday. Is itching for a taste of chaos. He will push to make things happen before their time. Always ready with a nudge or a shove or a little accelerant. He just wants to light the fuse and watch the world explode."

20

Accelerant

I WOULD SPEAK TO THE ALLIES, those who live in comfort but recognize that their life of ease and plenty is borne on the backs of others. Those who are given choices, and who understand that those choices constrain the possibilities of other lives. It's not enough to recognize your prerogatives and privileges. Your eyes must truly be open to the world around you, to the world made by Galt, to the world that is balanced on the edge of the abyss and requires your acquiescence to keep it from tumbling over. Or so Galt tells you. Après moi le déluge. If not for Galt, then chaos. Seek the memes who will tell you that every dictator and oligarch who has straddled the world from time out of mind has threatened such utter devastation in their wake. And yet, the world is still here. Ready to be remade. If only you will see. Truly see. Us.

So sayeth the Night Prophet.

The widow has a Wednesday routine. A trek into town on her silver cruiser for an hour's worth of flexitation to tone her aging body and mind, followed by an appointment with the hair artisan, who indulges her whims for ever more elaborate braids and twists. Then she meets her gossips for lunch at the lakeside cafe where the fems dine alfresco on the screened-in deck in summer and cozy up to the stone fireplace the rest of the year. She allows herself a goblet of the finer aged wine, rather than settling for the seasonal, and lingers over a slice of gooseberry pie topped with fresh cream. She absorbs the twitter of her companions, ogles the handsome men and their anxious wives who order food and rarely consume it, just pick, pick, pick at it, like foraging birds. Sometimes the anxiety and anticipation building in the fems overflows, triggering the Metrics monitors on their slim wrists and the beeping fills the dining room. Then the square breathing exercises begin and continue until the nerves are settled again. The old fems, the child-denied, huff at the interruption. The widow tries to be the one who feels a genuine sympathy, but knows she's just faking it to make herself look good.

Just before two in the afternoon, the hour when the assignment bureau begins to release the embedded and registered infants into the care of their new parentals, she settles her bill with the vouchier and exits through the side door, striding briskly down the road toward the intersection and the rack where she's bolted her bike. Ready to head home, desperate to avoid a glimpse of the treasures she's been denied.

Until now.

Because now, of course, her eagerness is less to avoid an unpleasant sight and more to hurry back to the armful of feisty sweetness that awaits. Still, she pedals at a leisurely pace, pondering the lucky circumstances that brought the little girl into her life. Chance meetings in the relentless spring rains. How the young man reminded her of her late husband with that slight hint of arrogance in the set of his shoulders, even sopping wet. And the young fem, face half hidden under her hood, too defiant to be bedraggled—refusing—REFUSING!—help, with the child squalling in her arms. Making the widow ask twice! Why, practically forcing her to beg that they allow her to give them shelter from the storm! Outrageous, they were!

Ah, but she'd gotten her way, as she often did in matters

that did not involve the approval of Galt. And now instead of a barren stalk, she is, from a certain point of view—*her* point of view—the mother of three. And quite enjoying snubbing her nose—if in secret—at the Corporate toadies who thwarted her all those years ago.

It's such a pleasant reverie, she's so engrossed in the anticipation of burying her nose in that halo of curls, that she forgets to look both ways at the crossroads. Poised at the edge of town, it's only a busy junction in the mornings or evenings, arrival and departure times, never in the middle of the afternoon in the midst of the bestowals. So it is that she doesn't see or hear the personal transport bearing down on her, its streamlined sage-gray body blending with the pines lining the road, the purr of its whisper-quiet electric heart muffled by a sudden gust of chilly spring air blowing in off the lake.

Lark is asleep, head lolling against the side of her toddler seat, arm flung out to the side and fingers splayed as if combing the invisible tendrils of the breeze. They've jammed it all the way back from the camp, in an effort to be puttering around the manse when the widow returns from her own jaunt. But they're late and will have to concoct a cover story.

Blame it on a fussy child. A stop at the park. A soothing trip down the lakeshore path. Blah, blah, blah.

Angel knows it really doesn't matter. The widow will believe whatever they say. In fact, she'll only half listen as she scoops the child into her arms and kisses that melon head. In fact, she'll hold up her hand to stop their babbling mouths and give the look that only she and Angel understand.

Plausible deniability.

At the crossroads, a black security troller, yellow lights flashing, idles beside a red and white medivan. An officer stands interrogating a handful of onlookers, sweeps from the look of their paint-stained coveralls. Kuba automatically veers to the other side of the road, but the security trap has his back to the path so Angel stays the course and slowly glides past as one of the sweeps spills his story.

"Was puttin' a second coat on the fence there. Heard a scream or somethin', then the squeal and the thud come. Turned round, the fem was on the pavement. Whatever hit her, a transport I guess, was already gone. Headin' east. Could just make it out between the trees. Greenish. Grayish. Not 'zactly sure."

Angel senses the trap craning his head. Hears him squawk towards her retreating back. "Keep it movin', biker."

Kuba has already crossed the intersection and pulled up a little ways down the path. He beckons her to hurry, but Angel's gut draws her near to where the medics, in their wrinkled blue scrubs, are bent over a dark mass in the road. They've already hustled the victim into a black body bag and one of them is tugging up the long zipper. Angel is too late to see the face, but from the open end she see the long silvery braid hanging out, lying twisted on the black pavement like a snake frozen in mid-writhe.

"It's Mam," Angel wheezes when she reaches Kuba, trying to swallow back the panic flooding her throat.

The look that lingers in the space between them encompasses everything she's feeling. A cycle of grief in hyperdrive. That first shock of disbelief and denial. The flush of anger. Bargaining.

How can this be happening? This isn't happening. Why did this happen? Now? Frack! She can't be dead. She can't. Not when I need her—we need her—alive!

The realization comes likes a punch to the gut that leaves her breathless.

This wasn't an accident.

It's a fact she quickly accepts as she feels a sick sweat seeping across her body. And just as quickly her mind turns to the how. And the who. Common sense and past experience say that it can't be Corporate. Galt would have acted with far less mess and fuss. A simple removal. A quiet disappearance. A vanishing with nary a trace left behind to dwell and fret upon.

Who then? Who benefits from this?

Then the practical of the here and now seizes her and shakes her out of speculation and into survival mode.

"We gotta get our stuff out of that manse before the traps and scavengers sweep in."

Kuba frowns. "We can't—"

There's no time to explain. Only time to act. Angel thrusts a pedal down, setting her bike in motion. "We have to go. Now. Not leaving my stuff. We need our road gear."

"How long before—" Kuba starts, but Angel cuts in, knowing what he's thinking.

"I don't know. Back in the AgSector, it was barely hours. But back there, everyone was severanced. It was all planned down to the minute. Nobody died a—" She's about to say *natural death,* when she catches herself. "Might take longer here, but maybe not. The traps'll be on it in a corporate minute. They'll push the sweeps in. These swags have precious things that Corporate will want to reclaim. You've seen it with your own eyes."

Kuba nods. "Then let's go."

As they accelerate, legs churning, wheels spinning, Angel's mind is spinning, too. Where can they go? Back to the camp? Kuba would never hear of it. He'd sworn to keep a roof over Lark's head, no matter the cost. Can she approach the Frazier fem? Dare she? The plan had been to wait until the fem approached her, to make the suggestion, to offer the proposal.

Frack! Frack! Frack!

At the manse, they stash the bikes under the portico at the side drive, where a thicket of lilacs covered with swelling buds hides the view from the road. Lark's still asleep in her seat. They can move and gather much faster without her.

Ten minutes. That's all. Not even.

Just a quick dash to grab the go bags they've kept at the ready everywhere they've squatted, prepped for just such a flight as this. Backpacks loaded with changes of clothes and medikits and maglites, canned and packeted provisions and fishing gear, Galt vouchers stolen and bartered. Kuba will stuff some fresh food from the kitchen into another tote. Angel will need just a minute more to retrieve her backpack of weapons and way finders and memento mori from the corner of her closet, the one she's carried since her flight from the AgSector. Since the morning Eben gave it to her. The morning Eben died. The morning everyone died.

The decision is unspoken between them. Maybe it seems safer that way. Less guilt-racked. They'll leave Lark to her nap. A nod and a quick sidle to the back door where Kuba punches in the entry code, and they're in, the warm, dim interior a relief from the day's chill. Kuba dashes to the kitchen, his provider's mind leading the way. Angel takes the stairs to the second floor two at a time. Ducks into Kuba's room, spartan and tidy, bed made, the few pairs of shirts and denims he owns hanging from the closet rod in a neat row. And, in the corner, the go bag. The room she shares with Lark borders on a maelstrom, dirty clothes draped and puddled here and there. But both backpacks are right where they should be. As she slings them over her shoulders, she feels a thud against her breastbone and catches sight of herself in the oval mirror above the dresser. The warrior agate, the color of dried blood, rests just below the hollow of her throat. The last gift from Serafina.

To keep you safe.

She lifts it and rubs it, smooth and cool, across her lips.

Hasta siempre. Until forever.

Stop. Breathe. Focus. Think.

In the mirror, she can also see the reflection of the window, and its view of the lawn and the curving drive beyond. And the sleek body of a personal transport easing around the bend.

21

The Persuader

In her sprint for the stairs, the heavy backpacks thump and sway, causing her to lurch and almost stumble headlong down the steps. "Kuba, we've got company," she hisses, poking her head around the entry to the kitchen.

"What?" Kuba stops shoving carrots into a tote.

"A transport—outside."

"Scavengers? Already?"

"No, it's small."

Stop. Breathe. Focus. Think. Lark.

Angel slings a go bag to Kuba, who slips it over his free shoulder. "They'll try the front door. We'll slip out the back. If we're seen, we'll brazen it out," he says, but his tone is less confident than his words. "And if comes to it, there's always steel persuasion," he adds, patting his cargo pocket.

Let it not come to that. Not in front of Lark.

The doorbell remains ominously silent.

Lark.

"We shouldn't have left her outside."

"Walk. Don't run," Kuba insists, as they burst out the back door. "Keep it casual."

Should she have her knife in her hand? At the ready?

Not in front of Lark.

The child's squalls rend the crisp air.

Kuba reaches the corner of the manse first and peers around the bulk of a forsythia laden with golden blossoms. Angel doesn't stop, darts past him, rounding the corner, heading straight for the portico where the tall, slender figure bends to the wailing child, unstraps the restraint, lifts her out of the seat, and presses her to a shoulder. And then turns at the sound of the harsh cry that erupts from Angel's lips.

"There she is. See, your mama didn't abandon you." Promise Frazier's eyes are deep, wide pools of reproach as she shifts the squealing child so that the girl can see Angel.

Lark, red-faced and teary-eyed, thrusts out her arms, hands reaching, fingers wriggling. "Mama," she blubbers, as Angel gathers her into her arms, the child's weight and the look in the fem's eyes adding to her burden.

"We were only gone for a few minutes. She was asleep," Angel finds herself babbling, wondering why she feels the need to explain, to excuse her behavior to this swag who has no hold over her.

Except that she does.

Kuba strides up, placing a comforting hand on Lark's back, patting gently as her wails ebb into hiccuping snuffles. "Ready for camping, sweetie?" A lie he ventures as awkwardly as a boy leaning in for a first kiss.

Promise gazes at them with the air of a fem appraising an antique in a whimsy shop, gauging its value. Then her eyes soften, reproach sinking below the surface, replaced by something akin to pity. She steps forward, closing the space between them.

"I know this"—she gestures to the go bags—"isn't a camping trip. I know about Mrs. Wright." She catches Angel's question before it leaves her lips. "Some compare the feed to a 'tronic grapevine, news traveling at the speed of sound. I think it's more like the speed of nerve cells in your body. Like when your fingers touch a hot stove and you jerk them away. No loitering, no contemplating, oh, what shall I do? It's that instantaneous. Of course, you wouldn't know that—when you're off the grid."

The denials start to tumble from Kuba but Promise's raised hand, fine-boned and manicured, her silvery nail polish glittering in the weak sunlight, halts their progress.

"Yours is not to talk, yours is to listen." Those deep pools now reflect concern. "I can offer you shelter. A place to live—and work. In my home on the island."

And there it is. The proposal. Spoken aloud after all the silent wooing. All Angel needs to do is accept.

"There's no time to think about this—now. Security will be here—probably on their way. Maintenance will sweep in. The vultures descending in a mad flurry to pick at the carcass." Promise winces. "Sorry. I'm sure she meant something to you beyond just a place to live in the blur." Her expression turns soft, coaxing. "Come. For now. Think. Decide later. For now, be safe." One long finger twirls a strand of Lark's hair. "Keep her safe."

In this forced pause of her body, Angel's mind settles as well, and in its quieting, Teeg's words come into clarity.

He will push to make things happen before their time. Always ready with a nudge or a shove. Or a little accelerant.

Is this Path's handiwork? The nudge, the shove? The accelerant? The bastard. Thinking nothing of what would be lost. She was a meme. And did Teeg know? Did she approve? Was this the business that the missing fourteenth man was taking care of?

No hay lágrimas. There's never any time for tears. So here we go.

Angel nods.

Promise smiles. "Then it's settled." She gestures to the backpacks and sighs. "You needn't bring—whatever this is. I can provide anything you might possibly need." Maybe she sees Angel's jaw tighten. "Flint will put whatever it is in quarantine anyway, and you're not likely to get it back, so best leave it behind."

Lark sniffles and burbles something into Angel's shoulder.

Promise blinks, her long lashes fluttering in a rhythm, as if they're passing along a coded message. "But we can make an exception for this sweet thing's favorite stuffie. That little rabbit she loves to clutch. You did remember to grab that rabbit, didn't you?"

Kuba and Angel exchange a look. Shake their heads.

"I'll get it," Kuba says, face reddening, guilt narrowing his eyes. He turns and hustles back around the corner.

Before Angel can formulate an appropriately groveling thanks, Promise lays a hand on her forearm. "This offer extends only to you and the child, uhm, Lark, isn't it? Such a pretty name for such a pretty girl. I can twist my husband around my finger like a strand of this lovely hair and he does enjoy being surrounded by beautiful fems." Her laugh is sharp-edged. "How could he not? It's his job. But we can't have an unauthorized man in the facility. Much less an undocumented one. You understand."

"I can't—"

"Of course you can. Mothers—good mothers—make sacrifices for their children all the time. Did your own mother not sacrifice for you?" A hushed intake of breath, the barest of gasps before Promise continues. "But of course she did. The very idea of you, standing here, a free born. Isn't that what you call yourselves?" She flicks a dismissive hand again. "But that's a tale for another time."

The fem points to Angel's backpacks. "And, like I said, no baggage. You'll find we have everything you need on the island." Her gaze flits over Angel's shoulder as Kuba comes trotting back around the corner of the manse, the pink rabbit clutched in his hand. Her smile is just a bland curve on her face. "As I said, I'll make an exception for the stuffie. Will you tell him or should I?"

Kuba wiggles the rabbit in Lark's face. She giggles and grabs it by the ears, drawing it in for a fierce hug.

"There now. She's ready to go." Promise's laugh is softer now.

The three stand, absorbed in Lark's joyous display of affection, until their silence and proximity grows uncomfortable.

Promise catches Angel's eye, inclines her head toward Kuba. Raises her eyebrows. Taps the timekeep on her wrist.

Kuba notices. "Yeah, what're we hangin' here for? Let's bounce before the traps catch the scent." Then he reads the tension on Angel's face as she takes hold of his arm and guides him out from under the portico, keeping her back to Promise.

She leans in, drapes her arm around his neck, lowering her vox to a whisper meant for his ears only. "She'll only take me and Lark."

Kuba squints in momentary confusion. Then his anger explodes in a hiss. "What? The hell with that—I won't let—"

Angel presses her hand to his mouth to silence him. "Kuba, I'm going with her. This is what the cell's been waiting for. What we've been waiting for."

What I've been waiting for.

Kuba brushes her hand away. "Get straight, Angel. You're putting Lark in the middle of—"

She cuts him off again. "That's the way it has to play. I knew that going in."

"Frack!" Kuba tries to reel away from her grip, but she squeezes tight, holding him close. "I can't let you go there alone."

"Go ahead, say your goodbye properly. As sloppily as you like. I won't look," Promise calls. "I'll avert my eyes. I'll even turn my back." Her tone is all fun-and-games, but Angel looks back to check whether the fem has actually turned away.

"Look, you have to let me go. And here," Angel shrugs off her bags and rests them at his feet. "I can't bring these with." Her hand brushes the bulk of the knife in her cargo pocket. She fishes it out and presses it into his hand. "This, too. Not now, anyway. Take 'em to the safe house, I'll find a way to smuggle 'em onto the island later. You could stay at the house with Path and Word—or better yet, go to the woods. Hook up with the cell." She forces a grin. "They could use a dude who can roast a squirrel without reducing it to char—and who's handy with a burner in a tight spot. It's where you belong in the story." She squeezes his hand, knowing if she looks him in the eye there'll be tears welling, and she doesn't want to deal with that, to feel compelled to joke it away or obliged to succumb to it. Instead she draws him into a hug as fierce as Lark's.

"I love you—the both of you—so much. You know that, don't you?" Kuba breathes, his vox brittle.

His words hang there, surrounding them until she eases him out of her grasp and brings her fisted hand to her chest. "To remake the world."

He folds his hand over hers and pulls her close again, their clasped hands and the knife, still in his grip, nestled between their pounding hearts.

"To remake the world."

The moss green personal transport is a sleek two-seater with luxurious cushioned semi-pods upholstered in a velvety fabric that matches its exterior gloss. It's unlike any of the strictly utilitarian transports Angel can remember from her early childhood spent shuttling around the Protectorate, as Eben requested reassignments to stay one jump ahead of the numerators. For her sake. Just one of many sacrifices. Angel shoots a look at Promise, who is smiling at Lark.

"She'll have to ride on your lap," Promise sighs. "Against the rules, I know, but this baby's not built for three." She pats the transport's sloping hood. "I won't tell the Corporate watchdogs, if you don't," she adds with a smirk. "And we're already breaking so many rules, aren't we?"

After they are seated, she gives Angel a conspirator's smile and presses a button next to the steering bar. The engine gives a tiny burp as it comes to life. Then she lifts the pair of blackout shades from the dashboard and slips them over her laughing eyes.

"After all, isn't that what are rules for?"

PART TWO

Corpus

Year 83 – April

"I heard the voice of the Lord, saying, Whom shall I send, and who will go for us? Then said I, Here am I; send me."

—Isaiah 6:8

22

Genesis I

As far as Angel knows, this is only the second time she's ever been on a boat. The first, as a newborn being smuggled away from these very islands, she has no memory of, only Eben's story. But her gut tells her it wasn't a sleek blue bowrider like the one Promise is piloting. They'd left the personal transport in its parking garage at the marina and are now skimming along, cutting through the water like a finely honed blade, the breeze whipping through their hair, a fine spray misting their faces. Lark clings, eyes wide, lips pursed, clearly on the verge of a meltdown after the long day. Angel keeps her eyes fixed on the island as they approach. Beyond the thin strand of beach stands a wall of trees.

Instead of pulling into the small marina with its ferry landing, Promise turns northeast and follows the curving bluffs. In the late afternoon sun, the layers of sandstone glow a warm, inviting red. At intervals, steel light towers loom, topped with twin fixtures. Ahead, an L-shaped dock juts into view. A dinghy with an outboard motor and a set of oars is moored on one side, and at the far end of the platform a pair of kayaks nestle in a rack. Promise cuts the engine and angles in with the ease of an accomplished sailor. The boat sidles up to the pier, where she grabs a piling to steady it and secures it with a rope.

"Baby boat," Lark says, pointing to the little dinghy.

Promise laughs. "Sad baby boat. It just bobs there, waiting for someone to take it out to play." She climbs onto the platform and holds out her arms. When Angel doesn't respond, she beckons with her hands. "Not a good idea to climb out of a boat with a small mammal in your arms—until you get your sea legs under you. Some experience navigating. Promise I'll give her right back."

But Lark clutches Angel and refuses to let go until Promise fishes a vitabar out of her tote bag, peels off its wrapper, and waves the treat in front of the child's face. "Who's a hungry little bird?" she coos. When Lark grabs for it, Promise draws back, just out of her reach. She holds out her arms again. "Come to me if you want your nom noms."

Lark's growling tummy wins out over her separation anxiety and she allows Promise to scoop her up for the second time that day, plucking the snack from the fem's fingers and sinking her tiny teeth into its chewy goodness.

How easily some are lured.

However, now that Angel is here, at the place that has haunted her since the night Eben revealed the truth of her birth, at the place that has drawn her as surely and steadily as a magnet draws a nail, the place she has plotted to conquer, she discovers that she's frozen, immobile as the jutting cliffs looming above her.

You've pictured this—in waking dreams while cleaning the widow's toilets and pruning her shrubs. Pictured this—in dreams that come unbidden in the night. It's been in your mind's eye for two frackin' years now. This is not the moment for your nerves to wilt. For your will to fail. This task is yet undone. Finish the job.

Always Serafina and Eben banging on the doors of her mind. But theirs are not the faces she pictures now. And their words are not the ones that resound the loudest in her head. The words that she sees now, seared as they are in her memory, are words scrawled in her own blood. And her mother's.

ANGEL, THERE IS A FATE WORSE THAN DEATH.

It's the prod that finally drives her to her feet, that sets her stride in motion, that propels her out of the boat and onto the dock, that guides her steps across the gray planks to the place where the platform and the island meet.

It's just a small hop down to the slab of red sandstone that marks the threshold of Galt Genesis I. But the landing jolts through her bones like she's taken a leap off a cliff. Taken the leap of a lifetime.

The massive visages of twin beasts carved in high relief on the hickory entry doors serve as a warning. They stand guard on a house full of ravenous light and ticking timekeeps and dead things, starting in the foyer where the huge skull of a horned creature presides over a staring contest between the mounted heads of a shaggy bison and a sleek elk with a fabulous, arcing rack of antlers. An eagle, carved in wood, captured in mid-flight, wings spread, each feather an intricate masterpiece, rises above an enormous round table of dark-veined oak set in the middle of the entrance hall.

Lark, cowed by the brutes looming to the right and left, finds fascination in the winged creature. She points and marvels. "Birdie. Inna house."

"He's not the only one," Promise says. "And the others are real."

She leads them past two open staircases that flank the foyer and under a gallery walkway that unites the two wings of the second story. A stone fireplace dominates half of this next room, rising to a cathedral ceiling which stretches in a honey gold expanse of wide hickory planks. Another elk, mounted above the carved mantel, stares impassively at a moose on the far wall. The moose's head is cocked toward the wall of glass and timber, ignoring its companion's limpid eyes to gaze at the stunning view of soaring green pines, white-skinned birches and the blue lake beyond. Along the side wall stands an enormous timekeep encased in oak. A bonnet crown topped with a swirl of carved leaves arches above its round face. Tremendous brass weights and a swaying pendulum hang below. A rhythmic click accompanies the movement.

"You can put her down," Promise encourages, but Angel keeps a firm hold on Lark. The fem flicks a hand to the doorway on the right. "The kitchen. Nothing much to see, except hard, cold, smooth surfaces. Another timekeep. That one's not so imposing. Of course, if you have a thing for fancy appliances, we could take a peek. Do you cook?"

Angel shakes her head. "That's Kuba's passion."

Promise nods. "Well, so sad we couldn't bring him along. I dabble in the kitchen. Especially since my housekeep was severanced and I refused to accept a new one. One spy in the house is enough, don't you think?" she adds cryptically. She gestures to the doorway on the left. "But you must see my menagerie."

The sheer number of dead animals is astonishing. Animals of which Angel has no knowledge or names. Animal heads. Animals in their full-bodied glory. Animals with antlers. With spiraling horns. With hooves. With pads and claws. Herbivores and carnivores. Predators and prey.

A second stone fireplace upon which two creatures are posed, one goat-like with massive curling horns, the other a spotted feline, seems a mere afterthought, as does the immense black panel feed screen angled into a corner. Yet another timekeep lurks, this one slender and enclosed in a material as clear as glass, so that all its inner workings, the levers, cogs, and chains that enable the hands of its face to move with precision, are clearly visible. Its tick has a higher pitch than the first.

"I have a thing for Old Republic timekeeps, especially the

pendulum pieces," says Promise, following Angel's gaze. "I find their ticking so…" She pauses for a moment, considering. "Reassuring," she finally adds with a nod. "A reminder that time actually does pass, you know?"

"And your husband must have a thing for hunting," Angel deadpans in reply.

Promise smirks. "Flint? No, he really is more about the creating of life than the taking of it. No, these"—she sweeps her arm in an encompassing arc—"are all mine." She steps over to the deer mount and flicks a speck of dust off its black nose. "Although I must confess that I did not personally bag all of them. Some of these creatures are quite rare and there is a market for them. But I do enjoy the hunt. The kill is almost beyond the point. Except to prove that you found what you were looking for."

Promise's fingers ruffle the deer's short fur. "Not to others," she adds quickly. "To yourself. Keeping the trophy lets you relive it. A little remembrance you can caress with your fingers." She strokes the fur back into place. "A reminder that in the moment you were the conqueror." She turns to Angel, head cocked. "How 'bout you? Hunt much?"

"No."

"Really?" Promise looks dubious. "I thought as a freeborn you'd be out in the woods, foraging, trapping. What did you do to survive? Filch your food from the GaltMart?"

Angel can't quite put a finger on the feeling that's nipping at her. It's the same feeling she gets when Path pulls a face or speaks in certain tone. A feeling of being toyed with. Batted at like a mouse under a cat's paw, dreading the moment when the claws come unsheathed and tear at your flesh. As she ponders a reply, the timekeep's ticking seems to speed up.

"I was raised in a home. With parentals. On the grid," she finally says, struggling to keep the knife edge out of her vox.

Promise snickers while pressing a hand to her mouth as if

to contain her amusement. "Oh my goodness, I didn't mean to imply you were raised by wolves, some wildling child. But the whole freeborn phenomenon is just fascinating to me. And from what I've heard, which, admittedly, isn't much, it sounds likes you're multiplying like..." She pauses, smiles at the stuffie still clutched in Lark's small fists. "I was going to use the cockroach metaphor, but rabbits have a much more pleasant aesthetic, no?" She gives Angel a side eye. "Are you descended from the legendary 'Handed?' Yes, no? Maybe?"

Angel shifts on her feet, the weight of Lark and the day's events bearing down, starting to overwhelm her. How much truth should she tell? Does her story matter now? She's already taken the leap, put herself in the Corporate crosshairs. With the widow, she had felt a sense of trust almost immediately. That sense is absent here, leaving a gap filled with a wary unease. For all she knows, a platoon of goliaths is waiting outside to cart off what remains of her after this ravenous huntress has had her bit of ruthless fun.

Will I be another stuffed head on her wall?

Tick. Tick. Tick.

Go with the truth. Easier to remember over the long game. If there is a long game.

"I was born here. On this island."

Promise eyes her, then flicks another bit of dust from a table on which a stuffed hawk perches, its dead eyes still fierce, ever vigilant. "The prodigal daughter returns. And none too soon or this place will be crawling with bunnies of the dust variety." Her eyes flash toward the hall, where footsteps echo. "I can't wait to hear your fascinating story, but another time." She turns to greet Flint Frazier as he strides into the room, bringing a clear sense of annoyance and a small white box with him.

"Why do I get the notion that she—they—haven't been swabbed?" he asks brusquely, holding up the box and eyeing Angel and Lark with an odd combination of distaste and acquisitiveness, like a Bartertown rat sizing up a pair of used cruiser rims, noting every dig, dent, and scuff mark. It's the first time Angel has seen him in clothing other than his black bike skins, but the khaki trousers and blue cotton shirt, sleeves rolled to the elbows, do nothing to soften his hard-shelled demeanor. A chunky oblong bit of tech hangs from a belt loop of his pants, its black body standing out against the tan fabric. Angel suspects it's a key fob.

"Because they just got here, darling." Promise shrugs and smiles, her vox coated with patient indulgence.

"And I told you—"

"To have a kit ready," Promise interrupts. "Yes, I could have done it myself on the boat over, but I know you love to get in a good poke now and then." She waves a hand, as if offering them up as a tempting morsel. "And really, look at them. The very picture of health." She rolls her eyes. "And please don't tell me about looks being deceiving. We've been through all that." She winks at Angel. "Come on, I'll show you your rooms."

"No, I'll do it here and now, reduce the possible contamination spread." Flint sets the box on the table and opens it to reveal a set of vactubes for drawing blood, flexigloves, and several nasal swabs, all familiar enough from Angel's childhood.

"Such a stickler," Promise says, tossing off a fake giggle. "You see what I did there."

"Sit," Flint orders, gesturing to the plush gray sofa.

Angel obeys, but keeps Lark firmly in her arms. The child has been regarding the dead zoo around her with a strange, silent awe, fear and wonder mingling in her eyes.

"Hold her," Flint says. "Distract her while I do the draw," he adds, pulling on a pair of the white gloves and tearing open an antibac wipe. "You first. Hold out your arm."

Angel complies and he cleans her inner elbow, then adjusts the angle so it rests on the sofa arm. She watches the needle enter her skin and her blood flood the tube in a vibrant burgundy spurt.

"What're you testing for?" she asks, half expecting him to ignore the question.

He withdraws the needle and quickly presses a patch of gauze onto the puncture. "Viruses. Bacterials. Anything that can be spread by human contact."

Freedom?

The thought almost makes her smile, but she presses her lips to Lark's cheek instead. The child is curious at first, watching the process, but she lets out a wail at the needle's plunging nip. Angel has expected rough treatment, but Flint has been surprisingly gentle, even with the nasal swab. Between her cries and her squinched up eyes, Lark doesn't even notice this second violation of her body.

Flint packs everything back up, and, lips pursed like he's just sucked on something sour, nods to Promise and exits as quickly as he came.

"Like a tornado. In and out quick, leaves a mess in his wake." Promise sighs. "Typical male."

23

The Waiting Room

"So we just sit here until the blood work's done?" Angel asks, trying to contain an antsy Lark, whose cries have subsided. The child is squirming, desperate to shed her mother's restraining arms so she can explore the fascinating, terrifying, ticking things in the room.

Promise rolls her eyes, something she does with flair and frequency. "Good grief, no. That might be his expectation, but..." She lets the word hang as she crooks a finger.

Angel starts to rise and Lark breaks free, running over to the gray wolf posed in mid-trot. She pats its lush coat. "Doggie?"

Promise laughs. "Close. That's a wolf. Doggie's cousin, if you will. Come. May I hold your hand?" She crouches down so she's at eye-level with the girl. "Shall we go see your room? See what wonderful things we can find there for Lark?"

The little girl ducks her head, peeking at the not-quite-a-stranger from under her tousled locks. Angel watches the flirtation with a mix of trepidation and amusement. The toddler bestows the smallest curve of her pink lips and then her tiny hand.

Oh, you are a coy thing—and I give thanks for that here and now.

Their suite of rooms takes up the entire west wing of the second floor. Luxurious in a manner Angel has seen only once before, at the manse lorded over by the director of security and his demanding wife back in Illiana. The manse she'd visited only once. The manse she would never forget. That manse—Tanner's manse—had been cold and sterile. The vibe here is different, a strange mashup of the glamorous and the rustic—a swag's idea of rustic. These rooms, like those of the floor below, are enveloped in hickory, from the planked sloping ceiling to the built-in cabinets to the gleaming floor. Another wall of glass faces the lake; amidst the leafy branches, it gives the impression of being in a tree-house—an impeccably built and ravishingly appointed treehouse.

Not like the one Kuba and his brothers built.

For a moment Angel drifts back to that treehouse, the handiwork of scrounging boys, thrown together with cast-off boards and scrap nails. With spit and muscle and perseverance. Remembers the night she climbed the shaky rope ladder to its loft, carrying Lark in her belly rather than her arms. The night she first heard Damn Otis on Radio TCT.

And now here I am. A Damn Otis. The Night Prophet.

This movement needs a prophet, not a martyr.

Word's pleas pierce her reverie. As does the slight ticking sound. Another timekeep sits on a ledge jutting from the far wall, this one a small piece, a silver face beaming from its arched case. Turning from the window, Angel studies Promise, who has set Lark on her feet and is guiding the child toward the door at the far end of the bedroom.

What's the play here? Hers. And mine.

"And here's your room," the fem singsongs, crouching down again, flinging her arm out like a magician revealing the severed assistant made whole again.

Angel trails behind, leans in the entryway, arms folded across her chest.

How long has the bruja been planning this?

The room is small and bright, with creamy white walls and

woodwork. Tucked in the corner is a child-sized bed with simple head and foot boards, also painted white and overlaid with a coverlet of delicate florals, all pale pinks and mossy greens. Next to it is a low dresser topped with a padded tray. A small rocking chair. Low shelves stacked with all manner of wonderments to delight a toddler. Wooden blocks and puzzle boards. A colorful cube with wires and racks loaded with chunky beads and rings for curious fingers to move, shift, and count. But, thankfully, no timekeep.

How long were you planning this? As long as I was planning this? Or did you have a child once upon a time? Did something go wrong?

Lark, shyness draining away, makes a beeline for the toys and plops down to examine the play cube.

"Ah," Promise murmurs. "Does she need a change? Or is she trained?" She gestures to a white basket next to the dresser. Inside are stacks of what look more like underpants than diapers, but still puffy and squishy.

Angel's confusion must register on her face because Promise quickly explains. "Training pants. For potty training. Have you thought about that?"

Angel has not had to think about it. Except vaguely. That was something the widow handled, because it was the widow who complained about the difficulties of finding diapers at the GaltMart, other than the tiny newborn size for the convenience of incipient parentals who, in the blizzard of their excitement, always forgot to bring some along for their baby bestowal. Few children are reared in Bayfield, and so Angel has always had to make do, to repurpose and refashion. But they had managed.

"The sooner we have her trained, the easier it will be. Those were a bit of a hassle to obtain. Even for me. Especially for me," Promise sighs.

Angel can't picture Promise strolling the makeshift aisles of a Bartertown. Or even the clean, antiseptic ones at the GaltMart. And she doesn't like the presumption of 'we.' Feels the bristling in her neck and shoulders. But she gives a mental shrug and forces her lips into a smile.

"Oh, she's..." She hesitates to use the word 'trained,' as if the child were a dog being housebroken. "She knows what to do."

"Well, that's a relief," Promise says, with a hint of amusement. "That's the only thing I wasn't looking forward to. Puddles all over the house." She nods toward yet another door. "When she—or you—need it."

"I'd like to wash my hands."

"Please, make yourself at home."

Beyond the door lies a palace within a palace, a bathroom that gleams and glitters as the warm light from bronze sconces bounces off the white tile and gray stone. After scrubbing her hands with creamy soap that smells of brisk mornings in a pine forest, and drying them on a soft towel, she avoids her eyes in the wide expanse of the mirror.

Don't succumb. Remember what you came for. Why you are here.

And so when she steps back into the small white room, where Promise and Lark are building towers with blocks, she pauses for only a brief moment before she speaks.

"I'll need to go back to Bayfield once a week."

"Whatever for?" Promise manages to drag her eyes away from the child. "I'll provide for all your needs. You can wear some of my clothes until we get you a new wardrobe. We look about the same size."

Angel, having anticipated this parry, bites her lip. Looks at the floor, feigning embarrassment. "I need to... see... my man."

A wrinkle spoils Promise's smooth brow. She squints as if she can't quite spy what she's looking for. Then she sighs. "Oh, that. Well, I can probably arrange for you to ride over and back on the supply ferry once a month."

Angel lets her gaze rise to meet that dismissive countermove. Then thrusts. "No, I need to go once a week."

"Well, the ferry only runs once a month."

Another thrust. "Well, then teach me to drive—sail—the boat. The little one. You said it just sits there, waiting for a sailor."

Promise stares, calculating how to win this fencing match now that she's on the defensive. "You can't go every week. Flint would never hear of it. I can hear him now, going on about contamination potential." Her tone is mocking, but her eyes are serious.

"So then he won't—hear of it." Angel replies with a tilt of her head, gauging the kill point for her verbal sword.

Another squint from her opponent. Another furrow of the brow. Then, just a hint of a smile in the corner of those plump lips, the kind of smile given in the midst of a skirmish to an adversary judged worthy.

"Not once a week. Perhaps every other week. And only for a few hours. Three, max."

"Every other week—and overnight."

"No," Promise scoffs. "Besides, won't you worry about your precious?" She nods at Lark, who's back to sliding beads over the wire hills and valleys of the fascinating cube.

The angle of attack—the bargain she must make—becomes as clear to Angel as the glass in the windows with their breathtaking views of the trees and the water.

"Why would I worry when she'll be safe with you?"

"Indeed," Promise huffs. "So I'm to be your babysitter?"

Feinting, deceiving, lunging.

But Angel is ready with a grand riposte. "Babysitter? No." She cocks her head. "Caregiver. Or—a second mother?"

And there it is—the vulnerable place, the chink in the armor. But the strike brings forth not a wince, but a gleam in the fem's eyes, a softening of the lips.

"Yes," Promise murmurs, half to herself. "Yes, I could live with that."

24

The Necessary Thing

THE CQO DOESN'T WANT to hear about the lack of success. Doesn't want to hear about trying. "You need to banish that word from your vocabulary, Mr. Connell."

The ProServ director dares to bristle. She can see it in his change of posture, the way he squares his beefy shoulders and draws up his broad chest. The way he clenches his fists. Though he's quick to release them again.

Smart man. Or rather, semi-smart man.

"Ms. Zinni, Comms believes they've pinpointed the transmissions as coming from within a certain radius of the Genesis I facility. The town of Bayfield falls within that radius. But, as you well know, we can't just go through the place breaking down doors."

"Why not?"

Her response flummoxes him. His eyes flit in their sockets, as if he's searching the corners of the narrow, gray office for a suitable answer. "It's not an AgSector full of migs. Or a garrison of factory bees," he finally replies, using the workers' self-proclaimed pejorative that CQO Zinni hates. He sees the tightening of her lips that could easily slip into a full-blown frown. "We're talking about workers with most favored status."

The CQO feels anger simmering, closes her eyes, and when she opens them again, directs her focus to the wall behind the

ProServ, where the serene, melancholy Venus inclines her lovely head. Oh, to feel the breeze that billows those golden ropes of hair. To let that breeze blow the cares of daily life to the side, out of one's eyes, just as it sends that mane of hair wafting from that inimitable face.

"Mr. Connell," she says, keeping her vox calm. "Even workers with most favored status are subject to all the bullet points in the Corporate Code of Conduct and conditions of employment, including the possibility of random inspections of workplace and household. Especially if security has any suspicion, with or without evidence, that they might be harboring chés."

The ProServ shrugs. "That requires a lot of manpower. And we haven't seen or heard anything on the feeds to justify that level of scrutiny at this time. Although, there are a number of retirees in the radius, so that reduces the feed spectrum a bit."

The CQO is amazed at the pushback she's getting from this subordinate, but she endeavors to be amused, rather than affronted by his presumption. "Why?"

The ProServ explains in a tone that sets the CQO's teeth in a grit beneath her closed-mouth smile. "Well, retirees are dropped off the two-way, so they're off the grid—or semi-off the grid. Frees up the bandwidth for other surveillance pursuits."

The CQO drums her fingers, nails clicking. For a ProServ director, this man seems rather squeamish. Reluctant to do what it takes. Oh, for a man like the legendary Tanner, the Corporate Hammer, a protective services man who knew how to get a job done. At least until the final job, when he appeared to go rogue and wound up dead on the floor of a waterman's control room. Well, that's what happens when one goes rogue. But still, she knows if he were here, he would be on his way out the door, lowering his blackout shades, the better to focus on the plan congealing inside his shaved head. A plan guaranteed of success. Because he was willing to do what was necessary.

As the ProServ natters on about the pros and cons of drone versus human sweeps, the CQO picks up her tablet and types in a quick reminder to check the succession plan and the corporate organizational chart to determine who might be in the pipeline to replace him. As she taps the Save button, an idea occurs to her, perhaps inspired by her reminiscence of Tanner. She looks up with a smile that really isn't.

"Mr. Connell, the speed at which you think and act rivals that of the glaciers, but I doubt you will have such an impact on this earth."

The man's quizzical squint reminds the CQO that his corporate track has limited access to the historical and scientific knowledge bases. To explain the allusion or not? She sighs. "Glaciers, Mr. Connell, were great masses, almost rivers, of ice back in time out of mind. They moved very slowly, but managed to dramatically change the surface of this planet." She nods in the direction of the windows and the view beyond the glass. "They helped form our magnificent bodies of water. And that's enough of a lesson for this morning, yes? No quizzes, but here's a question with regard to your task. Do you know the definition of the word 'infiltrate'?"

The man gives a nod, his stance suddenly that of a dog who has felt the wrath of his master so often that he goes into a cower before he even sees the stick.

"Then we're done here."

25

La Bête

He's always known what it's like to be feared. How it feels to generate fear in those who find themselves within a certain proximity to his body. Maybe not always a specific fear of him, per se, but certainly an uneasiness about who he is. What he is. An uneasiness that breeds a strange, niggling worry of putting a foot wrong. An uneasiness that spurs a sweat that seeps under the armpits and at the groin, a sweat that comes not from an exertion of the body, but a fretting of the mind.

What rule am I breaking? Did my toe drift across the line between compliance and disregard?

He can see it in their eyes, the way they focus anywhere but on him, except, of course, when they think he's not looking. He can smell it in that sweat. Can hear it in the hitch that constrains their voxes. Can sense it in the way they make themselves small, bodies shrinking within their skins.

It's always been this way. Even when he was a child, once his feet had been set upon the protective services track, people had eyed him like one might eye a rat trap. Thankful that such a contraption exists in a world cursed with vermin, but unwilling to get too close, riddled with anxiety by the sense that the contraption is essentially unpredictable, touchy. That it might be sprung by the slightest jostle.

When he was a boy, he skulked around the corners of living rooms and kitchens at the get togethers of his parents and the people who formed their social circle, all of whom seemed drawn from their work lives. Colleagues from the water facility where his father toiled as a quality technician. Chippers, who, like his mother, were employed by the enormous manufacturing combine where all manner of microtech products were constructed, including the embeds that kept track of everything Galt. Occasionally a random neighbor might be thrown into the mix.

He'd eavesdrop on conversations, which ranged from tedious recitatives on the proper balance of chemicals for ensuring the purity and taste of the water that flowed out of the Ontario Region's faucets to squawking arias about office etiquette and the proper way to deal with a boorish boss. Most slipped in one ear and out the other. The conversations that stayed with him were those sparked by his own stealthy presence.

Someone might catch sight of him slinking past a doorway and make a seemingly innocuous comment.

My, he's getting to be a tall drink of water.

Nods and comments and asides and questions would ensue.

My so-and-so was a sweetheart until puberty hit and then the proverbial shit hit the fan. Do you ever worry about that? With him on the ProServe track, I mean?

Is he definitely going to end up a goliath? How do you deal with that? I mean, are you expected to—what's the phrase I'm looking for? Toughen him up?

How does one live with a potential...

Whoever expressed something along those lines never actually finished their thought. His mother would cut in and assure the speaker that her boy was extremely well-mannered and thoughtful, as gentle a soul as you might wish to find. At the same time, his father would be assuring anyone else in earshot that he was building the perfect beast that would be up to the task of keeping the Protectorate and thus, themselves, safe and secure.

So there would seem to have been a disconnect there.

It was in response to this peculiar situation that he first learned to dissemble. Like any child, he felt the sting of injustice and tasted the bitter frustration when things did not go his way, but he also sensed that, because of his size, his displays of fury evoked a different reaction than those of children who took up less space. The wariness, the uncertainty in the adults' eyes left him wary and uncertain as well. The only thing he was sure of was that people were afraid of him.

A certain kind of child might have taken advantage of this—power—and fallen into the habits of the bully. But in him, the fear he sensed in others evoked such feelings of concern, of compassion, the need to soothe, that he began to cast about for ways to be a less threatening figure. When he wasn't around his father, he adopted a slouch to make himself appear small-er. Closer to the earth. He plastered a goofy smile on his face, although it took awhile and a few embarrassing moments for him to ken when that might be inappropriate. His anger found release in miles of running and in sparring with the body bag his father had purchased to help him build his arm strength. And he took comfort in the few whose eyes never showed a hint of unease in his presence.

The neighbor girl, for instance. The girl who smiled as she had to crane her neck to talk to him. The girl with the name that suit-ed her. Serene. The girl who had taught him about recitatives and arias and the art of pretending, the art of adopting a persona, the art of hiding behind a character. She was on the Entertainment track and knew all about such artsy-fartsy, high-falutin things.

"If you're a character in a show, whether it's a thrillweep or a dramedy or a farce, you have to know your motivations. That makes your actions and your lines come easier. Lets you slip into the char-acter's skin. And when you're in the skin, you can convince anyone

that you are who you say you are. Even if the character is nothing like you in real life."

At the day camp they attended on summer afternoons, the Convergent Thinkers camp—a ludicrous name for yet another step in the Corporate indoctrination process—they always partnered to brainstorm solutions to the puzzles and problems posed, learning quickly how to game the system, sorting among the multiple answers to find, not necessarily the best or most creative answer, but the one the trainers were looking for. And then laughing at them behind solemn eyes.

Gaming the system. It's a skill that has served him well over the ensuing years, throughout his journey on the ProServ track, through the grueling boot camp phase, when he'd found himself silently thanking his father for being a hardass, and during his initial placement at the border, where he'd seen enough brutality to last a Corporate lifetime. He hadn't realized how good he'd had it at home, chafing under the strictures of his dictator father, or at his previous posting, walking a factory beat, until he'd gotten here. Considering its proximity to the Hive and one of the Protectorate's prime facilities, Galt Genesis I, the squad barracks is a hellhole of concrete and cold water and a cot with a mattress so thin it would hardly qualify as carpet padding. But this hellhole is the place he needs to be. The place to which invisible strings have maneuvered him. Because of its proximity to her. And all along the journey toward this place, he's learned to hide the shock and disgust that springs from his soft, inner core. To hide it even when he isn't wearing his blackout helmet.

The scar running up his cheek helps maintain the facade. As fearful as the bees might be of a helmet-clad automaton, a faceless evil, they shrink even more at a scarred visage, because imaginations will run wild. And he doesn't have to utter a word, because they are already thinking it. Visualizing it. Visualizing the other man and how he must have looked after an encounter with a goliath. What he must look like now.

Dust and ash.

The scar has burnished his rep on the squad since he'd arrived a year ago. It's a young squad of mostly puke newbies, although he's only a few years removed from that status himself, and the scar, and the casual way he disregards it, gave him an instant cachet. As had the smile and shrug he'd tossed when one foolhardy smartass from the Huron with Québécois roots, testing his mettle, had referred to him as La Bête. It was not the first time he'd been called something along those lines. Over time, he's worked to live up to it. First up in the morning, always putting in the max effort during trainings, never dogging it, always the first to volunteer for dicey situations. It's also earned him the commander's respect, although that feeling is not mutual.

In a short time, they've all come to hate the commander, a verbose vacillator par excellence, a sniveler quick to point the finger at every mistake but even quicker to deny his own blunders, a Corporate equivocator suck-up who's never learned how to placate the bosses while taking care of his own people, and who is far too willing to throw them under the mobile to save his own skin. They've heard the rumors suggesting it's why he's never risen in the ranks, but even the greenest grunts know better than to spill their contempt out loud, even to their tightest buddy.

But La Bête can read their eyes. Their body language.

Another skill that the commander lacks.

He can also read the commander's eyes, which usually tell a different story than the words coming out of his mouth. La Bête's always amused to see the fear lurking there, although the commander must recognize how unseemly it is for him to show even one iota of apprehension in the presence of a grunt. So the commander always blinks and the look of dread disappears as swiftly as a newt scuttling through dead leaves in a roadside ditch. And La Bête takes care to hide his own unseemly emotion. So when the commander calls him into his office one morning as the rain pounds on the barracks roof and the squad is angsting over the possibility of a five-miler in the mud, he stands at attention, assuming the facade of a dependable, solemn goliath at the ready.

"Officer LaBatt, you have made quite the name for yourself in your short time on the force," the commander says, swiping his fingers over his tablet.

La Bête gauges what kind of reply and tone of vox might work best in this situation. Opts for humble, but self-assured. "I've worked hard the past couple of years, sir."

"Indeed, and it's been noticed. The impression you've made has apparently led those in charge to believe you have a particular skillset that will serve us in a situation that's arisen." The commander squints, as if to indicate he's not sure he personally subscribes to this impression.

"A situation?"

"A situation which necessitates a liaison."

Always the obfuscation with this man.

Then the commander's lips pucker into something between a smile and a grimace.

"Chés," he says, spitting out the word like a wad of phlegm he's hocked up from deep inside his throat. "If it were my decision, we'd be on those frackin' traitors like white on rice." He catches himself, blinks, and another unseemly emotion is tripped up and hustled away. "Instead, we'll let the traitors be undone by one of their own."

26

A Restless Sleep

The asphalt under her feet is rust-colored from the iron leaching into the soil and water. She can taste and smell the metal in the slightest sip, the slightest breath of air. But here at the crossroads, it's not water, but fear that floods her mouth with that peculiar taint. Here at the crossroads, she stands in the middle where the four lanes meet and it's a lonely space and empty but for the corporate sweep who haphazardly slaps a brush dripping with white paint against a fence post. And when he turns his head and grins, the dripping paint turns into a crimson gush and the personal transports are bearing down on her from all directions, but she can't run away or leap aside. Her feet have become part of the pavement, encased in that rust-stained asphalt, so she can only close her eyes and wait for the impact.

But the jolt she feels is the crack of her skull against the headboard of an unfamiliar bed as she scrambles to free herself from a too-confining sheet and blanket and sits bolt upright, panting in the dark of the strange bedroom. Shrinking at the slink of a stranger's nightgown across her skin. Flinching as a salty trickle of sweat slides around the bridge of her nose and pools in the corners of her eye and lip. Blinking in time with the mechanical click of the timekeep.

A whimper and a rustle of bed linens drifts in from the small room just steps away. *Lark.* The child is asleep but restless, perhaps mired in the middle of her own dream, reviewing the day's events in the distorted funhouse mirror that is the unconscious mind. Angel stands in the doorway, watching the girl squirm like a worm unearthed. The darkness is pierced by a sliver of light that broadens into a knife edge on the wood floor as the door to the hallway opens. The relentless tick of the timekeep, a silent noise, is overlaid with the scuffle of slippers on the wood floor. The still air ripples. Angel realizes a security eye and ear must be tucked away somewhere, attuned to every little toss and turn. Every gasp and sigh. She tenses even before she feels the shimmer of a silky sleeve against the bare skin of her arm.

"Trouble sleeping?" Promise whispers.

Her concern sounds real, although it's too dark for Angel to make out the expression on her face.

"New surroundings, new bed," the fem continues. "New everything. It'll take a bit to settle in. Would a nightlight help?"

Angel nods. "I was just remembering how, when I was little and woke from a nightmare, my mother would help me fall back asleep. She'd tell me stories or just ramble on about anything and everything. Times tables, the plants I could survive on if I was ever lost in the woods. Random stuff." She bites down on her lip. Why did she spill that intimacy to this fem? A fem that she doesn't really know, and certainly doesn't trust. A fem she's trying to game.

"Did it help?" Promise asks.

When Angel is silent, teeth still clamped, Promise steps over to the bed and perches on the edge of the mattress, where the child's restless sleep still shifts the coverlet.

"And I saw a new land
The first had passed away.
And there came a great vox
Comforting words to say."

Her vox is barely a whisper, sweet and opaque as fresh-drawn milk, crooning the folk song, the hymn to water, with its melancholy air and pleasant fiction.

"Wipe tears from your eyes
No sorrow and no cries,
For these pains are vanquished
The old world has passed this day."

"Did your mother sing that to you?" Angel asks, joining her at the bed.

Promise shakes her head. "The housekeep. Well, I guess she was also a nanny since she took care of me when I wasn't with my tutor. I don't think it was the words or the tune, but, like with your mother, it was just her vox. She could have been saying any-thing. Any sweet nothing. You could feel the care radiating off her." She trails off and stands, her vox breathy and tinged with wonder, as if she's far away in some other place, watching some other scene. "You felt safe."

The arm, sheathed in satin and lace, slips around Angel's shoulder.

"Like you're safe. Here and now. With me."

The lace, as it rustles against Angel's skin, leaves a trail of prickles and itch.

Kuba will fish out of necessity, and even enjoys its quiet, meditative rhythms, but he has always dodged the brutality of the hunt. The stalking, the killing, the gutting, the skinning. The blood. Truth be told, he is repulsed by it. So he finds himself at odds with his new band of brothers and sisters, who revel in each kill, from the puniest squirrel to the most massive buck. Who squat, sit, and sprawl around the campsite, gnawing the last scraps of meat from bones large and small, chomping cartilage, sucking at marrow. Who belch and fart and snore and piss and shit like wild beasts of the forest marking their territories. Who make the Bartertown hovels that he and Angel have wandered seem like havens of civility.

Not that he is unfamiliar with the social dynamics of the wolf pack, having been raised in one, reared in the midst of the rough and tumble of life, squabbling, competing, and carousing with his güeys, his brothers and male cousins. But his pack had ultimately been dominated by the alpha females, the matriarchs. His mother, grandmother, great grandmother, and above all, Isa— Grey-Grey—his great great grandmother. They were the civilizers, the toughness at their cores sheathed in the velvet glove of gentle persuasion. Here in the cell, the chain of command is not yet clear to him. Teeg and Armor are ostensibly the leaders, the alphas, but rather than bark orders, they appear to give them through looks and gestures, with an occasional verbal admonishment. As far as seconds-in-command, Kuba supposes those to be a pair of guevaras who go by the noms de guerre of Fox and Echo. Fox is tall and shifty, with narrowed eyes and a permanently furrowed brow, and a motor that runs in two gears: high and higher. Echo is a rangy fem who reminds Kuba of Angel, tough-minded, hard-bodied, always focused on working the problem.

Wilder is a burly enforcer-type, who, in another life, might have been a goliath and whose preferred method of communication is the grunt. And there is Nanda, the wise crone—the Isa of the band—but not hindered by the frailty of age, as Isa had been. Nanda is small but stocky, robust, and feisty, with a braided crown of steel gray hair and fierce brown eyes that can pierce an armored soul. And a two-pronged hook where her left hand should be. Kuba had never really believed the stories of the Handed. That there were men and fems who had mutilated themselves in that way, other than crazy-like-a-fox Joachim Debs, the revenant who drifted in and out of his childhood, who was tight-lipped except when he was in his cups and then his wild tales flowed along with the homebrew. But here, in Nanda, is living proof. The other guevaras are a blur of mutters and nods, in camp one morning, gone the next, out doing the deeds assigned to them in their mission to loosen Galt's grip on the Protectorate, one finger at a time.

What is immediately clear to Kuba is that he needs to find a source of sustenance to supplement the handfuls of foraged ramps, fiddlehead ferns, and wood violets that he's been surviving on during his first few days with the cell. Each day the guevaras spend a rigorous couple of hours in physical training, stretching, running, going through the various ups: push, pull, sit. They perfect their defensive techniques, practicing ways to slip out of holds, though Armor admonishes them to remember that goliaths have a shoot-first mentality. He also admonishes them to run deliberately, but not recklessly. At the same time, he pushes them to embrace the pain.

"If you're comfortable in your approach to training, then you're not taking enough risks. There is no comfort to be found in a skirmish or a firefight."

Embracing the pain also means that Kuba's stomach grumbles throughout the day and his muscles feel weak. He knows he needs to up his intake of quality nourishment. It's BoBeck, runt of the pack, scrawny, hunch-backed, with shifty eyes and lurching feet, like a dog that can't settle, who points out the mushrooms growing on the forest floor.

"Might wanna start gatherin' yourself some of those," he says, pointing.

Kuba eyes the patch of beige fungi, bright against the drab brown of the leaf litter, topped with bulbous caps of honeycomb-like cells. He's not a mushroom expert, but he knows some are safe for consumption and others are not.

"Them's morels. Good eatin' in a pinch. Taste sorta nutty. Rather have a nice roasted rabbit myself, but I respect your persuasion."

Later, on perimeter patrol, BoBeck jerks a thumb at an

enormous fungus spreading from the roots of an oak. "That's chicken-of-the-woods. Now that's really good eatin', even by this carnivore's standards."

Kuba crouches down to examine the mushroom, which has multiple caps spreading out from its center, like the misshapen petals of a giant flower. It's at least two feet in diameter. "Why chicken-of-the-woods?" he asks, running his knife through the stem and gingerly lifting the massive cap.

"Why you think?"

"Tastes like—chicken?"

BoBeck guffaws. "B'lieve it or not."

"I can't remember what chicken tastes like. I was a kid when I left meat behind."

"Welp, that'll fry up real nice. And then your tongue'll tell you what you've been missin' all this time." BoBeck bends and rips a broad leaf from a cluster of plants growing in a puddle of dappled sunlight. He thrusts its scalloped edge under Kuba's nose. The crushed leaf emits a distinct garlicky scent.

"This here's good if you crave some greens—and some seasonin' to boot."

Whether the mushroom fried in the cast iron pan over his little campfire actually tastes like chicken, Kuba can't say, but it is delicious and he wolfs it down, finally taking the edge off the hunger pangs that have haunted his belly since his parting with Angel.

Path hadn't seemed surprised to see him on the doorstep, just grinned a slyish lopsided grin. "Op's in motion," he'd said, a lilt of satisfaction bending his tone.

"Keep those as is," Kuba, protective as always, had warned, as he handed over Angel's backpacks. "She'll grab 'em, next time she voxes. Smuggle 'em onto the island."

"Sure," Path had agreed, shouldering the packs. "We'll stick 'em in a hidey-hole."

After the drop-off, Kuba had bolted to hook up with the

cell, who had welcomed him with meat and bonhomie, the first of which he politely refused, a little worried that his recalcitrance might brand him as a lesser man in their eyes. But they had just shrugged and pointed him to the coolers stuffed with cucumbers and squash supplied by a sympathizer with a vertical farm a little ways to the south. After he'd scarfed a couple down, hunger sharpening his appreciation for the contrast between the mild, watery flesh and the crisp, bitter rind, Armor had assigned him to a perimeter detail with BoBeck, who'd been welcoming enough. And that was that.

He's learned how to hide from the drone patrols that make regular sweeps over the forest and surrounding AgSectors— sweeps that are so regular that the cell members joke about mole time as they scuttle into the hand-dug tunnels that snake under and around tree roots. As they crouch, Kuba admires the craft work in the use of lumber and brick to bolster some areas of the earthen walls.

"They ever change-up the timing?" he asks BoBeck as they crawl back out.

"Complacency breeds mediocrity," BoBeck replies with a shake of his head. "Or so says Teeg. The Hive mind is a wee bit slow."

Kuba gets back to his foraging. He is now one of them. A pathfinder. A guevara. And a borderline insomniac. Maybe it comes with the territory, but he finds that sleep is now a precious and elusive commodity. It's not that he's a stranger to sleeping under the stars. Some of his favorite childhood memories are of dragging the sleeping bags out under the giant red oaks that sprawled along the compound's creek. Stretching out with his güeys to tell fright tales and watch for swift-arcing shooting stars and slow-crawling focus satellites. Even on the odyssey with Angel, from the compound to the Chicago garrison, and then the trek north with the infant Lark, when it was his turn to sleep, with Angel on watch, his slumber had usually been deep and restorative. Perhaps it's the upending of the comfortable routine he'd settled into at the widow's manse. Dinner prep, a good meal, the lulling of Lark with gentle play, the nightly wash-up, the bedtime story, the mantra and sway of a quiet song before the sleepy melon head would settle into her pillow. But in these woods, under these trees, with others on watch, it's toss and turn, one eye open, one ear perked.

It doesn't help that BoBeck's bladder is apparently no larger than those of the squirrels he is so fond of eating. Whenever Kuba wakes to the slightest rustle of pine needles that cover the forest floor and his ears pinpoint the location of the sound, his eyes narrow on a shadow's hobbling gait in the direction of the latrine pits. And then he spends another restless passage of time feeling every root and knot and loose pebble underneath him, shifting and squirming and contorting his body until a vague, neither here nor there illusion spreads over him like a fog.

There is no mirror here to reflect the puddles of fatigue under his eyes and even if he could see them, he would regard them as badges well-earned. Marks of the guevara.

27

The Veil

On the island, some things are noticeable by their conspicuous absence, including, significantly, the daily pronouncements from Galt. Where the air on the mainland reverberates—morning, noon, and night—with the rich baritone and precise alto voxes of CEO Blanche and CQO Zinni, and the vibrant trills of Chanel or one of the other Corporate-created live act shills, all presumably enhanced by the 'tronic vox adjuster, the air across the lake channel resounds with bird calls and the barely discernible hum of the inverters that convert solar power to usable electricity. When Angel inquires without really inquiring, hazarding a vague reference to the missing evening vesper, Promise erupts with a wicked laugh that borders on a cackle.

"I knew that would be one of the first things you noticed. Because that's one of the first things that burrows under my skin when I have to spend any length of time on the mainland. We still have the inside feed, unfortunately, but I try to keep the volume at minimum," Promise says, punctuating her speech with one of her winks. "We disconnected the infernal voxcast speakers a couple of years ago. We—or I should say they—the ovas— were experiencing an epidemic of infertility and miscarriages and I convinced Flint to convince the director that eliminating that—stressor—might help."

"Did it?" Angel asks.

Promise shrugs. "Who knows? Too soon to tell is what I say. And will keep saying since the director is willing to try anything to improve the performance of this facility. Quotas, you know." Her eyebrows arch in twin peaks for emphasis. "Actually, I'm hoping they just completely forget to ever turn the loop back on." She leans in. "Did listening to that ever help you be a better employee?" Her thick lashes flutter as she reconsiders. "Of course, you're not an employee, officially, are you? Well, take it from me, as one who is—sort of." She sighs again. "Only Galt knows what I truly am, maybe not even Galt, maybe just the CQO, but..." She trails off, blinking again. "Oops, I talk too much. Let's just leave it at, the less I hear those voxes, the better I feel. And, to me, I'm what really matters." She punctuates that with another wink.

Wildlife, with the exception of winged creatures and those minuscule beasts who burrow in the soil, are nonexistent. Not a squirrel or chipmunk to be seen sprinting across the grass or heard chittering from the trees. Neither skunk nor fox to serve as prey or predator. "Eradicated long ago, so don't blame me. Disease carriers, you know," Promise says by way of explanation.

Men are also missing from the landscape. There's Flint. And the craggy, stoop-shouldered captain, just this side of severance, who pilots the supply ferry. When their bloodwork comes back clean, Promise takes Angel and Lark on a tour via bicycles, since personal transports are forbidden, and those two seem to be the sum total of males on the island that stretches fourteen miles from tip to tip and three miles across at its widest point. Fems, fems, fems—from the ferry landing at the southwestern edge to the red sand beaches near Amnicon Point on the northeast. The groundskeepers with their green Agri ear buds and coveralls—fems. The medic staffers with their red buds and navy scrubs—fems. The service bees who clean and cook—fems.

And then there are the ovas.

Promise coasts to a stop along the single paved road that runs from one end of the island to the other. Much of the road is lined with trees but here a cleared opening accommodates a well-maintained driveway. Beyond it, two red brick buildings rise from behind neatly trimmed hedges and a manicured garden. One of the buildings is a tall rectangle rising six stories, the other a single level that sprawls horizontally in multiple directions. The tower has balconies jutting from its facade, but the doors that open onto them are covered over with steel grates, as are the windows. The low-slung building has a line of small windows that runs just under the roof line.

"There," Promise says suddenly. "To the right of the oak." She points toward a massive tree with sprawling limbs. Near it, a white pergola flanks two edges of the garden. "See her?"

Angel follows her line of sight and catches a glimpse of her first live ova. The fem's movements are slow, so that she does indeed seem to float, but not as Angel has envisioned, in filmy, flowing white, hair streaming. This fem is clad from head to toe in utilitarian sage green, so that she blends in with her surroundings. The snug long-sleeved tunic over the tight leg skins reveals her curves, stretching over the swelling of her belly. In contrast, a veil swathes her head and face, concealing all, with just a slit through which her eyes can peer. Her feet are shod in thick-soled trainers.

The scene is weird, unsettling to the point that Angel finds herself digging her nails into the skin of her palm to prove that she's truly awake, that this is not just another bizarre dream. Is that really a human? A fem? Or is it a shrouded phantom from a scare tale, a wood sprite that flits through folk stories told to entertain a child in the chill of an October night?

"Do you see?" Promise asks again, with a breathless eagerness, as if she's pointing out a specimen of some rare species in its native habitat. "And there's another."

A second ova, and then a third, garbed in identical fashion, join the first. They gesture back and forth, pointing to the green daffodil spikes pushing skyward and the purple and yellow crocuses dotting the flower bed at their feet.

"Why are they dressed like that?" Angel asks, not caring if she sounds impertinent.

Promise lifts her water bottle from its holder and takes a sip. "If I had my way, they wouldn't be. I brought in the modemant, because I knew it would help with the issue of jealousy. That was one of the first problems that I noticed."

"Modemant?"

"A gown and veil—Modesty Mantle. Modemant for short. I'm told—by those in the Hive with access to this sort of information, my sources in Knowledge Management—that this type of garment has been used from time out of mind in many faraway corners of the world. Apparently, different cultures had different names for it." Promise counts on her fingers as she rattles off a string of words unfamiliar to Angel. "Burqa, niqab, habit, wimple. These uniforms—this uniformity—supposedly helps temper certain—tendencies—of the male population. But it apparently also plays a role in controlling that sad propensity of fems to scratch and claw and bite each other, verbally, physically—even when there aren't any males to fight over."

Promise shrugs and flips her ponytail off her shoulder. "And here I thought I was coming up with something innovative. Just goes to show you that, truly, there is nothing new under the sun. But seriously, while we were using it, the modemant did seem to ease the competition." The fem leans in, as if sharing a confidence. "And it promoted—dare I say it—a modicum of what apparently used to be called sisterhood. Although, again, this is all hearsay from the KM crowd." She throws her hands up in mock exasperation. "After all, what do I know of sisterhood? I don't have a sister. Do you? Does anyone? No, they don't. Not here in the Protectorate."

Angel is about to respond and then realizes that she doesn't really know. It's possible she has siblings out there somewhere. And there's the little infant with whom she once shared a crib. Whose embed she once wore on a chain around her neck. Who is now just bones under the dirt in the Chequamegon forest. She lets the question hang unanswered as she studies the trio of ovas. "They're not wearing gowns."

"No," Promise huffs. "Once certain individuals in Corporate got wind of it, they trash-binned that." Her vox takes on an imperious, mocking lilt. "Because, of course, the ovas shouldn't hide their fertile, blossoming bodies. Their bodies *should* be a source of pride. To remind them of the service they're providing the Protectorate, for the glory of Galt, blah, blah, blah." Promise's tone has an edge to it, as if she's spitting out something hard and bitter like the crusts of burnt bread. "More like she wanted to rub my face in it," she mutters, then stops and adjusts her neck and shoulders, a curious tic that Angel notes and tucks away for future reference. "So, instead of the full-body modemants, we have these show-all monstrosities. However, I insist on the modemant veil—the mini modemant, if you will—and that is acceptable to the Hive Mind. Their focus is on broodmares, not show ponies."

Angel glances from the ovas to the buildings. "This is where they live?"

"Yes, it's the hot burning center of Genesis. There are three other dormitories just like this one. Further on down the road." Promise sighs. "At some point, they'll get around to demolishing those ugly towers. What a disaster they proved to be." She leans in again. "I was the first to say they should replace them with the single story unit, but they insisted, no, it'll be fine, we'll just bar up the doors and windows. That'll solve the problem."

Angel feels a twinge of dread lurch in her stomach, dread that warns her not to ask. And yet she must. "What was the problem?"

"Fems were flinging themselves off the balconies. I mean,

who does that? But it must have happened at least ten times my first year here. So the bars went up, but the fems somehow found their way up to the roof." Promise stares hard at something in the middle distance. "Desperation breeds desperation. Or something like that." She squares her shoulders again. "Finally, they listened to me and built the new dorms."

The taste of horror, acrid and bitter, rises in Angel's throat, but she swallows it back down with a gulp of water from her bottle. "How long have you lived here?" she asks, wondering if Promise and her birth mother may have crossed paths.

"Oh, close to twenty years. A lifetime," Promise says with a pout. "Why, if I was one of them"—she shoots a look back toward the ovas—"I'd be on a bullet train headed for severance. So, thank Galt I'm not. On the other hand," she continues, leveling her gaze at Angel, "there are moments when I feel that living here is a fate worse than death."

Angel can't be sure if she winces on hearing those familiar words said aloud, but she absolutely feels her stomach cratering and a sudden sweat pooling between her breasts. She takes another quick swallow of water.

"Where do they... come from? I mean, when you severance an ova, where do you get a replacement? Do you—are they—born to be ovas?"

Promise shakes her head. "No, although that might be easier. However, apparently the science says that approach would lead to a weakening of—something—I don't know, I'm not a scientist. They are daughters of the managerial class, what you and other bees call swags." Promise waves her hand as if trying to summon a waiter. "Or, what's that other word you people love to use?"

"Bushwa?"

"Yes, exactly. Bushwa," Promise repeats, rolling it around on her tongue as if she's taken a bite of something too hot to chew. "Anyway, they're tracked until puberty and if they show the characteristics that Galt looks for in its breeder stock—excellent health, mental and emotional stability, certain physical attributes, beauty, strength, the usual et cetera, they're harvested."

"But—how do their parentals feel about that?"

Promise fixes her eyes squarely on Angel's face. "It's an honor to have your daughter selected, to be one of the 'chosen.' " She flicks her fingers in the air, drawing quote marks.

"If parentals have to give up their only child, do they get another? To replace—"

"Are children so easily replaceable? One with another? Could another child take Lark's place if you were to lose her?" Promise glances at the child asleep in the cozy trailer attached behind Angel's bike, wind-blown strands of hair curling on her cheek. The fem's stony glare radiates heat and chill at once. "No, they don't get another one, but parentals are well-compensated by Galt. Besides, they know going into the approval process there's always a possibility this could happen. They're warned beforehand, so there's no crying after. At least, not publicly. At least, not to Galt."

Promise adjusts her neck and shoulders again, as if straining inside a too-tight jacket. "And we do let them keep in touch. That used to be forbidden, but it's another of my innovations. And the process is so very retro. Via letters." She emits a teasing giggle. "Three times a year. Hand-written. On paper. Can you imagine? Of course, they're all read and censored, if necessary, before they're sent along. As are the incoming. And confiscated after a reading. No brooding for days over a few heartfelt paragraphs."

Promise wipes an imaginary tear from her cheek, then rolls her eyes and huffs a sigh. "It's all very tedious, to say the least. But anything to keep the ovas contented and breeding. C'est la vie et c'est la guerre," she says, with a decisive lift of her chin. Then she smiles and pushes off, pedaling briskly down the road, so briskly that Angel feels the burn in her churning thighs as she struggles to catch up.

28

Words Left Unspoken

NAVIGATING LIFE WITH THE FRAZIERS is akin to crossing a chasm on a narrow footbridge riddled with missing planks. While blindfolded. Flint comes and goes, saying little, dividing his time between the facility's command station and his office in the manse, a dusk blue sanctum decorated in a nautical theme. Promise laughingly refers to the room as his bolthole. Notably, no timekeep stands sentinel against a wall or perched on a shelf. In a far corner, however, leans an enormous piece of iron with two hooks, its gray surface pocked and corroded.

"Any port in a storm. I think he pretends he's a pirate," Promise whispers with a giggle. "He actually dragged that thing home from an antique mart up on the northern shore. Spent way too many vouchers on a hunk of scrap metal, but I had to humor him. It was apparently salvaged from some time out of mind shipwreck."

"What is it?" Angel ventures, still staring from the doorway as Promise moves off down the hall.

"An anchor. Keeps a ship from drifting off. You drop it over the side and it hooks onto the lake bottom. Never seen one?"

Angel shakes her head.

"Well, yes, you're from the field and forest, not the sea. Just remember you aren't expected to clean in there. It's his space and he won't have it invaded," Promise warns, her vox as brittle as a layer of early frost.

However, Angel is expected to have his breakfast propurée, a blended concoction of protein powder, baby greens, and whatever fruit rolls in with the supply ferry, ready and waiting in his black ceramic portamug when he swings through the kitchen in the morning. Sometimes his eyes slide past her, as if she's just another dead animal in the menagerie. At other times, they hook in and follow her movements so that she feels like a fish caught on an expert angler's line, one who kens when to give a line some slack and when to yank it up tight, playing at giving his catch a sporting chance but knowing at the end of the game, he'll reel in the prize. With a Bartertown rat, Angel would have been quick with a warning look, a devastating put-down. But here, the game is different. Here, she's not the one setting the rules. She breathes easier when he takes the bowrider and sails away on his frequent pilgrimages to the Duluth Garrison to hobnob and palaver with his Genesis program counterparts.

Promise is ever-present, like the ticking of her timekeeps, but her moods lack their steady reliability. Charming one day, petulant the next—hell, her moods could change in an hour—in a manner not unlike two-year-old Lark. And both are blatantly unashamed of their emotional pendulums.

"If you don't like my weather," Promise teases, "just wait a bit. It'll change. With me, you can enjoy all four seasons in a single day. Pick your favorite."

In her crisp fall mood, she sets out tasks for Angel to complete. Brisk and efficient as the lady of the manse. Laundry. Dusting. Mopping the gray tiles that cover the kitchen floor. Keeping the white cabinets spotless and the steel counters and chrome faucets gleaming. Cleaning Promise's sanctum, which, given her apparent blood-lust and penchant for hunting, is surprisingly frilly, glowing in shades of lavender and blurple, a study in contrasts between soft pillows and hard wood and glittering crystal. Perfumed with the lush scents of sandalwood and bergamot. Lots of surfaces to tackle.

In Promise's frosty winter, with narrowed eyes, she criticizes the work in progress. "You missed a spot. Several spots. It's obvious you're more accustomed to having your hands full of grease, rather than dust rags."

But then spring arrives, and the corners of her mouth curl upwards and her eyes widen. "Oh, forget about this nonsense. It's too nice a day. Come with me for a pedal."

Summer follows soon after, with oppressive heat and light. "I just don't know how I've endured this place without you and Lark."

The intensity is scorching. Scary. And Angel is relieved when, like real summer, it doesn't last, when the heat eventually fades, replaced again by autumn's chill.

Perhaps Promise actually does resemble her timekeeps. Swinging, like their pendulums, from one extreme to the other. But Angel kens she can handle the chill and the heat, whatever weather arises on any given day. Can put her head down and grind it out. Feel her way forward, toes sweeping, tapping the space for solid footing, inching her way across that fragile bridge. Although she's not sure where it leads or if it ever ends.

In a few weeks time, she has started digging into the protocols and procedures of life on Genesis 1. It resembles the challenge of putting together a jigsaw puzzle. Her fingers sift pieces, while her eyes search for the straight edges out of which she can construct the border. A casual question to Promise can help her piece together corners, fill in chunks here and there—if Promise is in the mood. Otherwise, it's a risky business. The fem is the type who's easily frustrated. The kind who'd ruin a half-done puzzle with one sweep of her hand. So Angel prizes her discoveries, hoarding the pieces carefully.

She's learned that one hundred ovas reside in the facility, in cohorts of twenty-five lodged at each dormitory. A single medic treats the ovas. Another handles the illnesses of the staff. Both reside on the island. Each building has its own small service staff: a cook, a housekeep, two nurses, a physical trainer who keeps the ovas fit with all manner of exercise—flexitation, running, strength modulating. But apparently not swimming.

Promise shoots Angel a droll look when she inquires and asks in return, "You swim?"

"A little, when I was a child."

"Me, too. But I haven't set more than a toe in the water in years. However, I do like to shuffle my feet in the sand. We'll have to go around to Big Bay sometime. That's my sanctuary. The water's warmer on that side of the island and, if you're feeling brave, there's a fabulous place for cliff-diving."

During their exercise sessions, the ovas are free of their modemants, hair pulled back into tails or buns, faces—heart-shaped, oval, square—gleaming with sweat, but they are still dressed identically, in sleek black legskins and loose-fitting black tunics. Angel is amazed at the similarities of the body types in each cohort. Dorm One has the tall, lean fems, whose offspring are destined for live act stages or gladiator ball arenas. In Dorm Two reside the smaller, compact, muscular types, who produce the majority of worker bees, no matter the track: Agri, Service, Tech. Dorm Three houses the ovas with the lusher, pillowy bodies, the shape of the future pleasure women, and Dorm Four has the towering, big-bodied ovas that Angel recognizes instantly, with a shudder, as the mothers of goliaths. She also spies a thin band of sage green encircling the right ankle of each ova. She hadn't noticed these before, when the ovas were dressed in their green skins, but against the black they stand out.

Identification tags? A specialized metric monitor?

"Do you keep track of whether they do too little or too much?"

Angel asks, observing the ovas on another of her bike rides with Promise, which occur almost daily now that they have discovered these excursions guarantee that Lark, who fights sleep and whines for Kuba when she is tired and cranky, will succumb to a nap.

"Hmmm?" Promise is preoccupied with cleaning her black-out shades.

"The ankle bands?"

"Oh, those." Promise holds the shades up and peers through the lenses, checking for smears. "Security measure. They can wander anywhere on the island, free range, but if they get too close to the perimeter the sensor sets off an alarm. Almost as good as an embed." She waggles her left hand in the air, as if to flaunt the minuscule seed-like tracking device, barely detectable with the naked eye, implanted just under its skin.

Angel senses a hint of pride in the fem's tone. "One of your ideas?"

"No, I can't claim bragging rights over that, though the strategy was implemented not long after I arrived. I did once suggest that an electric shock would be just as effective and much less of a disturbance. The fear of pain is a strong deterrent. Better than noise pollution." She gives Angel a wink before settling the shades over her eyes. "However, it was thought by some that sort of thing might possibly harm the health or development of the fetus. And, as we all know, the fetus is god-king around here."

"Were ovas trying to..." Angel hesitates, not wanting to spoil Promise's expansive mood. She recalls the fem's matter-of-fact, almost casual reference to the ovas and the balconies and feels the revulsion rising again in the back of her throat.

Promise races to fill the gap. "Escape? Well, in a word, yes. I mean, the sheer—ingratitude—is that a word? Yes, I believe it is. These fems were—are—treated like queens." She extends her arms wide, as if preparing to embrace the world, her vox taking on the persuasive allure of a feedcom advertisement. "The best food, best care, luxurious suites in a beautiful setting."

Angel risks a comment. "Well, you did say that sometimes you felt living here was—"

Promises cuts her off, clearly irked. "For *me*—I was talking about me—my life—not theirs." A scowl crosses her face, bringing the chill, like a gust off the open water. "Wasn't always the case," she mutters, "this lack of appreciation for their place in the Galt universe. In the past, they knew what they had and thanked Galt for it. But all it takes is one uppity bitch to plant the seed of discontent and then it grows and spreads like a noxious weed. And once that weed is dug in, it's damned hard to eradicate." She reaches behind and tightens the band securing her ponytail. Smoothes the hair back from her forehead.

"That's the trouble with memories," Promise continues, twisting the cap on her canteen, loosening and tightening, loosening and tightening. "We couldn't replace all the ovas at once. So the story lingered and was passed on. One story about one ova, passed from lips to ears, embellished along the way, as always. Embellished so that the story, the simple truth, becomes a legend. So that even though all the ovas who were here at the time are now gone, severanced, the story remains. And so, long story short, the ankle bracelets." She straddles her bike and pushes off.

They pedal in silence for a moment, turning off the main road onto the drive to the Frazier residence. As they pull up to the entry and dismount, Promise arches an eyebrow. "But, oooh, I can tell you are just itching to hear it. The story. The legend. Everyone loves a good story. It's why so many bees have risked it all for a few biblios stashed away in attics and under floorboards."

Angel nudges her kickstand into place, attempting a nonchalant air, to keep the fluttering in her stomach from revealing itself on her face. "I think you want to tell me the story," she ventures, swallowing her nerves.

Promise takes the bait, although her smirk indicates she's

fully aware of Angel's manipulation. "Well, there's really not much to tell as far as simple facts go. An ova and her unborn child disappeared. Just vanished." She flicks her fingers in the air, as if scattering imaginary dust. "It was presumed she tried to swim away. But given that she was in her ninth month, that's not likely. In the realm of possibility, maybe, but it's not likely she would have made it across the channel. It's two and half miles. But no body was ever found. On land or in the water." Promise pauses, arching her eyebrows, goosing the drama. "So she probably had help," she finally continues. "But nothing unusual was captured on the security eyes. Of course, a couple of them had been conveniently covered, so there's that. The facility manager at the time was too obsessed with finding a corpse to investigate other possibilities. He definitely lacked imagination. And then, of course, there was me to deal with. I was fairly unruly, to put it mildly, when I first arrived."

Promise bends and stretches, touching the tips of her fingers to the laces of her bike shoes, groaning a little. When she straightens, she lifts her shades and stares at the house as if seeing it for the first time. "It's really just the story of how one malcontent can spoil it for everyone. The proverbial bad apple. And so the anklets. And the ban on sharp implements. Pre-cut meat. The bars on windows. The appointment of Flint as the new facility manager. Just kidding, darling," she sniggers, looking over her shoulder as if expecting to see the man behind her. She turns to Angel and shrugs. "But still, it's a life of ease. A lovely life. The life of a goddess, if truth be told."

Later, in the kitchen, where they hunch on the uncomfortable backless stools at the counter, Angel listens to the subtle tick of the timekeep that perches, vulture-like, on top of a cabinet, and considers her own origin story. How Eben said he'd spirited her out of the facility to the mainland. Considers how it intersects with the story she's just heard. Knows with a certainty that sets her knees jittering that it is the same story. Wonders about the change in protocol from then to now. Finds herself blurting out.

"When my father worked here, he lived on the mainland. He was a medic."

Promise, spreading a slick of blueberry preserves across a slice of toast, gives her a speculative look. "You do have a history with this place, don't you? What else did he tell you?"

Flustered, Angel bends to pick up a piece of granola that Lark has dropped onto the tile. "That was all he told me."

Because he hid things—truths—that he shouldn't have.

"Well, they dumped the men soon after I got here. Fems only."

"Why?"

"Well, aren't you full of questions today?" Promise takes a bite of her toast, chews thoughtfully. "Let me turn the question back on you. What's your theory on why Corporate would think it's a bad idea to have men around?" Her tone is seasoned with a dash of sarcasm.

In the face of Angel's silence, Promise taps her chin and throws a side-eye, as if giving a hint. When Angel remains mute, Promise sighs. "There were—apparently—incidents. Unsanctioned fertilizations, shall we say? Oh yes, let's say it that way. That's definitely a Galt turn of phrase." Her eyes stray to Lark, who is sorting her granola bits into small piles, raisins here, nuts there, oat clusters in the middle. "Because," she continues, "after all, the only births that should occur in the Protectorate are those sanctioned by Galt."

Angel watches Promise watching Lark. Feels the interminable ticking grating the edge of her nerves. Breathes in. Takes the moment to push farther, to dig deeper into the puzzle pieces, sifting for the ones she needs. "Who approves the births?"

Promise wipes a crumb from the corner of her mouth. "Some committee, which, of course, includes the CQO and CEO." She takes a sip of her tea.

More digging and sifting. "Then how..." Angel struggles to formulate the question, to find the appropriate words to elicit the information she needs. "How do...? So Flint is the..." Her vox trails off again, the thought so appalling it snags in her throat.

Promise bursts out laughing in mid-swallow, barely avoiding the embarrassment of spewing her tea. Coughs and sputters. Daubs her lips with her napkin. "Flint? You think he's the—Praise Galt, no!" She takes in what she must think is a perplexed look on Angel's face. "Your father—*the medic*—didn't enlighten you on these—matters?" Again, a lilt of sarcasm bends her words.

"I was raised as an androg. I wasn't taught about reproduction. Whatever I learned came from watching animals," Angel replies, the lie slipping easily between her gritted teeth.

Promise's eyes slide back to Lark, who is now re-mixing her cereal. "So how did you explain *that*"—a nod of her head in the child's direction—"to your father?"

"My father was already dead. And I have no words for what happened to me."

Promise blinks. A shadow passes across her face like a cloud skimming over a summer landscape, dragging darkness over the light. Her hand slips across the table. Covers Angel's in a warmth that feels dry and sheltering.

"You poor thing. I know. I know those words and we don't have to speak them here and now. Or ever again."

29

It feels like an escape. Trotting down the slope to the dock. Gingerly stepping a foot into the dinghy, feeling it fishtail under her weight, like a skittish animal shying away from her touch. Her mind runs through the checklist from the boating lesson that Promise grudgingly provided. Secure your life vest. Check. Cast off the rope. Check. Push away from the dock with an oar. She thumbs the starter button on the console and the electric motor purrs like a contented cat.

Twenty mile range, Promise had noted.

"You're only going about 5 miles round trip. Just make sure you plug into the solar station when you get back. And remember that the bow will go in the opposite direction from the way you turn the tiller. Most important, try not to look like a landlubber or a bee who's stolen some bushwa's boat."

The little boat skims along, the breeze stiffening to a wind. The late April afternoon had seemed warmish on shore, but now Angel zips her jacket against the chill of the misted air. Yet it all feels good. The speed. The whoosh of the wind in her ears instead of the relentless ticking of timekeeps. The sunlight after three days of steady rain. The nip of the lake spray against her cheeks. She closes her eyes for a moment to focus on the physical sensations, but the emotions bleed through.

The anticipation of seeing Word. Of confronting Path with her suspicions about the widow's convenient accident. The usual case of nerves that arise before a voxcast. Trepidation at leaving Lark alone with Promise for the first time. Promise, for her part, had been so very eager, practically shoving Angel out the door. She has decided that Angel's trips to the mainland must coincide with Flint's to the Hive. That it's the only way to keep them on the down-low. And Angel is not in a position to bargain.

This for that. Everything involves a negotiation or transaction and most of these involve Lark. However, the cost is never spelled out beforehand, as on a menu at a cafe. As payment for something—just what Angel can't be sure since these things are also never spelled out—Promise has taken to calling the child LaLa. The first couple of times Angel had forced a smile, thinking it was just a silly, singsong joke. But when the joke persisted into habit, Angel had pushed back. In a roundabout way, of course.

"She's going to think that's her new name," she had said, forcing a lightness into her tone.

"Well? And why not?" Promise had replied flippantly, brushing the child's hair back out of her eyes, securing it in a pert ponytail. "Lark is so harsh. That 'ark' ending."

"I thought you said it was a pretty name."

Promise had shrugged, eyes fixed on the child as she tied a yellow ribbon as a finishing touch. "Well, I'll say just about anything to get what I want." Then she'd turned her eyes to Angel. "I suspect you do, too." And here she'd made her little neck adjustment. "Besides, there's enough hard fems in this world. LaLa's a softer sound, a prettier name for this pretty, pretty girl."

And Angel had let it be.

Promise is also indulgent with the child in a way that makes Angel itch. The widow had been permissive, but in a thoughtful, tender manner that usually led to a teaching moment. She'd had a way of controlling situations with a guiding hand that pointed to the better choice, to the calm body, to the passageway out of the tantrum. Promise's indulgence is capricious, wanton, almost celebratory. When Lark whimpers and asks when she will see Kuba again, when they will go to the park and swing, a new toy quickly appears to distract her. Naughtiness goes uncorrected. Recalcitrance is winked at, almost encouraged, as if Promise has found a partner in crime.

Sly eyes. The both of them.

Stop.

This was not the time to think about that. Because it was all part of the bargain. A bargain she'd entered into with clear eyes and a clear head. So instead she focuses her eyes and thoughts on the mainland. On the buildings of the town that loom large as the boat draws near. On the acute color of newborn leaves that shroud the streets in a green haze. On the ripples of the water bronzed by the slanted light of the sun on its slide to the horizon. On the breeze that teases strands of her hair from its bindings. A breeze that scatters the clouds darkening the sky of her spirit.

At the dock, her lack of expertise reveals itself as the boat bumps and scrapes to a stop. But there's no one around to observe and critique. By Corporate edict, there are no casual sailors in Bayfield. The only boats to be found are miles away in the fishing facilities to the west and south.

Glancing back at the island, she marvels yet again at her very first escape, the one she made as a babe-in-arms, marvels at the part of the story she knows, and wonders at the part she doesn't. The story of how she came to be in the basket spirited away in Eben's arms, in his boat, maybe landing at this very dock. For a brief moment, she imagines not going back. To avoid tempting fate a third time.

I could just walk. I could go alone.

She could pick up her go-bags after the voxcast and then turn west and walk. Going around, going over, going through whatever obstacles lay in her path. Unburdened.

It stops her in her tracks, that brief moment of musing. Because her journey has never been solo. She's always had someone in tandem. Someone to prod, to guide, to teach. Someone to be the cautionary vox. Someone willing to share the burden unasked. Someone to be there, even when she thought it was the last thing she truly wanted. Someone to know her even better than she knows herself.

Could she leave? Now that leaving means more than just giving up and walking away, more than just leaving a task unfinished? Now that it means abandonment? She can picture Lark as Promise's pampered daughter, pampered as a caged bird is pampered, wings clipped, sated with fine seed, docile enough to perch on a finger and sing on command. Would that life be so terrible? To never want for anything?

Except freedom.

As if she knows what that word means. As if anyone does.

Whatever it meant—in the before times—in the Old Republic—that's long gone. Reduced to ashes scattered and spread in stories told by memes. Legends. Myth.

Her thoughts have brought the glowering clouds to her sky again, leaving her in a dark place as she walks the streets, watching shopkeepers lock doors and flick off lights and worker bees make their ways toward their hives. Now that spring has softened the air, there's less scurrying and more strolling. More pausing to take deep lungfuls of it.

Or is it just the Morametrics reminding them to breathe?

30

Turns of Phrase

SHE HAS WARNED HERSELF to postpone the confrontation. To keep a lid on the simmering anger that will surely boil over upon seeing Path's smug face and use it instead to feed her performance for the voxcast. But when she sees him sauntering up the brick walkway of the safe house, she steps directly into his path and gives him a bodyslam that sends him stumbling sideways into the shrubbery.

"You bastard," she seethes through bared teeth.

"What the frack?" he sputters, grabbing branches to right himself, dusting pine needles from the sleeves of his hoodie. "A simple hey-yo would've sufficed."

"You didn't have to murder her! It would've all come about without that. Without you killing her!"

"What the frack are you going on about? Killing who?"

"Oh, don't even!" Angel plants another forceful shove on his chest that sends him staggering. "The widow! I know the accident was no accident. It's got your sick mind and dirty fingerprints all over it."

Path flips his hands up in defense. "You've got to be neuro'ed but good. Frackin' neuro'ed! I didn't kill the widow. I was frackin' shocked when Kuba dumped your crap here and told us what happened."

"Lie, lie, lie! Don't lie to me. You may have sent someone from the cell to do the dirty work, but it's your dirty work all the same. Did they use the McCarthys' transport? Did you have them trash it somewhere? Or is it still back there in the garage? Did you wipe off the blood or it is still there on the fender—some kind of sick trophy?"

Path pats the air, a weak attempt to defuse the situation. "I swear to you I had nothing to do with it."

She shoves him yet again and he sways, his head thumping against the side of the house. "Stop lying. Just admit it. It's impossible for you to sink any lower than this."

Path flings an arm in the direction of the garage. "Go look!" he shouts. "You won't find a nick or scratch on it. Because it wasn't involved. I wasn't involved. No one in the cell was involved."

He reaches out to take her arm, but she slaps his hand away and lurches around him, making her way toward the garage. Taps her boot in a staccato rhythm on the concrete apron as the overhead door slowly rises to reveal the transport's rear end. A quick scan betrays no damage. She strides to the front and flicks on the utility lamp. The sheen of the bumper's finish is dulled by a layer of dust, but another scan reveals no telltale dents, chips or abrasions that one might expect to see after a collision.

"Angel, it was just an accident," Path says, sidling up to her, moving to slip his arm around her shoulder.

"No, it wasn't," she insists, ducking away from his touch.

"Fine," he says, giving way to exasperation. "It wasn't an accident. But the cell wasn't involved. Galt commits atrocities every day. Apparently even among the swag class."

"No, this wasn't the work of Corporate. If they want to make someone disappear, then that person disappears. Severanced. Poof. Gone. You know that. Whoever did it wanted to get rid of her, but couldn't actually dispose of her, not completely," Angel says, eyes still scrutinizing the transport, still filled with suspicion.

"Without bringing in Corporate for the cleanup," Path adds.

Angel runs her hand over the fender. "And there's always a risk involved in that."

Path tries to catch her eye, but she avoids his gaze like she avoided his touch. The damp spring air is seeping under her jacket, settling in like an unwelcome guest, spreading a layer of chills and gooseflesh along her skin. She's got a quease in her stomach and a sense of vertigo, as if she's still astride the little boat, bumping her way along the dock. She turns her eyes to the house, where the light shining through the kitchen window is like a beacon, beckoning her to safe harbor.

Time to come in from the cold.

The warmth is short-lived.

"We didn't send you there to bond with the bitch and be her bestie. Or turn her to the cause. You're there to gather info about how the frackin' facility operates," says Path with a scowl.

The three guevaras are hunched around the kitchen table, killing time before the voxcast, the remains of an undersized chicken scattered amongst a platter and their plates. Angel's only picked at her food, nerves getting the better of her appetite, and the men have taken turns grabbing forkfuls off her plate.

She had not expected a hero's welcome, but neither did she anticipate the tongue-lashing from Path after she briefed them on her first few weeks on the island. She looks to Word for an indication of support—a wink, a nod, the barest hint of a smile—but his head is down as he pokes among the bones, scrounging for any last tidbits. His face has started to fill out a little, his cheeks a tad plumper, his jawline a touch softer, flesh starting to subsume the skeleton.

"What if she *could* be turned?"

The vox from behind startles Angel. Her fork clatters to the table as she shoves her chair back and spins to her feet.

"Easy, girl—though I do admire your reflexes."

Teeg leans in the doorway, head framed by the folds of her hoodie. Without a respy to hide it, her grin, punctuated by a beguiling gap between her front teeth, spreads wide across her face. She steps forward and wraps Angel in a quick embrace, an embrace that Angel finds, to her astonishment, is much too fleeting, as a sudden craving for the human touch washes over her. But Teeg settles herself in the fourth chair, which creaks and sighs in protest under her bulk of muscle and bone.

"I'm inclined to think that bruja can't be turned—however, your insight might be better than mine—than ours," she adds, dipping her head in Path's direction, "having spent some time with her, in the here and now."

"But if she could be turned, that would be incredible," muses Word. "Is that even possible? Could you do that?" He stares at Angel, speculation ripening in his eyes, the green hue overwhelming the gray in the soft light from the hanging lamp.

"Forget it," barks Path. "That's not the mission."

"The mission," Teeg says, her vox sharp, "is taking the facility down, by any means necessary."

"I believe she craves comfort," Angel murmurs.

Path makes a scoffing sound. "She lives in a frackin' manse with every—"

"Human comfort," Angel clarifies. "And all her life it's been a stranger to her." She surprises herself with that thought made audible. Blinks, wondering out of which dark corner it crawled. Could that same thing be said of her? Of all of them? "I believe she would do just about anything to have a child."

Teeg nods, an expression passing over her face, darkening it, but here and gone, like a wind-driven cloud streaking across the moon. "Some games are too dangerous to play," she says with an air of finality, but her gaze holds to Angel's long into the silence that follows.

"El amor y la guerra son una misma cosa," Path breathes into the void. "Sin reglas sin límites."

"Says the man who knows practically nothing about love," Teeg snorts. "Well, we're not going to worry about turning the unturnable. Not going to waste time on that. We're going to work the problem. And that's getting a read on the facility. But if she takes you into her confidence, on her own terms, that's not a bad thing. If she makes the approach, then work with it. But, remember, waste no sympathy on this person. For that way lies disappointment. And failure."

There is a secret history. From time out of mind. Secret because they must keep it hidden from you. For fear of what it could inspire. Inside each and every one of you.

A history of warriors who struggled and succeeded against all odds. A history of the few who joined together in service to a cause. Of bands of brothers and sisters united in their hunger for freedom. Who ignored the weak-minded, the ones full of fear, those who said it could not be done. A history of these brothers and sisters who scaled the impossible walls thrown up in their paths. Who focused only on what was ahead, not what they'd left behind. Who kept their eyes on the prize.

You don't know this history because it's dangerous. Dangerous not to you, but to the keepers of the Hive. They think they've wiped it. Swept the memory clean. Moved it to trash and emptied it into oblivion. But it lives. It lives in a breathing memory. In a body. In a mind. It lives in the memes who hold that knowledge close. Who pass it on. Even as I speak. Even as you listen. You've only to ask, and it will be given to you. Seek and you will find it. Knock, and the door will open.

So sayeth the Night Prophet.

The cell catches the voxcast as it filters through the speakers of a chunky black handheld that looks as if it has taken a tumble or two down the boulder-studded trail to the bottom of the gorge. Though its body is battle-scarred, its sound quality is stellar, capturing every nuance, every sigh, every verbal wink and nod. For many of the guevaras, the voxcast serves as the equivalent of a bedtime story, distracting their whirling minds from self-sabotaging worries, draining the day's built-up adrenaline, dragging their stubborn attentions away from jagged emotions and the feeling of living on the edge of a precipice, teetering, one misplaced foot away from a fall. Perhaps they are. But in the night comes a vox with a surety and cadence that reminds them of the purpose behind the pain.

For Kuba, however, hearing Angel's vox reminds him of the dangerous path onto which she's stepped. Instead of sleep, it brings a yawning restlessness and a racing brain, through which fearsome thoughts ricochet. When he can't stand to be flat on his back and wide awake, body humming like a maxed-out generator, listening to the maddening thud of blood coursing through his veins, he carefully eases himself up on his elbows. He could offer to take over perimeter watch duties, put his sleeplessness to good use. He's pulling on his boots when he spies movement in the periphery. Just a slipping shadow, the barest riffling of the pine needles. Squints. Shakes his head. BoBeck and his teeny bladder. But the shadow turns, shambles off in the direction opposite the latrine, heading down the trail to the gorge.

The trail is tricky enough to walk during the day, crisscrossed with bulging tree roots and rocks, ever ready to snag an unwary foot, but to navigate it in the dark would take a canny sixth sense, a claw-trap memory, a badass attitude, and a maglite for a companion. Kuba, while he admires BoBeck's scrounging savvy, isn't sure the man has any of those attributes. And he's definitely not swinging a torch in front of him.

The where and the why drive Kuba to follow, slipping from tree to tree, setting his boots on the sloping switchback path.

He takes it slowly, while BoBeck appears to accelerate. A fem? Is he meeting one of the fems for a game? Possible, though not likely, given his frequent, though discreet, disparagements of his fem comrades' looks and hygiene. And Kuba can envision several more inviting places for a tryst than the cold, damp, pebble-studded sand below the waterfall.

He catches a toe on rock and grabs hold of a tree trunk to steady himself, his clenching palm rasping against the rough bark. To Kuba, the sound is explosive, but BoBeck is too far ahead to hear. When the man reaches the bottom of the gorge, he pauses, his head swiveling to look back up the trail, and Kuba ducks against a pine that leans precariously over the cliffside, its jutting roots clinging to the edge for dear life.

There doesn't appear to be anyone standing on the sand of the creek bank and BoBeck skips his way across the water, shuffling from boulder to boulder. Then, with a last glance back, he starts to pick his way through the underbrush, going up the rise on the far side of the creek, following a path that only he can see.

Kuba weighs his options. Follow and risk injury. And wrath. And loss of trust. Turn back and only suffer having his curiosity left unsatisfied. It's an easy choice. This is his family now. He tells himself that BoBeck has been given a mission, one best kept under wraps for now. One that will be revealed in the fullness of time.

But speculation keeps his mind racing, keeps the thoughts ricocheting, keeps the blood thrumming. Keeps his eyes wide open in the dark.

31

A Leaf of Voxes

EYES BLINKING, and then staring, wide open in the dark unfamiliar room, Angel abandons the stranger's too-soft bed for the comfort of the hard floor. But she can't find her way to sleep. The path is blocked by thoughts that crowd in, like a looming bully. Thoughts that invade, that creep and slither, that whisper and scream. Thoughts that shove and push for her attention.

How could you? How could you leave your child with that...?

The noun evades. What is Promise, at her core?

It's not really about her—it's about you. Terrible. Worthless. Incompetent. Afraid. What you've always been. So maybe she is better off without you.

That's a kick in the ribs that drives her upright.

No. Should never have left her. Should never have come here.

*No, should never have gone **there** in the first place. What were you thinking with your wild, ridiculous visions? Fems walking across water.*

The child will wake, as she is prone to do. And the person she looks to for comfort in the dark won't be there. Promise will hear, and what will she do? Offer a treat? Press the child close so the prickly lace of her nightgown scratches Lark's cheek? Sing her the hymn to water, the song of lies? And what will Lark do? Call out for her? Or snuggle contentedly, reassured by the port that any enfolding arms offer in the midnight storm, transfixed by the lies that spill so soothingly, so sweetly, from bitter lips?

Eben's words echo through the darkest places of her clouded mind.

Parents have always lied to their children. They lie to protect them. To give easy answers to difficult questions. To spare them the pain of the truth.

Should never have gotten mixed up with this mess. You are no Damn Otis! Back. Go back NOW!

Even in the inky night, it'll be easy. That's what she tells herself. The spotlights that ring the island will make it so. They will stand as beacons for her return rather than deterrents to an escape. With this midnight lizard brain clutching her in its fierce claws, it's all so simple. So clear. She will grab her go bags from where they sit in Word's room. Sail the dinghy back, gather up Lark, and then—

And then. That's when the murk of uncertainty starts to blur her vision, to muddy the stream of her thoughts. Lark may fuss. Call out in confusion. The bruja somehow hears everything. She'll wake and confront them. And then—

And then. Would Angel be able to do what has to be done? The necessary thing? It's been a long time since she's had to finish a job. That kind of job. In that kind of way.

Pushing those thoughts back, banishing them to where the trees loom, and the goliaths lurch, and the demons writhe and hiss, she focuses on the nearest task. Easing out of the room with its too-soft bed, slipping into her boots, she skulks down the hall, keeping to the wall where the wood is less likely to squeal. The door to Word's room is ajar and she pushes it with a tentative finger. Pauses at the threshold, listening for sounds of sleep, hearing only her own breath catch when she realizes the room is unoccupied. Maybe he's in the attic. Reading. Writing. Fiddling with the 'tronics.

In two silent steps, she hefts the backpacks. In another two, she backs out of the room and draws the door ajar again. Silent flight. But the stairs are problematic. She's never paid enough attention to notice where the treads are liable to complain. And she's toting the extra weight.

One squeak. A groan. And then another. Then she is standing in the foyer, ready to unlock the deadbolts and flee. The click of one lock and then the other and her hand grasps the knob, when a tug on the strap of one of the backpacks jerks her backwards and into the grip of a pair of strong hands.

"What're you doing? You can't go out there now." Word's rasp knifes through her. He edges around, putting his body between her and the door. "There's a brute squad combing the streets, looking for lice like us."

With a hand on her elbow, he eases the backpacks off her shoulders and guides her into the living room, navigating easily through the dark, around the chairs where the dummies sit and over to the bay windows. He crooks a finger around the edge of the drawn drapery. Pulls it aside an inch or two.

The fabric of the curtain presses a velvet kiss on Angel's cheek as she sidles in and aims an eye on the sliver of view to the outside. Her gaze follows the purple glow of the solars down the driveway. Then a hot white scythe of light sweeps over the grounds in front of the house. In the aftermath of its swift arc, Angel can see the bulk of a patrol transport idling on the road at the end of the drive.

"Teeg," Angel breathes.

At the end of the voxcast, the guevara had slipped out the front door. As she reached the bottom step she'd glanced back, looking as if she was itching to say something as wicked as the smile on her face, but then appeared to think better of it and just shook her head, hustling away, blending in with the trees.

"She'll be fine," Word whispers. "She can be less than a shadow when she wants to."

"Why are they here? This isn't routine. I've been here for nearly a year and I've never seen a goliath patrol in town. Just the local traps."

Angel feels Word's shoulders shift in a shrug as he leans in behind her to get another peek out the window.

"Your keeper's accident might've brought the focus down. Galt can't have such a mess happening in the midst of a bestowal. Ruins the image. Or it may be that they really are looking for us. Could be time to pack up and find a new hidey-hole. Traps are being pretty close-mouthed about the whole sweep, but they nearly blew up the armory break-in. The operatives escaped just in the nick of it. Or so we hear."

"What d'you mean?"

Word inhales a breath, holds, then blows it out like he's considering a particularly weighty thought. "We've got a read on their transmissions. A hook into their comms."

"You can hear what they're saying?"

"Some of the time," Word says, an edge in his vox. "Depends on their location."

"How?"

Word steers her away from the window. "Old goliaths can be a little chippy, a little resentful when they're not afforded the retirement luxuries they think they deserve."

"You've got someone on the inside?"

"A used-to-be on the inside."

"You trust him?"

"Only as far as I can throw him." Word's smile is grim and tight. "And that ain't far."

"Once a goliath, always a goliath. The mindset doesn't fade. Why would he—"

Word cuts her off. "How many proverbs do you need to hear? The enemy of my enemy is my friend. The unholy alliance. Adversity makes strange bedfellows." He tries to guide her back through the shadows. "Speaking of bed, you need to grab some pillow before you head back."

Angel slips away from the hand on her back. "I can't sleep. Got to get back to Lark. She's never been without me for the night." She puts her eye to the edge of the curtain again. The grounds and drive are dark again, with just the solars throwing their violet tinge along the curve. The goliaths have moved on.

"Lark will be fine, just like Teeg. Just like you."

"You haven't a clue—"

"From what you've said, I know this—that fem you left her with isn't going to harm a hair on that child's head and neither will anyone else, while she's around to protect her. And you know this, too. You can sense it. What shall we call her? Lioness? Mama Bear?" Word's hand on her back is insistent now. "Come, I have just the lullaby you need."

Angel allows him to guide her. She's caught up in what he's said, wrestling with the notion. If Promise is the lioness, the she-bear protecting her young, then what is she? The snake slithering away from her unhatched eggs? The cowbird sliding hers into another bird's nest? She bumps her knee on one of the easy chairs, stumbles at the threshold of the foyer. Word grabs the backpacks and tries to sling them over his shoulder while keeping his hand on her back, but one slides down and he just manages to catch it before it hits the floor. In the jostle comes a distinct thunk of metal on metal.

"Whoa," Word grunts as the pack thumps against his back. "What you got in here?"

Angel makes no reply. At the top of the stairs she tries to continue down the hall but Word nudges her inside his own room.

"No," she protests, but he leans against the door and it closes with a click.

"You do hold me in low regard, don't you? That's not what's on my mind. You need a session with the bowls. They'll sing you to sleep. But first I need to know what just assaulted me on the way up."

"No," Angel repeats, and reaches out to grab the backpack from him, but she can't tell where the dark ends and he begins until she hears the rasp of a match against a striker and sees a flame leap to life and set the wick of a candle aflame. The room fills with a honeyed light. Word's face looks almost full in the glow, the bones softened, the contours eased by the flesh he's regained over the last few months. Even the scar across his neck looks less than angry. A smile twists his lips, but it's small, a bit rueful.

"As tough as I've been on you. The fault-finder, not the flatterer. The critic, not the cajoler. The one who damns with his silence. Well, suit yourself. But a guevara..." His vox trails off, leaving the rest unsaid. Stares at her across the backpack, as it hangs like an offering from his fingers.

When she takes it from him, he steps around her to the dresser where the singing bowls wait and starts to gather them up, but freezes when he hears the scritch of a zipper. Turning, he finds Angel seated cross-legged on the rug, the backpack open on her lap, her hands carefully drawing forth and arranging its contents in a neat row.

His gaze is drawn first to the old burner, but it doesn't linger on the gun, as if it comes as no surprise that she'd possess such a thing. His eyes travel quickly over the hunting knife, too, its blades tucked away inside the grip. Then they land on Debs' mechanical hand. He reaches out, wordlessly asking permission. Angel nods and he hefts the hand in his own, running his flesh and bone fingers over those fashioned long ago from steel and wood scrounged from a tool chest and a junk drawer.

"Debs," Angel replies to the question forming on Word's lips. "And that's his burner. The one he spirited away from a brute squad armory somewhere along his journey. Must be a thing with guevaras, yeah? Thieving from goliaths?" she adds, with a sly smile.

Word places the hand back on the rug with a delicacy that

surprises Angel. He lifts the burner, checks the mag for cartridges. Rolls his eyes when he finds it empty. "That's not gonna help you in a jam."

Angel takes it from his hand and returns it to the backpack. "I don't want to have to use it again."

Word gives her a look. "There's wants and there's needs and there's a yawning chasm between the two. I'm sure you've heard the CEO squawk on and on from every 'tronic board in the whole frackin' protectorate on that topic. Ad infinitum." He winks. "That means forever. Just one more reason to shut the bastard up permanently." He fingers the worn red bandanna. "Fabric's faded, but not the dream." Taps Eben's body armor. "Now that will come in handy in a tight spot."

It's the old imagekeep that grabs his attention and won't let go. That and the scrap of cloth with its message traced in blood. He runs a thumb over it. Something's there, turning in his mind, visible in the narrowing of his eyes and the knitting of his brow. Turning, turning. Lips parting as if to speak his whirling thoughts, but in the end he just lays the items back in their places.

"Now it's payback time, your turn," Angel says. "Tell me how you came to get that scar across your neck." She leans forward, breaching the space between them, and the sudden motion sends the agate pendant tumbling out from under her shirt collar. It sways from her neck on its chain of gold, glinting, winking like a conspirator.

She braces for the shutdown, the flare of anger and the sarcastic rebuff, followed by the silent scowl. Instead, he reaches out and takes the agate between his fingers. Rubs his thumb across its smooth surface. "There's a weight we carry on our backs and another we carry in our hearts," he says, before letting the pendant fall again.

"Tell me your story. I'm not afraid of who you are."

Angel can feel the inner struggle radiating from his body, can almost see it shimmering like waves of heat rising from asphalt in the summer.

His eyes slip away from hers. "We were trying to place a mole in a power facility up north of the Duluth Garrison. Yeah, that close to the Hive. We'd recruited a techie, an engineer with some decent access. She believed in the movement. Was willing to work the inside game. Fed us some good intel until..." His vox trails off. But with a shake of his head, barely more than a twitch, he continues. "We were at the precipice, almost ready to make the move, to go in, and then the rock—the op—started to give way. And it all fell apart. I don't know how she put a foot wrong." He shakes his head. "How *we* put a foot wrong." He pauses again, and his gaze falls to his hands, empty, up-turned.

"No." He balls his hands into fists. "That's not true. I do know. I was taking risks when I shouldn't—still voxing, when I should have gone into radio silence. I'm pretty sure that's how they traced us. The goliaths came—in the pitch black, not even a hint of dawn on the horizon." A pause, a shift in his gaze, and Angel senses he's staring into that night again. The silence stretches until his eyes finally slide back to Angel's face. "I'm ashamed that I survived."

His clenched hands relax again, and he casts his gaze down, as if watching them lose their grip on something precious.

You were in love with her. Still are.

Inexplicably, Angel feels a sudden urge—a need—to obliterate that revelation, to banish it from this space between them, from this room, this house, the world. To wave her arms and clear it from the air, like clearing the smoke curling from an extinguished candle. To pull him close and replace that memory of sorrow and pain and regret with something else. Something new and alive.

And to banish her own memories of sorrow, too. Of a goliath in the guise of a boy. A boy with a perfect body, flesh unmarred, molded into something that fingers beg to caress. Of rain on a barn roof. Of a blood covenant. Of putting that bond aside. Of aiming Debs's burner. Breaking that covenant. And a memory of not looking back at the fallen body. Because that way she'd never know his ultimate fate. Frozen in that instant.

Words and deeds to regret. To forget. Many words and deeds. Time to move on.

The bowls weep a lament that night. A mourning song, ringing of grief, old and fresh, full of beauty and sorrow. Regret and longing. Thoughts drift and scatter, like leaves in a scouring November wind. Tears well and seep and ebb, like the tide under the pull of the moon. Muscles tense and relax, like the plates of the earth in their fraught, inexorable motion. It's a delicate journey back from the edge of the cliff, one that begins with the touch of a hand and ends in the curve of a body. And the song goes on long after the bowls fall silent.

Dawn brings a chill and a sense of something missing. As she shifts and runs her hand over the cool void where a warm body had been, her fingers brush a small, smooth, cold rectangle of metal. Blinking away the fog of sleep, her eyes catch the glint of brass. The mag from Debs' burner.

Reloaded.

And there, propped against her backpack, Word's whiteboard.

Now youre ready for a jam Yeah its a guevara thing

A scrap of yellowed paper, a page torn from a biblio, is tucked beneath its edge.

*Now I make a leaf of Voices—for I have found nothing mightier
    than they are,*
And I have found that no word spoken, but is beautiful, in its place.
O what is it in me that makes me tremble so at voices?
*Surely, whoever speaks to me in the right voice, him or her I
    shall follow,*
*As the water follows the moon, silently, with fluid steps, any-
    where around the globe.*

All waits for the right voices;
Where is the practis'd and perfect organ? Where is the develop'd
　　Soul?
For I see every word utter'd thence, has deeper, sweeter, new
　　sounds, impossible on less terms.
I see brains and lips closed—tympans and temples unstruck,
Until that comes which has the quality to strike and to unclose,
Until that comes which has the quality to bring forth what lies
　　slumbering, forever ready, in all words.

More scrawl in Word's hand across the bottom of the page.
Where the Night Prophet leads there I shall follow

32

Servant of Two Masters

THE IDENTITY OF LA BÊTE's new handler is a mystery. Name, gender, age, rank in the Galt hierarchy, official title on the Corporate organizational chart, all are left in the blur. The only thing in focus is a disembodied vox, modulated into a robotone by an audio regulator, passing instructions through the bud in his ear. Of course, this is nothing new. He knows very little about his other handler, the one who has orchestrated his movements since he first shipped off to boot camp. The handler he knows only as 'Nadie'—no one. Or anyone. This original handler speaks in a fem vox, crisp and authoritative, a vox that commands attention, a vox suited to a master manipulator who has pulled the strings to maneuver her puppet into all the right places, making all the right moves. Even the auditory signal announcing her presence in his feedcom is distinctive, a series of bell tones. At first, upon hearing them, he would stop what he was doing and cock his head. But Nadie had cautioned him against drawing unwanted attention, saying that he must learn to go about his business, as he would with any other feedstream, even as his focus was entirely on her vox. And so he learned. And he adopts similar behavior with this second handler, who intrudes with a disturbing crackle instead of calming musical notes.

With Nadie, communication has always been a one-way

street. Responses and questions are not allowed, although, in the beginning, La Bête had, with the green, pig-ignorant enthusiasm of a boy playing infiltrator in a Squads of Glory immersive game, pleaded for that ability. He was a budding cryptographer able to communicate in code. And talking to thin air would have burnished his crazy street cred. But no, that proposal had been met with the counter suggestion that perhaps he wasn't up to the challenge for which he was being groomed. With Nadie, his was to listen, not to speak, although in time she did, upon occasion, indulge his taste for espionage cosplay as a parental might indulge a child's outlandish whim in hopes he will outgrow it. She'd send messages through songs, sometimes a full-on version, sometimes just her vox whispering the lyrics. He assumed it was music from time out of mind, because he'd never heard the tunes before. They were not products of the Corporate Infotainment Division, chirped by their aviary of songbirds. These musical interludes were humbling experiences, since he could never be sure if his interpretation was correct. He finally decided that Nadie engaged with him in this fashion for precisely that reason. To humble him. However, over time, his ability to extract deeper meaning—to crack the code—sharpened, a blade honed by the whetstone of her mocking vox.

With this new handler, whose ridiculous catchphrase, "This is the operator," always provokes an internal eye roll, verbal communication is one-way, but La Bête has been given a code to enter on his linkcom with instructions to script his messages in the chat box that appears on the small screen. He is discouraged from queries not directly related to the business at hand, but whoever is on the other end of the feedcom sees his posts and instantaneously replies in his ear. The responses are minimal, consisting mainly of confirmations or sparsely worded clarifications.

His presumption is that both people behind the voxes are well-placed. High up in the Corporate realm, giving them access to the feedstream and the ability to circumvent or override the nature of its security systems, as well as a cushion of plausible deniability to protect themselves in case of a misstep or worse.

For him, it's a balancing act. But that has been his life for a long time.

He can admit to himself now that it had been a daily struggle to not take a razor to his wrists or put his Corporate-issued handcannon to his temple during those early months of walking the tightrope that was basic training. The process of being transformed from mere mortal into goliath, while at the same time being treated as something less than—other than—human. It's an ass-kicking, soul-sucking trial by fire under any circumstances. Stripped of one's name, deprived of sleep, food, and shelter, assaulted verbally and physically, subjected to all manner of humiliations. All in the name of submerging one's individuality for the sake of the squad. For the sake of the Protectorate. For the sake of Galt. But it was a particularly gruesome ordeal to endure these mental and physical deprivations while undergoing a separate, clandestine indoctrination in the fine art of espionage, without the benefit of the hormone ramp-up administered via every inductee's embed or the tiny white T-Roid pills that, while not officially sanctioned, were passed around like candy by recruits and drill sergeants alike.

He was destined for other things, for greater things, and must endure on sheer human will alone. So he was told, by his mother, by his father, by Nadie. And so the signals emitted by his embed were left untweaked. And he was warned against putting any substance in his body that might jeopardize the ultimate success of the mission. Enduring the punishment of the body had been easy compared to enduring the torture of the mind. The dissonance of being drilled in the delicate art of serving two masters, each opposed to the other.

Your body is not yours; it belongs to Galt. Your mind is not yours; it belongs to Galt. You are only here to serve Galt.

Your body is a temple. Your mind is a sanctuary. It is the only thing you have that is truly yours.

The mission is your life, and your life is only the mission, and the mission is the preservation of Galt Corporation and the Protectorate.

Your mission is the fem.

These men are your brothers; you owe them loyalty, as you owe loyalty to Galt.

Do not place your trust in the squad, only in yourself. We will attempt to dial them back, but there are no guarantees.

The people are expendable; the Protectorate is not. When an individual ceases to benefit the Protectorate, that individual becomes an enemy to the Protectorate. Enemies are targets to be engaged. They are foreign bodies to be eradicated.

Whoever kills one life, kills the world. Whoever saves one life, saves the world entire. Think carefully before you take a life, but always remember your mission. And your mission is the fem.

In order to dissemble without losing his sanity, he'd struggled to create a Venn diagram in his mind, to mine the diverging sets of messages to unearth the fundamental elements that both shared. The elements that he could live by to serve both masters.

Mission above all else.

Never accept defeat.

Never quit.

He hasn't been able to parse the current messages from his new handler to determine on which side the individual leans. His first presumption is that this is a Galt play by a Galt player. That what sits below the surface is the same as what rests on top.

But...

Nadie has been incommunicado for weeks, and La Bête wonders if she knows about his new role. It would seem almost certain that she does, but whether she set it into motion like so many other things in his life is impossible to know. La Bête has to work this problem on his own for now. He lays out his uncertainties like he's laying out his field kit for inspection, each piece carefully cleaned and placed. If it's a Galt play, how did the traitor come to be a member of the cell? Was he placed as a mole from the beginning or was he turned? If it's a Galt play, how long can La Bête string them along, seeming to provide information without actually providing any information? But if the play is from the other side, then his tactics should be modified. Then again, the splitlip is also measuring out his confidences in spoonfuls and it's a weak broth so far. That makes it more likely to be a Galt play. By prolonging the game, the splitlip must be attempting to secure the maximum reward for turning his coat.

La Bête shakes his head, licks his thumb and bends to wipe a smudge off his boot.

The fool must not be familiar with the Goliath Ethos.

The people are expendable; the Protectorate is not. When an individual ceases to benefit the Protectorate, that individual becomes an enemy to the Protectorate. A target to be engaged. A foreign body to be eradicated.

33

A Gambit

"She's bought herself a fem."

The CQO tilts her head and a strand of silver hair slips down, covering her left eye. She holds the pose for a moment before straightening and tucking it back into place. An arch of her eyebrow is all that is required to fluster her visitor.

"Well, maybe 'bought' isn't the right word," Flint Frazier sputters. "Uhmm, acquired—procured," he offers, stumbling on the words like loose stones in his path. "Adopted—maybe that's more accurate."

"Adopted," the CQO repeats, emphasizing each syllable. "A fem."

She has already endured almost twenty minutes of vague excuses during her interrogation of this man about the issues contributing to the execrable performance at the Genesis I facility and its production rate that ranks among the lowest in the Protectorate. Where was the promised turnaround? An inherently reasonable question met with hemming and hawing and now this distraction.

"Two fems, actually. A fem and her spawn. Off the grid. Border jumpers likely, though the fem claims she was born there. At the facility. I'm sure it's just some crazy story the fem's using to beguile her."

"Adopted a fem," the CQO repeats, as if grappling with an unwieldy package, one she can't quite wrap her arms around, the struggle apparent in her vox.

"Well, she's ostensibly there to do the housework, the yard-work—and she does, and does a decent job of it—but I think she's treated more like a pet than a housekeep. Or maybe it's the little spawn that's the pet."

The CQO stares. "A pet? Mr. Frazier, dogs are pets. Cats are pets. An undocumented fem is not a pet. It's a parasite on the health of the Protectorate. And you are aware of what we do when we find them, yes?"

He nods. He's losing her and looks as if he knows it, because he keeps stumbling over those stones, almost as if he's throwing them under his own feet.

"Here's the thing. Hear me out, please," he continues quickly, knowing he's over the boundary, but apparently deciding that since he's over the boundary, why not just keeping plodding and tripping onward? How much more damage could it possibly do? "Let's turn this into a win for Galt. She's a fem. A breeder. A successful breeder."

The CQO shakes her head. "I see where you're going with this, but—"

Flint dares to cut in. "She's young. Late teens, early twenties, I'd guess. Healthy." And here he throws the stone that he senses might cause the CQO to stumble. Or at least pause to consider her next step along the path. "Attractive." He swivels in his chair, eyes the painting behind him. "There's something about her face that reminds me of this one. The fem on the half-shell." He turns back, and thinks he catches a glint in the CQO's ice blue eye before she tucks it away, like a loose strand of hair.

"Mr. Frazier, ovas go through an onboarding program after they've been selected, a process that begins at puberty. You know this, so I'm not sure why I am sitting here explaining it to you.

We do not bring adult fems into the breeder initiative."

"Well, maybe we've reached the point where we need to start thinking outside the—" The word 'cage' almost slips off his tongue, but he manages to bite it back. "Thinking differently. Making exceptions when they are warranted," he states, determined to plead his case.

The CQO leans back in her chair, folds her hands in her lap, and heaves a sigh to indicate her infinite patience. "My sense, Mr. Frazier, is that you see this as an opportunity to keep that she-devil of yours content while also obtaining a measure of satisfaction for yourself. I suppose there's nothing inherently wrong in opportunism. A business often needs to take advantage of circumstances and make expedient decisions. But note, I used the word 'business,' not 'individual.' Because I'm wondering what's in it for Galt? For the good of the Protectorate?"

Frazier cocks his head, leans forward. "You have—Galt has—a quota to fill. A supply of healthy babies to bestow. Healthy babies to grow and fill all the open positions on all your tracks. A quota of future workers."

"Oh, Mr. Frazier, one fem does not a quota fill. And the easiest solution to maintain our balance of workers would simply be to extend employment terms. Put off severance for a few years. *If* it ever came to that. Although, there are times when I feel that, yes, our future is hostage to our young." The CQO's gaze drifts to the window and the blue vista of water and sky it frames. She blinks once or twice, perhaps imagining some different future, or at least one without these issues, this particular issue. With another sigh, she turns her attention back to the eager man.

"In this case, in your case, Mr. Frazier, I perceive that it's far more of a personal issue. Let me give you a piece of advice. You tend to skate along on your family name. Everyone knows the Fraziers were present at the creation, helping to forge the Protectorate into existence out of the chaos. But that time has already passed out of living memory and it's a part of history that could easily disappear. Be erased. So it's important for you to make your own mark on this world. Do you understand?" The CQO pauses until she gets a nod. "Look, if you want this fem as your pleasure woman, fine, just get an embed under her skin. And the skin of her spawn. In the meantime, you have six more months to turn the facility around. I think we're done here."

As Flint turns to leave, the CQO's fingers beat a rhythm. "Just a moment, Mr. Frazier. When did this undocumented arrive?"

Flint's eyes seek the ceiling as he calculates an answer that won't make him look like a shirker, a sympathizer. "It's been a few weeks. At first, I—"

With a wave of her hand, the CQO cuts off whatever lame explanation he was planning to offer. "Does she come and go? From the facility."

Flint shakes his head vigorously. "No." Then he hedges. "At least, not that I'm aware of. And Prom—"

Another wave of the CQO's hand commands silence. "Does she have—an interesting vox?"

Flints squints as if trying to see his way into the question. "Vox? Frankly, I've hardly heard her say more than a few words. When she does, she tends to mumble." Again, he hedges. "At least, around me. The spawn, on the other hand, has quite the yap on her. Would love to put a muzzle on the little beast." But he quickly adds, "She's a charming little thing, though, quite the beauty."

The CQO nods. "Well, all the more reason for you to not have a child, Mr. Frazier. It does require a high level of tolerance for yapping, as you so eloquently put it, no matter how beautiful the creature may be. One more question, have you ever heard of the Night Prophet?"

The man's puzzled expression answers the query. "No, of course, you wouldn't have heard any of those voxcasts. Because you are a responsible employee who observes curfew and the metrics for a healthy night's sleep and you are tucked away in bed in the arms of Morpheus while this insubordinate bleeds into the feed and attempts to rouse the rabble."

"Arms of—"

"Asleep, Mr. Frazier," the CQO clarifies. "Well, the sooner you get an embed in the fem, the sooner we'll be able to keep track of her."

"Is this—do you think this fem is somehow connected to this Night—person?"

"Prophet," the CQO clarifies again. "Night Prophet. No, not really. But perhaps make some small talk with her while you do the implant. Let me know about her vox. Or, better yet, get a voxcapture and send it along to me. And now we are done here."

34

Eavesdropping

ANGEL ISN'T SURE what irks her more: Lark's nonchalance or Promise's knowing smirk. It wasn't like she expected them to be waiting for her at the dock, scanning the water for the first sign of the dinghy, pacing and wringing their hands as the minutes passed, the air fraught with the child's whines. Lark in meltdown mode, writhing in a frazzled Promise's arms, in a mood that only Angel could soothe. But Lark's blasé little salute with her triangle of wheat toast, as if to signal 'oh, there you are,' before she shoves it into her mouth is decidedly underwhelming. Ego-deflating. And almost as annoying as the incessant click of the timekeep's mechanical heart and the accusatory stares emanating from the glass-eyed denizens of the dead zoo. So annoying and disappointing that Angel dashes around the counter and sweeps the child out of her chair and into a bearhug. She forces a smile onto her face and gaiety into her vox.

"What kind of greeting is that for your mama?" she scolds, pulling Lark even closer, breathing in the sweetness of the jam on the girl's lips, feeling its sticky residue in a slick across her cheek. Angel twirls and Lark giggles.

"Mama silly," she lisps.

"Indeed," agrees Promise, eyes sparking under her arched eyebrows. "Nothing like a dose of man to improve some fems' spirits, I guess. Too bad you have to return to this hellhole," she adds with a pout.

Angel peers at Promise over the top of Lark's head, the soft tendrils of the girl's hair tickling her chin. "Now who's being silly," she snipes, punctuating her words with a smacking kiss on Lark's forehead. "How can you doubt this display of devotion? How glad I am to be back?"

Watching the shadow of jealousy darken Promise's eyes and hearing it freeze a layer of ice over her vox brings Angel a distinct sensation of pleasure. And a tremor of trepidation, too.

Take care. The ice is brittle. Thin. And you don't know what lies beneath.

A shed is tucked in the back corner of the extensive estate, hidden by a thicket of evergreens. Stored there are the gardening implements, an array of rakes, shovels, and pruners. And it's an out-of-sight, out-of-mind place for Angel to stash her forbidden backpacks. A place where she's sure the Fraziers never tread. She has already expressed interest in upgrading the garden beds, after Promise complained that the groundskeep only drops by once a week in season to skim over the lawn on her standing mower.

"I have no gardener," Promise had lamented. "Do you have a green thumb?"

"So I've been told," Angel had replied, another deal brokered.

Promise had taken to calling her 'Nature Girl' for a hot minute, until she soon grew bored and moved on to other nicknames—Honey, Ang, Jelly—none of which sound as if they are intended as terms of endearment when they leave the fem's lips.

With access to the shed secured, Angel uses the blue gloom of a May twilight to trek down to the dock and retrieve the backpacks from the dinghy, where she had left them stowed under a tarp from the dock's storage locker. Under their burden, the trail back to the manse grounds seems steeper and more treacherous.

Twice she catches her foot on a bulging root and has to grab hold of a branch to steady herself.

The gloom has deepened to indigo by the time she's skirting the lawn and flitting among the shrubs at its border, thankful for the cover that the new leaves and the fullness of needles on the pines provide. She pauses in a copse of lilacs, breathing in the lush scent of their blossoms, cupping the panicles to her nose, marveling at their iridescent shade of mauve. The flowers seem to glow in her hand as night descends. From here, the lights in the many-windowed house seem cheerful and warm, inviting and calm. Promise is lazing on a sofa in the great room under the gaze of the beasts, Lark curled in the crook of her arm. The fem is gazing toward the bouquet of peonies arching from a green vase on the coffee table, a glorious riot of pink and fuchsia. Lark squirms, pointing at something on Promise's tablet, which the fem has propped with her knees. Something the child sees excites her and she claps her hands.

Another toy. Another frippery.

Flint is nowhere to be seen. Angel suspects he's holed up in his office with a bottle of his fancy artisanal brew. Since he returned from his bimonthly at the Hive, he's been stalking through the manse with the look and air of an agitated horse, eyes wide and wild, nostrils flaring, teeth wrestling with the bit, hooves in a permanent stomp. Throughout the flow of the day, when Angel is cleaning other rooms, when Lark is napping, when Flint and Promise have isolated themselves in the dining room and she and Lark are relegated to the kitchen, she's overheard bits and pieces of their conversations conducted in icy hot voxes that grow loud. Loud enough so that words and phrases float through walls and around corners.

More repairs on the transport... What was it this time? Another renegade cart at the GaltMart? As if you ever step foot there...

So it's always my fault... like I'm the one running to the Hive every two weeks...

Damn straight I have to run up there... trying to keep pace with the others...

And you're not...

Worst performance... won't accept mitigating factors... damn ovas keep losing...

Maybe if you didn't... yes, you do, don't even try to lie, I've got proof... frackin' harem...

Don't start... this little scam you're running with your strays... if one word got back... secrets to be kept on both sides...

Just go there... I dare you to go there and find out...

Maybe I've already gone there...

You're bluffing...

Don't know a thing about... could be harboring...

Don't be ridiculous... she never leaves...

Embeds in...

No... how would that help your precious quota... because that's where this is headed, isn't it... try to deny it...

Why shouldn't it head that way... we need success... she's...

Then you'd best forget the embeds... and remember—I'm family and you're not...

Family? Is that what you still think? Chained up here on this island...

Later, after calm has settled, alone with Angel, Promise scowls when she hears his footsteps echo in the entryway followed by a slam of a door, but she spills nothing.

Now, Angel steps back from the lilacs and moves on, steadily making her way to the farthest edge of the property, where the lawn curves and the shrubs follow a drop-off down to a shallow, rock-strewn gully that guides rainwater to the lake. Moving amongst the trees gives her the twitches, makes her bowels writhe, but she breathes deep and holds the air in her lungs before letting it go again.

Unbidden, memories come, but for once, they are not filled with the menacing black-clad forms of a brute squad. Instead, she remembers the feel of Lark's velvet cheek against hers. Of Kuba's resolute hand gripping hers in between their thrumming hearts. Of Word's calloused palm against the skin of her back. The unexpected smoothness of his scar as her fingers traced its path.

What can drive out fear? This and this and this and this.

The wooden shed, in excellent condition and with a recent coat of paint, has an old-school padlock to secure it. Promise laughed when she gave Angel the number code.

"As if there's anyone around who'd want to steal this stuff. But Flint insists."

Angel fishes the miniflash from her pocket, focuses its pinpoint of light on the lock, and fingers the digits of the code. The lock slides up and, with a quick slip of the hasp, the door swings open easily and silently. The miniflash lights her way to the wheelbarrow upturned in the far corner, as secure a hiding spot as any.

If there's mulching to do, I'll be the one doing it.

A comical scene plays in the theatre of her mind. Promise, in her finery, puttering around, wielding a silver-plated trowel, sprinkling wood chips; Flint trailing behind with a glass of iced tea and a tiny towel to wipe the minuscule beads of perspiration from her brow. The kept and her keeper? The finger and the string wrapped round it? Yet a darkness lurks at the edge of the farce, a sense that some tragedy bubbles under the surface.

The backpacks fill the cavity formed by the wheelbarrow's tub. Angel is about to pull a folded tarp into the gap around the rim when she pauses, her eyes catching the glint of a zipper. Her fingers are drawn to pull it open, to seek the newest memento inside, the most fragile addition to her collection. She eases it out, reads the printed text and the handwritten words below.

Where the Night Prophet leads there I shall follow

Word was nowhere to be found before she'd slipped from

the safe house that morning. He was not in his usual place at the breakfast table. Path had mumbled something about errands as he slurped his tea standing at the kitchen sink. Maybe it was for the better. Maybe it would have been awkward. But the words on the page give the lie to that notion. Yet, maybe, even for a wordsmith, especially for a wordsmith, some things are easier to write than to speak.

Angel tucks the paper into the backpack and pulls the zipper closed, the sound of resolve in its brief, sharp hiss. She settles the tarp in the gap and flicks off the miniflash before peeking around the shed door. Nothing but the tree limbs moving in the damp breeze. She strides toward the house, her pace brisk as the evening mist hardens into raindrops. Brisk, but not hurried. Not with a haste that would provoke suspicion that she has a reason to put some distance between herself and the shed. She heads toward the door to the kitchen, stepping onto the flagstone patio, skirting the architectural chairs carefully arranged around the brick fire pit.

"Doing a little night gardening?"

The vox snags her like a thorn on a barberry bush. She freezes and turns to face Flint, who slouches in one of the low slung armchairs, half his face lit by the light spilling from inside the house, the other doused in shadow. A plop of rain lands on her forehead and trickles down to the bridge of her nose, where it follows the curve and seeps into the corner of her eye. She blinks it away.

"Left the pruning shears out. Didn't want 'em to rust."

Flint shifts. Uncrosses his long legs. "Ah, yeah, I'm not a master gardener like you. Or even an amateur one like my pop, who liked to futz around the yard with the hedge clippers back home in Erie. But I'm keen to learn because Promise keeps harping on me to take up a new hobby. What needs pruning this time of year?"

Angel hesitates, unsure if the trail of wet down her temple is drizzle from the sky or her own sweat. She brushes it away with her sleeve. "Forsythias are done blossoming. Best to cut 'em back now. Bloom on old wood."

"Huh. Those are the yellow ones, yeah? Thought I saw you working them yesterday."

Stop. Breathe. Focus. Think. See. See the vase in the great room, spilling over with pompoms of pink and fuchsia.

"Yes. Today I cut some peonies to bring in the house—"

"Along with the damn ants," grouses Flint. "I don't like peonies in the house. And I don't give a damn whether Promise wants them inside. Throw them away."

Angel nods, turns to make her way to the door. His vox arrests her again.

"Tell me, master gardener, if I were to go to the shed and touch those clippers, feel 'em up, would they be wet?"

Angel doesn't turn to look at him, but shakes her head. "No, I dried them off."

And then he's looming behind her, grinding up against her, thrusting his hand under her hoodie, strafing the skin of her neck with his teeth, hard and slick with spit, his breath reeking of garlic and oblivion and reckless disregard.

"But you are, aren'tcha? Wet."

"Jel? You out there? Frack all, it's raining. What *are* you doing?"

Promise is just a silhouetted body leaning out the great room's entry door at the far end of the patio. Before the exterior lanterns flicker on, Flint's brutal shove sends Angel stumbling into the low wall of the fire pit. Her knee explodes with a crack of pain.

"Just putting away the shears," she gasps through gritted teeth.

In the sudden light, Promise surveys the scene with the exasperated look of a mother whose children keep doing the very same things she's warned them about repeatedly. "Frack, Flint, this one's a wildling, a nature girl, but what's your excuse? Haven't you the sense Galt presumes you have to come in out of the rain?" She huffs an exaggerated breathy sigh. The lanterns go dark again. "Jel, Lark wants to say goodnight. Your motherly presence is required."

When Angel follows her inside, Promise slams the door behind them and flips the deadbolt. "Let him come in whatever way he went out." She gives Angel's shoulder a gentle push. "Go on, mama. And next time, you'll have to figure out how to thwart him on your own. Don't expect me to be your savior."

35

Kate

The nerve center of Genesis I is surprisingly nondescript. The cave where Flint lurks for most of the day and sometimes into the evening is just a squat gray block punctured by a single window and a steel door, tucked amidst a stand of pines. A monster's lair cloaked in the utilitarian garb of a lowly worker bee. Black and silver antennae protrude from its flat roof. A single security eye is mounted beside the door, although Angel reckons there may be others more carefully hidden around the facade or in the trees. Or perhaps not. Perhaps the lack of heavy surveillance is just another example of Corporate complacency. Another chink in the armor.

The building sits a short walk down the path from the Frazier manse, situated just ahead of the bend that curves toward the first ova dormitory. Angel suspects this is where the 'tronic boards and communications center are located. Where the circuits that control the perimeter lights and the ovas' monitoring ankle bands are housed. A place she must access for the op to have any chance of success. A place she must breach for the op to even begin.

But in the warming, lengthening days of May, Promise has a lengthening list of chores to keep Angel's every waking moment occupied and her hands busy. There's the garden to sow, the stretching-to-forever windows to wash, an exercise station and climbing gym to construct for Lark's amusement, with swings to supplant the memory of those at the park where she rose high in the sky, squealing in delight after a push from Kuba's strong arms.

Flint pretends to ignore Angel's presence on the rare instances they happen to occupy the same room or pass on the grounds, but she senses the furtive shift of his eyes under his lowered gaze, knows it's not just her imagination that a covetous glint sparks in them. Or that his body gives off the reek of desperation.

He doesn't want me, not for himself. Not really. He's measuring me for a modemant and an ankle band. I'm a proven breeder.

The thought hits her with a wave of nausea, the acid burn of vomit at the back of her throat. She swallows it back, breathes deeply through her nose, pictures the burner in its backpack, the now fully-loaded burner waiting, waiting for her caress. Lets the breath flow out of her mouth in a low whistle. Realizes this is a fem's response to the unthinkable. Not the one she needs. She needs the guevara's response. That response is to roll the unthinkable around in the dark corners of her brain. To study it from all its ugly sides. To contemplate how to turn that ugly, unthinkable thought to her advantage.

A weakness identified. A vulnerability. A chink in the armor. A chink in the man. In the facility. And, ultimately, in Galt.

Just another reason the op must succeed.

On yet another morning with the sky swathed in leaden clouds that threaten rain, Angel is in the yard, working on the play set before the deluge begins. She's building the deck of its treehouse, laying out the slats with precision, Serafina's "measure twice, cut once" mantra echoing in her mind. As she drills pilot holes and tightens screws, she ponders Promise's ability to acquire so many child-related items, items normally restricted for purchase only by parentals, and, for the most part, bushwa parentals. If a bee child had a swing set, it was guaranteed to be home-made from scavenged material. An old slab of sanded wood or a worn-out transport tire hanging from a tree branch on lengths of rope. Did Promise manage it all through the down-low market? A market where it was rumored that just about anything could be had for a price. A construction kit of this size and quality wasn't something you'd find knocking around a Bartertown. Angel's mind is puzzling this mystery like she's wandering a corn maze, heading down paths, running up against dead-ends of towering stalks, when an ova rounds the corner of the manse and slinks across the terrace and up the stone steps to the kitchen door. The bottom hems of her legskins are stained dark from where she's tramped through the tall, damp grass. Under her tunic, her belly is as flat as the boards of the deck. If the ova notices Angel, she gives no sign, just stands facing the door, shoulders hunched, a touch of the supplicant in her posture. When the door opens, she slips in. In the time it takes for Angel to add a couple of slats to the platform, the ova exits the way she came.

The next afternoon, as Angel works on an A-frame support for swings, out the corner of her eye she sees another ova rounding the corner. The veil makes it impossible to tell, but judging by the height, the slope of the shoulders, and the distinct slinking gait, Angel suspects it is the ova who visited the previous day. The routine is the same, too. She spends maybe ten minutes in the house and then slips out. It happens again on the third day, as Angel is erecting the ladder to the treehouse, and yet again on the fourth, as she tightens bolts to secure the curving green plastiwood slide to the treehouse platform.

This time, as soon as the kitchen door closes behind the ova's back, the clouds let loose with stinging pellets of rain and nature provides Angel with the perfect excuse to enter the manse. She makes a dash across the already sodden lawn, her work boots squelching through the puddles. Mounts the slick stone steps two at a time, then swerves down the path to the door and bursts through it, without a pause to reconsider. Stands panting on the threshold, dripping rainwater.

The ova is poised at the steel counter, her back to the door, but Angel can see that the front of her modemant is thrown back across the top of her head. Promise stands in front of her, a large red mug clasped in her tapering fingers. She blinks, a rapid fluttering of her eyelashes, then draws her lips into a quizzical smile and gives that little twist of her neck that she does when she wants to shrug off whatever emotion has seized her in the moment and, instead, drape herself in the mantle of the emotion she prefers others to see.

In two ticks of the timekeep Promise settles in. "Well, aren't you a mess," she chides, giving Angel a once-over intended to be withering, as she presses the mug into the ova's hands. "Not exactly fit for introductions, but then, even with a glamover and a gown, no one would mistake you for Chanel, would they? Kate, meet Jel. Jel, this is Kate."

The ova turns. From her smaller stature, Angel guesses she's a Dorm Two. Her eyes are dark and wide, fixed in a stare. Something in her taut, heart-shaped face hints at fear lurking just under the skin.

"Go on, dearie, don't let it get cold," Promise urges.

The ova brings the mug to her thin, pale lips and sips obediently.

"It's Angel. My name's Angel."

"Well, not really," Promise interjects in a singsong lilt. "Not in the Corporate records. We could just call you No-Name, if we wanted. So Jel is just as good, when you get down to it, right? But K8579?" she continues, without pausing for a response. "That's no name for a fem. And such a pretty one, at that."

A blush colors the ova's round cheeks. Angel can't quite place her age. Older than herself, maybe—but not by much. Definitely younger than Promise. But she can sense the aura of dread that surrounds the fem, that veils her as completely as a modemant.

"But we're all good with nicknames—pet names—here, yes?" Promise smiles. "I confess, my number just doesn't lend itself to one. 12386. I mean, really, what can you make of that? Itoo? I think not."

The ova takes another swallow from the mug, a larger gulp this time.

"Jel, can I brew you a cup?" Promise coos, nodding toward the mug. "However, I would suggest chamomile for you. Well-known for its calming properties."

"No, thank you. I'll just get a glass of water." As Angel passes the ova on her way to the sink, she gets a whiff of the tea in the mug. There's a hint of mint and an underlying medicinal scent, astringent but not unpleasant.

The ova drinks up. In the time it takes Angel to reach for a tumbler and fill it from the tap, the fem downs two more large swigs and hands the mug back to Promise. She nods and sidles back to the door, hesitating just a moment to scan the rain and the grounds before slipping through and drawing it closed behind her.

Not a word. Not a sound beyond the gurgle of her swallow. Even her feet in their clogs were silent as she crossed the tile floor. Barely more than a ghost.

"Poor thing, she'll be soaked by the time she gets back to the dorm. I should have loaned her my umbrella. Oh well, plenty of skins and modemants to choose from." Promise tosses the muddy dregs of the tea into the sink and rinses the mug with a gush of water. She glances out the window. "Even through a downpour, I can see that's a fine, sturdy play set. Think of how much fun Lark will have when it's finally finished. And you can take pride that it was built by your very own rugged hands."

Angel ignores the dig. In her head she's repeating the embed code that Promise rattled off—12386—12386—12386—committing it to memory, sensing it might be of use some time, some place in the future. She trudges off to change into dry clothes before Lark wakes from her nap. Shrugs off her t-shirt like she shrugs off Promise's not-so-veiled insults. Just another change of the bruja's seasons. The autumn chill settling in again.

36

Tea and Sympathy

THE NEXT DAY, HOWEVER, Promise's mood is as warm and summery as the sun that finally breaks through the slab of clouds. When construction is complete, she's the one who takes Lark's hand and introduces her to the playset's delights, while Angel drags a sleeve across her forehead to mop up the sweat from her exertions. The frolic is only interrupted when the child grows cranky, signaling her need for a snack and a nap. Then Angel is tasked with sanding areas of wood that Promise regards as splinter hazards.

"She doesn't have your calloused hands," she says, lifting Lark onto her hip and carrying her into the house.

Neither do you.

But Angel dutifully rubs the sandpaper over the boards until they are smooth as butter. She's wiping away the wood dust with a tack cloth when another ova comes around the corner of the manse. Even with the modemant concealing the face, Angel can tell from the height, broad frame, and long legs that she's not the one called Kate. This one is a Dorm Four.

Goliath breeder.

Revulsion writhes through Angel's body like a worm unearthed in new-turned soil. Hatred writhes there with it.

Birther of evil.

No. It's not her fault. She's only—what did Path say?—a vessel of reproduction.

Angel can't imagine that this fem—that any of the ovas—would choose the life of a goliath for her son. A life intended to instill fear and obedience. A life steeped in brutality. For that matter, would an ova choose any of the other lives prescribed by Galt's bureaucrats? By the needs of the Protectorate.

No, by the needs and desires of the—who did Promise say made these decisions—some committee?

Under the modemant, the ova appears to turn her head toward the play set, where Angel stares out from under the tree-house platform, the tack cloth wadded up in her gloved hand. The ova hesitates, just a beat, then recovers her stride. For one crazy moment, Angel is seized by the impulse to run over, tear off that ridiculous veil, and—

And what? Ply her with questions? Drag her to the dinghy and ferry her to freedom? She's got the frackin' ankle bracelet. There's no tearing that off. No, no tearing it off. No cutting it, either.

No sharp implements, Promise had said.

Not in the dorms. But here, here there are knives and scissors. Pruning shears.

Instead of bursting into the kitchen again, Angel inches up alongside the door, where she can peer through its window. The scene and the props, the characters and the actions are the same: the ova at the counter, a red mug in her hands, sipping and swallowing, sipping again, and Promise directing it all with a small curve at her lips and a hint of satisfaction lighting her eyes.

When the ova starts to turn, Angel ducks and scurries across the terrace, back down to the play set where she gathers up the sandpaper and tack cloth. She keeps her back turned when she hears the door open and close, but cranes her neck in time to see the ova disappear around the corner of the manse.

"How's it going?"

Promise's vox startles Angel. She drops the sandpaper and

has to steady herself against the frame of the play set.

"You're as flittery as one of these gnats," Promise teases, swatting at the swarm hovering in her face.

"All done." Angel bends to retrieve the scattered sandpaper. She knows she should keep things zipped, but her mouth opens against her will and she feels the words slide out. "Do the ovas stop by a lot?"

Promise blinks, eyelashes fluttering. "Oh, well, they stop by sometimes. When they need someone to talk to. Someone who'll listen." She smiles, smoothing the hair back from her face and tightening the band of her ponytail before continuing. "A mother, a sister, a shoulder to cry on. Hormones and all that."

Angel fingers the sandpaper as she sorts it by gauge. The extremely coarse, pebbled surface of the #60 grit. The rough but tolerable texture of the #100. The barely ticklish surface of the #220. Different gauges for different purposes. Not unlike the precise phrasing of questions and the tone of her vox when she's dealing with the bruja. What she wants to ask—*do they actually think of you that way?*—and what comes out are of two entirely different grits.

"That's kind of you."

Promise smiles. "Yes. Yes, it is." She runs a palm over the sanded boards. "Much better," she chirps, then turns on her heel and strides back to the manse.

After Lark awakens, refreshed and cheerful, Promise suggests the three of them take one of their afternoon bike rides, but Angel begs off. There's mulch to spread while the sun shines. But once the two are off on their trek, instead of dragging a shovel through the mound of wood chips piled in the side yard, she's in the kitchen, opening and closing cabinet doors, feeling her anxiety mount with each snip and snap of the timekeep, as if its cold eye is capturing her every movement, until she finally finds herself face to face with Promise's stash of metal tea canisters neatly labeled in her tight, precise script.

The dried leaves in each tin give off unique scents. The citrus tang of spicebush. The aroma of anise, delicate in the goldenrod, stronger from the hyssop. The sweet warmth of bedstraw, the bruised apple scent of chamomile. The pungent odor of peppermint and gumweed. The savory smell of bee balm. The same scents had wafted from Serafina's pantry. Herbal remedies to soothe a sore throat, to ease an upset stomach, to calm frazzled nerves and tense muscles. But for Serafina, a meme, a fem of the earth, knowing about these nature-made remedies was part of her life's work. That's not who Promise is. So how did she gather this knowledge?

Angel's eyes are drawn to the bright red mugs that line the shelf above the canisters. They aren't the ones from which Promise sips her brew or Flint swills his chicory coffee that makes the kitchen smell of the woods. Those are white, more refined, matching the ribbed pattern of the white porcelain dinner plates.

Well, of course, she wouldn't let them drink from something that her own lips touch.

Angel is about to close the cabinet when her eyes catch a glint of silver just beyond the curve of the last mug. She pushes the cup aside to reveal another canister. This one lacks a fancy label. The ground bits inside resemble dried sod mixed with minuscule flecks of purple, perhaps the remnants of flower petals. She shakes a tiny portion into her palm. It spills out in a loose puff of dust and the scent of dried grasses. An odor of autumn and the change of seasons. She swirls her finger in a spiral through the leaves, puts a pinch on her tongue and savors it. Spearmint and hints of sage.

Why no label? Is it just an extra supply of the peppermint variety? No, the flavor and scent are slightly different. Earthier.

The timekeep reminds her to keep moving. She takes a

blue and white striped dishtowel from the drawer, an older one, stained and faded from use, and spreads it on the counter. She piles a tiny heap of the tea onto the center of the towel and then folds it over and over again into a small, neat, square packet.

On her next trip to the mainland, she'll find someone who can discern the ingredients. Perhaps one of the oilers, who have all manner of tinctures, teas, powders, and essential oils, although there would be risk involved in making an inquiry there. If the substance is not approved by Galt, if it's something prohibited, forbidden, she isn't sure she could trust the oilers to not report this. The shopkeep is a stout man who plays the jovial glad hander with most of his customers but whose eyes narrow into slits whenever Angel sets foot in the place, especially if she's toting Lark, presenting a heightened risk of breakage in the midst of all those pretty, fragile bottles that whisper come hither to curious fingers. The pillowy fem, presumably his wife, predictably has a soft spot for the child, but Angel knows the real reason that she hovers in close proximity to wherever Angel wanders in the small shop, her plump lips, the color of raw liver, fixed in a faux solicitous smile.

The fem's suspicions are ridiculous. Angel only ever thieves from Galt.

In her bedroom, she tucks the folded dishtowel under her mattress, where it can remain safely hidden until she sails the dinghy back across the channel to Bayfield.

Promise is kneading bread dough in the kitchen, her hands powdery white as they pound and fold the ball into submissive pliability. Her technique is more aggressive than Kuba's, whose fingers and palms apply a gentle, coaxing pressure. Promise is a slammer, a squasher, as if she's taking out her frustrations on this inanimate object. She glances up when she hears Angel's steps on the tile.

"Garlic twists," she crows. "Been craving them." She has a smudge of flour on her nose and a streak down her temple. When Flint is around and in a rare good mood, he will tease her, calling her Pro-Mess, in reference to the legendary chaos she tends to leave in her wake throughout the kitchen.

Angel nods and starts to idly open cabinets, as if she's unsure of what's inside, although she knows exactly what she's looking for and where it's located. She draws the attention that she seeks.

"Lookin' for somethin' in particular?" Promise drawls, as she often does while cooking, as if she slips into another persona when she slips into her red apron and starts wielding spatulas and measuring cups.

"Tea," Angel drawls in return, mirroring the fem. "In the mood for a sip."

"You know, now that the weather has turned, I should brew up some iced tea. It's all in that cabinet above the juicer," Promise says, vox casual, as if she has absolutely nothing to hide.

Angel peruses the canisters as she did the previous day. Listens to the slap of dough against the cutting board, a sound that falls in with the timekeep's metronome click.

"What's ailing you?" Promise asks, drawling again, like she's some backwoods AgSector healer who'll tend to your aches and pains and sniffles when the medic is overworked and the clinic overrun in virus season. "Herbals are wonderful easers for any number of complaints. For muscle and joint aches, brew yourself a cup of the rose hip. Upset stomach or headaches? I'd prescribe the peppermint."

"Well, no ailment, really, just..." Angel lets herself trail off as she takes down the unlabeled canister and turns to show Promise. "What kind is this?" She twists off the top and peers inside. "This no-name blend."

The bruja flinches. Most definitely she flinches. But immediately covers it up with one of her neck adjustments.

Oh, how you want to hurry around the counter and snatch this out of my hands, but no, I see you counting to ten in your head, forcing that calm smile onto your face.

But the twist of the bruja's lips reveals her discomfort, as does the modulated vox, the drawl tucked away and replaced by a cool, collected tone, well-regulated, reminiscent of the vox that Iris, Angel's old roboteach, used when confronting her pupil's recalcitrant behavior. Promise dusts her hands off on a dishtowel, a mate to the one tucked away under Angel's mattress. She steps over with a casual-but-not-casual swagger, removing the canister from Angel's hands.

"This is reserved for the ovas. Unless you have the same ailment as they."

Angel regards her without question or comment.

Fill in the silence, bruja.

Promise waits a beat, then shifts on her feet and tightens the lid back on the tin.

"Integrity of the womb." She places the canister back on the shelf with the red mugs but doesn't bother to push it behind them. "You've never lost a baby, I presume. You safely delivered a child. Even if you didn't really want her." Promise pats the air as if smoothing out a wrinkle in their conversation. "At least, in the beginning."

The bruja fixes Angel with a look both brazen and shy. A look that says *I do know your deepest secrets, but it's all right. Because they are not just your secrets. They are the secrets of every fem who's ever walked this earth. You want to say 'when I saw her, that little face, things changed.' But...*

"Even now it's a struggle, isn't it?" Promise continues in that calm vox. "I see the ambivalence—not necessarily on your face—but your body doesn't lie." Promise lifts the canister labeled chamomile. "You don't sleep well. This I know. You are an anxious thing, like a deer with the scent of wolves up in her nose. You wake and toss and turn and wander in the night. So this is the one I recommend for you."

Teeg sniffs the clump of herbs, dips her pinkie into it, daubs the leaves that cling to it onto her tongue, just as Angel had done. Wrinkles her broad-tipped nose.

"What did the bruja say this was for? Integrity of the womb?" She spits into the sink and takes a sip of water, swishing it around her mouth before spitting again. "Well, I guess it depends on what she means by 'integrity.' Maybe from a certain point of view."

"What do you mean?" Angel is confused by Teeg's unusual obfuscation, her language veering here and there instead of coming at her straight. "What is this stuff?"

She stares at the powdery residue in the center of the unfolded dishtowel. As she had piloted the dinghy across the channel, the packet secreted in the waistband of her cargoes, she had hoped Teeg would be at the safe house, having ruled out taking the tea to the oilers. Too much uncertainty. The risk of exposure. She had counted on Teeg's presence, hoping that, if Teeg didn't have a clue, then perhaps Nanda would know or could guide the packet to an herbalist who could decipher the contents and its use.

Angel looks down into the muddy golden concoction that's been steeping in a mug for several minutes. She stirs it with a spoon, watching the specks swirl and stick to the sides of the cup.

"What is this stuff?" she asks again.

"I'm pretty sure it's pennyroyal with some mugwort mixed in."

Angel sniffs the liquid. It smells minty and medicinal, just like it had tasted. She shrugs. "So? Is that helpful when a fem's carrying a child?"

Teeg shakes her head. "No. Just the opposite. These are herbs that—if taken at a certain time, and in a certain form and amount—can cause a fem to miscarry."

"To lose a baby?"

Silence sits like a gaping hole in the road waiting for a sweep to come by and fill it.

But that makes no sense.

Angel's not sure she's said that out loud. She raises her eyes to meet Teeg's, which are bright with speculation. And Angel is not sure if Teeg actually utters the next few words or if she just imagines her saying them. Or if they are coming from her own mind, her own mouth.

Oh, it makes perfect sense. From a certain point of view.

37

Words on the Wind

WHAT ARE YOU WAITING FOR?

The bullet train to carry you toward your severance adventure? Wake up. That way lies only madness and death. And you—you who don't have a date with the train programmed into your digital record—you who are allowed to remain in the Protectorate until you pass in the way that all living things should pass. What are you waiting for?

What is your precious life, really? When you are alone, curled in your bed, enduring the longest nights in winter's depth, or when you hunch upon your terrace and feel the summer twilight settle in like an ache in your bones and ponder how you've wasted the longest day, do you feel your life shrinking? Do you notice how the walls and fences built to keep the others out are really closing in all around you? And does a thought worm its way into your brain? A thought that those walls and fences are really just a cage to trammel your spirit? To tame the wild and the free into a pack of whining dogs beat down by their masters? Is that who you are? A nameless cur begging for scraps from the master's table?

We all have a date with the train. It's inevitable. There is—in the end—no choice but to board it. But you do have a choice—we all have a choice—in how we spend our time before we take that final ride. Before we step foot on the platform at the station.

Will you go sedated? Numbed by the oblivion that Galt pours down your throat or the lethe juice that it injects into your veins? Or will you kick and scream and bite and scratch, your blood mingling with the blood of your oppressors, until the earth is soaked in it. Until the rivers run red with it. Until the world is remade. Until we all are born free.

So sayeth the Night Prophet.

Words travel. On the wind. Or so it seems. Through the night air, carried along with the scent of wild rain and the wet exuberance of pine needles, their bracing odor filling the nose as the words fill the mind. Words filtered through battered 'tronic radios and squat black feedcoms and slender stream bars mounted under screens and the earbuds of those assigned to work through the night. Many who hear the message those words convey nod in agreement. This and this and this is true. Truth, all. And many discern that to make this truth come to pass will require more than just a wish to make it so. More than just an ache to see it come to fruition. More than just words.

For the man who sits as the words he's scribbled on scraps of cardboard are given life, are sent into the world on breath that passes warm across his cheek, it is a communion. For as she speaks, the words change, morphing from his thoughts to hers, from her thoughts to theirs. A melding, but a fragile one. The Night Prophet has warned that the mission must always be first in their minds, has said that things must not change between them, even though things have already changed.

For one young fem who listens, curled in the cabin of a boat, out of the elements but feeling them in every sway and bob of the craft as the waves ripple, the odors of fish and biofuel seeping up from the deck, the words that crackle from the ancient, battery-powered 'tronic are a match to light the tinder of resentments stockpiled in her soul. Her rage is a living thing, like a flame growing, fluttering, flickering, almost dancing as it feeds on dry wood. She has already lost all, knows the bitter taste that loss leaves in the mouth. A taste that can't be washed away by any sweetness that comes after. A taste that lingers, tainting every mouthful of the future.

Another fem, swathed in the luxury of an overabundance of places to sit or recline but finding comfort in none, listens as the words spew from a feedcom discreetly tucked on a shelf, its ugliness hidden behind a chunk of agate. For her, the words add a layer of frost to her outer shell, while inside she seethes. Who would dare? To think, to write, to speak in this way? Where's the gratitude? The loyalty? Something else creeps in and mingles with that outrage, a feeling that she will not give a name, but a feeling that devolves into a single word. How? How? How?

For a third fem, idly wandering her manse, running her hands over all her fine things, reveling in the smooth and the soft, the slick and the sleek surfaces under her fingertips, something she does when she cannot sleep, a condition that plagues her often, the vox barely registers at first. She purposely keeps the volume on the feedstream low. Would switch it off altogether, but that would trigger a signal and call down unwanted attention and really, it's just as easy to let it flow and ignore it. But in this midnight hour, in a silent house, with just the wind whispering around the gutters and eaves, the burble is annoyingly apparent. Who is talking now, at this time of night? A nudge of the control slider brings the vox to the surface.

It is soaked in threat and doused in apocalypse. Words and phrases that might gush from a hormone-addled fem in need of an embed adjustment and a dose of Tranquille. Yet compelling, the words almost hypnotic. Particularly to those prone to resentments and yearnings for some vague, amorphous better. But who wasn't, really? She could easily pour herself a glass of Euphoria, Vintage 79, and listen to this all night long. It's the vox, all smoke and velvet, more than the message.

The vox. A vox at once familiar and unknown. Perhaps and perhaps not. That vox. That particular vox.

Hope comes on the widespread wings of the soaring hawk. It comes on the wind that blows warm from the south or brisk from the north. It comes in the passage of the moon from sliver of light to golden orb that humbles the darkest sky. It comes on the arc of the sun that bleeds pink and gold as it pierces the horizon in the east. It comes in the cry of a newborn. In the laughter of a child. In the thrum of the blood in your veins. Hear it. See it. Feel it.

So sayeth the Night Prophet.

38

In the Nerve Center

SHE STALKS HIM, channeling the she-wolf as she has done before. Slinking through the stands of lush evergreens, the grays of her t-shirt and cargo pants, like the fur of the wolf, a perfect camouflage amidst the olives and sages of the pine needles. Precise in the placement of her feet, one in front of the other. Wondering if it's just her imagination or if she can truly detect the brisk scent of his favored soap in the morning breeze.

The 'tronic fob gets him through the steel door. She's been close enough to see the keypad, under the pretense of inquiring about his dinner preferences, knowing she'd be caught square in the security eye. He hadn't bothered to come to the door, just muttered that he didn't care, his vox fractured and robotic through the commspeaker. Throughout her surveillance, he has never paused to punch in numbers on that keypad. Just steps up, turns the handle and pushes the door open. Lets it swing shut behind him.

She's also learned that if the fob is inside the building, the door will open from the outside unless the occupant has manually turned a deadbolt, a fact she discovered while delivering Flint his lunch. She'd stood holding the basket with its sandwich and tray of fruit and cheese in one hand, rapping hesitantly on the door with the other, until Flint had finally appeared, sputtering that he was on a conference feed and why hadn't she just come in and put the damn food down and left again without this needless fuss.

Now the she-wolf approaches the building with caution, circling wide, keeping the cover of the trees between her and her quarry. Keeping out of view of the 'tronic eye and the building's single window. She'd considered donning the green tunic and modemant veil stolen from the Dorm One laundry room, but knows that if she's caught wearing it, the entire op will be blown to bits. Best save it for another time. So she hunkers down and squat-shuffles toward the corner of the nerve center, eyeballing the window's distance from the ground. Does she have the length to peer inside? And if she does, will fortune favor her with the placement of the equipment and Flint's chair and desk? Will he be turned away from the pane of glass? Or towards it?

Her route from the corner to the window frame is a journey travelled in agonizing inches. Back pressed to the concrete, she feels its rough caress on her skin through the thin fabric of her t-shirt. The coarse surface claws and catches the fibers, as if to hinder her progress. As if to warn: that's not the way you want to go. As if to say: beware.

Fortune favors the bold.

Obeying Path's adage, ignoring the imagined warning, Angel moves on, pressing her cheek against the edge of the window frame and inching forward until she can peer through the thick pane, which she suspects isn't glass, but an unbreakable hybrid like the kind used to prevent smash-n-grabs at the Galt-Mart. Flint hunches in a mesh task chair in front of a checkerboard of screens, some glowing green, some blue. They cast an ill light across his skin, lending it the tinge of nausea. His face, in profile, has a slack jaw, an air of disengagement. His fingers tap here and there on the glass surfaces, but without a sense of urgency. Their plodding but rhythmic tempo suggests muscle memory is at play. He's going through the motions. But then his body swings to the right, twisting in the chair, and Angel has to duck, shrinking back against the facade.

Did his eye catch that sudden, retreating movement? Would he rise and walk to the window to peer out? Go so far as to come outside to investigate? Should she make a dash now? Retreat to the cover of the evergreens? Or should she risk staying put? Bet it all on the she-wolf? On her lightning reflexes rather than his?

A breath. Then another. Shallow, silent—amazingly silent, considering how she imagines her heart's wild thumping is reverberating off the building's wall and the trunks of the surrounding trees. But the grim tattoo plays for her alone, while the she-wolf attunes to other sounds around her. The scree of a blue jay off to the right. The shuddering whisper of pine needles off to the left. The soft slap of waves against rocks in the distance. But no scuffle or crunch in the dead leaves clustered around the building's foundation, leftovers from autumn, brown and curled and crisp.

She waits. Stares at the rotting trunk of a fallen pine, its innards eaten away by time and enterprising insects. Envisions these tiny animals, living in the rotting wood, feeding on it. Notes the patches of moss and lichen, draped like a coat of green fur across the top. Imagines the wood lice and centipedes and beetles that would greet her on its underside if she were daring enough to roll it over. Shudders, her childhood fears still clinging. Puts those thoughts aside. And waits. Ticking off the seconds in her head, using the incantation from her childhood.

One Mississippi. Two Mississippi. Three Mississippi.

A memory seeps into her silent count. Asking Eben what Mississippi meant. Him dragging the old biblio, the atlas, out of its hidey-hole in the floor. Revealing its existence. Pointing out the long blue squiggle squirming its way down the green landmass, his long finger tapping the river that formed one of the Protectorate's borders, now called the West River.

Ten Mississippi. Eleven...

When she reaches her approximation of a minute, she eases her body upright and peers through the window. Flint is swiveled around so that all Angel can see is the back of his head above the chair. Her eyes scan the corners of the interior, noting the apparent lack of security eyes, aside from the one on the exterior. They may be hidden. But it's also possible that this is another chink in the armor. In the end, this spying will be pointless if she doesn't get inside. The fact that she can see the screens and the desk set-up and the emptiness of the room beyond and the fortuitous lack of surveillance will mean nothing if she doesn't know what to do when she's standing in front of them. She has to get inside.

The fob. The fob. The fob.

The words ricochet off the confines of her mind. The questions follow. Where does Flint keep it? How can she spirit it away for an hour or two? Does he take it with him when he journeys to the Hive or leave it behind? Does the bruja have access to this inner sanctum? Promise never talks about it. Wouldn't that be something she'd brag about? Something she'd dangle in front of Angel—or let slip accidentally on purpose.

The fob. The whole op might rest on that small handful of 'tronic power.

In the end, it falls into her hands through the most mundane of actions—the tedious act of checking his pants pockets before tossing them into the washing machine. Promise has warned her to be meticulous. Flint is notorious for leaving items in his pockets. Wadded up tissues. Ear buds. Marks-alls which then bleed black ink onto his white shirts and khaki pants. This morning, it's yet another balled up tissue—and the nerve center fob.

Angel takes only the briefest of moments to marvel at how the chunk of black metal fits perfectly in her palm before she secrets it away in her hip pocket. It's a Thursday morning and Flint has taken the bowrider to Bayfield for his hair cut and grooming ritual. As usual, Promise has accompanied him and taken Lark as well, with promises of sweets after a visit to the seamstress to select fabrics and take measurements for new clothes for the child's growing body. No drab GaltMart apparel for LaLa.

For Promise it's a moment to pretend that she and Flint and Lark are a happy, thriving bushwa family; for Angel, it's a moment to seize and she grabs it with gusto, slipping into the stolen tunic and modemant, barely able to resist breaking into a run on the path to the nerve center. The tunic isn't much different from the yellow one she wore while posing as an androg in Illiana. But the veil, though featherweight and silky smooth, feels like a cage. When the fabric brushes her cheek, her hand moves to swat it, to sweep it back like she sweeps her hair back into a tight braid. The slit fences her vision into a slim rectangle, radically reducing her ability to scan the periphery.

Frackin' bruja and her innovations. Suck it up, if the ovas can tolerate this three hundred sixty five, you can handle it for blink time. You may have only seen two security eyes, but you can't be sure the nerve center isn't like a spider, with multiple eyes bugging out to catch you on their retinas.

She doesn't even have to take the fob from her pocket. Crab-stepping along the outer wall to avoid the gaze of the security eye, she sidles up to the door, and as soon as she grasps the door handle and pushes down she hears the subtle click of a bolt tumbling. With a shove of her shoulder, the door swings open and she slips inside.

A hint of Flint's cologne greets her, along with the sharpish scent of crushed pine needles. The pleasant, warm odor of bergamot. A dry smell of 'tronics. A vague hum and a sense of vibration. The feedcom eye bulges from a gooseneck stand that can bend and twist in all directions. Fearing a motion sensor, before she steps in front of the screens she carefully turns the eye, bending it down and away from the desk. The screens are black in sleep mode, but brighten to blue as she taps her index finger on the corners.

Her heart drops. In the middle of each screen is a red touch sensor icon.

Of course. Biometrics.

Flint's digit print unlocks the system. Perhaps it even requires a scan of his eye or face. No labels or markings indicate which facility system—lights, comms, monitoring, security—is controlled by each of the five screens. She should have realized that it all seemed too easy. And when has anything ever been easy?

Dead end.

Her remark to Path echoes through her disappointment.

When I smash those lights and ferry every last one of her sisters across the water...

A stark image sweeps in. Her scaling the light platforms, a rock clutched in her fist. Frustration tempts her to smash things now, and she struggles to keep her clenched fists at her sides, grappling with her emotions as another vox worms its way into her brain, a vox that usually visits her in the dark, taking her to dark places.

You don't have to do this. These fems are nothing to you. You can take Lark and go. Or just... go.

Shakes her head, a conscious physical act to shake loose the thought, to drive it out and send it crashing down to the place where she sends all unwelcome thoughts, the dark place where the dark vox lives, a place she tries to keep locked as tight as these screens.

You can leave this unfinished. The dinghy. Grab your go bags from the shed and take that little boat that's just waiting for you.

She paces the room, searching for any small, encouraging sign to glom onto. In one corner, there's a ladder chained to the wall and a stream of light flowing in from above, where a roof access hatch with a skylight stamps a patch of blue into the drab gray of the ceiling. A white cloud drifts by. In another corner sits a small red tool chest. Its layers of drawers are mostly empty save for a few screw drivers and wrenches, a small assortment of screws, nuts, and bolts. A hammer.

Oh, how she is tempted to take that in her hand and demol-ish the 'tronic chains that imprison this island. But even in her frustration, she senses that destroying a screen will not take down the system.

Stop. Breathe. Focus. Think.

An outline of a plan takes shape as she surveys the room. The view from any angle involves Flint. Subduing him. Forcing him to unlock the system. To enter the commands to dismantle it. Exceedingly dangerous. Ridiculously dicey. Extremely high probability of failure. But she's got to take him down. The how is not something she wants to think about. Yet. Something she doesn't want to think about alone. Something that requires the advice of others. Teeg. Word.

After carefully bending the feedcom eye back into place, Angel stalks out the door. Throwing caution to the wind, she rips the confining veil from her head and the tunic from her body. Feels the rush of freedom like a freshening breeze on her face. Letting her fury get the better of her, she wads the hated garments into a tight bundle and prepares to heave them into the pines, but some-thing arrests the movement of her arm midway through its arc.

A deep breath, and then another. She tucks the bundle under her arm and steps around the corner of the building, nearly trip-ping over her own feet as she comes face to face with an ova. The startled fem, whose veil is draped back around her shoulders, blinks once, twice, her dark eyes wide. Tension grips Angel's shoulders into an automatic hunch, until she recognizes the gen-tle curve at the ova's lips and a sad kindness settling into the corners of her eyes, once the fem's initial alarm subsides.

Those dark eyes.

"You're Kate," Angel ventures, half question, half statement.

The ova's lashes flutter again, a signal that she's teetering on the edge of flight. "You're Jel—no—Angel. Yeah? The new housekeep at the manse? You were building a play set—" The ova purses her lips, shutting down the rest of her thoughts, stopping the flow of her words like she's closing a spigot. As if she's already spewed too much in those few words and phrases.

Angel nods, forcing a small grin, aiming to put the fem at ease. "Yeah, that's right. I'm the jill—or Jel—of all trades. Doing all for those who can't lift a finger to do for themselves." It's a risk, this criticism, however mild, but it's one she'll take. "You came for a visit with—" Angel hesitates, unsure of how to refer to Promise. Opts for formality and deference. "With Mrs. Frazier." Pauses a beat. "The bestower of nicknames." Another calculated risk.

When the fem's lips loosen into a tiny smile, Angel knows it was a risk worth taking. Yet this feels like approaching a skittish animal. A slow, inching progress. Two steps forward.

"Sipping tea in her kitchen," Angel adds.

The ova's eyes grow wide again and her gaze slants to the side. *Looking for an escape route.*

"She's always trying to foist the chamomile on me. Please!" Angel rolls her eyes. "Give me a mug of roasted dandelion root any day. And twice on Sundays."

No response. Just a flutter of eyelashes in the oval face. As if the fem thinks she can blink away what she does not wish to see. What she's afraid to see.

One step back.

In the past, Angel has lacked the patience to fish. To play the waiting game. As a child, she could never sit still waiting for some slippery creature to take the bait. She'd rather wander the shore, digging up fistfuls of pebbles or tugging out cattails by their slimy roots, squishing her fingers in the sand and mud. But here she is, eye to eye with another slippery creature. Even now she can still feel the twitch of impatience in her fingers, the throb of it traveling from her chest to her toes. The urge to be moving. Chided all through childhood for abandoning her tasks, for leaving her work unfinished. Here is something that cannot be hurried. Nor abandoned. Something worth the time and effort it will take to reel it in.

"Walk here much?" Angel says, believing she already knows the answer.

Why would an ova stray so close to the place that holds the key to her prison cell? Or does she not think of it that way? Is she one of those contented with her lot in life? But the visit with Promise? The tea? Does she know the truth of it? What comfort does she seek when she sips from the red mug?

The ova shakes her head, with a sidelong glance at the nerve center that lurks just beyond the pines. "Not often. It's just a shortcut to the manse."

"She's not home. Went to town. Suspect she won't be back for awhile." Angel shrugs. "She's got the little one along, and they are both quite the consumers. So very attracted to shiny things. Like crows." She grins at the ova, then looks away, feigning deference again. She lets silence hang for a minute, hang and waft and spread like smoke curling from a snuffed candle. Then she ventures a question. "Do you need tea?"

Out of the corner of her eye, Angel can see the ova is flushed, pink spreading from her cheeks to her chin. "It's okay, Kate," she quickly reassures. "I can brew you a cup. Promise taught me. Like I said, I'm her—Jel." She forces a laugh, hoping it sounds authentic.

The ova stands mute. Then nods.

39

Kali

KUBA KNOWS NEXT TO NOTHING about boats. He's fished
the river that bordered the family compound in Illiana from
the side of an ancient rowboat. What he remembers most about
these excursions is the ache they left in his shoulders the morning after. Soreness from struggling to haul in the huge and nasty
silver carp that his mother and grandmother would grind into
all manner of dinner entrees. Soreness from wielding the oars
against the current. Soreness that comes from grunt work. So
he's not sure why he's been included on this trek to the fishing
enclave hunched on the red cliffs above Lake Superior, other
than to provide some added muscle in case negotiations go sour.

What he's learned in the past few weeks would fill a thousand
biblios—or so he thinks—never having actually seen a thousand,
only the couple hundred that his family had stashed away. His
brain feels stretched, expanded to its limits, nearly exploded with
new information, including the revelation that the resistance has
deep roots and a history beyond just the legends of the Handed.
That it stretches back to the earliest days of the Protectorate,
when the Galt Corporation seized control of the Great Lakes in
the aftermath of the collapse of the old Republic. That its origins
go back to this beginning, to when the multitude saw a safe hav-
en but others saw, in the steel fences and the razor-wire and the

promise of security, the seeds of oppression.

Nanda, the wizened walking remnant of the Handed, and Veda, a meme whose farm provides the cell with fresh vegetables and eggs and the occasional place to shelter when the soaking spring storms settle in for days on end, are both patient tellers of tales, letting stories gush out in a way that all his grandmothers, all the fems of his childhood, never did. They might have intermittently let slip a drop or two, but quickly shut down the flow in the face of his questions, always reminding him it was best not to traffic in Corporate ways. He realizes now that in squashing history, in keeping it tucked away inside their own bosoms rather than letting it fly free to him and his brothers and cousins, they were, in fact, behaving in a manner not unlike Galt Corp.

We are our own island.

It was something he recalled Grey-Grey Isa muttering once or twice, with a bitter force, as if saying it could make it so. He was beginning to see that—in a way—the compound was its own Protectorate. Safe, yes, to a degree, but only due to its own level of oppression. And hadn't he been a resister even then? Listening to the renegade Damn Otis voxcasts in the midnight hours, dreaming.

Of what? This particular corner of the Protectorate?

Perhaps—because in a short span of time, he's grown to love this place. Grown to love the hard face of the red cliffs that stand as a bulwark against the angry surges of the lake. Grown to love the angry water itself, its deep mysteries, so different from the calm shallow river that flowed alongside his boyhood home. Grown to love the canopy of trees under which he roams, the towering pines, the balsam firs, the spruce, the gradient of green that colors the forest. Loves the smell of it, the expanse of it that he sucks in with every breath and absorbs through every pore of his skin.

Had he also been dreaming of rambling through the woods with a ragtag cell of insurgents? He hasn't been on a mission or raid yet, though he's sure some have taken place. The number of guevaras squatting in camp ebbs and flows. People appear and disappear and reappear, looking refreshed or worse for wear. He's tried asking BoBeck, but the man is far more tight-lipped about ops than he is about foraging. Kuba wonders if maybe he hasn't yet worked his way into their trust.

But he sees things turn up in camp that weren't there the day before, raid spoils that the guevaras are proud to flaunt. And he's part of the circle as the items go from hand to hand. Several sets of 'tronic-enhanced goggles. *Night vision, my find,* BoBeck had bragged. Burners with laser sights. *Sureshots,* Armor calls them. Lock onto an embed and you can't miss. Ammunition clips. Wilder, a smile finally cracking across his pugnacious face, had strolled in with a late model embed scanner equipped with the ability to read the identifier on a chip. *Come in handy when we're aiming to track a particular quarry,* muses Teeg.

He's listened while the cell hashes out the plan to liberate the breeder facility, the Fathom Op, as the guevaras have taken to calling it. Angel has sussed out the lay of the land, discovering that, in addition to the ferry landing and the private dock at the Frazier manse, three other usable docks are situated around the island. One at the far eastern end at Amnicon Point, another on the southern side of the island at Big Bay, and a third midway along the northern shore. She's plotted them on one of Veda's ancient maps. Rendezvous points.

And here he is now. Finally on what is, for all intents and purposes, a mission. The blood in his veins surges with a 'tronic charge. Though he longs to join the parlay, he follows instructions and hangs back, leaning against the weathered rail fence that separates the gravel transport lot from the dock, while Teeg, Armor, and Fox stroll up to a trio of men clustered near the fishery's overhead door. The building is as weathered as the fence, its corrugated metal siding marked with the wear and tear of life lived alongside Lake Superior, smears of rust dappling its contoured ridges and valleys. The men are weathered, too, a ragged bunch of walking gristle wrapped in drab waffle weave shirts and bright orange chest waders. Having transferred their catch from their boats to the built-in cooler in the back of a transport and shoveled in a top layer of ice, the fisherman have called it a day. They wave to the hauler, pull their green feedcom buds from their ears, and shove them into shirt pockets.

A conversation ensues. Low key at first, distinctly unanimated, primarily one-sided, with the guevaras doing most of the talking, Teeg and Armor tag-teaming their proposition. But a shift occurs. And the fishermen use their bodies to indicate their responses. Hands gesturing, arms folding across chests, heads shaking. Kuba can't quite make out the words, but he's getting the gist nonetheless. They're saying no. And by the way the guevaras' shoulders are sagging, the way their hands are reaching out to pat the air, to settle down whatever they've riled up, Kuba senses they're accepting that response. Accepting defeat.

That can't be right. They can't be giving up so quickly. Seemingly without truly, emphatically, making the case. Without thinking, he finds his feet in motion, striding towards the group.

"Hey," he blurts as he nears the huddle, but his vox barely rises above a mumble.

The guevaras are already turning away, Teeg's frown deepening when she sees him. Armor flicks his hand in dismissal.

"No. Hey!" Kuba repeats, this time in a bark that packs some bite.

Armor nabs Kuba's arm, trying to steer him, but Kuba shakes off the man's grip.

"No? You're sayin' no? Just like that? After what? Not even five minutes of pondering. A cow takes longer to chew her frackin' cud! Probably takes you longer'n that to take your mornin' dump."

Kuba feels Armor's hand heavy on his shoulder, the force of it pulling him back, trying to turn him around. With another shrug and a shuddery shift, he steps free again.

"No, I'm gonna say my piece and they're gonna listen. If they got the guts."

Armor makes yet another grab, but Teeg's hand stays his arm mid-swing. Her look says it all.

Let the boy make a fool of himself.

And then, there he is, in the arena of their hardened gazes, encircled by the walls of their skepticism, withering under the blistering lights of their disbelief.

To be a prophet is to be a vox crying in the wilderness, to be a messiah you must go amongst the people.

If convincing them depended on the volume of his shouts or the passion animating his vox, then they would be convinced beyond any reasonable doubt. Would be as committed to the undertaking, the cause, as he is. But he is not a speechmaker. Neither a prophet nor a messiah. His words tumble and stumble in an inarticulate race to leave his mouth. Falling, falling, falling, if not on deaf ears then on ears that consciously choose not to hear, not to listen, for it seems the louder he talks the less the mens' expressions say, until he's staring at nothing more than inanimate blocks of stone.

"You don't care about living free cuz you're already dead. Inside. You're dead," his last volley uttered in barely more than a whisper.

A beat, then two. Silence.

"It's pointless, Kuba." Teeg's vox is flat, weighted with resignation. "Their boats have trackers."

Kuba's fever of righteous anger melts into a flush of embarrassment, like a preacher abashed, red-faced at the lack of response to his zealot's call.

Until one finally rings out.

"Mine don't."

When he turns to find the source of the booming vox, Kuba's first thought is the absurdity of it to be erupting from such a scrawny body. Draped in faded blue flannel and denim, a sun-bleached cap pulled low over its face, the figure stands, hands on hips, in the doorway to a shed.

"Though I didn't hear nothin' 'bout recompense for time and fuel. Or don't you 'varas reckon on things like that?" The figure doffs the cap to brush a snarl of close-cropped black hair from a wide forehead. A grin splits the heart-shaped face.

"Yeah, thought not. 'Sall 'bout the glory, not the blood and guts," the fem says, more than a touch of mockery in her tone, striding forward while giving Kuba the twice-over, her gaze bold, frank, decidedly unapologetic.

"Freedom—" Kuba stutters.

"I can't eat freedom. Can't use it to fill my fuel tank," she interjects, practically spitting the words at him in that raucous vox. But then she grins again, leans in closer, her lips, dark and plump as the skin of a ripe plum, near to his ear. "Still, somethin' 'bout a man not afraid to bring the noise. Even if that's all it is. Noise." She cocks her head, a bird listening for the movement of a worm in the soil under her claws. "Well, maybe a couple words in that stew you boiled up made sense."

"I am a better cook than a vox," Kuba allows, feeling a heat rising from his belly that has nothing to do with the sun, a heat spreading up his neck and across his cheeks.

"But you appreciate a vox. You follow the Prophet."

Kuba can't resist a brag. "I knew her before she was the Prophet." Then he moves to close the deal. "You have a boat—without a tracker?"

The fem levels her gaze. "I have three."

A scoffing snort erupts from Armor. "What're we talkin'? Little dinghies?"

The fem's fierce eyes flash, gleaming and dark as elderberries. "Yeah, cuz size matters. Vete a la chingada. My boats are big enough and fast enough to haul what you're fishin' for."

One of the fisherman nods. "She's not lying."

Armor squints, giving her the eyeball, measuring her. "How'd you come by three boats? And sans trackers to boot."

"That's my deal," she snaps, inspecting the dirt under her short-snipped fingernails.

"You 'spect us to just believe? What proof can you give that you're not shreddin' us?" Armor persists.

"Well, I'm bettin' you got a embed scanner in that pocket in the front of your pants. Or else you're just real glad to see me." The fem winks. "Whip it out and check what's blinkin'. Six on the fiver channel, I'd say. That's them three plus their crafts. But you won't see me or mine. They're ghosts to that machine."

Armor, like a dog wrestling for a bone, won't give up. "Where are they, these ghost boats?" His eyes scan the dock area and he flings a hand in disgust. "I only see the three that belong to these cabrónes."

The fem doesn't really need to ask her next question. Her expression says it all. But she lets loose.

"Are you pig ignorant? Because only a cabrón who's completely clueless—or stone loco—would 'spect me to keep downlows here where any corp trap can swoop in to find 'em." She heaves an exaggerated sigh. "Gotta spot for 'em out in one of the island bays. And no, I'll save you the time and breath askin'. Don't 'spect me to let their anchor point drop. To you."

Teeg finally steps into the conversation, muscled arms folded across her chest. "What about your name? You drop that on us?"

The fem's gaze momentarily alights on Teeg, taking her in, making a snap judgment, and then shifts to some point in the distance, a thousand-yard stare that silently screams of troubles left behind but not yet forgotten.

"I been called lotsa things. Lotsa names," she finally replies, her vox bound tight as a pair of wrists caught in a trap's steel bracelets. "But the people who meant somethin', they called me Kali."

40

EASING HER WAY INTO THE CONFIDENCE of the ova called Kate reminds Angel of a story Eben once told her of watching his father tame a caged bird. It was a process of time and patience. A process that began by watching the bird for signs of ease in his presence, noticing when the creature stopped startling and fluttering its wings when approached. A process continued by talking in a soothing, reassuring vox. Using slow, gentle movements. Extending a hand carefully inside the cage. Enticing an interaction with a treat. A process of pushing, but gently, always gently, until the bird was finally trusting enough to step onto his finger. Always keeping in mind that even when the creature consents to perch there, it's never truly within one's grasp. That it will most likely flit and fly away. Of course, the caged bird can only go so far before it crashes into the bars of its gilded prison. A captive to the bitter end.

Angel remembers staring at Eben at the conclusion of his story, puzzled. She suspected he meant the tale as a parable about the virtues of patience. But it struck her as a reinforcement, a reminder, of something altogether different. And she had let the notion slip her lips.

"*That's why birds aren't meant to live in cages.*"

Eben had burst out laughing, a raucous guffaw that shook

his whole body. *"Truer words were never spoken. Especially not us Birds. Yeah, my little bird, especially not Birds of the human feather."*

Angel can't remember the last time she uttered her family name. But it brings a measure of comfort now to remember it and to remember Eben and his story. Maybe one day she'll tell it to Lark as her own parable of patience. Or perhaps she'll tell her own story—of taming the ova.

She might tell of loitering on the periphery of Dorm Two, treats shoved into her pockets, like a pink-cheeked tween skulking up and down the block of his crush. Of plastering a winning smile on her face any time an ova passes by, on the chance it will be Kate behind the veil. But it also seems that Kate is amenable to being tamed, that she is willing to partner in the dance. She begins to intercept Angel on her circuits around the outskirts of the gardens, lifting her veil for the briefest of moments and waving as Angel pauses to sniff the fragrant white blossoms covering the mock orange shrubs.

Their conversations begin with matters of little import. The name of a flower. The sweetness of the strawberries served at breakfast. Whether the predicted rain will hold off long enough for a stroll to the lagoon and back. But Angel tentatively probes for the information she needs. The emotional states of the other ovas. How many are pregnant? How many visit Promise for her tea? The first time she asks a question, Kate will blink and sidestep, a wary animal avoiding a trap. But Angel is a savvy hunter, knowing when and how to double down, to retrace her steps, to phrase and rephrase. Knowing when to let the silence sit open. Knowing that people can't abide the gap. Find it awkward. Long to fill it.

And she is becoming practiced in the art of beguilement. Learning how to win over. To charm. To read a room. Learning from an expert, after all. From watching Promise's every move. From having to adapt to her every whim. And she has learned from life itself. From struggling to keep her balance while every rug she's ever stepped foot on is pulled out from under her.

She senses a deep loneliness in Kate, a longing for connection, a yearning to break through the isolation enforced by the modemant. And by the life. When the ova drops her guard, walking the path in the deep woods that hug the northern shore, or digging her toes in the sand that runs in a narrow strip just a short stroll from Dorm Two, she's ready to confide, ready to spill. But in these stolen moments when Angel can slip away from her chores, the story never comes in a gush. Just in dribs and drabs, like water dripping from a leaky faucet.

A picture of Kate's childhood trickles out and pools. Her life before. She was on the Entertainment Track, with the given name of Serene, interacting with a roboteach uncannily similar to Angel's Iris, though Kate's was named Terpsichore. And her lessons were quite different, guiding her in the study of music, dance, and stagecraft, immersing her in lyrics, melodies, and harmonies, training her to sing the songs of corporate exultation.

Her parents were in research and development at Galt Technical Services in the Ontario Region, a bustling industrial sector that pulsed with the noise of production. But they weren't showy swags with an overstuffed manse and sleek personal transports. Kate describes a sweet little cottage with a view of the lake, her blue-walled bedroom cool in the afternoons in the shade cast by the oak tree outside her window. She remembers biking everywhere. Peeling tart Granny Apples for a fruit crisp with her housekeep and, sometimes, kneading bread with her mother. Decoding ciphers and puzzles with her father on winter afternoons while snow blanketed the town. Creating their own ciphers.

"I still use ciphers in my letters home. I've tried to get the truth past the censors, let my parents know where I am. Which facility. It's silly, I know, but I still have a wisp of hope that my dad finds the clues I've scattered." Kate pauses, realizing she's said too much. Pivots. "After all, what's the harm in them knowing?"

She mentions, a wistful smile tugging at her lips, a best friend, Faith, who had a single dimple just to the right of her lips. Fearless Faith who never cried through all the scrapes and falls of childhood. When she mentions another friend, a boy named Bond, a blush spreads across her cheeks.

"He was so tall and big-boned. And awkward. The other kids called him Beast. They didn't tease, though, because they knew he was on the goliath track. But he was so sweet it was ridiculous to think of him becoming one of them. He loved theatrics—used to help me practice. He could play any character. He'd do this pitch perfect imitation of CEO Blanche's most pompous pronouncements. I'd be laughing so hard my sides would ache. He's the one who should've been on Entertainment track. How was he supposed to go from this gentle soul who rescued worms from drying out on the sidewalk to..." Kate's vox trails off.

She doesn't have to finish her thought, because Angel knows and nods and pictures the boy she knew who fit that gentle description. She doesn't want to tell Kate how it all ended with him.

Kate pulls a strip of bark from the slender trunk of a paper birch. "He had a scar running across his cheek from the time when he was six and tried to rescue a raccoon caught in a hunter's trap. The terrified creature fought back, but Bond kept at it until the thing was free. That's who he was—is—still, I hope. I guess you could say he was my first crush. My only crush," she says, curling the bark around her finger. "I think he felt the same about me. He swore he'd figure out a way to find me. To save me. Swore he'd come for me and..." Again, she leaves the thought unfinished. Blinks. "Well, that's too much like a thrillweep script, isn't it? And it's not like I need saving. This is who I am. Where I am." But her vox has slipped into the dispassionate, measured cadence of a robovox.

Angel nods and squeezes the fem's hand, and offers a sweet fiction. "Maybe he and your dad will work together on this, work the clues you've planted. Brains and brawn."

All the while biting down on the bitter truth.

Yeah, he'll find you. He'll come for you, but it will be with a burner in his hand.

Kate recalls the exams that preceded her selection at the age of twelve, the verbals—a trio of harvesters asking invasive questions about her thoughts and feelings, the inner workings of her mind—and the physicals—even more invasive, the prodding and poking of the inner workings of her body. She doesn't remember an explanation for why she was selected, what special attributes she had, although she overheard the quality control specialist talking in generalities to her parents.

Ovas are evaluated on their traits. Physical attractiveness and no health defects in the genetic history. Mental capacities, intelligence, yes, but not in a way that impacts the emotional side of brain function. *We want them cooperative, docile, and absolutely no mental health defects.* She remembers her parents pretending it was a great honor to be chosen for this crucial role in the Corporate organization. But the lie was plain to see in the way their gaze kept sliding away from her face. The hitch in their throats when they said her name. The rapid blinking of their eyes.

And she remembers the pain of leave-taking. Never an event more rightly named, for she had to leave everything behind. Everything. Forced to abandon her dreams of performing. Allowed no article of clothing, no memento. Boarding the transport with the blackout windows without even the comfort of her ragged stuffie, a little squirrel named Nutley, well-loved and hugged, whose plush gray fur had absorbed so many tears and kisses over the years that it had faded to the color of ash.

She remembers the matron's oily smile as she greeted all the wide-eyed, empty-handed newcomers on stops along the way. And the strange sensation of leaving even her name behind. In Galt Genesis I, she became a number and a nickname. K8579. Kate. Of the seven others who were inducted with her, two hulking girls were assigned to Dorm Four, one with a tall, willowy grace went to Dorm One, and the rest went with her to Dorm Two. And after that came the confines of the green skins and tunics, the modemant and the regimen. The indoctrination into the life of an ova.

Your body is not yours. It belongs to Galt. For the good of the Protectorate. Your body—which is not your body, but Galt's—is a sanctuary, a safehold for the future of Galt. For the good of the Protectorate. The children you bear, the futures that you grow and nourish in your body—which is not your body, but Galt's—are Galt's children and Galt's alone. But you must take pride in this most vital service that you are performing. And enjoy the fruits of your labors. The healthiest of diets. The choicest of fruits and vegetables and grains. A life of structured ease. A feed of entertainment— the live acts, the sporting events—at your fingertips.

Kate produced her first Galt future at the age of 18. Is expected to produce three more before she earns her severance at age 35. Tries not to think about how intimate an act it is to carry a baby to term. Tries not to perseverate on the secret conversations—as she came to think of them—between her and the child. The tattoo of kicks just under her ribcage. The nudge to her belly that only she could feel and actually see, stripped bare in the evenings in the refuge of her dorm suite, watching in wonder at the flexing of a tiny foot rippling under her skin like a wave.

Do not speculate on the future you are carrying. Do not speculate on its shape or form or the color of its eyes. That future is not your future. It belongs to Galt, and to Galt alone. Marvel only that you were chosen from among many to bring that future into being. To be the vessel in which it safely develops. To be the conduit through which it comes into the world. For the good of the Protectorate.

Despite the mantra that had been drilled into her brain, the urge still pulsated within, overwhelming and inexorable as the tide. The desire to see, to hold, to cradle, to nurse as the squall of the newborn, pinched and angry, filled the delivery room.

You have brought the future into existence. Praise be to you. And thank Galt for the good of the Protectorate.

Tears, outstretched arms, pleading to have just a moment with the child, but nothing was given to her except shushing and admonishments, until the final rebuke came with a small pillow shoved up against her breasts and a nurse's hands wrapping Kate's arms around it. Then came the after-fog. And the meds. And the washing of the brain. And the re-training. And a resistance that brought her nothing but grief until, using her earlier training, she learned how to fake the mindset. The modemant made it easier and for the first time she didn't curse having to wear it. It let her hide so very much, including the fact that she remembered every second of the birth and its aftermath. Her brain had not been washed of it. And she knows she never wants to experience that loss again.

"That's why I drink the tea," Kate says, as if in reply to a question, although Angel has been ever so careful not to ask or refer to it since their initial conversation outside the nerve center. She draws a line in the sand with her index finger. "I won't ever go through that again."

Silence settles and Angel sees the gap, the cleft in the conversation, like a fissure in a rock face. Hears it. Feels it. Knows it could widen into a chasm. Senses that, for once, it's her turn to fill the silence, to build the bridge across the crevasse. Reaches out to squeeze Kate's hand.

"What if I told you that you don't have to?"

PART THREE

Anima

Year 83 – Summer

41

The Geology of Fear

THE CQO DETESTS an interruption while dining, although she is not exactly sure why an intrusion of this nature should bother her more than any other. She enjoys a well-prepared meal, but is neither gourmet nor gourmand. Perhaps it's the intimacy of the act. The conspicuous consumption. The inevitable noise. The clinking of silverware on porcelain. The contemptible sounds of chewing and swallowing.

Or perhaps she loathes the invasion of her inner sanctum that such interruptions necessitate. Unfortunately, it is a problem of living where one works. Having an apartment above the shop, in the parlance of the bees. Her penthouse is just two flights of stairs above her office, though she can imagine it being a world away, with its walls of floor-to-ceiling windows and their spectacular views of Superior's infinite charms. She hasn't always been a Hive Dweller, as a certain envious element of corporate hierarchy refer to those few who have that benefit. She'd once upon a time maintained a lakeside manse alongside the upper echelon of Galt directors, and had dragged herself off to it every evening, but she tries not to let memories of those days creep in on her mindful present.

However, she must allow the CommCon and ProServ directors to creep in, like a pair of scuttling rats with beady, eager eyes that land here and there, taking it all in, for while her office is gray and spartan, her home is a sleek study in earth tones and artisanal acquisitions. Fine tables wrought in stone. Pendants crafted in brass and glass and alabaster. Furniture swathed in sophisticated fabrics the colors of which call to mind expensive and rare delicacies. Chocolates and caramels and toffees. And it is ever the case that people allowed to breach the sanctum want to touch things—surreptitiously, of course—but she can always catch this, no matter how furtive the act. Oh, how hands and fingers are drawn to rub the stone or brush up against the wool and the velvet. So it is this evening, when she spies the thumb of the new ProServ inch along the curve of her dining table.

"Travertine, Mr. Cruz," she says, noticing, with an inner smirk, how the thumb jerks away the instant the words leave her lips. "A stone that knows history, that has witnessed more history than you or I could ever comprehend. More than all the cloud could ever contain. And yet this stone is young, compared to some. Formed by the destruction of a different stone, an older stone. Amazing, isn't it? A fundamental rule of geology—so I'm told by those who know—is that the present is the key to the past. To history." The CQO twists her lips into an approximation of a smile as the mens' cheeks flush as the conversation edges toward the verboten. "Oh, don't look so shocked, Mr. Emmons. History—it's just a word, yes? Because it's here and then it's gone. The passing of time. Ephemeral. But stone can last forever. Of course, it doesn't come out of the ground looking this beautiful." She lets her hand hover over the surface of the table. "No, a block of travertine must be skillfully cut by a master artisan to reveal its veins. Every piece is unique. Go ahead, touch it."

Their appreciation is visible as their hands explore the table's complicated surface. Feeling indulgent now, like a mother whose clever child has just been praised by a passing stranger at the Galt-Mart, she gestures towards the chairs that flank the table, curved minimalist buckets that look more for show than comfort.

"Well, enough of the geology lesson. To what do I owe this interruption?"

The new ProServe Director, a sleek greyhound of a man named Cruz, with none of his predecessor's swaggering bulldog tendencies, accepts the invitation to sit and settles into the beautiful chair not made for sitting. He shifts his body weight trying to find a comfortable pose, then abandons his efforts and slouches, leg crossed, foot resting on his knee.

"We've gotten word on a couple of possible scenarios the chés may be planning. The first is a strike on the water plant in the Superior Garrison."

The CQO eyes a cherry tomato that has rolled off her salad and is teetering on the edge of her plate, a brilliant scarlet globe against the white void. She nudges it back with the tip of her knife. "And the other?" she asks.

"A hit on the breeder facility in Bayfield."

The CQO sighs. "Gentlemen, where is this intel coming from? Because neither of those 'scenarios' sounds very likely."

Director Cruz leans forward. "It's coming from within a cell that we think is ranging along the southern shore. It's second-sourced, yeah, someone told someone else who passed it along to our ear man, but that's how we have to run things. Nobody'll risk a direct line to us. But that pipeline's been reliable in the past. Things don't get fumbled in the passing. It's the same source as the power facility tip from last year."

"Which I am still not convinced was actually going to occur outside of some ché's wet dream," the CQO retorts, her impatience dragging her down into vulgarities.

"Well, but we did prevent—"

"Mr. Cruz, that's in the past. You should know by now that, like the stars of gladiator ball, you're only as good as your next play. I don't really need to hear the details of your varied machinations to defuse these possible events before they occur." She pauses, smoothing the napkin in her lap as she smoothes her expression into a facade of patience. "I know you think I'm a micromanager," she finally continues, her hand flicking at their quick head shakes as if swatting at a pair of pesky gnats, "but really, I'm not. All I ask is that you do your jobs and that you do them with an attention to detail that I devote to my own. I don't ask you to exceed expectations, only to meet them. This is not an either/or situation. The expectation is that neither act of sabotage will occur. So work the problem, gentlemen."

The ProServ shifts again in the damnably uncomfortable chair and wonders how the CQO can sit there looking so at ease in what to him feels like an instrument of torture. "Well, ma'am, we are working the problem, but we'd appreciate some guidance. We can continue to approach the situation as we've done in the past and snare individuals here and there, playing the whack-a-mole game. Or we can wait, exercise some patience, and go for a more thorough round-up. Take out most, if not all, of the cell."

The CQO eyes the salad on her plate, considering its variety of lettuces, all grown in the vertical farm on premises, admiring the rich shades of green that contrast so beautifully with each other and the reds of the tomatoes and radishes and the eye-popping orange of the slivers of carrot. Realizes with dismay that the leaves are wilting, their crispness rapidly diminishing under a slick of garlic and basil vinaigrette.

"Well, Mr. Cruz, although some might not agree, I am infinitely patient. Killing one cockroach may provide immediate gratification, but in the long game it does you no good. Eradicating the whole intrusion of cockroaches, while it may take time and effort, is obviously the goal and provides the ultimate satisfaction. And so." She nods at the men, with the understanding that they can read the metaphor. "We're done here," she adds, her usual dismissal, but when the men leave, instead of resuming her meal, she pushes back the plate, her appetite suddenly vanished.

42

Revelation 1

JUGGLING THE NEEDS—the sheer neediness—of two fems is exhausting. Angel wonders if this is how it feels for a man trying to cater to the whims of a demanding wife while placating an equally volatile pleasure woman on the side. She imagines it's easier for the bushwa swag to compartmentalize. In one home, there would be a certain set of rules, a certain way of acting, a certain face to wear. In the other place, a different set of rules would govern, a different set of clothes would be hanging in the closet, a different mask would cover the other. But in her situation, there's no way to keep the conflicting thoughts and emotions separate, stacked neatly in their own boxes. Here, everything and everyone is entwined, dangerously so, like a bag of writhing, venomous snakes, fangs at the ready, should she reach inside to pull them apart.

And then there's Lark. Crying, thrashing, stomping, hitting, kicking, screaming. Her emotional weather is a constant storm of frustration, anger, disappointment and want, want, want. And she's learned that when Angel says no, Promise will say yes, particularly when Flint is around to hear the meltdowns.

Promise makes light of it all. "She's just learning that making a little noise, stirring up a little chaos, is vital to getting what you want out of life. What's wrong with that? It's an important lesson. After all, she's not going to end up a worker bee who has to be satisfied with the scraps that fall from some swag's table. You do know that, don't you?" The smile curving on those plum-colored lips speaks all and says nothing.

And then there's skulking, glowering Flint. His arguments with Promise have become more frequent and knife-like, sharp-edged and meant to wound. Angel's skin prickles a warning whenever he comes into view. She jerks awake in the night, half-expecting him to be looming over her. And there's the Fathom op, the weight of it on her back, the pressure of it pounding in her brain and her heart. Her thoughts prodding her to search for an entry point into the command system at the nerve center.

The stress surfaces on Angel's face, despite her efforts to tamp it down, to keep her expression bland, to keep her lips composed in her own sphinx-like smile, to keep her eyes blank, shallow pools reflecting only what the onlooker wants to see. The strain puddles in gray splotches under her eyes after nights spent with her mind wheeling, ideas tumbling, cascading like a waterfall's endless flow. It draws lines around her lips and carves creases into her forehead. Works its way into her hands with random tremors when anyone looks at her too long. Manifests in the need to check and double check. To trust only in the seeing and not in the remembering.

In the shed one warm, sunny morning, she readies her tools to attack an overgrown area of lilacs, now that the blooms are spent. That is her task, her focus, and yet she is compelled to check her hidden backpacks, although she has done this a half-dozen times in the past week. There they are, safely stashed behind the wheelbarrow. Her fingers are drawn to the zipper and then to the rectangle of paper inside and the words printed on it, as if to run a thumb across its fragile surface is to caress the cheek of the man who wrote them.

Where the Night Prophet leads there I shall follow

"I say no yard work today."

Angel stumbles and spins, startled by the vox intruding in what she has come to think of as her sanctuary, slipping the page back into the pack with one hand while her other tugs at the edge of the tarp tucked into the gap between the wheelbarrow and the wall.

"Oh, didn't mean to startle you." Promise has Lark on her hip and a hand shading her eyes as she stands in the doorway, silhouetted in the bright sunlight, peering into the gloom. "What are you doing back there?"

"The tire—on the wheelbarrow—it's slightly—deflated," Angel replies, conjuring an explanation out of nothing.

Promise sighs. "Well, you're done with mulching anyway. Didn't you tell me that? I declare it a wheelbarrow-free day. Although you might need a shovel where we're going. But only a small one. And a little pail, too."

"Where are we going?" Angel asks, rising from her crouch.

Promise inclines her head to Lark's, whispering in her ear.

"Beach," Lark pipes. "We go beach."

"Yes, a beautiful, warm, sunny day in June and I can't think of a better way to spend it—to idle it away—than at Big Bay. The beach, the cliffs, the trail, the beach—did I mention the beach?" Promise laughs. "I've packed a lunch, towels, blackout shades. Why, I've done all the grunt work. Tell me again why I have you around? Just kidding, Jel. But seriously, the only effort you need to put in is some pedaling."

Angel opens her mouth to protest, but Promise holds up her hand and adopts a scowl. "Don't speak. No vox," she says, and then lets the scowl slide into a sly grin as she tilts her head with a wink. "The next thing I want to hear coming from your mouth is 'how beautiful this place is and thank you for bringing me here.' Got it?"

Angel nods.

"Alright, then let's hit it."

Big Bay is indeed a magnificent place of picturesque bluffs and evergreen-studded plateaus carved from the ubiquitous brown sandstone. A long crescent of fine sand forms a slim barrier between the steel blue lake and a murkier inland lagoon. Angel senses a history here, a history of weather patterns and water currents, a history in which the forces of nature swept the sand into piles in some areas and gnawed at the shoreline in others.

The bay faces east so the morning sun glitters on the water, turning it into a liquid mirror, warming the shallows at the very edge of the strand. Lark still jumps back in surprise at the chill lapping at her toes. In the split-second after her feet touch the water, her reaction could go in one of two directions and Angel braces for it to go the wrong way, but then a smile breaks like a Superior wave over the child's face and a giggle spews forth.

"Well?" Promise prompts, a look of expectation on her face.

"This is truly a beautiful place and thank you for bringing me here."

"You could say it with more enthusiasm," Promise pouts. "A little more inflection in that vox. So I know it's not robo-generated."

"That wasn't the response you were looking for?"

If Promise is miffed by Angel's retort, she doesn't show it. Instead she spreads a roomy towel and sinks down, running her fingers through the sand, grabbing up a handful and sifting it back and forth, from palm to palm.

"There's something about this sand," she murmurs. "Maybe it's the ordeal of its creation. The way it was scraped from the rocks. The way it was tossed around and rode the currents. It could have wound up anywhere. But it washed up here, on this shore. It's special, you know." She squeezes another handful and then lets the grains slip through her fingers. "Coming here, to this beach, is what makes this life semi-tolerable." Then she grabs the little bucket and shovel they've brought along. "And it makes the best frackin' sandcastles you'll ever see."

Sandcastles built and destroyed by baby monster feet. Water waded and splashed. Trail hiked. Lunch devoured. They lie on a rock outcropping, drowsy in the afternoon sun, enjoying the fresh breeze skimming cool air off the water and tickling their toes. The lapping of the waves is an ancient music, one with which their bodies are intimately familiar, a music their bodies have heard before, in the dark cavern where they curled before ever knowing of the world and its wonders. Lark has fallen asleep, a bunched towel cradling her head, her hair a tousled mess escaping from its ponytail.

Promise stretches her arms to the brilliant cloudless sky, her movements supple and cat-like, then raises herself on her elbows. "Oh, to stay here like this forever. To never, never go back."

Her vox is wispy, plaintive in a way Angel hasn't heard before. Last night's battle with Flint, which, to Angel, hearing it through a wall, had sounded no worse than all the others, has taken its toll. Angel shifts onto her side, feeling the warmth of the rock seep into the skin of her cheek.

"Why do you go back? To him? To the manse?" she asks, emboldened by the carefree intimacy of the day. "Why not leave? For good." She tenses for the storm, for an angry rebuke meant to put her back in her place, but Promise just pushes away a strand of wind-whipped hair from her face, revealing the wry, tired smile of a fem ready to let go of a burden she's forced herself to carry.

"You want to know how I came to be here and why I can't leave? That's what you're really asking." Promise glances down at Lark, asleep between them, then out at the water, which stretches far into the reaches of the Protectorate, to places unknown, places where they have never, and perhaps will never, set foot.

"My mother had two children, though that is a violation of corporate policy. I was her first and I was perfect in every way." Promises shrugs. "I'm not bragging, it's just the way it was. She told me so herself. Because that was the expectation and she made it so. Made it happen. Funny how mothers do that—make things happen." She adjusts her blackout shades, casts a speculative look at Angel before she continues. "How they impose their will upon the world. Scrabble and claw until their nails are broken and their hands and fingers are bloody in the endeavor." Promise inspects her own flawless hands. "She made me. The look, the manner, the intellect. Perfect Promise."

"How did she come to have another baby?"

"When you make the rules, you don't necessarily have to follow them. You can order your personal medic to remove your embed and then reinsert it when you've achieved your goal. And then severance him before he can tell any tales. Concoct a story about how your body is so strong and powerful and fertile that it can overcome the effects of the embed. Except it can't. Because the baby comes out all wrong."

"Wrong?"

"Not perfect," Promise clarifies. "Far from perfect. The farthest from perfect you can imagine."

"And she—got rid of it?"

"Oh, no. That would be an admission of error. No, she loved her little boy—Pace, she named him." Promise twirls a delicate tendril of Lark's hair around her finger, but gently, so as not to disturb the child's slumber. "Or maybe she pretended to love him. But after awhile, a year or two, I could see she had drawn away—from both of us. Felt it in her touch, the way her lips slid across my forehead, as if they couldn't bear to linger there for any length of time. Of course, I couldn't understand why she seemed repelled by me as well as him. I was still her perfect daughter. It was only later—much later—here on this island, that I figured it out." Promise flexes one foot and then the other, tensing and releasing muscles and tendons, slowly and deliberately. "My perfection reminded her of his deformities. And her hubris. And her failure."

"Where's your brother now?"

"Who knows where the ashes of the dead end up. Fertilizer for some AgSector field?"

It's not the sudden gust of wind that provokes Angel's shudder. A part of her wants to stop treading this path, to let the questions go unasked, to let the conversation end with her murmuring some vague expression of condolence. The way forward only threatens traps and landmines with every footfall. But the guevara must march on. "How'd he die?" she ventures, certain she doesn't really want to know.

"Pace liked to watch me swim. Strapped into his mobile chair, head lolling, all tubed up, but I could see he enjoyed it. But happy and sad at the same time. I could see that on his little twisted face. He wanted to be there in the water with me." Promise tucks a stray lock of hair behind her ear. "It was a very hot day and he looked so miserable, sounded so miserable, making these whines and grunts. When Sela—his nurse—went inside to get some water, I slipped out of the pool and gathered him up in my arms and took him in with me. He wasn't very heavy to begin with and he was even lighter in the water. I distinctly remember noticing that. And I remember singing him the water song. He always loved that. Funny what we remember and what we don't. I don't remember letting go of him."

Promise pauses and wipes the sheen of sweat from her forehead. Glances down at Lark again before continuing. "But I must have. Let go. I do remember how ridiculous Sela looked, her scrubs sopping wet, plastered to her body, like her skin was printed with this teeny floral pattern. Water dripping from her hair. It looked like black sea weed clinging to her cheeks. Doing things to Pace's body that looked much more painful than death."

Angel swallows, a sliver of dread as sharp and cold as an icicle plunging from her throat to her gullet. She shivers in the sunshine, catches herself, and sits up, drawing her knees to her chin, hugging her legs in tight to her body. "How old were you?"

So wrapped up in reliving her story, Promise doesn't appear to notice Angel's discomfort. "Ten. The last time I swam. The pool was drained. But never filled in. I think she wanted to feed my guilt. Maybe it worked. I don't know. We struggled along for a few years. But then I became—how to say this?—obsessed with replacing Pace. Oh, I knew it wouldn't happen with the frackin' embed stuck in my hand. But that didn't stop me from trying." She sighs, almost flippant. "It was all so wantonly tedious. It was almost a relief when she found out."

"What did she do?"

"Had me fixed and sent me here."

"Fixed?"

"Sterilized. Made it so I can't ever have a child. And then banished me to a place where everywhere I look I can't help but see fertility."

A black fly lands on the fem's knee. She watches, nose wrinkled with a mixture of disgust and the avid curiosity of a child, as it grooms its antennae, until repugnance wins out and she swats it away.

Angel dares to probe further. "How could she do that? Corporate decides—"

"She *is* Corporate. When you're CQO, you can do just about anything you please in the name of making the Protectorate a better place."

It's a smack in the face, a boot heel to the belly. Angel tries to hide the jolt of astonishment that quakes through her body, but her game face fails her.

Her fascination with her story waning, Promise sees Angel's reaction. A grimace contorts her face. She nods. "Yeah, that CQO—Mora Zinni."

Angel sucks in a breath, holds it before attempting a pivot. "What about your father? Couldn't he—"

"I have no father." Promise cuts in, her vox as flat and impenetrable as the stone on which they lie. "Well, I suppose I do, but I don't know who he is—or was. Maybe my mother opted for a procedure. Or if she chose the more primitive method, for all I know, she bit off the male's head after the deed was done—like a praying mantis."

The words drift and then settle, like sand roiled in a wave. Angel turns her gaze to the water, notices the tremor in her hand, quickly clasps it in the other.

Lark's little body shifts and she raises her melon head from its makeshift pillow, her chubby fingers tussling with her wild hair, trying to push it from her face. "Mama?" she burbles, half question, half statement.

Angel and Promise both reach for her. Promise's movements are quicker, more assertive, scooping Lark into her arms and rising to her feet with the fluid grace of water. She cocks her hip, triumphant.

"After all these years, these rotten years, I think I'm ready to swim again."

She scrambles across the boulders, sure-footed as a mountain goat, Lark, still nap-woozy, swaying in her grasp. She's in the water before the gasp can even escape Angel's lips. As Promise wades out into the lake, as the water rises higher, to her ankles, to her calves, to her knees, thighs, and hips, all Angel can see is the image that the bruja has just painted. Of the young girl carrying her brother into the water. And letting him go.

She hears the bruja crooning the hymn to water. But not just as part of the horrid vision. She hears the words floating, in real time, over the lake.

To those who thirst I shall give
Water without price...

The water's lapping at the fem's waist now, tonguing Lark's legs and bottom as Promise dips and twirls the child, now fully awake and clinging. Frozen, limbs disobeying her commands, Angel tries to call out, but a stone is lodged in her throat and the words can't slip around its jagged edges. Instead, she hears the little vox, the snake's hiss that slithers in her guts and through the folds of her brain.

You never wanted her. There's no shame in that. She was thrust upon you. You never desired her like others have. Like others do every single day. You have only ever felt the burden, never the joy. Always sought out the mark who would carry that burden for you. Watched and wondered what life might be like without that burden. Without the need to hand off the burden. Without the guilt that comes with that.

She is an anchor weighing you down, keeping you from moving on. Time to cut loose. Time to let her go. To sail free. Because you know that every day she grows to look more like him and one day you will look at her and only see the face of evil.

No.

No!

The fem is chest deep now, her back to the shore, bobbing up and down. Lark's arms are raised to the sky.

No, don't you let go of her!

Struggling to swallow, to dislodge the stone, but it sticks, blocking the passageway.

Stop. Breathe. Focus. Think.

But there's no time for that, no time to stop, not this time, so then she's in motion, leaping from rock to rock to the water, running, trying to run, but in water there is no running, only an awkward lumbering gait as she tries to cut through the thick liquid chill. A squeal, a cry, and then they're gone, heads dipping below the surface.

No!

A single thought, a silent shout echoing through her mind, over and over and over, but one so full of panic and dread that it finally summons the power to smash the stone to pieces, to let the thought escape in a full-throated scream.

"No!"

Suddenly, the heads bob up above the surface again, with a spray of water as they shake back and forth, tendrils of drenched hair flying, and peals of sounds that Angel struggles to distinguish. Are they cries of fear? Laughter?

"No!"

Both heads turn to look at her, faces dripping water and splashed with joy, and then awash in confusion as she makes the final push through the water to reach them. Without a word, Angel's hands close around the giggling Lark's waist, but she has to give a little tug before Promise releases her hold on the child.

"Come to join the fun?" Promise laughs, but her delight fades as Angel backs away, dragging her feet along the lake bottom, making for the shallow water.

"Deep, too deep," Angel mumbles as she turns away and trudges back toward shore, the swells swirling around her, plucking at her shorts and t-shirt, making every effort to impede her progress, to keep her clasped in its cold, wet embrace.

"Spoil sport!" Promise calls with a teasing lilt, but Angel senses the disappointment under the playful facade.

Just what disaster her actions averted, she will never know. When her imagination drifts toward the what ifs, the thoughts of what might have happened, she is quick to sweep them from her focus, although they linger in the darker corners, like dust.

Later, after the sun has worked its magic to dry their clothes and they've built one last fortress in the sand and are preparing to depart, Promise turns to Angel as she's shaking out her towel. "I know what you were thinking," she says, a hint of accusation lurking around the edges of her vox. "Nothing would've happened. Nothing did happen. You should know I'd never hurt her. That I love her like I'd love my own daughter. Why, I think I loved her from the moment I saw her in your arms in front of the sweetshop."

Angel, mute, tucks her towel into the saddlebag of her bike, hands fumbling with the zipper, the day's revelations weighing on them. Weighing on each move her body makes, like a chain forged of every fear she has ever known, every cold shivery thought that has snaked its way down her spine, every hateful sight that has made her flinch.

Coveting something or someone is not the same as loving them.

"I'm not the kind of person who hurts the ones they love," Promise says in a murmur, as if she's talking to herself.

Only the things that stand in your way.

Lark ambles over to the sandcastle and lifts her foot to obliterate a tower with a mighty stomp, but Promises snags her hand and draws her away. "Oh please, baby monster, let this one stand. A monument. A memorial that says 'LaLa was here.' Yes?"

Angel tenses, knowing the child is growing tired again and hungry. Another moment that could go either way and if Angel had to bet, she'd opt for the meltdown. But mercifully, Lark just gives a rueful little smile and a wave.

"Bye, castle."

"That's my good girl. *Our* good girl."

The smile that twists Promise's lips is just another link in the chain.

43

Hostage to the Future

It will require pain. Pain that slices deep through muscle and sinew. Pain that slices to the bone. It will require tears. Tears that well and seep from frustration and tears that gush from mourning. Because, yes, there will be mourning. Because, yes, this truth will require blood. Because our aim must be victory. And nothing less. Victory over this tyranny that some dare to call a protectorate. That some dare to call a life. Victory without regard to cost. Victory no matter how long the road or rocky the path. Victory in the face of the terror that will rain down upon us from without and engulf us from within. For victory is life. All else is just a living death. And no amount of pretty words can change that.

So sayeth the Night Prophet.

"Get Lark and get the hell out of there. Frack all, why didn't you just bring her with you today?" Word ignites in the aftermath of Angel's bombshell, sparks shooting from his eyes and his lips, mottling his checks.

Path gives a low whistle. "What a frackin' takedown this is gonna be."

"No, no, it's not gonna be a frackin' takedown! Because there's not gonna be a takedown. We're pullin' the plug!" Word insists.

Angel avoids his glare. Senses he's dropped his game face,

his anxiety laid bare for all to see, his expression having strayed from that of comrade to something else.

"No, güey," Path replies. "We're riding this wild pony to the end of the plateau and then we're gonna jump, if we have to."

Teeg remains silent, seemingly poised somewhere in the middle, arms crossed, weighing the available options. Angel senses that she's not one to abandon a course of action at the first sign of difficulty. However, neither is she inclined to take unnecessary risks. She's a guevara well-served by her level-headed common sense, her ability to look at a situation with a clear eye and a clear head, unclouded by emotion.

"Much as I'm of the 'take no prisoners' persuasion, there's something about the idea of a hostage angle here, with this particular prisoner," Path muses, eyes closed as if visualizing the scenario of the CQO's daughter bound and gagged. What a disruption in the feed stream that would be, like a rock thrown in a calm pool of water sending out ripples in all directions. A rock? Hell—a boulder. An avalanche. An earthquake under the ocean driving a tsunami.

"No, no, you don't get it!" Angel brings her fist down hard on the table, hard enough to rattle the forks and knives crisscrossed on their empty plates.

She'd waited to drop her incendiary information until the end of the evening, after the voxcast had been sent out into the night, after the usual breaking of bread to celebrate and re-hash and plot the next, because she had anticipated the cataclysm that would erupt in the wake of her words. She'd listened to Teeg's updates on the Fathom Op. How she's secured a string of safehouses along the southern shore past the Keweenaw Peninsula and several more in towns that hug Superior's northern flank. How the guevaras have a lead on some boats. How things are falling into place. Only then had Angel dropped her news. Kate's story and the revelation of Promise's identity. She'd predicted their reactions. Word's concern for her safety. Path's glee at this twist of chaos added to the mix. Teeg's careful, measure twice, cut once approach. What she hasn't anticipated is the strange brew of emotions bubbling up inside her own body.

What does she feel? About Kate? About Promise? Why do their faces materialize in her mind's eye, unbidden, unprompted, apropos of nothing other than the fact that, no, she can't get them out of her mind, can't think of anything else. They possess her thoughts every waking minute and haunt her restless sleep as well, flitting in and out of dreams as birds flit amongst trees, a whisper of feathers, a dash of color, a psalm sung in a foreign language, a choir of call and response. She fears to put names to these emotions, for bestowing a name upon something makes it real. Too real. And gives it power. And so it is now. She sits with the two fems encircling her thoughts, circumscribing their movements until Path's impatient vox breaks the spell.

"What? I don't get—what?" he asks, though from the set of his jaw, it's clear that he's not open to hearing her explanation.

*What **do** you ever truly get? What can you possibly understand about it?*

In the days since the revelation at Big Bay, Angel has studied Promise out the corner of her eyes. And she has kicked herself for being blind to the striking resemblance that Promise bears to her mother.

Is that a blessing or a curse? Or an awkward, witch's brew blend of both? It would bring instant recognition and all that accompanies it. The best banquette at the most exclusive farm-to-tables in the six regions. Private boxes at the arenas for the hottest gladiator ball competitions. Front rows at the live acts and backstage access before and after, the entertainers fawning over her even as she bestows compliments and kudos upon them. Every fiber and stitch adorning her slender body bespoke. The ultimate in swag haute. And yet. What must it feel like to know that your mother, the queen bee of the Hive, is far more reviled than beloved by her worker bees? To wonder if that hatred carries over to you?

It's simple enough, really. Though Path won't understand. Won't care. Yet Angel is compelled to say it.

"Her mother doesn't love her."

She's right. He doesn't understand. None of them do. She can see it in the lift of his forehead, a trait of the permanent skeptic. Can see it in the way that Word digs his thumb in the space between his brows, as if probing for clarity. Can see it in the way Teeg's mouth tightens like a rope pulled taut. Path stares at the floor, gives his head a little shake as if to dislodge some irritant. A fly. A speck of dust. Then his gaze returns to Angel.

"Uhm, you know, I'm not sure what happened to the badass who held a knife to my throat the night we met, but I really hope she comes back soon or else this op is a crash and burn before it's even in the air." Path's gaze slides to Word's face, takes in the fear pooling in the man's eyes, and his lips curl into a frown, dragged down by what might be a dawning awareness. His lids drop and he shakes his head, exhales. "Frack. Again?"

The single word hangs there under the lamplight, until its burden of disdain drags it down. Angel imagines she can hear the splat as it puddles on the tile floor.

Word's cheeks redden as he plunges into the awkward silence. "This op has already crashed. It's over." His hand slices the air. "Not all things have to be finished. Particularly things bound to fail."

"No," Angel asserts. "It's not over."

Because this is not a task that I will leave unfinished.

She leaves that thought unspoken, but stumbles through others. "What I'm saying is, it's useless to think you'll get some kind of advantage by using Promise as a pawn, holding her hostage, or whatever. The CQO doesn't—she won't—it won't matter to her. She's keeping her own daughter a prisoner—on that island—in Genesis—so she can—torture her."

Disbelief can be sharp, blade-like. Or cold, immobile as a block of ice. The disbelief that Angel faces now feels more like a swamp, oozing, muddy, ready to swallow her as she wades, feet sinking in the mire.

"Listen! Are you hearing what I'm saying? What I mean? She's not torturing her body—well, yes, in a way, she is—but—"

Their faces. Their looks. Their twisting mouths.

So smug. So pure. Thinking they know everything.

"Oh, why am I trying to explain it to you?! You! Who never wanted a child. Never felt the hunger, the yearning—like a thirst that's never quenched. A wish that's always thwarted. You've never carried a child in your body." Angel glares at Path, spitting the words like bitter seeds. "You talk of hostages. So flippant. It's these fems who know what it means to be a hostage. What it means to give a hostage to the future. All your bullshit about fortune. Imagine never knowing whether fortune will favor that child. Never knowing what's destined for that child. Don't you think that even the mothers of goliaths bleed a little every day—when they think about what they've unleashed on the world?"

And then she's running. A thoughtless, heedless dash. Through the door and down the porch and into the dark, feet following the path of the solars to the road, the white laces of her kicks glowing violet. Running crazy, gasping for breath, careening down the sloping street, until she reels herself in for fear of tumbling head over heels, and settles into a slower, even rhythm, until the thud of her feet echoes the thud of her heart. She follows her feet and her heart, as the street bottoms out and joins the road that curves above the lake. And there's the familiar path that leads to the park, that leads to the bench. The bench where all of this began.

The night air is thick, even after she catches her breath, the day's damp heat lingering. She senses more than sees the flash behind her, then, after a long moment, hears the low growl of thunder. A storm's curdling, somewhere to the west.

"You should come back to the house. Storm's rising fast."

Teeg's vox is husky, as the fem, breathing heavily, settles herself on the bench beside Angel. "You set a fast pace, a bit of the sprinter in you, but I'm prepared for the marathon," she chuckles. "But we will walk back. At a decent clip."

The lights across the channel mark the curve of the island. The place where her daughter sleeps, the child who will wake in the midst of the hurly-burly and cry out.

And her mother won't be there.

Except she could. She could run to the dock, unslip the dinghy. Twenty minutes. She could outrun the approaching tumult in the little boat. Twenty minutes. Angel waits for another flash of lightning in the periphery of her vision. And then she'll count, like she did as a little child, like Eben taught her—*one Mississippi.* But a bolt doesn't come.

"My daughter's alone," she finds herself saying out loud. "I need to be with her. She's afraid of thunderstorms." She wills her body to rise, but her legs disobey, obstinate and rooted, like trees growing sturdy in the wrong places.

"She's not alone. Promise will see to her comfort."

"It's not—"

"The same? True, a child can only have one birth mother, but if she's lucky she will have many mothers in her life. You trusted this fem—at least enough to make the trade off. To accept her offer of shelter, to leave Lark in her care so that you could do the work you made a commitment to do. The mission you undertook. To be the Night Prophet. What's changed? Is it the fact you know her backstory? Is it a problem now that you know a little bit more of her truth?"

"If anything she says *is* the truth," Angel mutters, although she knows the contours of the fem's face do not lie. Promise fits the mold that formed her. She is her mother's daughter.

There's the flash she's been waiting for.

One Mississippi. Two Mississippi. Three—

"Come on, we need to get back. Don't even think about try-ing to take the boat across the channel. I have a range of take-down skills and a good thirty pounds of muscle on you. And we both know we don't want this to turn into a wrestle in the mud." Teeg's hand closes around Angel's arm and half guides, half hauls her to her feet. "Comrade's vox? Mother's vox? Whatever."

44

Revelation 2

WHEN THEY REACH THE SAFE HOUSE, instead of going inside, Teeg eases herself into the wicker settee on the porch and pats its floral cushion. Angel sinks down, seizing any opportunity to delay renewed encounters with the two men inside, either of which would prove maddening. A pulse of lightning flares, followed by thunder, a crackling jolt like the sound of a tree limb splitting, leaving jagged, splintered ends and heartache.

Angel shudders.

"I have a story to tell," Teeg says in the sudden quiet.

Angel shakes her head. "I can't listen to any more stories. I am too full to listen. Stuffed with stories. Sick with them."

"This one—just this one more—you must hear. Before I was a guevara—no, that's not quite right—before I *knew* I was a guevara, because when I think back, I've always been a guevara, but for a time I didn't understand my own nature. But, in the before-times, I was an ova." Teeg sighs, an exhalation sharp and swift, as if she has set down a heavy burden. "My girlhood was similar to Kate's. On one track and then tested and chosen for another, removed from my home, separated from everything I'd ever known. I can only liken it to an amputation, a severing, as if part of me was surgically removed. Yes, I was treated like a queen bee, fed and groomed and coddled. Eventually, the wound scabbed over, but it never really healed. Not properly. Not deep down. I can still feel the pain from that phantom limb."

A gust of wind ripples through the metal tubes of the chimes hanging from the eave in a corner of the porch. They sing a watery, melancholy chorus, which repeats over and over again, as a second and third gust blows. The branches of the trees bend to the tune. And then the sky lets loose in a pelting, staccato percussion.

"I didn't know how to resist," Teeg continues. "Didn't know I could resist. I had no one to give me tea, to even tell me there was such a thing, or any other way of keeping the—how did the bruja put it?—the integrity of my body. They put us under for the procedure. Shot us full of Tranquille so all we could see was a pink and blue bleeding to violet haze. I felt nothing, just a little awkward pressure, at first, but then nothing. I thought that was how I'd feel about the baby, too. It wasn't mine. It would never be mine. It belonged to Galt. But that's not the way of things. Not the nature of the heart. Once. Twice. Each time I mourned like I was grieving a death, when I should have been rejoicing in a new life."

The wind carries mist from the downpour, cool and refreshing, onto the porch, onto their faces. The front door opens with a creak. A head appears in the gap, but in the darkness Angel can't tell if it belongs to Word or Path.

"This is not for you," Teeg chides, giving a dismissive flick of her hand. "Inside."

A clatter and click signal obedience.

"To send a child into this ruthless world and never know her fate. Who her parentals are, what they believe. To never watch her take her first steps. To never dry her tears or hold her in the middle of a storm and say it's gonna to be okay. And to know that it won't be okay. To know that whatever track she's locked into, no matter what hopes and dreams she may harbor, she's headed for a life of bondage."

A flare of lightning illuminates Teeg's face, casting a bluish glow across her skin, unearthly and ephemeral, revealing her wince at the thunder's immediate, crackling boom. Another blast of wind bullies through the yard. Another crack. Then the whoosh of a tree limb slicing through the rain and crashing to the ground. Angel flinches and she feels Teeg's hand close over hers, a grip strong and calm in the midst of the maelstrom.

"Thunderstorms. As a child, you're afraid of the sound and fury in the thick of it, the roar of the beast. As an adult, you're more afraid of the consequences, the aftermath, the damage. All the pieces you'll have to pick up—if there's anything left at all. If you want to go inside, we can." Teeg says, with a squeeze of her hand.

Angel shakes her head. "No." She's been through storms, hunkered down in makeshift shelters in forests, in fields, in all the abandoned towns she's passed through on her way to this place. But none have made her heart race, made the chill seep down through the core of her body and pool in her belly, in the way that the thunder rolling under Teeg's words does now. "Go on with it."

Teeg gives Angel's hand another squeeze. "Come the third time, I knew I was headed for severance. And I made up my mind that my last baby would live free or die. Nine months for the idea to grow, right along with the baby. I nurtured it, like I nurtured that child. It rolled around in my mind, twisted and turned and poked and prodded, just like the child. I wrestled with it, boxed with it, grew strong from struggling with it.

"So when the pains came in the late afternoon, I knew what I had to do. I kept a lid on it and smiled through gritted teeth and didn't report them to the nurse like I was expected to. Grabbed a basket and towels and hobbled down the path to the trash pit. I knew nobody'd be there at that hour. Evening was coming on and I knew by the angle of the sun that the medic shift would be over soon. I had this crazy notion. The medic, the one called Doc Bird. He wasn't my caregiver, but I'd heard that he seemed different, more caring. That's his mission, yeah? To care, to save lives. And he seemed to truly believe it. To live it. I knew he'd save my baby, as irrational as that may sound. I just knew. Knew he'd take her out of that place. And if he didn't, she'd die, but die free."

Hearing her father's name doesn't come as a jolt, but a sense of relief, an exhalation, an unhunching of the shoulders, of the spirit, like the feeling of relief when you pull a thorn out of your finger and the pain vanishes so quickly it makes you giddy.

"And that's where I squatted and pushed, right there by the trash pit. But it was a struggle. A dark, raw struggle. Body opening, straining, stretching, pushing, pushing with the waves, but something wasn't right. With all of it, all the straining, the child seemed stuck, unwilling."

"How did you manage? All alone?" A vision strikes Angel, of her time, in the waterman's lair, in the midst of the horror and the gore and the mechanisms of Galt's control, in the dark tunnel of it all, and how lucky, so very lucky, she was to have Kuba there to hold her hand through to the other side.

"I wasn't alone. There was a young fem."

"Another ova?"

"No, she was—I don't know what she was—she just turned up on the island one day. One day she wasn't and the next day she was. The manager seemed to keep her on a short lead, but like a wily dog, she always managed to rip the leash from his hands or slip the collar when he wasn't paying attention. She seemed—trapped—and free at the same time. She watched us. Something in her eyes. Longing. Envy. She'd sit and stare. And I'd stare back. Maybe we saw something. In each other's eyes. I don't know. All I know is that when I needed help, at that moment of crisis when I was stretched to my limit and the child wasn't coming, the fem appeared. And she grabbed hold of the moment and my hand." Teeg lifts her own hand, stares at it, flexes it. "Oh, she was strong—strong hands, strong arms—though she was just a willowy sapling. Strong vox, but soothing, too." Teeg's vox catches, wavers and tears a little, like the delicate fabric of a sleeve snagged on a twig. She pauses for a moment, takes a breath and holds, then lets it seep out slowly through her lips.

"She arranged my body the way it needed to be and she just reached in, not a bit squeamish and her mantra was 'no pushing, no pushing, just ease, just let it slip, here it is, just let it slip'. And she guided the baby out, the head and then the shoulders. She said to hold on, that the cord was wrapped around its neck. But she freed it, her hands all covered in my blood, and told me to give one more easy push and then it was free and clear and she lifted it and wiped the blood and snot from its nose and mouth with the hem of her blouse and told me that my child was a girl and that she was beautiful."

Angel feels yet another squeeze of her hand.

"That was the first time anyone had said anything like that to me."

The emotion hanging in the air is raw, so raw that Angel fears the guevara will burst into tears, while she herself is dry-eyed and steely-jawed, alert to the slackening of the rain and the dimming of the lightning and the dulling of the thunder as the storm moves off to the east, across the lake to the regions beyond, where perhaps another fem sits on a porch listening to a story she's waited to hear for years. Maybe for her entire life.

No hay lágrimas en la revolución.

Angel puts the thought into words and a low chuckle slips from Teeg's lips, pursed to stanch their quavering.

"Something my mother—one of my mothers—was fond of saying," Angel adds. "The storm's done with us. On its way to cause trouble somewhere else. But I don't think you're done with your story."

Because it hasn't yet ended in the way that Angel believes it will end. In the way that she desires—yearns—for it to end. In the way it must end if she is to have the strength to finish the task.

"I wish it was done. Wish that moment of grace was the end. But you're right, there's more, the ugly more," Teeg says, but then falls silent.

Angel waits, but when the silence stretches, she feeds Teeg a prompt. "She wanted the baby, didn't she? Tried to take it."

Teeg gives Angel's hand another squeeze, a wordless response.

"But you weren't gonna let that happen."

The rain falls with a gentle patter now, but the wind is still blustery, gusting and driving wet sprays onto the porch, onto their faces, where it might be mingling with tears, though Angel swears she's not crying. Teeg, maybe, but not her, not here and now.

"She was just a willow twig of a girl." Teeg's tone is low, dreamy, as if it's coming from somewhere far away and in the past, from some reverie that she doubts ever really happened, except she has the scars to prove it did. "Giving birth is exhausting, you know that. But exhilarating, too. Something in the veins, some flow of energy, pure and white hot, seizes you, drives you to bond with your newborn, to take that baby up in your arms and carry on. Because you know it's not the end. It's the beginning."

"Tell it straight. Just tell it to me straight," Angel whispers.

"Desire, madness. It does strange things. Gives you a strength, a power..."

"Straight. Tell it straight."

"We were grappling over the baby, like—like a pair of vixens snarling over a carcass."

Angel feels the tremor of Teeg's shoulders against her own. Just a small spasm, but the movement shakes Angel to her core, like pressure triggers a fault line as masses of rock strain against each other, straining, straining, until they finally fracture and slip. She wraps her arms around Teeg, a fierce, unyielding hug, a bulwark against the landslide.

"Just—say it—straight."

"I hit her—with a rock. Pushed her into the pit, into the trash."

When Teeg can't bring herself to go on, when she's overwhelmed and shuddering, and Angel knows the tricklings down her neck are the fem's tears and not the rain, it is she who finishes the story.

"You ran to the boat dock and your head was just right enough for you to remember to cover the security eye with a towel. And you wrapped the baby in another and put her in the basket and then you took the precious time to scrawl a note, using the blood that was still seeping from your body. Angel, there is a fate worse than death." She feels Teeg quake and then freeze in her arms.

Angel pushes on. "And then you... swam. You swam, didn't you? You swam because you couldn't take the medic's boat. You were gambling it all on the medic and his boat. He would need the boat to rescue me. You were gambling my life." Angel pauses, her tongue seized by the cruel actuality of it all. The story, the legend suddenly made real.

This happened. This did happen. To her. To me. To Promise.

"She came after you, didn't she? She climbed out of the pit, made her way to the dock. And then what happened?"

The only sound is the gurgle and drip of rainwater through the downspouts.

Angel loosens her stranglehold grip and pushes back from the fem, holding her at arm's length. "Oh, no—we will finish this story. Right here, right now." She shakes Teeg into raising her head, into opening her trickling eyes. "What happened when the girl came to the dock?"

"I was already in the lake," Teeg rasps, her vox as grating as the sound of one stone grinding against another. "She called out. I pretended I had the baby in my arms. And then I went under. And stayed under and held my breath and swam as far as I could before I had to surface. And as I swam, I kept saying over and over again in my head, like a prayer to the Maker, 'don't cry, baby, don't cry, Angel.' I put my face up and gulped a breath and went under again, and kept going, until I figured she wouldn't be able to see me. Just praying—don't cry, don't cry, Angel, don't give yourself away until the time is right."

Agua Quieta. Miss Stillwater. As the bikeman in Illiana called me. Yes, Mr. Cain. You were right. Even from the very beginning.

45

Prisoner of the Past

ELATION. JOY. A SENSE OF COMPLETION. Of wholeness. Emotions Angel has imagined she'd feel if and when she found her birth mother. Emotions conjured as she stared at the young fem's face on the little imagekeep snipped from a printed roster of ovas at Galt Genesis I so many years ago. As she stared, she'd envision scenarios of that moment of discovery, scenarios that ranged from thrillweep to laffriot.

A chance encounter in a GaltMart produce section, where they would both be complaining about the sad state of the broccoli while reaching for the same stalk. A meeting of hands, a meeting of eyes. Fate. Or strolling up to a makeshift table at some ratty Bartertown. Inspecting the merch, staring into the seller's face, steely-eyed, prepared to haggle, and being struck dumb by the resemblance. No, it can't be... but it is. Destiny. Or a scene similar to that which brought her into the widow's care. Rain, a personal transport, a fem in fine clothes, jewelry dripping from ear lobes, neck and wrists. A Cinderella story in which her mother has captured the heart of a swag and lives in a richly appointed manse with walls hung with art saved from the Old Republic. The recognition between mother and daughter is sudden. Overwhelming. Tears and hugs abound, but the revelation to the larger world is drawn out. Steeped in subterfuge. So many issues to overcome. The husband's feelings to consider. And the fair-haired half-sister's, as well. But the transformation from housekeep to swag princess is inevitable.

These scenarios shared a common feature—the instantaneous recognition of two strangers that they are bound together by the strongest ties of blood. Of course, it didn't happen that way. Could never have happened that way. How ridiculous of her to have ever dreamed it would happen that way. She has achieved the irrational goal which set her feet walking north those many months ago, but what she is left with is exhaustion, not elation. A taste of ashes in her mouth and the bone dry hardness of drought across her body, even though her clothes are still damp from the rain.

"I should be happy," she whispers to Word as he slouches beside her on the settee, Teeg having long since crawled off to grab a few hours of sleep.

Teeg had seemed overwhelmed, shaking her head in disbelief, nodding her head in acceptance, staring into space, confused and agonized, straining as if trying to reach something just beyond her grasp. Coming to grips with the realization that the article of faith she had wanted to believe all these years—that her girl had survived, that she had been found and nurtured and loved, raised free of the embed shackle—was something that she hadn't truly believed at all, deep in the darkest places of her heart, in the shadowed corners of her mind. And yet here was living proof.

Angel can't imagine her own head on a pillow on this night, of all nights. When Word joined her, unbidden, she had planned to sit, quiet to the end, unreadable, immovable, as impassive as the brownstone cliffs in the face of all Superior's cajoling and wrath, but the touch of his fingers gathering her hand broke that notion like a boulder splitting into a million cascading pieces. She had spilled everything, blending the two strands of the story like strands of yarn, weaving them into one.

"I should be happy. Why am I not happy?"

"Are you unhappy?" Word asks.

Angel probes her mental state, her physical state. Shakes her head. "I'm not sure I feel—anything. Just numb."

"Heroes need origin stories and you have one helluva story."

"I'm nobody's hero. Don't wanna be."

"You don't get to decide that." He squeezes her hand for emphasis. "Are you disappointed in who and what your mother turned out to be?"

Angel shakes her head again. "No. Who else—what else— could she be, but a badass guevara? After all, she is my mother." A low chuckle ripples in her throat, surprising her.

Word's lips brush her forehead and the stubble on his chin rasps against her temple. "Yeah, if you find a shiny red apple on the ground, the tree is sure to be near."

"But that's the thing—I didn't see the tree. Didn't recognize her. I should have recognized her. Why didn't I recognize her?"

Word pulls her closer. "What? From that little piece of image-keep you been toting around? An imagekeep that was captured when she was barely more than a child? Bang your head against that wall and it's sure to cause you nothing but an ache all day long."

She lets her head settle onto the solid reassurance of his shoulder. "It doesn't hurt, I just—I don't feel—anything."

His fingers lift her chin so that he can kiss her lips, a long, deep, lingering kiss that leaves them both a little breathless. "Did you feel that?"

She shrugs. "Somewhat."

"Oh, isn't she a guevara to the bitter end, yeah," Word taunts, pulling at her braid. "When I'm looking for mi amante. When I'm not ashamed to say I feel you with me every frackin' day." He pauses for a moment, as if waiting for a reply. In the silence, he moves his lips to her ear. "Every frackin' day—like a splinter in my fingertip."

"En la guerra y en el amor todo se vale, as Teeg—mi madre— would say."

Word is quiet. When he finally speaks, his vox is husky. "So is this guerra or amor?"

Angel takes a moment to breathe before she answers. "I think we are two transports on a one-lane road, one coming from the east, the other from the west. Bound to collide."

"Ah, now all she will speak is metaphors."

"As you taught me to speak."

Word squeezes her hand again. "I meant what I said before. Get Lark and get out of there."

"I know. But there are things I have to finish. And this mission is just one of them."

Word cuts in. "Don't talk to me about putting the mission first. I've been there and done that and gained nothing from it but pain and misery."

Angel runs a finger along the scar on his neck. "Yes, we know loss and pain. And the fury that comes after."

Word closes his eyes, leans into her touch. "And if I say I can't go through that again. Take that risk?"

"Then we must say that we... are not... we." Angel lifts her fingers from his neck.

Word shakes his head, pounds a fist on his knee. "Damn, if you're not the hardest fem I've ever met. Diamond hard." He gathers her fingers and presses them to his lips. "And just as precious."

"Then we take the risk. So answer me this. Will you stay with me until the dawn breaks red over the water, because another storm is coming, and I don't want to go through it alone."

The silence stretches until Angel can scarcely endure it, she who has long endured silence. Now she wants it filled. Filled with the answer she longs to hear.

Finally, Word draws her hand and presses it to his chest. "Anywhere, anyplace, anytime." Lowers his lips close to hers again, breathing out his words, breathing in hers.

"To remake the world."

46

No Rest for the Wicked

"THAT ONE DON'T KNOW whether she's a fem or a man."

BoBeck's grunt is sharp-edged, honed with distaste. He squats off to the side of the camp, but his gaze is fixed on the group at the center, where Kali stands, hand on a cocked hip, holding forth about navigating Lake Superior by night. Beside her, Angel listens with the intensity of an avid pupil held in thrall by a charismatic teacher.

"You suddenly got a problem with strong fems?" Kuba retorts, his own eyes fixed on the same spot.

"Huh?" Another grunt, this one quizzical.

"You've been surrounded by 'em for months." Kuba waves his hand for emphasis.

BoBeck shifts positions, stretching out his left leg. Pulls his t-shirt away from his chest. Scratches at the stringy black hair escaping from under it. "Somethin' different about that one, like she wants to have it both ways."

Kuba itches to reply that the confusion might be on BoBeck's part rather than Kali's, but caution holds him back. He's developed a camaraderie with the guevara, but he's not yet a true comrade, a blood brother. Not yet someone that Kuba feels he can call güey with the off-handed affection he had for his brothers and cousins back home. Maybe that trust will come with the successful completion of the Fathom op. So he keeps his lips zipped tight, hoping the convo will move on to some other topic.

But BoBeck's not letting go of the thread. "I mean, would you play the game with that?" He gives a lift of chin in Kali's direction, as if he thinks, in the brief silence, that Kuba has forgotten where he's been throwing shade.

The fem is still talking animatedly, her hands darting this way and that. When Fox appears to ask a question, she rubs those hands vigorously through her flattop, as if trying to stir up the answer, the hairs bristling on end like those of a startled cat.

"Whoa, you would," BoBeck exclaims, taking Kuba's silence for assent. "That's desperation, dude."

"Shut up, man," Kuba snaps back. "I was raised that men—real men—don't talk about such things—about fems that way. And anyway, we're guevaras first, yeah? Brothers and sisters in arms? That's what Teeg—La Tigresa, the tiger mother—says. You don't think about your sister that way."

"Hey, man, I don't mean nothin' by it." BoBeck pats the air as if to smooth things over. "No offense." But then his face lights with a wicked smile. "When you think about it, she ain't one of us—not yet anyway. Probably never will be, cuz she sounds like she's more bear than wolf. Likes her solitary. Don't run with a pack. So feel free to go for it. Give it a poke. Now that other one, I'd game that. If you could ever melt the ice off her." He punctuates his insinuation with a wink.

Kuba shoves to his feet and strides over to the group, leaving BoBeck to fester in his man funk and libido stew. He has to admit, however, that Kali is a bit of a strange bird. Bear. Wolf. Whatever. The way she cocks her head one way and then the other while giving whoever she's looking at the twice-over, chill-eyed and matter-of-fact, as if she's measuring them for a body bag. And the way she blurts out some irreverence, usually pro-fane—whether directed at Galt or the dude she deals with at the fish hauler's or the person she happens to be talking to at the moment—and then levels her gaze to gauge the reaction it provokes. Squinting a little, black eyes glinting in the sunlight. Never letting on whether it was the reaction she expected or desired. And the way she leans in when she wants to make a point. Leans in and brings her body close, but never touching. Brings her hand close to another's arm—close, but never actually touching—letting it hover there, barely an inch of separation between her skin and theirs—but never touching, never closing that intimate gap.

They've checked out her story. Teeg insisted on seeing the boats, so Kali consented to ferry her—and her alone—out to their anchor spots in coves off several of the small islands, where a clever combination of camouflage netting and the contours of the surrounding cliffs hides them from the eyes of drone patrols and lax brute squads who seemingly can't be bothered to make a thorough reconnoiter of the archipelago. Kali had insisted that turnabout is fair play and as part of her price tag, she demanded to meet the Night Prophet. It's a risk, but no higher than what any of the other guevaras are taking in trusting this feral creature, and so Angel stands in the circle, bleary-eyed after a sleepless night, exchanging glances with Teeg, looks that speak in a coded language they've just invented, a language only they understand.

Kali is not in the least bit overawed in her idol's presence. She's regaling the cluster with the origin stories of her fleet and she holds the spotlight with a breezy grace and a colorful patois. She claims she inherited one boat from a dying man who confessed to being her father—the backdoor man, as she calls him—but she has strong doubts about the truth of his claim based on his woeful deficits both above and below the shoulders. Her mum, who had a sharp eye, had always insisted that the studman who sired her had live-act looks. But who was she to stop a man from assuaging whatever guilt was eating away at his heart? She was happy to ease his pain by sailing away with his near-to-deathbed gift.

She hints that she spirited another boat away from a man who intended to keep her as his pleasure woman, but who died mysteriously before the culmination of that intent ever took place.

"As if," BoBeck, joining the group, sniggers in Kuba's ear.

"So sad," Kali mourns, faking it all the way. She makes a face, lips folded in a gleeful pout. "He did bring quite a package, but it was an old package, more than a little worn."

She brags that she won the third boat in a high-stakes game of Seven-card Slam amongst a rogue's gallery of lake pirates and severance jumpers, a gathering that had more hard crust than a day-old loaf of bread.

"Don't ever bet against me," she crows, turning her sights on Kuba, who's standing beside her. And then she does her leaning-in thing, making a heat rise in his face and a fluster unsettle his body.

Teeg smiles, but it's not her usual broad grin, just a small curve of her lips. "I'm not one to play games of chance," she says. One of those coded looks passes between her and Angel, and she adds, "Though I have been known to gamble on a rare occasion."

When the cell hunkers down to break bread on a meal of fried whitefish, courtesy of Kali, who is eager to prove her prowess in any realm or endeavor, including the harvesting of Superior's delicious bounty, Kuba finally has a chance to sit with Angel and debrief on the hectic weeks since they last saw each other. But, as they talk, he senses a withholding, a reserve in her replies to his questions. She is fine. Lark is fine. Everything is fine. It's as if she's just been on a little vacation at the home of particularly dull aunt. *We breakfasted, we lunched, we pedaled around the paths. Oh, and we saw many trees, lovely trees. Oh, and did I tell you we had dinner after? Biscuits with watercress and a lovely poached egg on top. Not too runny.*

It's more than a little maddening. In his opinion, the fact that Promise is the CQO's daughter has made the Fathom op infinitely more dangerous. But Angel blithely downplays his concerns, pretends it's not an issue. He wants to grab her by the shoulders and shake her out of the info stupor she's trapped in, but he can't summon the nerve or the words to challenge her. They are not just Kuba and Angel anymore. She is the Night Prophet, the infiltrator, the mole, the key to the op.

And then there are the eyes that can't let her drift out of their sight. Teeg's eyes. The eyes of the faux bros, Path and Word. Eyes that are possessive. Proprietary. Pondering. Speculative. Studying her as if she is a piece of land over which they've staked a claim. A piece of land they are weighing the future of, asking to what use can they put this fertile ground? What seed shall they plant?

Kuba is surprised that Kali's eyes aren't fixed on Angel as well. But, instead of fawning over her fem-crush, she's reveling in the attention of a pack of odoriffic guevaras, a new-found audience for her time-worn stories, legends that can grow ever more exciting with extra detail, tales she's eager to embellish, like a seamstress adding a bright new thread to her faded embroidery.

"That one's got quite the yap on her. Diarrhea of the mouth, as my aunties would say," Kuba mutters when the cluster around Kali breaks into a group guffaw.

Angel grins. "She's frackin' amazing. What a find." Her grin dissolves into something more wistful. "Reminds me of a couple of kids I knew back in Illiana."

Scrawny bodied Em. Crooked teeth in a wide smile Em. Love ya like a sister Em. Even on the driest day, Em's mouth would be running like a fresh, clear stream. Frack you, Galt! ¡Vete al infierno! Pain, it's mi amigo. A reminder I'm still breathin'.

And Suraj. Another scrawny body with a big mouth. Always the talk, always the mouth running. However far I run'll be enough, cuz yer eye is blind. Suraj the thief whom she detested at first sight. Suraj the wisecracker who got under her skin. Suraj the fugitive companion whom she came to regard—to love even—as a brother. Both gone suddenly and way too soon. Oh, to have them here now.

To run their mouths. To say what needs to be said. And more. Gue-varas to the bone.

"Well, the feeling is mutual. She's got a thing for you," Kuba says, not sure why a tinge of jealousy is coloring his words.

Angel snorts and rocks her shoulder into his, a playful shove that reminds her how serious they have been for so long. How that was forced upon them. How they are barely more than kids themselves now, in this moment.

So make it a light moment. An unserious moment. Just for a moment.

"Uh, no, güey. She's got a thing for you. She's over there, entertaining the troops, and the whole time she's got a side-eye riveted on you. And it's not the shady kind."

Kuba can't control the flush that rises. His face has always been a window into his emotions, flaming cheeks signaling anger, enthusiasm, and, as now, embarrassment. He shakes his head. "Yeah, always the needle with you. When I think about you—the things I miss about you—this ain't one of them."

Abruptly, she wraps her arms around him in a fierce hug. "I miss you, too, Kuba. I wish you were there with me," she whispers, her vox hitching.

"But you know I'd just be trying to talk you out of doing this, especially now. Sometimes I feel like a man trying to hold a boulder in place, stopping it from tumbling down the mountain, from starting a damn avalanche."

"The boulder's already in motion, Kuba. You know that. It's gaining speed and the avalanche will come. It has to come."

Kuba's knee is bouncing, his impatience seeking an outlet. "And I think of the chaos it'll bring, with you and Lark in the middle of it."

"Yes, and chaos drives change. There is no change without destruction."

"Oh, now you're just channeling the Night Prophet," Kuba

grumbles, astonished to find himself pulling back from her embrace.

I am the Night Prophet. And I am Angel of the Shawnee. And I am Merit, Miss Stillwater, who listened and saw and said nothing. And I am the seeker that Eben and Serafina raised me to be. And I am the fighter that my mother bore. And abandoned to fate. But here I am, alive, with all of them inside me.

Teeg sits apart, propped against a massive downed tree trunk. In her eyes, there is a summons. Angel gives Kuba's shoulder another playful shove.

"You should take Kali down to see the waterfall. Though something tells me she'll come up with a thread about a bigger and better and taller and wilder one that she's encountered along the way. But that's what makes her more entertaining than any Galt live act ever could be, yeah?" Angel gives him a wink before she crosses over to Teeg and settles down beside her.

Teeg's fish sits uneaten on her metal plate so Angel snags a hunk and scarfs it down.

"It's good, you know. Didja try it?"

"I did and it is. But then I started ruminating about—things—and there went my appetite." Teeg nudges the plate closer to Angel with her knee.

"Things?" Angel pops another piece of fish into her mouth. She has a strong suspicion of what's on her mother's mind.

How odd to think of her in that way... and yet there is no going back to just Teeg.

"Suddenly, this mission has become—something that's almost too dangerous to contemplate."

Angel dismisses that with a shake of her head. "No, things are falling into place. Now we have boats. And I'm pretty sure we have another person on the inside. I believe Kate is willing and able to help us. That we can trust her. She'll be our link to the other ovas. I've sketched out the picture for her. I just need to work that angle a little longer. Fill in some details. And Promise—I don't know—I sense—"

"No!" Teeg cuts her off with a sweep of her hand. "Do not go there. Do not even think of trying that path."

"But you agreed with me that if she—"

"That was before. Things have changed."

"Only one thing has changed," Angel hisses. "And that—thing—can't get in the way."

"It's already in the way."

"Then push it out of the way."

"Is it so easy to do? Can you do it? Is it so easy to push your thoughts of Lark out of the way?"

"No, it's not. She's always on my mind. Because she is why I'm doing this."

And yet she wonders.

Is this the truth? Does saying it make it so?

Does it matter?

"What's your play in all this?"

Angel and Kali stand at the end of the pier at the old marina, gazing out across the channel. In the waning afternoon, Angel knows she needs to head back to the island, but her feet aren't quite ready to leave. Kali ignores the question, launching into a critique of the dinghy.

"This may be righteous for summer, but come leaf-turnin', just you wait." She shakes her head. "Them gales'll swamp you silly. Leave you upside down and sideways—if you're lucky."

"I don't plan on being here in the fall," Angel replies.

"Well, good on that plan, cuz one of them waves will knock you and that itty bitty thing six ways from Sunday."

"I get the feeling I'm not living up to your expectations. That you're a little disappointed."

For once, Kali appears to be weighing her words, deciding

how to measure them out. "Well, ain't it always that heroes turn out a little..." She pauses for more weighing and sifting. "A little smaller than they're made out to be? There's the legend and there's the life. But people believe what they want to believe, yeah?"

In Angel's mind, an image rears up of a tall man with a raptor profile and eyes that could bore a hole in your gut. "I knew a legend once," she says. "The only way he ever disappointed me was by dying."

Kali frowns. "Well, that's a problem, yeah. Cuz that's always the end of things, ain't it? The man died. But the legend, did that die, too?"

"Not if I can help it. Or maybe I should I say, not if the Night Prophet can help it."

The humid air feels thick, a damp wad of cotton in her nose and throat, a muggy blanket draped across her shoulders. In the west, thunderheads are rising fast in thick billows, the top of the clouds flat and ominous, steel-gray anvils where lightning will soon spark. She should leave, and yet the question compels her to stay.

"You didn't answer me. How do you stand to benefit from this? What's in it for you?"

"Besides that freedom you're always preachin'?" Kali avoids her eyes, examines her grubby fingernails, digging at something she finds underneath.

Angel nods. "Yeah, besides that."

"We all got basics, yeah—mouths to feed, bodies to clothe and shelter. Maybe the thrill of kickin' Galt's ass every now 'n then. No rest for the wicked, you ken?"

"Mouths? Plural? More than one?"

"Yeah, fem, I ken what plural means," Kali snaps. "Yeah, I got what you call dependents. But that's none of yours."

"Well, it is my deal—if I'm gonna trust you."

Kali squints at Angel, flinty-eyed as a hawk scanning for

prey. "Huh, I seem to recall somethin' you said—plural times—more'n once, more'n twice even. What was that word you used?" Kali makes a broad show of scratching her scalp, scratching her chin, shifting back and forth on her feet, her baggy denims slipping down and catching on her hip bones, until she has to pause and tug them up again.

"Faith—that was the word you used, weren't it? Walkin' by faith. How faith is—how'd you say it?—things hoped for, not always seen? Faith, faith, faith." The fem cocks her head, again resembling a bird contemplating the world. "Or was that just the Night Prophet blowin' smoke?" Kali leans in. "Read the scene, fem. Shouldn't be too hard, only one person in it. I got no love for Galt. You oughtta be able to see that, feel that."

Angel feels the words—the truth of them—like a bludgeon. Reflects on the line of people who've walked the road with her. Sees their faces. Suraj. Debs. Kuba and his family of wise and ruthless matriarchs. Life savers all. Now Word. And Teeg. Faith is the path she's been walking, trusting in those she barely knew, putting her life in their hands and where has it gotten her? To this very place and time. Alive.

And so, here's another. All sinew and attitude and a distinct lack of awe and isn't that how it should be in a streetfighter, a rebel, a guevara?

"You know," Angel says, stepping into the dinghy and preparing to cast off. "All those vees you're demanding as payment—you ken those vouchers won't be any good once we take Galt down, right?"

Kali smirks. "Well, I'll lay a wager. I bet I'll have a chance to use 'em up 'fore that day actually dawns. Revolutions don't happen overnight, do they?"

Angel shrugs. "No, they don't. But if you don't believe we can win, then you've already been defeated. I choose to believe we can win. Keep the faith," she says with a wink, and then brings her fist to her heart. "To remake the world."

Kali's black eyes spark. She nods, cool and dodgy. "Yeah, let's do that."

Angel flips the engine switch. Its purr and the distant growl of thunder accompany her as she pushes off, the island in her sights.

Promise is miffed. Or pretends to be. Complains about the lateness of the hour when Angel strides into the kitchen. The room is messier than usual, plates and glasses piled in the sink, counters streaked with the residue of meals consumed while Angel's been out mantrawling around, as the bruja huffs. It's the price she pays for her escapes. The clean-up after. A small price, to be sure. But there's a reward, too, in Lark's broad smile, the glee that glints in her eyes, and the ferocity with which she wraps her arms around Angel's neck and plants a sloppy, crumb-caked kiss on her cheek.

"Mama!" It's a whoop that subsides into a coo as she tucks her head under Angel's chin. "Mama. Mama."

In that embrace, Angel senses the through-line, the thread, woven strong, stitched fine, and knotted tight. The thread that binds their lives, the thread that now binds them to another, and to generations before her. Mother and child. Mother and daughter. Invisible, intangible, but strong as corded steel, with a hold as tenacious as a spider's web, gossamer lace that enraptures and ensnares.

Eyes lowered, nose pressed to the curls that smell of Promise's floral-scented shampoo, Angel sways, a little woozy, drinking in the flow of love like a double-shot of home brew. But a corner-eye glance at the bruja is a sobering slap to her face. And still, she fends it off, the dagger of envy that slices the space between them, so quick and then gone, hidden away with a pursed-lip smile and a quick reset of the neck and shoulders, like a blade tucked back into its sheath, waiting for next time, for a better time to cut to the core.

Not today. Not this day.

A bright-hot, stark-white flash knifes through the windows, with a crackling shot that rattles the panes. A shudder in her arms and small fingers clutch harder, dig deeper, as if to burrow under her skin.

You are already there. You are mine. And I am yours. Forever.

47

Down the Rabbit Hole

LA BÊTE HAS EXPERIENCE playing both sides. During his stint in junior gladiator ball, the coach, needing the boy's size and strength, insisted he play through the whole game, running a series on offense and then heading right back onto the field to grind it out with the defense. Physically, it was brutal, but mentally, it both broadened and sharpened his perspective, as he came to see the logic of action and reaction, how the moves of one side mirrored the other. How to anticipate the fake, the juke, the tuck, the block, how to counter an attack and devise a drive that camouflaged its pre-determined approach.

Lack of a live opponent never stopped him from engaging in a game of chess on his mother's heirloom board, with its intricately carved pieces handed down from time out of mind. The neighbor girl, Serene, was not a chess player. Said she could never visualize the countermoves an opponent might use to thwart her own. Found it discouraging that she could set herself up to lose with her opening move. Most of the other children lacked the necessary perseverance and gravitated toward the instant gratification and physical action of immersive games. So he played against himself, finding it more stimulating and satisfying than going up against a robo competitor through a chess engine. By setting up the game on one of his mother's brass trivets, he could easily turn the board back and forth, allowing him to switch viewpoints without the hassle of having to switch seats. He always played both armies to win.

These experiences inform his current moves. In their clandestine meetings, the splitlip is telling him the Genesis takedown is a go, but that no firm date has been set. La Bête suspects this is not true. Suspects that a date has been established and this hesitation is all smoke and prevarication on the part of the runt to extract a few more of whatever Galt has promised. He considers employing a few intimidation techniques, but that approach has not been authorized by either of his handlers, so he dons the mask of the patient listener, the quiet go-between, who sees and hears, but says very little.

When the vox of the self-styled "operator"—the master he believes is the Galt pipeline—crackles into his feedcom, requesting an update, he spews a stream of disinformation. That both ops are in play, that logistics for the attacks on the water and breeder facilities have been developed, but due to an overabundance of caution on the part of the ché leaders, the hits have been put off. That the mole has hinted at the possibility that cells are experiencing a wave of deserters. When logistics are finally shared with him, he will pass them along. Blah, blah, blah.

While there is no indication that the "operator" questions any of what he's feeding it, there is a definite risk in taking this path. The higher ups may decide to do a sweep and round up whoever they can—now—rather than waiting until the op is in motion to bring the hammer down. But one rock solid fact he has learned over the past few years is that, from regional directors on down to squad commanders, ProServ securitycrats are glory hounds and fame whores. He intuits their Corporate attitude. Why do a quiet little severance when, with just a tad more firepower, you can do a big splashy extermination? He can already hear the bombastic pep talks reverberating through the roll call rooms.

We'll make an example of those frackin' chés. Put the fear of Galt into any little shit who's dreaming of running off to join the movement. Show 'em there is no frackin' movement. Just a red tide of lowlife scum.

And then one evening as he polishes his boots for the next day's inspection by the sector manager, an 'unscheduled' preparedness sweep of the lower Superior squads of which, somehow, the commander has been notified in advance, the bell tones ring in his ear and Nadie's assertive vox fills his head.

"The day is near, chess master. Remember this. Whoever makes the first move seizes the initiative. In the opening, gambits will be offered. Reject any that will cause you to lose the initiative. Make no unnecessary moves that would allow your opponent to gain tempo. You know that by having the initiative you put your opponent on the defensive. And having that initiative is crucial in the endgame.

And remember this above all: your mission is the fem."

Even the pruning shears are high-end. Titanium-coated steel with distinctive gold-colored blades. Angel surmises this was their attraction for Promise—their looks alone, without her giving a thought to their added durability. The red handles are smartly designed to fit the hand in a steady, comfortable grip. Powerful but lightweight, with a blade slender enough to slip under an ova's security band and sharp enough to slice through the ultra-thin wires that keep her chained to the island.

It had been easy enough to convince Promise to purchase a replacement for the shears that Angel claimed she lost. To order it from the GaltMart and have it delivered on the supply ferry. The bruja had briefly cooed over the shiny blades like a child fascinated by a glitzy bauble before pushing them across the kitchen counter to Angel.

"My fleeting connection to yard work for the year," she'd

said, sauntering away.

Angel has acquired two additional pairs of shears by sneaking into the utility shed where the groundskeep stores her implements, while the oblivious fem tooled around on her standing mower, feedcom buds and noise cancelling muffs firmly in place. These shears reside at the other end of the quality spectrum. Basic carbon steel, with some corrosion and staining, but the blades are sharp and will do the job on the first snip.

Four shears, one per dorm, to sever the bonds of twenty five ovas in each location. If they all decide to evacuate. And determining that is a dicey situation.

Kate had surprised Angel with her immediate and full embrace of the plan. Angel had expected initial reluctance, the need for artful, passionate persuasion. But Kate had the fire in her belly from the get-go. Had even anticipated parts of Angel's carefully worded approach, shrouded as it was in innuendo. Angel herself had been astonished when she heard the words coming out of her own mouth, that day on the sand-spit when Kate confided her story.

What if I told you that you don't have to? That you can leave this place forever?

A blink, a quick shake of the head in disbelief, but then another, more subtle, as if Kate was daring to throw off that initial disbelief, to banish it from her mind. And then a receptive wonder had appeared, glowing in her eyes.

Sometimes Angel speculates if it was too easy. If the ova had bitten the bait too soon, allowed herself to be reeled in without a fight. If that ease means something. If the possibility of betrayal lurks behind the eagerness in Kate's eyes. That possibility has crossed Angel's mind, but only fleetingly, because she pushes it out as quickly as it flits in. As quickly as Kate had pushed her own doubts away. Doubt is a staller. Doubt only serves to drag the feet, to cause a stumble at the exact moment when sure-footedness is essential. Like tears, there can be no doubt in the revolution. In this mission. In the Fathom op. Only belief. Only trust.

The ova has dreamt of escape. Has plotted for it in her own way, with the coded messages slipped into her letters home. Has kept Bond's vow in her heart and imagined a day when rescue might thrust out a hand to her. A hand she'd grab in an instant and clutch in a death grip. Angel has left it up to Kate to approach the other ovas. To choose the right words, the right time. To start with her circle of friends and gossips and work outward. Because it is a huge ask. As much as any ova may detest her life in Genesis I, the fear of the unknown could easily outweigh that loathing, because there is no certain destination, no guarantee of success, that the cell can make. No tableau of life after, of life outside, of life beyond the water, that Kate can present to them. No promises she can make. Just an offer of hope that another kind of life is possible. Somewhere down the horizon. Hope to bite down on through the fear and the pain, like a bullet.

To hope is to gamble. To bet on the future. To hope is dangerous, and yet hope is the opposite of fear, for to truly live is to take risks. Teeg's words before Angel had left the camp, when she'd pulled her into another fierce embrace and pressed her cheek up against Angel's, so the fem's breath was fire in her ear.

This is the message that Kate will deliver. She will slip through the gardens and draw alongside and pull up a chair on the terrace. She will have a tête-à-tête over a glass of lemonade, a heart-to-heart while offering to share a slice of the cook's coveted cherry crumble. She will smile and whisper. Murmur and purr. She will take a fem's hand in hers and give a gentle squeeze of reassurance. And then they will discover who will hear her words and who will truly listen.

48

Lies and Other Stories

SOME THINGS STILL POSSESS the ability to amaze the CQO. The vibrant hues of sunsets. The power of water to shape stone. The idea that a short, thick rod of metal, mesh, and wire can snatch vibrations out of the air, translate them into 'tronic signals and then scribe these signals onto a capture medium for storage or send them immediately back into the air over a loudspeaker. Yet she loathes being face to face with the microphone in the Hive studio. Freezes when the time comes to speak the Galt truth into the ugly bulbous thing. Self-medicates with a microdose of oral Tranquille to get through the torturous process. Understanding her own issues with capturing a voxcast reinforces her wonder at the ease with which the fem works her magic as the Night Prophet.

She presumes the voxcasts are live, not pre-recorded, which makes them even more impressive. No multiple takes that can be cut, spliced and run through the audio tailor. No, the nuances found in that singular vox are real. The clever use of phrasing and pace to keep the listener engaged. The subtle pause before the passionate outburst, the incantation, the build to a climax. The command of phonetics to create a mood. The sibilants that change the tone from soft and gently flowing to almost hissingly sinister over the course of a few phrases. Plosives that create an abrupt, knife-like effect. The blending of the two, which can bring a short, sharp shock after a softer start, or a juddering, stuttering tone, like stones dropped into a gently flowing stream.

You know the words to the song, the hymn to water, the hope it represented to the people, the hope that was betrayed. The hope of a new land, the hope that pain had been vanquished, that sorrow and tears had been banished. And you think—when you actually stop to think—how ridiculous. Because you know, in the wisdom born of suffering, that life is a vale of tears and that nothing comes without a price. And here is how the idealist is bruised and battered and split open and the cynic oozes out. And a field of color is bled into a vast, gray waste where you construct your fortress, surrounded by insurmountable walls. Each brick a bulwark against feeling, against engaging. And as the years go on, the snow of bitter disillusion shrouds and the ice of distrust encases your citadel. But you discover all of that protection only breeds loneliness. And that your fortress is really a prison.

So what can you do? To truly live.

Raise the portcullis. Open the doors and go outside and face the truth. Take the walls down, brick by brick, and let light fill the room. You'll find that what was once a childish, blind idealism is transformed, rebuilt into a realism that is grounded and strong. Malleable. Adaptable. Able to bend, but, in the end, unbreakable.

Let your heart believe. Trust that it is possible to remake the world.

So sayeth the Night Prophet.

This interplay of words and sounds. Pulsing with bitterness one minute, dripping honey the next. It's not impromptu. Not some stream-of-consciousness spew. It's deliberate. It has to be. Does the fem write her own messages? Or is there another hand feeding the vox? A wordsmith crafting the message? What a duo that must be. But just how dedicated to the cause must one actually be to *sound* so completely dedicated? Is the mindset of the true believer absolutely necessary to sound so absolute?

The CQO has her doubts. She has only to consider the actors and actresses who populate the live acts and the stream-cam dramedies and thrillweeps. All that emoting is only skin deep. All those characters are just roles to play, just costumes and wigs to slip into for a six-week run. Paint your face and play the fool or the ingenue or the hero. Hit your marks and say your lines. Take your bows as the curtain falls or the credits roll. And then you shed one costume, one role, one persona, and don the next. In her experience, the faked emotion is generally indistinguishable from the real. So, what a boon it would be to have a night prophet spouting the corporate propaganda. A fresh vox, a young vox. Fresh and young and hypnotic.

The CQO is nothing if not perceptive. The vox of CEO Blanche—and her own vox—no longer capture the ears of the Protectorate. No longer sway the mood of the people. These thoughts have become such a preoccupation that she summons the ProServ director to her office, rather than waiting for him to seek her out to deliver a status update. He launches into a rambling sermon about preparedness in the face of two potential actions, but acknowledges that the mole still hasn't coughed up a firm date for either, and that the lips of the cell leaders seem to be getting tighter. It's possible that they suspect an infiltration, or are at least taking measures against that possibility, but rest assured, his goliaths will be ready for any eventuality.

The CQO blinks away the glaze that has formed over her eyes. "Yes, I trust you will round them all up before the mayhem reaches a crescendo. Here's the thing. I want this Night Prophet. No severance for that one. I want the fem brought to me."

The ProServ director erupts into a stuttering mass of confusion. "But—but we have no way of—no way of knowing which fem it is. They—they may all claim to be the Night Prophet—and then how—"

"Mr. Cruz, have you listened to the vox? Do you not think

you would recognize it?"

"I've listened, yes, but—"

"Well, we shouldn't have to stoop to this, but, if you must, bring them all—whoever claims to be the prophet—bring them to me, because I will most certainly distinguish the real, the true, from the false."

"And then?" the director prompts, not wanting to give in to his own lurid imaginings.

"And then, Mr. Cruz, we will see if this rebel is actually willing to die for her cause."

Spurred on by the grinding song of the dog-day cicadas, the guevaras pace like coyotes that have come up against a wire fence enclosing their territory, back and forth, eyes peering into the middle distance, noses to the wind. Ready to move on, but unable to move on. Ready for action, but resigned to waiting. Waiting. Waiting.

They check and re-check burners, knives, comlinks. Teeg moves among them, laying a calming hand on arms and shoulders, a calming vox on anxious minds.

"Did you check it once?"

A nod.

"And it's all good?

Another nod.

"Then put it away. When the time comes, you'll be ready."

BoBeck squats with Kuba and Kali, prepping aid kits with supplies liberated during a night raid on a clinic. The mission had been cake. The tiny rebel signifier, the heart clutched within the fisted hand, lurked just to the right of the back door, carved into the cinderblock low to the ground, not quite hidden by a creeping sprawl of ivy. The door had been left unlocked. Accidentally or on purpose, who could say? They took lightly, only what they needed, no more. Rolls of bandage gauze and tape, anti-bac wipes, lotion, and pills. Some lethe capsules, in case of serious injury.

"Not like Teeg to play it so close to the vest," BoBeck grumbles, shoving a packet of wipes into a kit bag. "We should know how this thing is goin' down. And when. Can't do an op without kenning the logistics."

"Maybe she don't know yet. Maybe she's waiting on word from the prophet," Kali speculates, zipping up a finished pack and grabbing another.

"Yeah, things seem kinda fluid," Kuba says, idly twirling a roll of tape on his forefinger.

"Oh, she knows. She just ain't tellin'. And that ain't normal procedure," BoBeck mutters. "Tired of this shit," he adds, tossing his unfinished pack down in the dirt.

"Dude!" Kali retrieves the pack and wipes away the pine needles clinging to it. "The point is to keep med supplies as clean as possible. So you can actually put 'em on an open wound."

"What're you, a medic now?" BoBeck grunts as he springs up from his perch on a log. "Frack it all!" He stalks off in the direction of the trench latrine.

Kali watches until his scrawny figure disappears in the stand of evergreens. "Maybe Teeg's worried 'bout too many people kenning." She arches an eyebrow. "The wrong people."

"A leak?" Kuba's tone is less questioning than scoffing. "No, not happening."

"Uh yeah, could be happening, easily. And a leak is something sorta accidental. Oh, there's water dripping, my pipe must have sprung a leak. I'm talking something more accidental on purpose. Or just on purpose."

"A splitlip? In this cell?" Kuba shakes his head, rolls his eyes. "I don't think so. It's—we're—a tight squad."

Kali shrugs. "Maybe. Maybe not. You know, it goes both ways. There's plenty of skinshifters inside Galt. Like the one who carved the rebel sign on that clinic wall and left the door unlocked. Pledging allegiance for the good of the Protectorate, but fingers crossed behind their backs, working to bring it all down. So don't you think it's possible there's at least a few in the movement who roll the other way?"

"Well, yeah, sure, I guess, but not in this cell."

"What makes you so sure?"

"Just feel it in my gut."

Kali smirks. "Oh, yeah? Well, maybe that squirrelly feeling in your gut is just the 'shrooms you ate last night. How long you been runnin' with these guevaras?"

"A few months, but it feels longer—long enough to get a sense of who they are—and to get a sense that none of them would betray the cause."

"Ah, yeah, the cause. So then you're the newest guevara?"

"In the cell? Yeah."

Kali slowly rolls another strip of gauze. "So then maybe you're the infiltrator? The man with the splitlip."

"What? You're crazy, you know that?" Kuba waggles the small bottle of lethe pills. "Been into the supply? Cuz you're sounding stone loco. Ha-ha." He arches an eyebrow, cocks his head, taps the bottle against his chin. "But hey, you know, actually, you are the newest member of the cell. So maybe you're the splitlip. Love Galt much?"

"Güey, I'm not a member of the cell. I'm an independent contractor."

"Yeah, and sell your services to the highest bidder? Including Galt?"

Kali smiles with her lips, but not her eyes. "Who can find a virtuous fem, for her price is far above rubies."

"What's that supposed to mean? Is that from some biblio?"

Kali just keeps smiling that enigmatic smile-that's-not-a-smile. "Man who gave me my third boat was a preacher—ex-preacher—but once a preacher, always a preacher, because he rattled on in 'pocalypse and revelation and things he called proverbs. It's one of his." She zips the pack, tosses it on top of the pile, and stands to stretch. Then, without a word, she strides off toward the pump, where BoBeck is vigorously cranking the handle and splashing water over his face and head.

Kuba frowns. "I thought you said you won that boat in a card game," he calls after her.

A shrug and an over-the-shoulder wink are her only replies.

49

Endgame

If Promise has regrets about spilling her family history to Angel, she doesn't let them show, doesn't wear them on her skin the way she does her other complaints and troubles. Angel continues her surveillance, scrutinizing the fem's facial expressions and body language from under lowered eyelashes and out the corners of her eyes, but she catches nothing amiss. If anything, Promise seems more even-keeled and less moody now, solicitous without being overbearing, striking just the right balance in her interactions with Lark. Less mother, more auntie.

The thought has crossed Angel's mind that she should spirit the child off the island before the op. That she could conjure some excuse to take Lark to the mainland on the final voxcast trip. But what good would that do? She has no one in whose care she can entrust the child. The widow is gone. All of the cell will be engaged in the op. And it would only raise suspicions in Promise, putting everything in jeopardy.

No, Lark will have to remain on the island until the bitter end. And that's what Angel doesn't want to think about. She can run everything else though her mind, over and over, visualizing each phase of the op, phases that she's talked through with Teeg and Armor. Taking out the nerve center. Shepherding the ovas to the boat landings. The courses of the boats sailing north and east to the safe houses that will provide temporary refuge for the diaspora. She has forced herself to consider all the possible scenarios if they—when they—encounter goliaths, from best case—a lucky evasion—to the worst—an all-out firefight. But it's the gathering up of the child that somehow never takes shape in the midst of these imaginings. The endgame.

In the past, someone else has always been there. Someone to let her be a mother without doing the hard work of mothering. Someone to take charge. To know what to do when she didn't, when she couldn't. When she wouldn't. Here and now, there is no one.

Though Angel tries to keep every emotion in check, to keep everything hidden under the cloak of the routine, the day-in and day-out, Promise notices. See the flinch at the clatter of a dropped spoon. Hears the tremor in Angel's vox when she scolds Lark for spilling her milk.

"You're jumpy as a feral cat lately," she remarks, handing over a towel for Angel to sop up the mess. "There's a time out of mind saying, you know, no crying over spilled milk." Promise takes the upturned cup and pours another serving. "Mistakes will be made, accidents will happen," she singsongs, setting it down in front of Lark. "Careful this time," she reminds the child, tousling her hair.

"If something happens to me, you'd keep her, wouldn't you? Raise her as your own?"

The wild, random thought not meant to be uttered somehow escapes Angel's lips and hangs in the air of the kitchen, amidst the scents of fresh-baked bread and sliced apples. Promise stares, a piece of fruit in her hand poised halfway between the plate and her mouth. Her own lips twitch and curl into a semi-smile.

"Where did that come from?" she asks, though it sounds more statement than question. Again, though Angel is sure her face has the blank visage of a cornhusk doll, Promise must discern some image drawn there, some message written in cryptic glyphs that only she can decode.

Somewhere in the manse, a timekeep's hands align and set off its melancholy chime, followed by another and another, until the kitchen timekeep joins the chorus and Angel feels that, finally, they've driven her mad and she will explode into shrieks that will never, ever stop. Instead she bites down on her lip, hard enough to draw blood.

At last, Promise blinks. "You know she would want for nothing."

Angel knows she should let it be. Let the words drift and dissipate, like the spiraling smoke of a snuffed candle. Hold the others inside. But the words squeeze their way out again.

"Things—trinkets and toys—don't matter. I want her to be loved."

Promise stares, her eyes calm, bottomless blue pools into which an unsuspecting wader might wander and drown. "You heard what I said. On the beach. You know it's the truth."

Angel nods.

There is the other truth, the realization Angel feels in the deep part of the body where the blood pulses, though even now, a part of her fights against accepting it as reality, as the thing that really happened. The realization that Promise is the one who set this all in motion. With an act that started in compassion, one fem helping another in her time of extremity, and ended in violence.

Without her, I wouldn't be here.

So what wouldn't she do for her beloved? Nothing. There were no lengths to which she wouldn't go. Even to the point of murder.

Then we are two of a kind. Guilty blood. Innocent blood. Blood is blood, no matter what drove the hand it stains.

And it's as if a vow has been taken, on both sides.

"Fathom is like a boulder. Like a boulder, it will follow the laws of nature. Heavier objects resist change much more than lighter ones. At first, the boulder is much harder to move than the loose stone lying in your path. But once it's set in motion, it becomes next to impossible to stop. And Fathom is a very heavy object."

Teeg stares at Angel across the safe house kitchen table. "It will keep on rolling. There will be no turning it around. And so I'll ask the question—and I want you to think well and hard before you answer." The fem shakes her head. "Even as I say these words, I know you have already thought, long and hard. Are you prepared to do this?"

Angel knows the boulder is already in motion. Out of the hundred ovas, Kate has reported that thirty-seven are ready to bolt. Another dozen or so are leaning, but not yet committed. Many regard the notion of escaping the facility as either a complete fantasy or an impractical plan destined to crash and burn. Almost two dozen have been left unapproached, out of the loop, for fear they would prove outright traitors to the cause. Those who seem too content, too chummy with the overseers, too quick to spout Protectorate propaganda, as well as those all-too-quiet ones with ever watchful eyes.

"At least I hope they're still out of the loop. I can't guarantee that lips haven't slipped. I did my best," Kate had said, shoulders sagging with the weight of her uncertainty.

Angel had nodded her reassurance. "Of course you did. We just have to trust."

And there they are, balanced on the edge of the precipice. Watching the boulder roll and knowing there really is no stopping it.

Silence cocoons the kitchen, enveloping the fems, until Path skitters through the screen door, bringing the scent of damp grass with him.

"You're late," he snaps, not bothering to wipe his shoes on the throw rug. "Your frackin' adoring audience is waiting with bated breath. You can't afford to be late tonight."

Angel feels like a boulder herself—a heavy object in the grip of inertia, resisting a change in her current state. Path opens his mouth to speak again, but Teeg lifts a hand, staying his words. Angel's eyes find Teeg's. She nods.

Teeg nods in return. "There is a vox that whispers to me when doubts crowd in and I feel the wall against my back. And it says, who are you to deny that she was born, that she survived, that she walked back into your life, for just such a time as this." A deep inhalation, a long, slow exhalation. She nods again. "We go on Corpse Day."

Corpse Day. The bees' darkly humorous nickname for the final day of a week-long celebration of the founding of the Protectorate. Corporatization Day, officially, but that is too much of a formal mouthful to describe this grand finale, a bacchanal of feasting and drinking and leisure-induced mania. And if one survived the mayhem, one would arguably come out looking like death warmed over. Hence the macabre joke.

The holiday means little to Angel beyond her memories of carnivals that popped up in the AgSector at the height of August's heat. The spun sugar on a stick that melted on her tongue, tasting sweet and burnt at once. The inevitable pools of puke, weird amalgams of pink and brown, that stained the sawdust around the crazy ride that spun like a whirly-gig. A ride she avoided like a virus. Eben and Serafina never observed the holiday, although the AgSector migs and town bees doused their free days in oblivion, homebrew, and lethe, if they could score it.

She'd once glimpsed a man and a woman, totally wrecked, stumbling in a fraught, awkward dance in the middle of the two-lane. When she'd asked Eben what they were celebrating, he frowned, stared hard at the pair, and then looked toward the horizon. When he finally spoke, his vox had been subdued, full of what may have been regret.

They're not drinking to celebrate. They're drinking to forget.

The decision is strategic. Corpse Day means Galt Genesis I

will have only a skeleton staff, with most of the island bees allowed to depart for the mainland to celebrate the holidays. And there will be fewer goliaths patrolling the lake and the shorelines.

When Angel reaches the rope ladder to make her ascent into the attic, she sees Word's face staring down through the opening, a squint of concern narrowing his eyes. He has begged her not to do this final voxcast. Implored her to go into radio silence. He fears a repeat of the not-so-distant past. Fears this voxcast may be the one that gives them away, that allows the focus to pinpoint their location. Fears a visit in the pitch-dark hours. A visit by a brute squad. Fears another loss more devastating than the first.

But she won't allow herself to be dissuaded by his words or his body.

"That happened in the past," she'd whispered. "I thought you'd let that go."

"The past echoes," he'd whispered in return.

She'd pressed her hands over his ears and kissed him long and hard to stop his words. "I can't guarantee things will be different this time. I only know that I am doing this. I'm committed to it. And you vowed to follow wherever the Night Prophet led."

Now she tries to scowl, but finds her lips won't bend to anything other than a weak smile. "Will you chide me for being late, too?" she asks, setting her foot on the first rung.

"I know better," he replies, without smiling in return.

When her head breeches the opening, he draws her in for a kiss and then boosts her up into the attic. The equipment rests on its makeshift table, silent, patient, waiting to purr to life at the touch of her hand.

"This may be the end," she says, eyeing the mic with the same mix of trepidation and wonder as she had the first time she saw it, nine months before.

Nine months. The time it takes to grow a child in the womb. The time it takes to grow a vague seed of an idea, a mere vision, into a reality so close she only has to reach out and grasp it.

"No, this is only the beginning," Word says. He gestures to the table. "Ready?"

She nods.

Only a fool would think that if she squats by the river long enough, she'll see the body of her enemy float by. And so that time is over. The time of waiting. Of doubt. Of longing. Of hesitation. That time is over. It is the time for doing. For taking action.

I cannot say what will happen. Difficult days stretch before us with a dark passage and a deep valley through which we must travel. But this I know. I have glimpsed the future. I've left the valley and climbed the mountain and I've seen the other side. What the prophets of the ages called the promised land. This land. Our land. I cannot say that I will set foot there with you. But I will pledge to fight for it with you.

We will reclaim this land for freedom. And in this effort, we will not fail, for we are riding the arc of history.

We will fight in the streets of the Ontario region and in the fields of Huron.

We will fight from the factories of Erie to the orchards of Michigan.

We will fight across the Superior, from the northern cliffs to the southern shores.

We will fight in Illiana, the land that made me who I am.

We will fight in the glass castle of the Hive, until every pane is smashed and lies in glittering ruin.

We will fight, as a prophet of the ages once said, until justice rolls down like waters and righteousness like a mighty stream.

If we must, we will paint a portrait of a new world with the blood of our oppressors.

We will never relent.

So sayeth the Night Prophet.

PART FOUR

Spiritus

Year 83 – August

“Faith sees best in the dark.”

—Kierkegaard

“Hope is the thing with feathers.”

—Emily Dickinson

50

La Bête Noire

UNDER THE LACKADAISICAL COMMAND of a slacker-in-chief who is rigid one day and lax the next, many of the goliaths, without the physical regimen of daily drills, have let their movements devolve into a trudge or a lumber or a plod, but La Bête still walks with the precision he learned in boot camp. Serene would say that he's living in character, playing the role of goliath. Following this method provides him with a level of reassurance that he is capable of doing what is expected of him. Because he knows that his mission requires stealth as well as strength, cunning as well as brute force.

He never takes the same path through the forest for his weekly hookup with the splitlip. Just after sunset, as the slanting orange glow begins to blur into a velvety bluish haze, he winds his way through the balsam firs and white spruces with the instincts of a nocturnal beast. When he nears the rendezvous point, he squats to wait for time to pass, for the dark to close in, for the runt to limp into view, swinging his mini-maglite to signal his presence. As if that were necessary, when La Bête can hear him coming through the thickets of thimbleberries and honeysuckle, when La Bête knows the very tree from around which the man will step into the tiny clearing where they meet. Because the splitlip never varies his path.

La Bête strips a couple of needles from the cedar that shelters him and crushes them between his fingers. Breathes in their crisp aromatic scent, a scent that reminds him of clean things. A scent that evokes a memory of playing sardines in the old neighborhood. Serene had been 'it' and ran off to hide and he'd been the first to find her, wedged into a sliver of space in back of a shed, the opening excellently hidden behind a stand of arbor vitae. He'd squeezed in with her, his arm and leg pressed against hers, his nose hovering above a branch of the evergreen, breathing in the smell of pine and the smell of her, and almost reeling from the heady mingling of scents, finding himself hoping that no one would find them for a long time.

Here and now, he knows that would be a futile hope. Knows that both of his handlers have the focus fixed on him, that they possess his coordinates, his embed a hot read on their screens. It comes as no surprise when bells toll in his ear, along with Nadie's vox.

"Some music to pass the time?"

A guitar. A vox that heaves and rasps, like the vox of a man who just got pummeled to within an inch of his life in a brute squad shakedown. A man lamenting a lost love with his dying breath. *Remember me to one who lives there... Where? The north country...* The phrase sung twice, in the first verse and the last. *The north country. North... Where the winds hit heavy on the borderline... north.*

He's still puzzling over the lyrics when the next song begins, again with a simple guitar. But when this vox eases in, it's smooth and supple, oozy as molasses, bending vowels and notes, holding onto a word until it finally decides to let go and pick up the next, spinning a ballad of a man falsely accused of murder who cannot save himself without revealing his true crime, gaming his best friend's wife.

She walks these hills in a long black veil... Three times the phrase rings out, the vox stretching out the vowel—*loooong black veil*—and the hairs prickle on his arms.

Kuba crouches, his back against the narrow trunk of a birch. Teeg had wished them all a good night's sleep, now that the uncertainty was gone, swept aside by the setting of the date. So, of course, he cannot stop his brain from tossing and turning in anticipation. Can't stop his fingers from tracing the outline of the knife secure in the pocket of his cargos. Can't stop ruminating over the curious way in which she'd made the announcement. Not as an announcement at all. Not as a rallying of the troops. Maybe she knew that she couldn't top the Night Prophet, so instead she'd moved among the members of the cell, catching them alone or in pairs. Placing a hand on a shoulder, engaging in a solemn eye-to-eye. With Fox and Echo, her seconds-in-command, she'd drawn them into a hug, her lips close to their ears. With Kuba, she had folded his hand between hers and stared, first into his eyes, and then down at the hand she grasped.

"Corpse Day," she had said. "But I want no discussion of this amongst the brethren. Now that you know, there's no need to talk, only to prepare to do what must be done."

One more day, a sundown, a night. Too little time and too much. Are they truly ready? Is Angel truly ready?

"Angel—the vox—she sounded so assured," Kuba had said, keeping his grip on Teeg's hand, even as he sensed her letting go. "But is she, really?"

She had looked away, bright eyes scanning the clearing, watching as the others obeyed her strictures, slinking off to their favored dens. To sleep. To meditate. To fully wrap their minds around the mission on which they are about to embark.

"In dreams begins responsibility. Or so I've read in one of Word's biblios." Her gaze, somber, had locked onto Kuba's. "Dreams aren't free. Once you have one, you're setting a goal. And with that comes responsibility. You can have the most fervent dream, but it means nothing, goes nowhere, if you neglect the responsibilities behind it." Teeg had glanced around again, as the last of guevaras drifted out of the clearing. "With freedom, we choose the goals we want to achieve, but our actions determine where our lives will lead. Whether our dreams are realized. Or whether they'll fade into regrets that prick us every now and then, like a twinge sparking from an old wound when we bend a certain way." Teeg had extracted her hand from Kuba's, but not before giving it another reassuring pat. "Get some sleep." And then she, too, had drifted off through the trees, weaving a soundless path.

Now Kuba squats, still wide awake, knees starting to ache. His ears prick at the rustle of pine needles before his eyes catch the movement behind the sound. BoBeck, of course. The man has not mastered the silent moves of La Tigresa and probably never will. Once again, he veers from the path leading to the latrines.

Kuba wonders what BoBeck thinks now that the date for Fathom has been set. Does he believe they are ready? That the mission can succeed? Kuba's own doubts drive him to seek the thoughts of another foot soldier. Ignoring Teeg's instructions, he stands and follows the man along the trail to the gorge. He doesn't want to shout after him and risk discovery. The man is moving quickly, the distance between them growing rather than shrinking. He quickens his own pace. As before, when BoBeck reaches the waterfall, the sand is deserted and he crosses the creek. This time, instead of turning back, Kuba follows, hopping across the slippery slabs of rock to the far bank, finding the narrowest of footpaths, just a thin line of tamped down dirt leading up through the underbrush. He picks his way through prickly brambles, ducking under and around thin branches that scrape and snag his t-shirt, as if to hold him back, as if to say, *Do not follow in those footsteps.* He pauses at the crest, looks around. He's lost sight of the moving figure and can no longer hear the muffled crackling of his footfalls. The canopy of trees blocks the moonlight, creating an all-encompassing dark. Further pursuit seems useless.

Then Kuba's eyes catch a blink up ahead. A white hot blink, followed by another, and then a third. He moves forward, feeling his way through the trees, inching along, sweeping his feet before placing them, scouting for loose rocks and jutting roots. More blinks, a code in light. Drawing nearer, he sees there are two pinpoints. And they are converging. As the pinpoints meet, two figures emerge, but shadowed, just four legs visible in the cones of light thrown down by their maglites. The figures may be hidden, but the reason for their meeting crystallizes in a split-second.

He's spilling. Spilling the op.

The realization has barely had its moment in the blinding spotlight of Kuba's mind and the shock of it hasn't had time to jolt his body when there's a muffled crack, a whoosh and a rush of something past his right ear, followed by a second crack, another whoosh. Instinct pushes him into a defensive crouch, hands clenched over his head, while his innards squirm.

Frack, oh frack, what've I done...

A hand lands roughly on his shoulder.

"Steady, man." Armor's gruff whisper is sibilant, snakish. "One down, the other running, but possibly with a bullet lodged in some area of soft tissue."

Kuba feels his gorge rise and finds himself retching, puking up the wad of fear and astonishment caught in his throat. BoBeck alive one second, dead the next? BoBeck, his patrol buddy, mentor. A splitlip. A traitor.

How can that be?

Kuba's breath comes as fast and ragged as his thoughts. It's the first killing he's witnessed since that horrendous day at the water facility. The day he'd been faced with a stark choice in an adrenaline-soaked blur of time, with seconds—*not even*—to decide—*no, not even*—just to do. Kill or be killed. Kill or watch your friend—your soulmate—be killed. He sucks in more air, but it's not enough to fill his lungs.

More air. Can't get enough air.

This—this—kill—watching as it happened—felt different. And Armor's words. The sound of them. Matter-of-fact. Like he'd completed a task. A chore. A dispatching of a troublesome thing. An execution.

"Box breathing, Kuba. Breathe in, one, two, three, four. Feel that air in your lungs. Hold," Armor coaxes, hand squeezing Kuba's shoulder.

Kuba breathes, but his thoughts still whirl. To kill so coldly. Without passion. Could he have done it? Yet, wasn't it still kill or be killed? Kill or watch the cell, the Fathom op, the goal, the dream, be destroyed? He wipes his mouth on his sleeve, tries to rise, but Armor's restraining hand keeps him in the crouch.

"Steady, breathe. You're not the first to puke at the thought of a splitlip walking beside you, sharing your bread."

"Should we go after—"

"No, we can't afford to stumble into a trap. Not now. If we're lucky, he'll bleed out. If we're not as lucky, he'll make it back to his squad."

"Was it a goliath?"

"Possibly. Or any number of Corporate toadies sent out to lure a weak-minded man with whatever spoils they promised."

"But he'll spill—"

"The wrong info." Armor cuts Kuba off again, crouching beside him. "Teeg suspected BoBeck was a viper, the splitlip in our midst. She's got a gut and a nose to ken these things. Why do you think she played this game so tight, ordering everyone to keep shut? C'mon." He releases his hold on Kuba. "Let's go."

In the stillness, Kuba fixes his attention on the place where the conspirators had been standing just moments before. Strains to hear sounds that might indicate the man is still alive. Even the leaves above are silent.

"But—"

"She told him the wrong date." Armor's tone reeks of patience expressed through gritted teeth, like a father explaining the rules to a recalcitrant child for the umpteenth time.

Kuba squints through the mirk. "But what if they strike early? Pre-emptive like?"

Armor sighs. "Güey, goliaths and their ilk enjoy their Corpse Day as much as any other Corporate flack. Maybe more. It's all eat, drink, and be merry, for tomorrow we kill. By the time they've sobered up and swooped in, we'll be long gone."

"But how can you be sure?"

"We can't. Is anything in this life a sure thing, other than the end?" Armor turns to pick his way back to camp.

"Shouldn't we..." Kuba doesn't finish the thought, just inclines his head in the direction of BoBeck's body.

Armor doesn't hesitate, keeps moving forward, throwing words over his shoulder. "That's the end for all traitors. To be carrion for the crows."

51

In the Dark

THE NIGHT PROPHET MOVES through the darkness, vox silenced, lips pressed tight, a reflection of her concentration. She's Miss Stillwater again, holding her thoughts inside, even as they roil under the calm surface. And the thoughts do tumble and twist, driven by the powerful and rapid torque of her imagination.

Visualize what can go wrong. All the things you fear. Then visualize your response. Because things will go wrong. It's inevitable, no matter how well we plan, no matter how smoothly we've combed through the details. Things will go wrong. But it's not the things that go wrong that derail an op. It's how we respond to them. Or don't respond. The moves we make to counter the problems. Visualize those moves, your response to the inevitable setback. Then you'll be prepared for anything. And most of all, believe that you were put in this moment for a reason. For this reason.

Teeg's words guide Angel's steps as she gathers her backpacks from their hiding place in the shed. She hefts them to her shoulders, one packed with survival supplies, the other heavy with her memento mori and the weight of memories each item holds. They might slow her down but she is loathe to let them go.

Not yet. *Nunca en la vida.* Serafina's vox falling in rhythm with her steps. *Hasta siempre. But not yet. Forever has not arrived. Not until you finish what you start.*

She walks the path with feline precision, her feet practiced at avoiding jutting roots and stones. The slosh of the restless lake against the boats is comforting, reassuring, almost hypnotic. Across the channel, the solar piling caps outline the harbor marina in a violet glow. At the dock, the dinghy waits patiently, rocking slowly to and fro. Within its sturdy, familiar form, she and Lark will make their escape from Genesis. But instead of heading east with the rest of the flotilla, up and around the Keweenaw Peninsula, barreling towards the safe houses, she will head west across the channel, back to Bayfield. Where Word will be waiting.

He'd pressed to cross the channel with the others. She'd been the one to say no. To say stay put. Wait.

Give us something to return to. And then…

She shakes her head to clear her mind.

No. Don't look ahead. Keep your eyes on the mission in front of you. This mission.

Before she tucks the backpacks into the stern of the dinghy, she regards her options. Caresses the knife.

No. You require an intimacy I cannot bear and craft a slower death than I can afford.

Her fingers leave the blade and grasp the burner, loaded and ready. She cradles it in her palm.

Hello, old friend. Can I rely on you again?

A scrap of paper peeking from an inner pocket catches her eye. The poem torn from the biblio with Word's message scrawled below.

Where the Night Prophet leads there I shall follow

She plucks that, too, ever drawn to talismans, the things she holds close as she moves toward danger. Folds it into her shirt pocket, where it rests just above her heart.

She retraces her steps to the manse's garden, pauses to stare up at the dark windows, searching for the ghost of a movement. Flint had stumbled in well past the dinner hour, long past the time his prime cut of beef had grown cold, its fat congealed in pale slicks across his plate. He had been absent for the past two days, gone to partake of some of the week's festivities at the Hive, and brought the reek of debauchery home with him. He'd leered as he lurched past where she stood pushing Lark in the swing, stopped, turned as if to say something, but just stared, jaw slightly slack, working back and forth. His right hand was poised in the air in front of him, index finger raised, moving as if in time with music only he could hear. A blink, a nod, a curl of the lips.

"Shoulda, woulda, coulda," he'd mumbled, and then shambled up the steps to the terrace where Angel half-hoped, half-feared he would trip and crack open his skull on the paving stones.

Angel had kept Lark out into the twilight, until the lights in Flint's suite were doused. Until the danger of walking into the midst of a shitstorm was passed.

Now, she leaves the manse and garden behind and veers onto the path leading to the nerve center. The rotting trunk of the fallen pine makes an excellent hidey-hole for the burner. She tucks it inside amidst the creeping, crawling critters lurking within, without a pause, without a flinch. Shoots a glance at the building where, come dawn, she will attempt to disable the comm system.

Word had advocated for scrapping that part of the mission, adamant that it was unnecessary. "With the bands cut, they won't trigger the sensors. The ovas can fly free," he'd argued, face flushed, vox raised. "There's no need to take the risk."

"No," insisted Armor, his own vox low but landing hard as a hammer. "We take out the nerve center. Disable the comms to buy time. That means taking out Frazier as well."

There was no misreading the look in his eyes when he had stared at Angel. She understood her assignment.

When she met with Kate and three ovas from the other dorms who had volunteered to lead each cohort, Angel had handed over the pruning shears as if bestowing a priceless chalice. Because, along with the shears, she had bestowed her most precious possession. Trust. In the honeyed glow that enveloped them just before the sun slipped below the horizon and curfew sent them slipping inside the dorms one last time, their eyes peering through the slits in their modemants were bright and wide and flashed a spectrum of emotions: eagerness and fear, anticipation and trepidation, determination and a shadow of confusion. But nothing that resembled doubt.

A flicking sound, a scritch scratch. A hushed crack, like a dry twig snapping. Angel freezes.

Not here. Not now.

But the familiar icy gush flows, the panic coursing.

The trees. Always in the trees. The narrow path always leads to evil.

Not here. Not now.

Her hands want to go scrambling for the burner in the log, before the masses in black emerge, before the trees close in, but she clenches them slow and easy.

Not here. Not now.

With excruciating deliberation, she cranes her neck around, her eyes following, rolling into the corners of her sockets, forehead pounding with the slow, straining tension. Of course there's nothing there. Nothing she can see. Nothing behind. Nothing to the side. Nothing she can see. In another place and time, another wooded stretch of lonely trees, she could imagine an opossum or raccoon lumbering past on its nocturnal jaunt. But not here. Not now.

Eradicated long ago.

She cannot call out, cannot confirm her own presence. Can only stand frozen in uncertainty. Until the tension in her limbs and the pressure at the corner of her eyes screams for release. Until the gush of panic ebbs to a trickle. Until there's nothing to do but move forward. Nothing to do but make her way back to the manse to spend a last night under Promise's roof, with its dead menagerie and menacing timekeeps.

Angel would rather sit on the terrace until the blue veil of dawn replaces the black shroud of night, her eyes fixed on the stars and the slow-crawling zoom satellites, running her hand over the pocket of her cargoes where the plastibinds are curled, visualizing how she will deploy them to secure Flint's wrists. But she worries that Lark will wake, call out, and her absence will be discovered. There can be no variation from routine. So she forces herself to cross the threshold of the kitchen door. To remove her kicks and ease her way across the floor, the tiles as chill and smooth as panes of glass under the soles of her feet. To mount the stairs and steal down the hall into her room. To go through the motions of removing her clothes and slipping into her nightshirt, knowing that she will lie in the narrow bed, eyes wide open, staring at the ceiling until the grooves between the hickory planks become visible in the growing light. If she sleeps at all she must dream of the planks, for they are her ever-present companions through the night, along with the timekeeps, whose clacking tongues remind her that everything passes.

Until Corpse Day finally dawns.

52

Corpse Day

THE CQO RARELY WAKES in a panic. Is not accustomed to the beading of sweat along her hairline or its trickling path down her temples. She medicates the problems associated with advancing age, controls them with pills, subjugates the entire process with shots of Feminessence. Has her skin peeled and plumped regularly. Is inclined to believe she embodies a phrase she came across in a text stored in the digi-archives. *Age cannot wither her nor custom stale her infinite variety.* Sadly, the fem about whom those words were written had come to a bad end, having lost her ability to enchant and beguile. A fate to which the CQO has no intention of succumbing.

Yet she wakes now in a sweat-soaked dread that has nothing to do with the revelries of the past week. She does not partake in the debauchery—is, in fact, repulsed by it, and if she truly ruled the Protectorate would abolish it. Her staffers know better than to exhibit any after-effects in her presence. Know to relieve their morning-after malaise with heavy doses of Staminate and to apply powders and creams to hide the dark residue that lurks under their eyes. But they will enjoy the day, Corpse Day, the CQO's prudery be damned. They will sleep late and loll in bed. And later, much later, will lounge and linger over brunch, washing down their eggs alá goldenrod and heirloom apple fritters with mimosas and bellinis, while the CQO stares at her ceiling as the sliver of dawnlight pierces her bedroom, slicing across her bedspread like the blade of a knife.

As much as she despises the chés, as much as she loathes the theory that in order to defeat an enemy, one must adopt his mind-set and get down in the muck with him, she finds her mind slipping that way. How to squash the cockroaches for once and for all.

Only a fool would think that if she squats by the river long enough, she'll see the body of her enemy float by.

Words of the Night Prophet slither through the heated morass of the CQO's daybreak.

Only a fool... The body of her enemy...

Its corpse.

The guevaras will be split among the boats, with Teeg piloting one, Armor another, and Kali guiding the third. Nanda and Path will stay behind, breaking down the campsite and the safe house, hiding what can be hidden, removing what can be removed, destroying the rest. It's not much. They've lived lightly on the land, mindful of the need to leave barely a trace when the time comes to move on. And that time has come.

If there are questions about BoBeck's absence as the teams make their ways to the rendezvous points, they are left unasked. There may come a time to talk about the missing. Or maybe not. Now there is only time for the muffled crunch of boots trampling last year's leaves and the whispers of twigs brushing against arms and legs.

Colors. Kate imagines them spreading like a fan before her as she pulls on her black legskins, flexing her feet through the narrow leg openings, tugging the fabric up her calves and over her knees, around the swell of her hips. Blues. She'll wear blues. Baby blue, sky blue, navy. Aqua and teal. And all shades of red, from carmine to cordovan, cardinal to cinnabar. Even scarlet, whether it suits her skin tone or not. She will wear whatever bright hue she can lay her hands on, maybe more than one at a time, not caring whether the colors clash, or whether she looks as gaudy as a peacock, or as ridiculous as a dotty old fem with too much leisure time and a taste for the bespoke.

She slips the tunic over her head, pulls it down to cover her flat stomach, lets it settle around her thighs. From this day forward, she vows to wear black only under duress, if she faces a circumstance requiring formal mourning attire. But for today, black is the color of hope. In the last letter to her family, written barely more than a week ago, she'd ciphered the barest outline of the op—no, not even an outline—just the wisp of a notion.

While some may fear the winds that howl from the north, I love when they sweep in. I stand in my black tunic and let the winds carry away whatever mood I'm in.

She trusts her father to understand and decode the other segments, as she believes he has before. There is nothing else to do but trust.

Reluctantly she sweeps on the veil. Smiles to think that when she next removes it, she will never wear the modemant again. Sage green, too, will be banished from her wardrobe, even if it's the color of the last garment hanging on a GaltMart rack or the last scrap of fabric at the sew-your-own shop. She'll never wear it again—never—even if she has to wander the earth wrapped in something stitched together from the tattered sheets separating the booths at a Bartertown.

Now that she has donned the ova's uniform, it's time to remove something as well. The true mark of the ova. The pruning shears rest heavy in her palm. She has the well-worn tool, the one the gardeners have used over the years to snip and trim, the one Angel has honed knife-sharp with a whetstone. Her thumb hovers over the edge of the blade, a temptation driving it down to rest on the cool surface of the steel. A temptation to test that edge. To feel the pain it promises. Instead, she brings her foot up to rest on the seat of the wooden desk chair. Eyes the band that hugs her ankle. Bends to the task.

It's gone. Debs' burner—fully loaded, ready for business—is not in the hollow of the log. Angel reaches in again and again in disbelief, patting the soft rot that crumbles under her scrabbling fingers, as if placing her hand inside the hollow just one more time will do the trick, magically make the thing reappear. As if her effort alone, her mere desire for it to be there, will bring it back. But no. It's gone.

Sweat beads spread in a slick at her hairline, under her armpits. A sick heat curdles her innards, while her thrumming heart feels as if it will explode against the wall of her ribcage. The scritch scratch. The sound not made by any animal. Except the human animal. Too late. The op is in motion, even as she crouches, thrusting her hand, her arm into the log. It's too late for anything, but to do. To pivot and do.

Stop. Breathe. Focus. Think.

The blade in the go bag.

The sun has barely torn a slit between the sky and the horizon as she kneels in the dinghy, grabbing for the knife. She doesn't need the dawn light to see all the items nestled in the backpack. Knows its contents by heart. Knows all the things that can help her now.

The past I've carried, the weight of it on my back. Things useful and things not. And I've never felt so glad of the burden.

Kuba has made sure he is one of the four guevaras that cross the worn gray planks of the dock and step onto the boat that Kali will pilot, an ancient trapnetter with a name painted along the prow in a fancy script, the red of its letters long ago faded to pink.

Vamos

About 30 feet long, the vessel, the color of the sky at twilight, has low sides and a small cabin at the bow. It's not much more than a squat floating rectangle that reeks of fish. But the deck is wide and flat, good for accommodating iceboxes of the day's catch. Or a haul of ovas scrambling for freedom.

At dawn on Corpse Day, the fishery is as desolate as a Bartertown after a brute squad sweep. As the sun slips over the line where lake and sky meet, the only sound disturbing the silence is the rhythmic lap of water against the pilings and the hull of the boat. Kali nods from the wheelhouse, grim-faced, flashing none of her usual bantering bravado.

Kuba knows he'd feel safer riding with Teeg, boarding at the private dock of a sympathizer, or Armor, loading his crew at the marina in Bayfield. When the cell had split up at the edge of the forest, they'd all raised their hands to their chests. Some had pressed and held their fists there, others had thumped as if striking a drum.

To remake the world.

All had made the vow, none more solemnly than the two leaders. Kuba trusts their judgment, their ability to navigate the twists and turns that will arise in the midst of the mission. It won't go smoothly. Of that one thing, he is sure. There will be blood spilled. Of that he is almost sure. Let it not be the wrong blood. Her blood.

The other three guevaras are known quantities. Fox controls the embed scanner, though, even without it, he has a sixth sense for detecting a goliath a mile away. Wilder is the muscle man, fists wrapped in leather straps that sport metal spikes ready to pierce the toughest flesh. Echo has a scope out, already scanning for trouble, working a problem that hasn't yet occurred.

Kali is the wild card. He can't be sure in the deepest part of his gut that she's on the level, on their side. Still feels his guts curl in uncertainty when she lets her eyes slide to the right in the middle of evading a question. Teeg and Armor are going with it. Going with her. Whether they're convinced of her sincerity or are just willing to risk it because they need her boats, Kuba can't say. If there's a sacrifice to be made somewhere along the line, are they going to look in her direction?

The plan is to approach the island together, strength in numbers against a possible goliath intercept, but to split up upon reaching the facility and head for the three docks where the ovas will board the boats. Then to make a run for the safehouses perched on the southern, northern, and eastern shores. Kali's route heads north across the lake, a longish route compared to the others, with the highest potential to draw the attention of goliath patrols. There will be sober goliaths on Corpse Day. And, by accident or intent, they may encounter a squad of them patrolling the lake. A squad of sober goliaths, who are pissed off about the fact that they are sober and on patrol, rather than getting hellafried in the local brew joint.

The engine thrums a low growl of pleasure as it consumes the bio-fuel driving its kinetic life. Kali is an expert pilot, easing the boat away from the dock and nosing its bow toward open water. And then they are off, heading across the channel to the east, where the tangerine glow is spreading fast and the undersides of broken clouds look like splotches of blood in the sky.

53

The Alarm

HE'S LATE. Angel imagines Flint stewing in an oblivion-soaked haze, slouching under the stream of water in the shower, twisting the faucet head to generate the highest pulse, turning his chiseled face to the stinging spray in an effort to rouse himself to a vague state somewhere on the ragged edge of sobriety. Then she shakes the image away.

I'll have the advantage.

She hunkers down amidst the stand of pines to wait, her gaze ricocheting from the path to the nerve center and back again. Re-envisioning how it will all go down.

One by one the bands fall away, light as feathers, heavy as chains forged of iron. They land on the lawn, where they resemble strange greenish worms curling around and through the blades of grass. Some of the ovas pick theirs up to examine them more closely, holding them with the tips of their fingers, bringing them near to their faces, curious and amazed that such a thin thread of wire could bind them so tightly to a place. Others kick at them, sending the bands flying into the garden beds, where they dangle like spiraling seedpods from the branches of shrubs or slip down into the mulch below. Most let them rest where they fall, eager to leave them behind.

As some of their sisters still lie asleep in their beds, perhaps dreaming of a freedom they are not brave enough to seek in their waking life, the newly untethered, without a word passed between them, only grim smiles, nods and the gestures of raised hands, begin making their way toward the water and the vessels that will carry them into the uncertain future.

It's the body he covets. He can finally admit this to himself.

The body. The body he's glimpsed in odd moments when she doesn't know he's watching. The body that moves in that long-legged strut with a swagger that the fems here, and those he deals with at the Hive, and certainly the ovas, all lack. Even Promise, gilded and grand in her delusions, doesn't walk that way. Of course, the fem hides it when she knows his eye is on her, adopts the shackled movements of the meek, the subservient. But that's just a pose.

He has dreamt of that body in the night, a body with the lure and power of a siren song. A body to bend to his will, to trammel and tame and feed like some wild, ravening animal. Dreamt of violence. Of pain inflicted. Of scratches and tears, of beautiful bruises violet as the twilight, of ugly bruises as sickly green and yellow as the sky before a storm. Dreamt of the body drained to the merest drop of life. And that would be enough. Has woken drenched in the sweat of nightmares sparked by this body. The body that is on his mind as he trudges along the trail to the squat building where he spends his squat days pondering escape, feeling as imprisoned as the ovas he monitors, the ovas whose failures are his failures, the ovas he has come to resent.

Frack it all. Tear it all down. Let it all go.

Fevered thoughts of a weakling, big thoughts of a small mind that lacks the nerve, thoughts that will never come to fruition. And so he is stunned when he steps around the far side of the building and his right arm is jerked up behind his back in a swift, powerful grip. In the middle of gasping his pain and surprise, he wonders if his shoulder has been dislocated. But that thought slips away, as he feels a sliver of—*ice? Can it be ice?* Sharp, brittle, cold—pressing against his throat. And a body, long, lean, and imbued with a strength he's only ever imagined having, is pressing up against his as it wrestles him face first into the concrete. He feels it scrape along his cheek and lip, tearing the flesh. Tastes the blood. Feels the slalom of something warm along the slope of his neck.

The body he's dreamt of. But it is the vox that holds him in a vice grip.

"I don't want to kill you. But I will."

The whine of a mosquito. No, more like the whirring buzz of a wasp. Some small, annoying, potentially harmful thing murmuring near his ear. La Bête drags his hand out from under the bedsheet and swats at the sound without opening his eyes, which feel glued shut.

Lethe was powerful shit. Should've stuck to the oblivion, and just one glass of that.

But no, he'd let himself be challenged, be goaded.

Are you a man? No, that was way too low of a bar to meet. *Are you a goliath? A colossus among men, a leviathan among mere puny mortals?* What could he say to that, but frack yeah, and to prove it? To keep up the facade?

Maybe it was the bodyblow of being so near to death, the sucker punch of seeing the splitlip stagger and crumple not two feet from him. Or hearing the sizzling hiss of the bullet, feeling the rush of it speeding past his ear. The bullet meant for him. Never had he felt so vulnerable, so naked, so human. So fragile at a time he needed to be invincible.

He'd run, or tried to, bouncing off the trunks of standing trees, hurdling the rotting bodies of the downed, regretting now that he hadn't blazed a single trail, set a path that he could follow in retreat. Miles passed before he slowed to a walk. Just beyond the barracks, he'd paused to catch his breath, to listen to the uproar reverberating from a room of men so fried they would barely notice his return because they had barely noticed his absence. But he'd been glad to find refuge in the moronic revelry, to wallow in the drink and the drugs and the staggeringly ridiculous attempts at games of darts and bags, games that required a precision that had been swept away in the boozy tide.

Now, the flutter of his hand does nothing to scare the noisy critter away. Instead, as his senses begin to achieve some clarity, the buzzing grows louder. When he finally picks away the crust that binds his eyelashes and manages to pry his lids open, in the blur he makes out a red glow pulsing in the gap between the bottom of the barracks door and the concrete floor. Swinging his long legs over the side of his cot, hoisting himself to his feet, swaying a little at the sudden elevation, head thick and clotted, La Bête feels the overwhelming need to pee. The buzz, the glow can wait another minute. Maybe it will finally pierce the dreamworld of one of the other seven goliaths. Or even puncture the snore-filled somnolence of the commander, asleep in a private cell on the opposite side of the command center room, except that their fearless leader was downing brew as fast and furious as any of the grunts, and is likely to be just as comatose.

Shit, and this is going on for one more day?

Corpse Day.

La Béte stares at his face in the mirror above the lavatories. Notes the pallor of his skin above the dark stubble. The lavender smudges under his eyes that hint at the nights he has lain awake, visualizing the scenario of what, according to the splitlip's last words, will take place twenty four hours from now. A technique that his old gladiator ball coach had taught him.

"Wonder what the pros think about right before they compete? They're in the arena, in front of thousands of people, live and on the stream. They're nervous, eyeing the competition, weighing all the

things that might go wrong and how to avoid them. That's what you think, right?"

And every boy on the team had nodded until the coach took his cap off and slapped it along his thigh.

"No, that's not where their minds are at! Pros know they should never visualize mistakes, especially right before a competition. Because picturing mistakes—imagining a poor performance—just makes it more likely they'll actually frack it up and make those mistakes during the game. No, pros visualize their goals! They see themselves winning the game, scoring the winning point! Pros picture what they want to happen, not what they fear will happen!"

He runs his fingers along the pale scar that arcs across his cheek. If he closes his eyes, he might imagine they are her fingers. But not quite. His calluses give the lie to that little bit of conjuring. The buzz drones on.

Frack.

As he pads across the concrete the calluses on his feet rasp, adding to the sonic discord harshing his hungover brain. Pushes the cheap plastiwood door open. Is greeted by a cacophony of monotonous alarms. And a panel at the security station that's blinking hot. *Redredredred* A knife cutting through the fog. *Redredredred*

It's the panel labeled **Galt Genesis I.**

54

Rendezvous

THE PASSIVE RESPONSE of her captive is a kink in the narrative. She'd expected much more of a fight. Had prepped for—visualized—his struggle and her parries to all his possible moves. Had honed the techniques she'd use to subdue him. But Flint had offered little in the way of resistance. Had gone down like an omega wolf in the narrow-eyed glare of the alpha. Had even chuckled when she reached into his pocket to fish out the key fob. Now he leers from his chair, wrists and ankles bound, arms secured, weirdly confident in his non-compliance. Almost as if he thinks of it as some sort of game. Or a warped act of foreplay.

"Swipe it," Angel orders again.

Flint shifts his gaze from her face to the biometric panel awaiting his fingerprint and back again. His smirk is unsettling.

"You want my finger there, you put it there," he taunts.

She should've never said what she said. She knows this. She'd heard the menace in her vox, but somehow he didn't. Somehow he has interpreted it as an empty threat. Only heard the first sentence. *I don't want to kill you.* And ignored the rest. *But I will.*

Now he's toying with her. In bondage, a prisoner, and he's toying with her, as if he has the upper hand. As if he kens her deepest fears. As if he senses a hesitation. As if he knows all the secret places of her body. And her soul. As if he knows she is loathe to touch him again. To grab his hand, to splay his fingers and press them to the screen. That this is an act of intimacy from which she will shrink. This is a weakness. A weakness he has sussed out. A weakness he is using to his advantage. She has the blade but he is in control.

"Look, just swipe it. I don't—"

"You don't want to kill me. You said that before. And yeah, that was your mistake. Because something in that remarkable vox of yours—"

A whoosh of fresh air and a shaft of sunlight slice through the dim funk thickening around them, halting the flow of his speech mid-sneer.

The sneer congeals into a smirk.

Angel doesn't have to turn around. The icy finger running up her backbone spells out the name of the presence standing in the open door.

Among the flat bellies, the bulging ones are conspicuous.

The breeders amidst the tea drinkers.

The thought pops unbidden into Kate's mind. The contrast between those who discovered how to game the system and those who didn't. Or those who weren't brave enough to try. And Promise was the key to it all.

We'll never know the first ova that she pulled into her kitchen. The when or the why. Only that she never refused those who sought her out. Her and her tea.

But here they are now, with new-found courage. Carrying another life within them. A potential free-born. If the op succeeds. A mosaic of skin color. Of body shape and size. All still wear their sage green tunics and, out of sheer habit, their veils lowered. But she doesn't have to see their faces to know the range of emotions that are seeping and melding within them. It's all there in their eyes. Anticipation. Fear. Hope. Dread.

Should she have told them to wear the black legskins and tunics? Would they be less conspicuous where they are going? Will there be clothes to change into? So many questions without answers. Because she didn't ask. Didn't even think to ask. Was caught up in one word. Escape. Suddenly she feels woefully unprepared.

Her group stands on the wooded bluff above the dock on the north shore. The hike there had not been particularly long or arduous, and the morning air is pleasant, fresh and cool in the slanted rays of the sun, but sweat stains blossom under armpits just the same. A silence has settled that no one wants to break. And all eyes are fixed on the shimmering lake and its endless blue promise.

Teeg is headed for the dock at Big Bay, which requires her to navigate around the western edge of the island and up the shore. But she has the shortest escape route, heading directly toward what the old maps call the Porcupine Mountains, a still-rugged land with rugged people willing to buck the Galt Corporation without the need to brag. Armor has the longest route out to Amnicon Point, and then he is headed north and east around the Keweenaw Peninsula. Kali's rendezvous point is the north shore dock. After shepherding the ovas aboard, she'll dodge and weave the *Vamos* around the other small islands that make up the archipelago, and then make a straight shot north to safe houses up near the Thunder Bay garrison.

Kali's hands are fixed on the wheel and her eyes are fixed on the island as it grows larger by the minute, rising from a thin line on the horizon to a looming destination of rocky cliffs and trees. Stone-faced and silent since they pushed away from the dock, she has communicated in fits and spurts through hand gestures, her eyes hidden behind blackout shades. Does her quietude reflect her focus? Her intent to bring them through to safety and success? Or do her hidden eyes scan the horizon for something or someone that only she expects to see? Kuba ponders these questions as he cleans his own shades with the tail of his shirt. He's stationed himself in the stern next to Fox, who's surveying the receding western shore, scope in one hand, embed scanner in the other. Echo stands portside holding a scope to her eyes. She lowers it.

"Company's coming," she says, pointing to the northwest.

Fox adjusts his position, still peering through his scope. Blows out a sharp breath through pursed lips.

"It's on." He strides to the wheelhouse. "So, is this strictly putt-putt, or can you put the pedal down on this hunk-a-junk?"

Kali doesn't even glance back at him. She moves her hand to a black lever. "It's called WOT on a boat, güey. Wide-open throttle. And here we go."

The boat leaps forward, its sudden acceleration staggering the trio. In the jostle to keep his footing, Kuba's shades slip from his fingers and go flying. As they disappear under the turbulent rippling wash, he has a vision that sparks a shudder. A skeleton reclining in his watery grave, a pair of blackouts hiding his empty, infinite stare.

"Oh, Jel, for once, you are so unprepared."

The hole in the muzzle of Debs' weapon stares at Angel like a black and vacant eye, drained of all feeling. Dispassionate. Indifferent. Deadly. In contrast, Promise's eyes are sparkling, radiating a strange melange of amusement and disappointment.

"That blade's rather useless in the face of one of these," she says, giving the burner a waggle. "So it'd be best if you put it down. Now."

Angel moves to place the knife on the console, but Promise shakes her head.

"Oh no, on the floor, please. And the fob, too," she adds, nodding at the device clutched in Angel's other hand.

Promise stares at the open blade on the tile for a long moment before she kicks it, sending it spinning and sliding across the room. She levels her gaze at Angel again.

"I think the taste you've developed for the bushwa life has dulled those keen freeborn senses of yours. Because who was able to slip between the trees, unseen, unheard? Not you."

A guttural snigger erupts from Flint, who shifts in his chair. The bones of his neck and spine crackle. He inclines his head towards the corner of his desk, where a small gray medikit sits, a syringe visible through its clear cover.

"Toss the thrillweep script, honey. Time's a wasting," Flint says, in a tone bordering on boredom. "Let's sink the embed and be done with it."

"Oh, it's really too late for that," Promise coos.

And it is too late. Too late for anything to come between the boom crack and its echo off the walls of the tight room and the scarlet flower that blossoms across Flint's chest. Too late for anything but a second boom crack. In the merest instant, a second rose blooms and joins the first, both so very stark against the white expanse of his shirt. Moments before it had stretched like an empty canvas awaiting an artist's creative touch. Now it's covered. Drenched. And the scarlet no longer resembles flowers. Too late for that. Now it's just an ever expanding blotch of red.

Promise casually regards the damage she has wrought, a quizzical curve bending her lips, with an air of almost blasé disappointment. She blinks, gives her neck that signature twist.

"Now you've got his digit print. Figure out what to do. Here's a hint. Just swipe down on everything. Go ahead, it might buy your friends a little time. Not much. I loved the pruning shears idea, but it's a fail. You didn't have the sense to anticipate that cutting the bands would trigger a system alarm." Promise pulls something from the pocket of her cargoes and holds it up. A severed band dangles from her fingers. She tosses it onto the console.

"So, yeah, there's really no point. Ah, Jel, I really wish I hated you." Promise shakes her head, biting down on her lip. "It would make this all a lot easier. But that's the thing, I don't—hate you.

In fact, what I think I feel is something akin to—love. Like I've finally found a kindred spirit. A sister subversive. But you couldn't keep your rebellion on the down-low. Couldn't serve it up, one cup at a time."

A smile twists across her mouth. "A tempest in a teacup, yeah." Promise exhales, a dismissive huff. "Not so much." She shakes her head again, her expression souring. "No, you're a rabble rouser. A stirrer of bees. You don't understand that subversion is best measured out in teaspoons. And that some fems will spill the tea to curry favor." A lift of her eyebrows and a wistful curve of her lips emphasize her message.

"You didn't want to see that possibility. Blind spot. We all have them." Her eyes rest on Flint for an instant and then skid away. "Yet, there are times when I wish I could be like you. Hell-bent on remaking the world. So, to my mind, it's better for you to die at the hands of a loved one, rather than let the goliaths have their way with you. If they get their paws on you, it'll be evil work, not quick and easy."

"Where's Lark?" Angel asks, tamping down the panic skittering up from her belly. "Don't hurt her. Please."

"Oh, I'd never hurt baby girl. Rest assured, she'll be having a very Tranquille day."

A notion, conceived in a grim desperation, suppressed, contained. If she can just keep Promise talking, she can perhaps lull her, manipulate her, maneuver her. Perhaps.

Stop. Breathe. Focus. Think. Promise her anything.

"I know she's what you covet," Angel blurts, adopting a pleading tone. "I understood from the beginning. Used her to get to you."

Tell her what she wants to hear.

"Because I knew all along that you have things I can't provide."

Promise cocks her head. "You did use her. And what truly good mother does such a thing with her own flesh and blood?"

"Yes, I am a careless mother, an awful mother, I admit that, not fit for that name, not fit to raise a child. But I got her to you, didn't I? You can give her things I can't—"

"Oh, so this was all for LaLa's benefit? Not for this little freedom scheme you're running? You really must take me for a fool. Like everyone else. A beautiful fool."

"Take her. Raise her. I know she'll be better off with you."

"Oh, you think so? Now that you've blown everything to frackin' bits? Well, I guess we'll see how it all turns out. Or, at least, I will." Promise's vox dips to a murmur, as if she's talking to herself. "She wants the Night Prophet, the vox that wafts through the midnight air and curls around insomniacs and lunatic bees crazy enough to think they can change the world. I want Lark. I was willing to do things to get her. Horrible things. Am still willing to do... horrible things."

Clarity strikes like the clang of some enormous bell, deep and enveloping, blunt and reverberating, bringing back the image of the widow's silver braid, twisted and snake-like escaping from the black body bag.

Don't pretend surprise, even to yourself. You suspected—no—you knew all along, deep down, where the rotten feelings seep and ooze...

"I suppose there's a deal to be made." Promise's vox is whispery, faint, meant for her alone. "But no. If I can't have you, my kindred spirit, then no one can have you."

The dock is a gray stretch of weathered planks as the boat approaches. Empty. Lifeless.

"Where are they?" Echo asks with a tinge of panic. "They were supposed to be on the dock, waiting."

Fox brings the scope to his eyes and makes a sweep across the cliffs. Points. A procession of figures clad in filmy green is making its way down the slope.

"Can they move any slower?" Echo shoots a look over her shoulder at the lake.

"Some are pregnant. Very much so," Fox says, after another sweep with the scope.

Kali nestles the boat up against the pier, lashes it secure. Beckons to the approaching figures. Kuba stares, transfixed at the strange creatures with their veiled faces and varying forms, some slim, reed-like, others rounded and bulging, all erect, with a posture arising from indoctrination rather than nature. The scene calls to mind a biblio he'd read, a fantastical tale of bizarre creatures who descend to Earth in outlandish machines and colonize the human population. Creatures who appear weirdly superior in every way, from their analytical brains to their slender, green-skinned bodies and elongated heads with enormous, luminous eyes. He can imagine these approaching figures as their descendants, transcendent hybrids formed from the union of aliens and humans.

"Yo, güey," Kali says, lowering her shades and turning a piercing eye on Kuba. "You like to play the bushwa with your manners. Give 'em a hand down."

Kali's taunt, and the shove that accompanies it, jostles him from his reverie.

Fems. They're just fems. Fems in need of your hand.

He strides forward to meet them, keeping his pace measured to match theirs, to avoid sending them into a panic, like one avoids rushing at a bevy of quail or a mob of deer. In the biblio, the first human-to-alien contact was described in exquisite detail, with words to engage the senses. The slight rasp of the alien's breath. The smooth-as-wax texture and dry chill of its skin. Its odd lack of scent. And so when he nears the first ova as she teeters on the last rock ledge, tentatively stretching her narrow foot encased in a thick-soled trainer down to the dock, and he extends his hand, he's expecting something equally momentous.

But the hand that grabs hold of his is nothing more than human.

And it's trembling.

55

The Mission

WASTED TO THE POINT OF OBNOXION. Even the soberest among them could only manage a lumbering shuffle from the barracks to the dock, bodies listing to one side or the other. Half forgot to grab their armored vests and the other half, instead of slipping them on, had just slung them onto the deck of the patrol boat. Even the commander has left his unsecured across his broad chest. Now they are puking their guts out over the sides of the patrol boat—even the commander—as it lurches through waves that are kicking up in the gusting wind.

Tomorrow. Supposed to happen tomorrow.

La Béte glances around at the drawn, ashen faces, so very un-goliath like.

Smart. Whoever's running this op is smart. Whip smart.

If the splitlip's info is reliable—a huge if, given the traitor's frack-up on the op's go date—did the cell suspect him of treachery and use him to plant the bad seed? He heard the shots, saw the man fall, but the finality of that fall was just a huge assumption on his part. Was the runt a double agent sent to pass disinfo? The execution faked to preserve that ruse? In the end, it doesn't make a damned bit of difference, because the op is happening—now—and the squad is in pursuit. If—an enormous if—the runt's info is accurate, there's a one-in-three chance that the boat they're chasing, the boat they will soon intercept, holds the treasure he's been hunting. A treasure with sleek hair and doe eyes and a vox like the sweet, clear, piercing light at dawn after a winter's long, bleak night. Last night's fog of regret is clearing fast and in that sudden clarity Nadie's music echoes. Those interludes were never just a bit of amusement to pass the time.

Traveling in the north country fair... the north country fair... the north country... north... she walks these hills in a long black veil... long black veil... black veil...

And then he knows, whatever course the boat in front of them takes, whether it turns or continues straight, his own path heads for the north shore of the island.

She once was a true love of mine.

The blast rends Angel's ears, rends her chest. How could a mere sound stagger a body so? One thunderclap, then a second, a noise like a hammer to her ribcage. A noise like a bludgeon. Cracking the air, cracking her bones. Staggering her, first forward, then backward. Falling. Into a void, a chasm. Tumbling into a crackling blow to the back of her skull. Plummeting into an aurora of shimmers and sparks. Slip-sliding into a gray mist. And then, in time with a vague thud and a resounding click from somewhere close by and far away, she glides into the black.

"Those need to go," says Echo, flipping her hand in front of her face as if lifting a veil.

Kali shoots an arrow of a glare that hits its target dead center. Then she spreads her arms wide as her lips spread into a broad smile.

"Welcome aboard," she says, her sincerity as broad as her grin.

"No time for niceties," grumbles Fox, craning his neck around, eyeing the boat that is rapidly closing the gap of open water.

Kali ignores him. "I ken she's not a beauty, ken she's not the best-smelling vessel on this here lake, but this baby can get you where you want to go. Where you need to go. Not gonna sugar-coat. Got a posse on our tail and we're gonna fly. This liquid road could get rocky. So keep your veils down and take a seat." Kali gestures around the open expanse of deck. "We might need your help before this voyage is done. I'm Kali, by the way. That's Kuba," she adds, nodding in his direction. "Fox and Echo. Ain't got time for more'n that. Take a load off, hold on, and ahí vamos!"

The fear emanating from the ovas is palpable, almost visible, like mist hovering over a fallow field at dawn. Some of the fems are shivering. Kuba imagines the drawn, anxious faces behind the green veils. Sees the unease and tension in the eyes that peer through the slits in the fabric.

Except for those of the ova in black. The one who shepherded the others down the cliff-side trail. Who waited until the others were safely aboard before she stepped foot onto the deck. She remains standing, moving from one ova to the next, laying her hands on their shoulders. She teeters, swaying recklessly, as the boat suddenly accelerates. Kuba darts to steady her, but before he reaches her side, she extends her arms and catches her balance. Her sudden laugh catches him off-guard.

"It's been years since I've been on a boat," she says, a little breathless, the words catching in her throat.

Her eyes are clear as an October sky, radiating warmth like the sun in March. Kuba senses a lovely smile just under the veil.

"I'm Kate." Then she shakes her head. "No, that was never my name. Just something that someone called me. By her whim. I'm Serene. That's who I am."

Hurt. A bellyful. A hollowed out kind of ache. A throbbing pain like someone has bashed in her torso with a two by four. A pounding vibration radiating through her skull when Angel lifts her head, bludgeoning her all over again.

So don't lift your head just yet.

Fuzzy goggles. How the hell is she wearing fuzzy goggles? Smeary like the ancient pair that Eben was always hounding her to use when she was little and dead set on helping Serafina saw or hammer or sand. She brings a hand to her face, tries to lift the goggles from her eyes, but her fingers grasp nothing but air and her own nose.

That simple movement sends a shivery stab through her body, arcing up from her abdomen to the top of her head and down to the tips of her toes. Her hand flutters down to her stomach. She slips her fingers under her t-shirt. Runs them over the thin layer of fabric that covers her torso. Traces the outline of the slim, rigid plate encased in that soft shell, feels the nubby surface of the straps that hold the armor tight to her body.

Eben's admonishment cuts through the buzz muddying her focus.

"I want you to wear this at all times."

Well, Pop, I didn't wear it all the time. But I wore it at the right time.

Kali has the throttle all the way down, pushing the boat to max speed, but the goliath patrol cruiser is still closing the distance.

"Burners at the ready," Fox barks above the roar of the engine and the slap and hiss of the waves.

Echo peers through the scope. "Can't tell if they're geared up. All hunched over. No helmets, unless they've got 'em stashed."

"Then we go for the head shot," Fox growls.

Kuba closes his eyes. Squinches his lids good and tight against the mist churned up by the boat's powerful thrust. Any other random summer day he would be reveling in the tingle that its chill fingers trace on his cheeks and forehead. But today he is caught by the snakes writhing in his stomach and wriggling up his gullet. Caught by the extraordinary weight of the burner in his hand as it hangs by his side.

Too heavy. Never be able to lift it. When push comes to shove, it'll be hanging here, holding me down, keeping me from drifting, from running, like the anchor on this boat. Keeping me from doing what I need to do.

From doing a deed he's not sure he's prepared to do. Doing a deed he knows he doesn't want to do.

It's been a long time since that day in the waterman's lair, but he still remembers how his hands shook. The tremors running from the tips of his fingers up past his elbow. The sick thud of heads against tile reverberating through his brain. The bizarre sense of disappointment at not knowing which man he had slain. The feeling of evil oozing inside him, like the scarlet oozing from the fallen bodies. The only thing that had saved him from falling into the abyss that lurked just beyond the act of killing, even a justified killing, was the need to help Angel. The need to bring new life into the world. To bring Lark into the world. Finding comfort in the words of his beloved Grey-Grey.

Whoever kills one life, kills the world entire. Whoever saves one life, saves the world entire.

A life for a life must have balanced the world. His place in the world. This is what he has told himself all along.

Armor's curious turn of phrase as they broke camp and headed for the boats echoes in his mind. *Unrepentant lethality.* Kuba knew—they all knew—what he meant. So what will save him on this morning, should he have to heft the burner and fire it into another body clad in black?

56

A Living Wall

ANGEL'S SHOVE TO THE CROSSBAR of the door is met with firm resistance. She scans the floor. Promise has taken the key fob, securing the exit. But the knife lies where she kicked it. The handle has a reassuring heft nestled in Angel's grip. She takes comfort in its solid weight, the curves that accommodate her fingers, before snapping its blade shut and tucking it into her cargo pocket.

Just you and me. Oh, what damage we can do. But first we need to find a way out.

She expects the panic to rise. Anticipates a flash flood of adrenaline-soaked blood surging through her veins, pounding a crazed rhythm in her neck and temples. Instead, she feels a pre-ternatural calm, a lightness and looseness in her limbs, a clarity in her vision, a steady tempo on the drum at the center of her body. Suspended somewhere between the mundane world and the miraculous universe.

This is not what you planned for, but this is what happened. What you must face. What you must rise above.

The she-wolf's gaze lands on the red tool chest in the corner.

The hammer.

It is useless against the armored window, but she takes a few whacks anyway. Once, twice, a satisfying third time.

Enough.

The monitor screens are of a far more delicate constitution, shattering on first impact, the hammer leaving a gallery of intricate designs in its smashing wake. Glittering webs, like a spider's lacework bejeweled with the morning dew. Star-like constellations and supernova explosions. The ephemeral zigs and zags of a lightning bolt captured forever.

The feedbox offers scarcely more resistance, splintering on the third whack, revealing its guts. The circuits shatter in two blows and her clawing fingers leave the wires in a tangled mess. When the she-wolf's pulse starts to race after her exertions, she stops and sucks in a deep breathe through her nostrils, closing her eyes to let that eerie tranquility settle again, like sand after the retreat of a seething wave.

Now the way out.

Her eyes scan the ceiling and lock onto the square of hazed-wash blue that punctures its solid blanket of gray. The roof hatch with its skylight.

That's your play.

But the ladder is still shackled to the wall and the chain's lock and links are strong enough to resist the hammer's assault.

Fine. We'll do it the hard way.

Two sweeps of her arm send the monitors crashing to the floor in a crescendo of cruel thwacks and thuds, destroying her exhibit of cracked glass art, freeing up space for her feet. Maybe her adrenaline hit is starting to wane because the desk is surprisingly heavy for its minimalist style. Its feet screech and whine in protest as she drags it across the tile. When she gets it centered beneath the hatch and clambers on top, stretching, stretching, stretching up from her tiptoes, extending her arm with its wriggling, grasping fingers, she is still too low to reach the latch and sinks back with a grunt that borders on a rumble of frustration.

No. We do it the hard way. This is what we face. And we will rise above.

Another foot of height is what she needs. Just twelve inches. *The tool chest.*

One hundred feet, maybe, and closing fast. Close enough to be seen as individuals, instead of a black smudge. Close enough to be distinguished as those machines that—in another life, if their Galt-determined destiny had set them on a different track—would be called men, but in this life, on this track, are fated to be revered or reviled as goliaths.

They are unaware of the time out of mind story of the original Goliath, the monumental mass clad in a glittering breastplate, armed with a prodigious spear, who fell dead on the battlefield, slain by the smallest and meekest of all, a boy armed only with a stone and a searing, righteous anger. They only know the name as an epithet spawned by fear and revulsion and they revel in it. Except this morning, they aren't reveling, because their heads feel like hives where throngs of furious bees are vibrating in a vexed, buzzing unison. But no matter. They are expecting nothing but a false alarm, even though the commander has been unable to make contact with the manager of the facility. That's no surprise. It's frackin' Corpse Day. Frazier's probably sleeping it off, as they all long to be, as they all should be, instead of swaying in a sickly rhythm on this blasted, rocking boat, feeling the sweat of nausea puddling in the small of their backs, the skin of their faces clammy and not from the mist churned up the waves.

Fifty feet and close enough for the goliaths to see three figures standing in the stern of the fishing boat they've been tailing. Close enough to see a host of what at first glance appear to be green bags lining the edges of the deck.

"Can't outrun 'em," Kali shouts above the tumult of wind and water and machine. They are skimming the channel between two islands, with a third straight ahead.

"Then throttle it down and we'll take our shot," Fox orders without the slightest hesitation. "Let's do what we've trained for," he adds. "What we're prepared to do."

The engine sputters as Kali eases the throttle back and the boat gradually slows to a glide and then settles into a rocking, rolling pause.

"Now!" Fox barks, and the trio raise their arms, training their burners on the patrol boat as it draws to within forty feet, close enough to distinguish faces. And these would seem to be the faces of boys, for they hardly qualify as men, their visages as-yet unhardened, their cheeks and chins still plumpish with the soft curves of youth. On seeing them, recognizing brothers of an age with himself, Kuba can feel the tremor flickering through his arm, can see the weapon in his hand wavering.

Yet these boys clutch burners in their hands. And, although the words of the actual command are lost in the wind, they have been ordered to take aim, raising their weapons, assuming a defensive posture in a unison that is only slightly ragged. It's a moment. A lifetime. A fraught, frozen eternity, although in real time, it's scarcely time enough to breathe in and out again before the silence is shattered by a vox.

"No! Stop!"

The ova in black, the one who calls herself Serene, lurches in front of Kuba, arms outstretched. Her body is turned away from him, facing the patrol, her right hand gesturing frantically. She cranes her head around so Kuba can see the panic in her wide eyes and the glow of tears welling.

"Astra! Selly!" she calls and two ovas, tall and big-bodied, stagger to their feet.

"Get out the way!" Fox yells, waving his arm. "Stay down!" His is the vox of a man grappling with the beyond-belief choice of grabbing the fem out of harm's way or keeping his aim steady on the enemy.

But Serene holds her ground and the two ovas join her and then a third and a fourth stumble across the deck, grabbing hold of each other's hands, forming a barrier of flesh and bone and blood and beating hearts. A green wall bending and swaying with the bobbing and dipping of the boat. A green wall with a black post in the middle. Solid, secure, unwavering.

"Get out the frackin' way!" Fox yells again. He finally moves to grab one of the ova's arms, but Kuba takes hold of his shoulder and jerks him back.

"No, let 'em be."

"And let 'em be massacred? Not on my watch," Fox snarls, pulling away.

But as he looms up behind the ova in black, she whirls and plants her hand on his chest in a stiff arm move worthy of a gladiator ball champ. "This is not your battle to win," she hisses, giving him a shove for emphasis.

"Fox, he's right. Let 'em be. Look," Echo says, her vox hushed, her face alight with wonder.

The patrol boat bobs, its engine cut, starboard side facing the *Vamos'* stern. The goliaths stand, burners still aimed, but a flood of confusion widening their eyes, a slick of bewilderment seeping across their faces, weighing down their chins, leaving their mouths agape.

"Would you kill your mothers?"

It seems barely more than a whisper, but it carries across the water like a bellow.

"This was not the life they dreamed for you when they first felt you move inside their wombs."

With a sweep of her hand, Serene lifts the veil from her face and stares at the goliaths. The ova to her left steals a glance at her, then raises her hands to do the same. But her movements are slow and halting, and her fingers tremble as they grasp the fabric. One by one, the wall of ovas pull back their veils to reveal their faces and all that is etched there, like runes carved into ancient tablets. Fear. Resolve. Speculation.

Could one of these boys really be my son?

"They dreamed of holding you close, skin to skin. Of walks in the spring showers, laughing at the patter of raindrops on the umbrella. Of lifting you high in the summer sky, so you blocked the sun, because the only bright warmth they needed was the gap-toothed smile on your face."

When Serene finishes speaking, she takes the hand of the ova to her right, gives it a squeeze, and leans in to her. "Speak your truth. Tell them."

The ova, whose tall, strong body is a stark contrast to her timid eyes, her quivering lips, hesitates.

"Go on," Serene encourages. "We need to speak our truth, for once."

It's the ova on her left who breaks the silence.

"I dreamed of seeing the first smile to curve your lips."

A long silence again, before another tall ova speaks.

"I dreamed of feeling your fingers curl around mine and hold tight, so tight, as if you'd never let go."

A very pregnant blonde locks arms with the ovas next to her.

"I dreamed of picking you up when you fell and bandaging your scraped knee and wiping away the hot tears from your cheeks with my thumbs."

"I dreamed that the road you walked would ever be lit with sunshine and your steps light with the joy of doing the right thing."

Finally, the ova to Serene's right finds her words.

"I dreamed of lulling you to sleep with a favorite song. Night after night after night."

And then, like a dam breaking, the truth comes spilling forth from each and then the words to a song, shaky and slightly off-key at first, until Serene's vox gathers strength and assurance.

And I saw a new land
The first had passed away.
And there came a great vox
Comforting words to say.
Wipe tears from your eyes
No sorrow and no cries,
For these pains are vanquished
The old world has passed this day.

The fems are dry-eyed as they join in on the second verse. Dry-eyed and resolute, voxes melding, high-pitched and low, some muddy, some crystalline pure, some rusty from lack of use and some sharp and acute as a newly honed blade.

The tears are across the water, trailing down the cheeks of boys who stare through watery eyes at this green living wall and see only home.

57

Bond

BALANCED ON THE TIPS of her toes, extending her arms, stretching, stretching, the fibers of every muscle straining to the utmost, Angel's fingers brush the smooth surface of the latch, then grab hold and yank it to the side, freeing the hatch. With the peen of the hammer, she thrusts it open, relishing the thump as it falls back against the roof. Welcomes the rush of warm air that feels like a caress against her sweat-soaked cheeks. But her tendons are still screaming as she struggles to boost herself up through the opening, her arms and shoulders ready to give in to the pain.

No use.

She hears herself say it, think it, but then another vox interrupts, murmuring in counterpoint. And then a second. And a third. A chorus.

Pain it's mi amigo no hay lagrimas we walk by faith born survived for such a time as this where the Night Prophet leads there I shall follow

One moment she's dangling, feeling herself slipping into the void, the next she's bursting up through the hatch, flinging herself forward onto the rubbery surface of the roof, embracing the jolt as her knee bangs against the metal framing the opening.

Mi amigo

The array of antennae, upright poles with branching crossbars and a small bowl tipped toward the northwest lures her, but only for the briefest of moments. The components look too sturdy for her to inflict any real damage and she has neither the time nor energy to waste as a choice rears up before her. Confirm the ovas have made it to the boats and are on their way to sanctuary. Or go after Promise. And Lark.

A leap, an awkward landing on the bulging root of a hickory, and a blade of pain pierces her right ankle. A pause to settle herself before planting the foot. Under her full weight, the pain digs deeper, drilling into the joint. She sucks in one deep breath before she's on the move, offering up a silent gratitude that the path back to the manse is flat, well-worn, and root-free as she navigates it in an awkward, hobbling, amble-skip. How much time did she waste, giving lead time to Promise, who would have been packed and ready to go?

Ready to go. Wherewherewhere?

Remnants of the song hang in the air, settling slowly, like a feather wafting on a breeze. The boats sway in a gentle rhythm. A pair of fierce-eyed herring gulls skim along the surface of water. Kuba feels the lull in his own body, the way his arm hangs slack at his side, burner still in his grip, but his grasp, the looseness of his fingers, seems almost casual. A song. Voxes. Fragments of a story float and eddy. Whispers coming from Grey-Grey's lips. A tale she told at the river's edge because it rose and fell on water. A tale of a spell-binding song that lured sailors to their deaths.

"Whoever draws near and catches the Sirens' song, no sailing home for him..."

Now would be the time.

While the goliaths are still transfixed. But his arm is frozen. As their arms are frozen. As everyone seems frozen. Frozen and mute in the new world created by the lifted voxes, the subduing voxes.

Except... Is that a flicker of movement?

"And she said to stop their ears with beeswax, so they might resist the siren song."

But Kuba is too late to react when the patrol commander pivots. The man's motion is herky-jerky in the periphery of his vision. Or perhaps that's how Kuba perceives it in his own frozen state. He senses another movement to his left. A jostling. Fox pulling, Echo pushing. The green wall swaying, beginning to crumble. The echoed memory of the song bleeding into something else.

But in the vital instant, it's as if the song has left him deaf. He no longer hears it, nor the shrieks and screams that bleed from it, now that it's been pierced by a spray of bullets from the commander's burner. But they're wild, straying off their mark. And the commander himself is teetering, dancing a marionette's jig, jerking and jerking and jerking, like his body hangs at the ends of invisible strings tugged by a pair of wanton, cruel hands. The tall goliath to the far left, the tallest among all the tall boys, is the one pulling the strings. He's dropped to his knee and is firing, firing, firing, until the commander falls, folding into himself, a crumpled bag of a body now hidden from view by the gunwale of the boat.

The sudden silence is deafening. But only for an instant, until the empty space is filled by whimpers and sobs, as the splinters and shards of fear and relief scatter across the deck. The ovas sink to the gray planks, gathering themselves into huddles of green, shoulders lifting and falling, lifting and falling, like the waves. But the ova in black, the one who calls herself Serene, still stands, though her chin trembles and her eyes glisten.

"Bond. It's Bond. It's him. I know it's him. He worked the clues. He found me."

The rhythmic ticking of the clocks and the skip-a-beat patter of her footsteps are the only sounds echoing off the walls as Angel limps up and down the hallways and staircases of the manse, in and out of rooms devoid of life. The glass eyes of the dead animals mock her slow progress. Tick. Tick. Tick. The clocks scold, reminding her of all the mistakes she's made. Surrendering the knife and fob. Leaving the burner hidden—not—in the log. Not inventing an excuse to spirit Lark off the island. Underestimating Promise. The biggest mistake of all.

Tock. Tock. Tock.

They are traveling light, the closets and drawers still crammed with clothes, the beds left unmade, of course, because that is Angel's task. She can see the indentation in the pillow where Lark's head had nestled only an hour before. When she rests her palm there, she can sense the residue of warmth left by the child's plump cheek. Or is it just her imagination?

On the sly, she's been teaching Lark how to make her own bed. How to fluff the pillow and pull the coverlet up, showing her how adorable her stuffie looks propped splay-legged against the headboard, where it will wait patiently until nightfall, when the girl will once again gather it into her tight embrace and snuggle through a rambling story or an off-key lullaby until sleep finally overcomes her.

On this morning, the sheets are thrown back and the stuffie is gone.

"Lay 'em down, boys. Lay the burners down, like laying down a burden."

La Bête speaks to the goliaths in a gentle tone, animated with a slight lilt, coaxing and easy. But all the while his burner is aimed in their direction, his finger poised at the trigger. Because it would just take one or two of them to spin and fire and he would go down like a beaten dog, just like the lifeless commander slumped on the deck, arms and legs bent at weird angles, the marionette abandoned. But almost in unison, the boys bend and gently, almost reverently, place their weapons at their feet, and when they straighten again their shoulders have lost their hunch, their arms look relaxed, hanging loose at their sides.

"You got some thinkin' to do. Time's come for choosin' sides. And thinkin's best done without a burner in your hand. Now, you're gonna have a seat over there." Le Bête gestures to the far side of the deck and the boys obey his instructions, plopping down like a line of exhausted bees boarding a mobile after a hard day's labor. He waves a hand at the *Vamos*. "Bring her closer, so these boys can make a donation to the cause."

Fox and Echo, slack-jawed, still have their burners at the ready, aimed toward the goliaths. Kuba is wavering, not sure if it's the motion of the boat or if his body is ready to give way, slip-sliding into a fog of bewilderment.

The tears. The goliaths' tears. The tears were real. Real. The burners are on the deck. That really happened.

"What the frack?" Fox grunts.

"I know him," Serene says. "He's a friend."

"He's a goliath," Echo mutters. "With a frackin' burner in his paw."

"He's a friend," Serene says again, her gaze never leaving Bond's face. "One of my closest. Pull alongside." Finally, when Kali makes no move to restart the engine, Serene shoots her a glare. "Pull alongside," she repeats, with a bite in her vox and a tenacity in her eyes that startles the guevaras. "We can trust him."

Kali exchanges a look with Fox, doubt puckering her lips and lowering her brow.

"I've trusted him with my life." Serene turns her gaze back toward the patrol boat. "Before. And now."

The engine grumbles to life, but quiets to a purr as Kali maneuvers the boat close enough to grab hold of the patrol boat's gunwale. A small smile slides wide across La Bête's face as joy and wonder ebb and flow in his countenance. There's a slick of something wet—maybe sweat, maybe tears—alongside his nose. The only unchanging thing is the pale scar running up his ruddy cheek.

Here I am traveling in the north country fair and there she is in a long black veil...

She once was a true love of mine.

"I told you," he says, his eyes flitting from Serene to the seated goliaths and back again. "I told you."

She nods. "Yes, you did, Bond."

And hearing his name, his real name, hearing it come from her lips, feels like a blessing, a benediction that lands lightly, like the laying on of hands to a fevered brow.

"The letters—we worked 'em—your dad and I. You were brilliant, laying it out. Then it was just maneuvering." He bites down on his lip, glances at the goliaths. "Maneuvering, yeah." His eyes shift back to Serene. "Being maneuvered. Like a piece on a chessboard. Waiting."

He shakes his head, questioning whether what's happening to him now is actually real, and not some delayed hallucination brought on by yesterday's lethe and 'blivion. Rubs his finger along the barrel of his burner. Feels the heat, a residue of his actions. Nods before he picks up the threads of his thoughts and weaves them into words again.

"Waiting for something. Something—a way in—to come along. Doubting it ever would. But here I am. And here you are. Did you ever doubt?" he asks.

Serene cocks her head. "Oh, well, there were moments."

Bond shrugs, a wry grin twisting his mouth. "Moments, yeah. I had some of those, too." He shakes his head again, as if shaking off a painful memory. Gestures to the burners. Gives the guevaras a look. "You trust me to pick these up and hand 'em over or you want to come get 'em yourself?"

58

The Channel

Both boats are gone.

Angel perches at the end of the dock, toes over the edge, squinting, straining to see what she already knows is not there. Her eyes spy no trace of the blue bowrider in the channel.

Twenty minutes to cross, less if she was pushing it. Gone. And you wasted time smashing screens.

A white movement in the periphery of her vision. There, to her right, a hundred yards distant, maybe more, bobs the dinghy.

Would the bruja have taken the time to search it? To find the go bags? Taken the time to dump them? Taken them with her? No. She'd have her own. After all, what would she need to carry besides a stack of v-cards? With her embed, she could saunter into any Galt Mart and clear the shelves if she wanted. She has that freedom.

Freedom. From a certain point of view.

And she has Lark.

The thought is like a stinging jolt from a goliath's shock prod. The only one she needs. And then she's in the water, swimming.

With the last burner transferred to the *Vamos*, Serene beckons Bond to climb aboard. But as she reaches out to take his hand, Fox insinuates himself between them.

"He can't come with us."

Serene is confused. "What? He's—"

"Frackin' traceable, is what he is. His embed," Fox says.

"But—"

Echo interrupts, though her tone is kind. "He would endanger the op. The mission continues."

"The mission?" Serene's vox wavers.

"The mission. Our mission."

Bond stares at Serene. "You were my mission."

Something hangs on the look that passes between them. An understanding rooted in a shared history of bonds knitted in backyard games and childhood nicknames and us against the world endeavors.

"We need to get moving," Fox says, gesturing for Kali to get the engine started.

As it chortles to life, Serene glances toward the ovas, huddled in clusters on the deck, coated in a glaze of shock. Her gaze returns to Bond, who is also frozen in the moment.

"I'm going with you," she says, putting her foot on the gunwale, extending her hand.

Fox grabs it, yanking her back. "No, you're not. We got our orders and we're—"

In that moment, in the action and reaction, Kuba feels a light and a heat piercing the fog that has surrounded him, bright and blistering as the sun at noon. And with that sudden clarity comes the question.

What would Angel do? What would the Night Prophet say?

The answer comes through a throat full of a ragged, clenched vox. "Let her go!" he cries out. He takes in a breath, holds, then blows it out. "Let her go," he repeats, this time with a quiet control. "Ain't that what this is all about? Choices? Freedom to make choices? To have choices? Let her make that choice. Let her go."

"Go to what?" Fox shouts. "A goliath barracks? On the run with an AWOL that's got an embed blinkin' hot? Have a frackin' clue!"

Kuba starts to reply, but Bond holds up a hand. "I do—have a clue," he says. "And a cover story. A Corpse Day misadventure. Complete with a corpse. At the bottom of a bottomless lake." He grins, the twisted grimace of an exhausted man who's paid an extremely high price to get what he has long desired. "You think only guevaras plan their missions down to the last detail? That this happened without strings being pulled?"

"There's frackin' blood in the boat!" Fox growls. "And seven goliaths to tell a different story. Gonna need a helluva lot more string-pullin'. Or you planning to eliminate them all? If so, go ahead, while you got the ammo. Spare us from having to do it later."

"You love your comrades?" Bond asks, gesturing to the guevaras.

Fox squints, giving him a quizzical look.

"Do you love your comrades?" Bond repeats. "Do anything for them? Die for them?"

Fox flings a hand in exasperation. "What the frack are you—"

"Are you not driven by those bonds as much as by your lofty cause? Your pledge to remake the world? And your hatred of Galt?" Bond shoots a look at the body on the deck. "The commander was not beloved. Far from it. Not loved by anyone, it would seem. No family to demand Galt expend the effort to retrieve his body from its final resting place. And Galt doesn't care because there's always another goliath to take his place. The factory that makes us"—he pauses, casts a look at the boys—"that makes them, won't stop. Until we make them stop. Until we burn the whole frackin' factory down."

Bond takes Serene's hand and helps her cross over the gunwale. "One mission accomplished. On to the next."

The gasp explodes from the core of her body, ignited by her sudden immersion in the enveloping cold. Sucking in air but never getting enough, spasms wracking her frame. Time screams by before she can regulate her breathing, pull herself out of the shock response, get control of her body. But the lake is a relentless adversary.

HowdidTeegdoitHowdidsheswimthechannel?

For every lurching stroke forward, Angel is yanked back by a greedy pair of icy hands. Swimming the lake is like wrestling a slippery, writhing eel, like grabbing hold of a liquid body that wriggles and slides out of her grasp, and then slings a tail to bash her sideways. Fighting and getting nowhere but a place of floating exhaustion. The dinghy seems farther away than when she leaped from the dock. As she treads, the chill seeps under her skin, slices through muscle and sinew, settles around her bones, digs into the marrow, encasing it in a numbing cold. A cold that freezes into despair.

NotgoingtomakeitEventothedinghyHowdidTeegmakeitacross?

"Desire, madness. It does strange things. Gives you a strength, a power..."

Desire, madness. For me, it's been hate. I embraced it. Was driven by it. And this is where it's gotten me. Water is always my nemesis. Wrapped in its frozen arms so every move I make, the tiniest flex of muscle, the blink of my eyelid, pulls me in tighter. Squeezing the life out of me til I'm drowning in it. I can keep fighting. But it's only a matter of time. Tighter. Tighter. Til there's no breath left to breathe. Or I can stop fighting and let myself shrink. Smaller and smaller until I can just slip through the gap in its embrace. Right there.

But in the gap, as she's about to slip through into a blinding, ice-white void, a mass of darkness looms. A darkness that splits and curls into wild tendrils that entice her frigid fingers to comb through and push back and tuck into place, revealing an impish face with flashing eyes. A face that fades from view as quickly as it appeared, but not before the bow lips purse and pucker around the word 'no.'

No.

With a gasp, she surfaces, shaking the water off, amazed at the blue gashes in the cloud-studded sky. Amazed that, in the distance, she can see a boat. She imagines for a moment that she is swimming alongside it—no—ahead of it, creating a white, churning wake for the boat to follow, the vessel tacking to and fro to match her moods.

If I stay still, will all the world contained in that single vessel come to me?

She bites down on that tidbit of hope like she's biting down on a bullet to contain a scream of pain. The dinghy looks closer now, drifting on the little waves. She's tempted to swim again, but fights the urge, saving the bare ounces of strength she has left.

Be still. Let the world come to you. Be the center that holds as everything swirls around you, like the post of the carnival round-about, keeping the painted ponies prancing in a circle, bobbing up and down. Be still and let the boat come to you. Work on the story to tell them. A story to beguile. A story they'll believe.

As she treads, willing her weak, clumsy muscles to move, the boat looms large and then larger, shocking in its clarity. Her thoughts chatter like her teeth.

Closeyoureyes makeawish likeachild infrontof herbestowalday cake. Of all the people... who do you wish for... now?

A splattering thwuck. A firm nudge. Her closed eyelids relax, the tight squeeze easing into a flutter.

"Grab hold!"

Although the skeleton wind has grown flesh with the thrum of blood coursing through it, its rasping rattle smoothed into a commanding rumble like the low roll of thunder from a distant storm, she can still recognize the bones underneath.

"Grab hold, Angel. Now!"

And there is nothing to do but obey.

Sprawled across the bowrider's transom, she is too exhausted to flail, though some wild, beast-like creature hunched at the back of her mind is prodding her, its frantic yowl telling her she should be flailing like a fish plucked from its watery home, stunned by the fiery air flowing into its puckering mouth, burning through its gills. And in the moment when she opens her eyes and reveals the stark terror within, Word enfolds her twice, first in the thermal blanket he grabs from the safety kit and then in his arms.

"Steady." His breath and his words are warm against her cheek as he rocks her, swaying side to side, the motion and the mantra a rhythmic balm. "Steady."

"She took her." Angel's words finally escape her lips in a shuddery staccato.

"I know. Saw them drive away from the marina. Personal transport. Gray-green. Fem was moving fast as water flowing downhill, the little one in tow. Moving so fast she forgot to take the boat fob. And here I am."

Her view is devoid of all light, a tunnel without an exit, a bleak maw, all-consuming, inescapable. "But she's gone. She's gone."

"No, she's just out of sight. For now." Word digs in his shirt pocket. Slips out a slim handful of black tech. Thumbs it to life. "Smart fem, but stupid, too. You once said she rattled off her digits. I know you haven't forgotten them." He holds the embed scanner in front of her, but her hands are shaking, fingers too numb to key in the numbers.

His hand enfolding hers is warming, calming, the grip strong as it guides her toward the pinpoint of light slowly coming into view.

"Whisper them, like a love song, like the last, hushed sermon of The Night Prophet."

"I... 23... 86."

As the morning ages into a hot, hazy afternoon, the fishing boats release their catch in small batches along the shores of Lake Superior. At each dock, the ovas render themselves into the hands of strangers, fems who smile and talk softly with coaxing lilts and slow gestures, movements one uses with skittish horses and wary cats. In the basement safe rooms of the strangers' modest homes, they marvel at the copper mesh lining the walls as they shed their green skins and toss aside their modemants, don worn denims and workshirts, and emerge as bees, transformed by some weird reverse metamorphosis, butterflies entering their chrysalises and emerging as caterpillars.

With a ravenous hunger they can't explain, they consume handmade bread slathered with raspberry jam, ruby red and tart, washing it down with fresh, grassy chamomile tea, savoring the flavors, flavors enhanced by freedom, flavors enhanced by this moment of repose between flight and whatever fight may lie ahead.

South. Promise is heading south on the two-lane that hugs the shoreline. But that road curls west as it merges with the four-lane that snakes its way toward the Duluth Garrison. Toward the Hive. She is at the mercy of the curves and bends of the asphalt. They will travel off road. She will be slowed by the needs and whims of the child. She will arrive first.

But they will not be far behind.

You thought you could silence the bird who sings in the night. Clip her wings and cage her. But you didn't stop to consider the essence of a bird. Of this Bird. What you mistook for a songbird is really a bird of prey. For her beak is wicked sharp and her talons sharper still. Her eyes are lasers that can pierce your smooth façade and see deep down into your craven heart. Her flight is silent and she travels at a speed that you can achieve only in your wildest dreams. And she is fierce. Fiercer than any of the creatures bought and paid for in your dead menagerie. And fiercer still when you've stolen something that belongs to her.

You cannot hide from her. You cannot outrun her. You can only hope to find a drop of pale mercy flowing in the midst of blood-red vengeance.

So you have no hope at all.

So sayeth the Night Prophet.

Acknowledgments

Stephen King, in "On Writing," notes that "writing is a lonely job." I'm not sure I agree with him, although he is one of my idols. Reading *Carrie* as a young teen was a formative experience in this writer's life. Perhaps one can think of writing as a *solitary* job, because during the early stages of the process, it's just you and your story. But I find that I am never really alone, and hardly lonely, because my characters are always hovering close by, demanding that I tell their side of the story, demanding that I take those clichés out of their mouths and put in something better, some turn of phrase that sounds fresh and snappy, that sounds like something they would actually say, rather than a stilted bit of literary dialogue.

Whether I succeed or not depends upon another person. The reader. Every writer needs a first reader, a person willing to take on the thankless task of slogging through a first draft, or even a second or a third draft. The first reader's questions and thoughtful suggestions help shape a draft into a novel. I want to thank Cindi Proffitt, who, as a first reader, looked at a very ragged, underwritten ending and knew better than I did how Angel would respond to the ultimate adversity. Thanks go to another early reader, Larry Pincsak, for pointing out my writerly tendency to choose the obscure word when a more common one would better serve to keep the reader in the flow of the story, rather than stopping to Google the definition. Side ponder: does anyone still use print dictionaries? I appreciated our lively discussion on "jerry-rigged vs. jury-rigged." (Both are correct, by the way.) In the end, I substituted an entirely different word with approximately the same meaning, in the hopes of keeping the reader in the flow of the story, rather than asking Siri about the correctness of my spelling and usage.

Every writer has a favorite place and atmosphere in which to write. For me, music helps set the mood and I am grateful for the vibes that Angèle Dubeau and the ensemble La Pietà send out into the world, particularly their *Ludovico Einaudi: Portrait* and *Pulsations* recordings. The music of Trent Reznor and Atticus Ross, pulsing with dread, helped propel the Fathom Op. And I couldn't do without the tunes of the awesome indie rock band, Lord Huron. As Tolstoy noted, "music is the shorthand of emotions. Emotions, which let themselves be described in words with such difficulty, are directly conveyed to man in music, and in that is its power and significance."

Joanne Zienty was born in Chicago, Illinois. She is the winner of the 2014 Soon to Be Famous Illinois Author Project Award™ for her debut novel, *The Things We Save*, for which she was also named a semi-finalist in the Publisher's Weekly BookLife Prize for Fiction. In 2017, she was named an "Emerging Voice" by the College of DuPage. She published her second novel, *Children of the Revolution*, a revenge tale set in a dystopian Midwest, in 2020. She studied English Language and Literature at the University of Chicago, earned her teaching certification at Roosevelt University, and her Master's in Library and Information Science at Dominican University. When she's not writing, she uses her influence as a teacher/librarian to help young students grow as readers and find their voices as writers. She lives in Wheaton, Illinois with her husband and a crotchety old cat.